NADINE DO...   2023

class family in Liv...
of her childhood living on a farm with her
grandmother, and attended school in a
small remote village in the west of Ireland.
She trained as a nurse, then followed with
a successful career in which she established
and then sold her own business. She is an
MP, presently serving as Minister of State
in the Department of Health and Social
Care, and has three daughters.

Nadine Dorries

The Velvet Ribbon

HEAD
of ZEUS

First published in the UK in 2020 by Head of Zeus Ltd
This paperback edition first published in 2020 by Head of Zeus Ltd

9 7 5 3 1 2 4 6 8

A catalogue record for this book is available from
the British Library.

ISBN (PB): 9781786697592
ISBN (E): 9781786697561

Typeset by Divaddict Publishing Solutions Ltd

Printed and bound in Great Britain by
CPI Group (UK) Ltd, Croydon CR0 4YY

Head of Zeus Ltd
First Floor East
5–8 Hardwick Street
London EC1R 4RG

WWW.HEADOFZEUS.COM

For my husband, Paul, who passed away at home on June 7th 2019

Chapter 1

Tarabeg

Shona the gypsy woman and her bad-tempered grandson, Jay, had slipped into Tarabeg under the cover of darkness and camped in their old haunt, up against the church wall on the edge of the seven acres. He had complained bitterly every step of the way. 'This is a waste of our time – why the feck are we here?'

'We have been sent for,' she replied, and Jay knew better than to ask for more. 'Wrap rags around the horses' hooves to muffle them,' she instructed as they reached the outskirts of the village. The light had just begun to fade and the moon appeared, large, bold and orange, close to the earth. At the sight of the blood moon, Shona finally knew in her heart why it was they were there.

'What use are the rags?' Jay grumbled. 'They'll see us

if they look from the bar in Paddy's and they'll drive us out again. Why are we even here?' he repeated.

Shona had not the strength to answer, even had she been inclined to tell him. It was where she had to be just one more time for one last curse; it was all she had left in her and she was waiting to be told how to use it. They had remained unseen, invisible, as she knew they would be, as they set up camp, fed the horses, lit the fire and settled down. But all the time Jay complained. 'What use are you when you can't even cook any more,' he said as he threw the rabbit he'd trapped the previous day into the scalding cast-iron pot. Without any further words, they both bedded down for the night.

In the hour before dawn, Shona lifted her head and took one last look through the parted oilskin draped across the rear of the caravan, down the hill towards the Taramore river. The wind raced through the trees as the river thundered down the steep slope then meandered round the base of the hill, hushed and deep over the Taramore table where the salmon came to spawn year after year, before whispering over pebbles in the shallows. She'd been woken by the voices from the dark, forbidding flow and they were calling her name. It was time.

The straw mattress crackled beneath her shifting weight, disturbing Jay, asleep on the pallet beside her. 'Lie down, you mad old crone,' he barked.

She wanted to answer him, to order him to speak to her with the respect she deserved. She was Shona of Erris, the head of the oldest gypsy family in the west of Ireland and the true owner of the land on which they were now camped. They'd parked up on almost the very spot on which she'd been born. But her strength, her powers, were ebbing away from her; she felt it and knew it for what it was.

She gulped down hungry, shallow breaths of the damp night air and tried to speak, but failed. She ignored Jay and his impatience as the sweet and pungent earthy smell of night grass rose, stung her nostrils and scorched her lungs, competing with wood-smoke from the fire to the side of the caravan steps. With supreme effort, she pushed herself up with one hand, grabbing at the bent-willow frame of the caravan for support.

Jay, blinking, offered no assistance. 'Have you finally lost your mind?' he grunted as he punched his straw pillow.

Desperate for his help but too proud to ask, she made one last attempt. Grasping and clutching, she leant her back against the frame and looked down on the scene below. The white Church of the Sacred Heart was just in view, on the periphery of her vision; the gravestones reflected the luminous full moon, and the stars shone in the cold, clear sky and danced on the surface of the river.

It was a perfect night to leave the place where she'd spent so many nights before. She knew every rabbit burrow that had kept her and her family fed, the fox that fled when she approached, and the owl that, perched and blinking, watched her now. 'I knew all your mothers before you,' she murmured to the bird. The smile of reflection slid from her face as a lone tear trickled down her cheek. The whispers of her ancestors were floating up to her from the banks of the river, in and out of the caravan as the wind grew stronger. She could hear the long past sounds of Daedio Malone from when he and the guards drove her and her family off the seven acres the old Lord Carter had given to her grandmother before his death.

Jay, tiring of her ramblings now, hearing nothing and exhausted after acquiescing to her demands to reach Tarabeg by nightfall, pulled the sacking and the old blanket up to his neck and turned onto his side. 'You'll be dead by morning if you sit there for much longer,' he said. His eyes, black, snapping, held no sympathy. He sensed she had almost lost her powers, and his respect, rooted in fear, had all but disappeared as a result.

Shona had a message for him; she could see it, hear it. The white walls, the fire, the money... It was the cottage on Tarabeg Hill, where the Malones lived. The voices were urging her to pass the message on before she left. The money was at the root of it all. It had given Daedio Malone the means to buy the seven acres, the reason they'd been evicted. Revenge burnt like a torch in her heart and she found her voice.

'The farm on the hill. The money. The fire. I can see it. They have brought it to me, to give to you. The American... Get the money. Avenge us all.' Each word came out on the end of a gasp.

A smile spread across Jay's face. 'You fecking mad witch,' he said, his grey lips curling in disdain. Within moments, his breathing told her that he slept once more.

She had failed. She had grown weaker as his contempt for her had grown stronger.

Shona and Jay Maughan were no longer as welcome in Tarabeg as they had been not so many years before. Back then, villagers had wanted to buy their pots and pans, have their fortunes told, get their knives sharpened or ailments healed. But the Maughans had been driven out by the Malone store, built on Shona's land, and by the priest who wrapped a band of prayer around the village as he strode around the periphery with his Bible each night after Mass, chanting as he walked. It was a force she could not break. Father Jerry blamed her for all the ills that had befallen locals, including the death of Sarah Malone in childbirth many years before, and he was right, Sarah had been cursed, but it was not enough. Sarah Malone's daughter, Mary Kate, must pay the final price.

Dark sins cast long shadows as the memory her ancestors had returned to her played out before her eyes. She watched the ghostly tableau of the eviction: not one villager lifted a finger to help, as with sticks and dogs the Maughans were driven from the seven acres, Daedio and the old man Carter beating from the front. She strained her eyes until she could see her young self, huddled there with her mother, her grandmother wailing, her father cursing, the wind howling. It was those same people, her own loved ones, whose voices were calling her now, their cries piercing the night air, carried on the wind. It was time for her to slip across to the other side and she felt the shame she would take with her. She had let them down and would die an outcast, hovering on the edge of the land she had never reclaimed. She had failed them.

'Help me,' she gasped. 'I cannot come yet, I have not avenged you.'

But they were insistent that her mortal work was done. She had wreaked havoc, and yet still she had failed.

The villagers had been right to blame Shona. Their ills had been her doing and if it had not been for Bridget McAndrew, the village seer and holder of powers almost as strong as her own, she would have completed her task long ago. But the priest and Bridget had been too much for her now she was an old woman, and they plagued her still. She'd seen in her crystal ball as they'd come into Tarabeg the all-knowing face of Bridget watching them arrive.

Shona's shoulders drooped and as she slipped a few inches down the wooden frame, the willow as sharp as a knife against her spine, the wind lifted the tarpaulin and she saw her mother on the steps. The night was clear, but her mother's hair was dripping down her face, just as it had on the day they were driven off the land, when a fierce rain had pelted the sorry band of evictees. There was no mistaking the message as her lips moved and her eyes burnt with a fire deep within.

'Come, Shona. It's time.'

'I can't, not yet.' Shona gasped, lifting her hand towards her mother and wanting to look to see had Jay woken. But there was no turning back. She felt a shift in her core, a lifting of the pain, a lightness, and she knew that the passing over had begun. It was all beyond her now.

That old fool Daedio, he had outlived her. The image of his great-granddaughter, Mary Kate, came to Shona and it occurred to her just what her last curse must be. She smiled. Bridget could not reach her here; it was her parting gift from the twilight.

She closed her eyes and felt death envelop her. The icy hand of her mother slid into her own. 'Wait,' she whispered. 'I am not done.' And with the rattling wheeze of her last breath, she uttered her final, deadliest curse.

Chapter 2

Liverpool, two years later

His starched shirt collar stood upright and his cuffs hung down, waiting to be secured. Breathing in, shoulders rising, a slight lift onto the balls of his feet – she could never understand why he did that – he tucked his crisp white linen shirt deep into the front of his trousers. She nuzzled her face into his pillow, pulling the recent warmth of him closer, and smiled up at him lovingly. She adored watching him dress. Even after two whole years of sharing the same bed, it was still a novelty, a pleasure that she never wanted to end as she gazed upon her total undoing.

He smiled back down at her, equally adoring, and the quizzical look that crossed his brown eyes told her that he was curious to know what she was thinking. His face was morning pink and freshly shaven and as he dropped a kiss onto the top of her head her space filled with the fresh aroma of his favourite Old Spice aftershave and the soap from his recent bath.

'Take me to Tarabeg, to meet your family, please?' he said as he lifted his smouldering cigarette from the ashtray on the bedside table. The smoke caught his eyes, made them sting. Blinded, he blinked furiously before stubbing it out. Slivers of silver ash exploded into the air before floating down onto the unmade bed.

Mary Kate lifted her head, frowned at the overflowing ashtray, its contents now scattered over the polished mahogany, and made a mental note to empty it as soon as he'd left. She threw back the sheet and flung her legs out of bed, collected her robe from the brass post and slipped the dove-grey satin edged in white Nottingham lace up her arms. His wife, Lavinia, had left it hanging on the back of the bedroom door when she'd departed in something of a hurry and had never asked for it back. Lavinia was a good six inches taller than her and as Mary Kate flopped down at the dressing table the robe trailed over the dark woodblock floor, covering the pink rose-patterned oval rug that kept the wheels of the three-legged stool stationary. She swivelled on the round needlepoint seat to face the mirror and do battle with her morning hair.

Her reluctance to answer had not deterred him. 'They all sound like such characters. I can see each one of them reflected in you every time a letter arrives and you chatter on about one or the other. They say the apple never falls far from the tree. Go on, darling, please, take me there. I so want to see the shop, and the farm on Tarabeg Hill. I've never even met your little brother, Finn, and I know this sounds odd, because I've never been there, but I swear that sometimes it's like I even dream about the village, you describe it so well.'

Mary Kate sighed, more to herself, not so that he could hear her. He'd asked her the same question only the week before and she'd guessed he was warming to a theme and would ask again soon. She stopped with the hairbrush halfway down a stroke of her long red hair and looked past the triple oval mirror, through the grey, rain-splattered window and down over the tops of the cherry trees that lined the avenue. They stood bare and dormant, their cold branches stretching up to the sky like the splayed fingers of the dead, grasping for the life-giving sunlight that was still months away. An image of her home and the view from her bedroom window in Tarabeg flashed into her mind. Her nostrils retrieved the memory of the green fields, her mind recalled the fast-flowing Taramore river, and her heart tightened in response.

She swivelled back round on the stool to face Nicholas, with the hairbrush, which had also once belonged to his wife, still in her hand. Her hair had not yet been tamed: red curls were hanging down over her shoulders, and the back was a bird's-nest muss, a consequence of their vigorous lovemaking the previous evening.

A kept and childless woman, she had the luxury of the morning to prepare for her day, but Nicholas had only minutes to spare. He hated to be late for work and was always keen to arrive at his GP practice long before his patients. His signed letters were waiting on the desk in his office across the landing from their bedroom, letters he had handwritten the night before just as soon as he had finished his supper, ready to be dropped into his bag and handed to his loyal receptionist, Bella, to post. He never liked to keep patients waiting for test results a moment longer than he had to. Some of his letters were asking patients to call in and see him, so that he could explain the findings in person. 'No appointment required,' he would write at the bottom in his almost illegible scrawl, and then Bella would scold him for overloading his surgery. The list of phone calls he would need to make that day sat next to his letters. As he became more popular and his surgery busier, the list grew. Dr Nicholas Marcus loved his work, and in his drive to improve the health and wellbeing of his poor dockside patients nothing was ever too much trouble.

His cufflinks lay on the dressing table in a lime-green lustre dish, next to Mary Kate's discarded gold crucifix. Long since abandoned, it could never save her now. He bent over her to retrieve the cufflinks, his apologetic smile always spontaneous, full of love and gratitude because he knew, or he thought he did, the price she had to pay for being in love with a man who was still handcuffed in law and in the eyes of God to the woman who had left him and taken his sons with her. In truth, he had no idea. How could he? How could she explain a way of life that was totally alien to him?

There was nothing more she would have loved than to alight from the bus and walk into Tarabeg holding his hand, taking him into every home and shop and announcing to the people she had grown up with all of her life, people who would greet her as though they had seen her just yesterday, 'Look what I did! This wonderful, kind and clever man – he's mine. Are you proud of me now?' But she knew that no matter how much time passed, that could never happen. If they walked in through the doors of the Church of the Sacred Heart, Father Jerry would see beyond her smile to the sin beneath, and at the very least a bolt of lightning would strike and the doors would slam shut behind her.

But Tarabeg was with her. She lived this life in Liverpool with the man she loved, but Tarabeg would never leave her. When she closed her eyes at night, the familiar rumble of Nicholas's deep, rhythmic breathing morphed into the rushing of the Taramore at the back of her old bedroom. It pulled at her heart and blotted out the caterwauling of the cats and the squealing of brakes as the buses came to a halt down at the bottom of Duke's Avenue. In her dreams she saw the grave of Daedio, her great-grandfather, even though she'd never seen it in person, having been too ashamed to attend his funeral. How had she done that, lied to her own family? In the darkest hours, the guilt came to haunt her. What price had she paid for love? How could she take Nicholas home?

'Nicholas, I cannot take you to Tarabeg. I've already explained a million times – it just wouldn't be right. We aren't married. The shock would kill Granny Nola and Granda Seamus, I've no doubt about it. I cannot even begin to imagine. They think I work here, that Lavinia and the boys still live here. Even if you were a single man, the fact that you aren't a Catholic, that would be enough. Father Jerry would be apoplectic with the shock.'

'That's the Irish in you,' said Nicholas with a grin. 'You're just exaggerating. None of that matters a jot to anyone. They will be happy for us both, because I love you as much as they do and more still, and isn't that all that matters to them, that you are happy?'

Mary Kate sighed, exasperated, but then grinned, unable to stop herself. 'I do not exaggerate, Nicholas.' She jabbed the hairbrush at him as she spoke. 'There is no divorce in the Catholic faith, it doesn't exist in Ireland. I've never met a divorced person in my life. Even if Lavinia does one day agree, it would never be accepted back home. Divorce is one unholy scandal, a terrible sin. Do you not understand? They've always known I'm strong-willed, but this... Not one of them would ever have imagined this. This me would be a stranger to them.'

She looked down and turned another woman's hairbrush over and over in her hands, felt the gold band on her wedding hand slide between her forefinger and thumb. They had bought the ring for appearances, for when they were out together. None of the other women who lived on the avenue were fooled, but thank God that Nicholas's surgery was down by the docks, away from the stuffiness of their Fullmore Park neighbourhood. And down in Surrey, at the Box Hill teashop they went to on the rare weekends they were allowed to visit Nicholas's boys at their boarding school, she passed as the proud wife of Dr Marcus. On those days, Mary Kate forgot the truth, became the real Mrs Marcus and revelled in the fantasy of being his legitimate wife.

Nicholas lived for those infrequent, intense weekends. There was so much to say to the boys, but when the time came there were often awkward silences and sadness in between the bursts of fun and chatter, especially for little Jack. As they drove the car down the drive of the school to return the boys to the housemaster, Jack always began to cry – 'Don't leave me, Daddy. Don't leave me here' – and Mary Kate could almost hear Nicholas's heart breaking beside her. Lavinia was in the driving seat down that long and winding driveway, not Nicholas. She was the boys' mother. The boarding school was at her insistence. Cold rooms and corridors. Stern hearts, scant love.

As Mary Kate looked up at the man who made her heart lift, the words of Mrs O'Keefe, her friend and neighbour, rang in her ears. 'If anyone ever reports him to the General Medical Council, he could be struck off for adultery. It's happened before. Be discreet, my dear. True love knows no bounds, but it can encounter many obstacles along the way.'

Mrs O'Keefe lived further up the avenue and Mary Kate had met her on the boat from Ireland. Her arrival in Liverpool had been disastrous and if it hadn't been for the kindly Mrs O'Keefe, and Cat, her great-aunt's neighbour, she might well have ended up back in Tarabeg within a week. Now those two women were her closest friends; their unquestioning support felt like a warm blanket draped across her shoulders.

The words echoed through Mary Kate's mind as she stared at Nicholas's reflection in the mirror. She would never mention that possibility to him. He was obviously blissfully unaware and had enough to deal with. His first thoughts were always for his patients, and as Bella often told her, 'He's the hardest-working doctor in all of Liverpool and his patients love him more than any doctor I've ever worked for – and I've worked for some very important doctors in my time. I saved the best till last.' Bella, who threatened to retire at least once a day, would place a soft hand on top of Mary Kate's and give it a little squeeze. 'Don't worry. I won't leave him,' she always said, 'if you don't either.'

Mrs O'Keefe regularly counselled Mary Kate to share her concerns over their morning coffee together and not to worry Nicholas. 'Don't burden him. His patients do enough of that, with all their problems. God knows how much he does for them. There are only so many problems one man can shoulder in a day. That Lavinia, she was a truly wicked woman, and thank God there aren't many like her. But, despite her wickedness, he has all the guilt and the shame to shoulder in this because he would wish it any other way for your sake and for his boys too. He would stop the tide for you, that man, if he thought it would make you happy, because you make his boys happy.' Wise and true words from the woman who had become the closest to a mother any girl away from her own home and family could have wished for.

Nicholas sat on the bed and pulled on his socks, his heart heavy with the words Lavinia had spoken to him the previous day. She had threatened to report him. He would never let Mary Kate know that she hounded him on a daily basis, and he had secured a promise from Bella that she wouldn't breathe a word about the intimidation or the telephone tantrums to a living soul. Even though Nicholas held a letter that proved Lavinia's adultery, she vowed to ruin him should he ever use it to sue for divorce. And because he and Mary Kate were living together, in sin, as man and wife, he knew he would be struck off the register and forbidden from practising again if she did report him. That nightmare possibility haunted him, along with the sound of Jack's pitiful tears; he was all too aware that he and Mary Kate were teetering on the edge of an abyss, their situation so precarious that it couldn't possibly last.

'Show that letter to a single person and I have nothing to lose,' Lavinia had hissed down the phone the previous day. She never called the house, always the practice. 'I will make sure every woman in the avenue knows that girl for what she is, do you hear me? It will take me one call to the golf club captain and another to the medical council. The captain always rather liked me, not that you'd have noticed. And don't you ever forget, the medical council will have to listen to me because she was a patient registered on your list. We all know the price a doctor has to pay for sleeping with one of his own patients, don't we? Never mind living over the brush with the little whore.'

She gave a shrill laugh that sounded like breaking glass and had the desired effect of sending a shiver down his spine. She was of course quite right. Mary Kate had been his patient.

'Had even you forgotten that little fact? She was registered on your list at the practice, not Robin's – at your absolute insistence, he told me. Your patient, not his, and he will testify to that now that his poor wife knows what happened. Ruined everything, you did,

Nicholas, because you couldn't keep your trousers up.'

The phone in his hand shook violently. His throat tightened and his mouth was dry. Fear made it impossible for him to speak, but at that particular jibe he almost laughed out loud. His wife had been having an affair with his partner for months. There had been others, for which he had always forgiven her, but not this time, even though Lavinia now had the power to ruin him and it was all in her hands.

'You will lose your job, the house, your reputation, your precious patients... And as for that harlot that you insultingly refer to in my presence, the mother of your sons, as the love of your life – you won't see her for dust. It'll be all over the newspapers and Mary Kate will be known forever as nothing better than a scarlet woman.'

The first time she'd called and made her threats, he'd driven twice around the park before returning home after work, asking himself over and over, should he tell Mary Kate? He had decided against it. She didn't need to deal with that, and besides, how could she? She was far too young and trusting, the opposite to Lavinia in so many ways. He would handle Lavinia in secret and shield Mary Kate from her intimidations.

'Use the letter that Robin wrote to me, that your little harlot stole, and I can tell you this: you will unleash the dogs of war. Neither of you will survive. You have committed the ultimate crime for a doctor, my darling, broken the absolute taboo, brought the Hippocratic oath into disrepute. Not fit to practise on ethical grounds – that's what they'll say when it's reported to the General Medical Council, so Daddy tells me. The only thing you have in your possession, Nicholas, is the ability to prevent me from doing much worse. Try me and I will destroy you both.'

Lavinia had been referring to the letter Mary Kate had inadvertently found; it was from Nicholas's former partner, Robin, with whom it had transpired Lavinia was having an affair. They still had the letter. It was all that stood between him and ruin and he thanked God that Mary Kate had found it because if she hadn't, he couldn't bear to imagine what Lavinia might have done to both himself and Mary Kate by now.

The noise of the radio in the kitchen broke into his thoughts and brought him back to the present. Joan was moving noisily about downstairs and the kettle was whistling. The pipes clanked as the water ran into the sink and Joan sang along to the radio, slightly too loudly, one of the many liberties she now took as payment for working in a house of 'the most unspeakable of all sins'. 'When my little girl is smiling...' her voice bellowed up the stairs.

'Look how hard it was to keep Joan,' Mary Kate said, gesticulating towards the open bedroom door with the hairbrush. She frowned. 'She still threatens to leave almost every day. If it wasn't for Mrs O'Keefe, we probably would have been run out of the avenue with all the wild gossip. As it is, no one here speaks to me.'

He covered the distance between them, threw his arms about her and hugged her into him, causing the stool to squeak and shift across the carpet. 'But it will be different once your family meet me and I explain everything to them...'

Mary Kate pulled away and shook her head. 'Do you know, one of the women in the avenue actually crossed to the other side of the road yesterday when Joan and I took the bus into town. Liverpool is a Catholic city, Nicholas. Can you imagine? This is just a small taste of how bad it would be at home.'

Anger flashed across his face as he turned over the first cuff. 'Who was it?' His tone was controlled, but his smile and happy demeanour had evaporated and his eyes were focused on her reflection.

'I'm not telling you because I don't trust you not to knock at her door and give out to her on your way to work. I'm not going to have them calling you a bad-mannered brute and damaging your reputation on my account – not likely.' She brushed her hair as her eyes still held him in her view. Then she smiled.

His face relaxed and he smiled back at her, although this time it didn't quite reach his eyes. She was right. He couldn't help himself. All he wanted to do was protect her and when he heard stories of how she was ostracised, he was filled with an anger he was wholly unused to.

'Are you seeing Cat today?'

Mary Kate laid down the brush and gathered her hair into a large tortoiseshell clip. This was far safer ground. 'I am. I'm going with her to take Debbie for her hospital appointment and then I've promised Debbie that as it's her fourth birthday tomorrow we will call into a café for cake on the way home.'

'What time is Debbie's appointment?'

'Eleven o'clock. Why? Are you at the hospital today?'

He struggled with the right cufflink, using his left hand. 'I am, but I'll be gone by then.'

'Come here,' she said. 'Let me help you.' She reached out and took the cuff with one hand and the link with the other. 'Think of it as a lucky escape then. Mrs O'Keefe is coming with me. She's knitted Debbie a cardigan for her birthday. You would have been surrounded by women and bored with us all.'

The arrival of the young widow Cat and her brood of children into Mrs O'Keefe's life had given the kindly woman a renewed sense of purpose. She had barely stopped knitting since.

'You are good to Cat and those children,' Nicholas said, secretly relieved that Mary Kate had them in her life to be good to. He often asked himself how unbearable life would have been for her if there had been no Cat, or whether she would have tolerated all

that she had since Lavinia had threatened to destroy her reputation, and thereby her life, even though Mary Kate had done nothing other than fall in love with a man whose wife had slept with his partner and walked out on him. Nicholas wasn't sure that Mary Kate could have borne the loneliness if Cat and Mrs O'Keefe hadn't been there for her. They were all the friends she had in Liverpool.

Cuffs fastened, Nicholas picked his tie up from where he'd thrown it on the bed.

'Here, let me.' Mary Kate moved towards him and stood at the edge of the bed. Her dressing him during his morning routine was as intimate as him undressing her at bedtime. The pink quilted satin eiderdown had fallen from the blankets and was now almost fully on the floor. The pillows were tumbled, the sheets a tangled knot. Her nightdress was carelessly thrown across the bedstead, where it had been since the night before, when he'd removed it not long after she'd switched off the lamp. While she looped his tie, he slipped his hands inside her robe and around her soft, naked waist, as he always did, and began kissing the tip of her nose. Then, lifting stray tendrils of hair out of his way, he moved down to her neck.

'Nicholas, will you stop.' She laughed as she tilted her head back.

'Okay, if you insist, I suppose I must – I can't be late today,' he said with reluctance as instead he began devouring every feature of her face with his hungry eyes.

Her sparkling blue eyes; the thickness of her red hair that all too frequently refused to be tamed; the bridge of half a dozen freckles across the top of her nose and along the line of her jaw; her lips, oh her lips. If there were any other way, he would give up his medical career and remain at home with his Mary Kate all day and every day, just kissing those lips.

'Nicholas, stop doing that too.' She could see him out of the corner of her eye and she was grinning.

'I can't help it. I love you,' he said and suddenly tugged on her waist and hugged her into him, tight, too tight, as he tried to cover every inch of her with his body.

'I love you too,' she whispered into his chest and for a brief moment time stood still and all they could hear was the beating of each other's hearts.

'How about I invite my new partner, William, and his wife over to us for lunch on Sunday then,' he said as they broke away and she threaded through the final loop of his tie. 'I imagine his wife would appreciate the change of scene, as she's got two little ones to look after.' He chuckled. 'You know, Bella and all the patients call him Dr William – they don't realise it's his first name.'

Her eyes met his. 'Do they know about us?'

'Well, not exactly, but he's a doctor – we don't judge like some others do. I'll explain beforehand and it will be fine.'

'Are you sure? Where are they from?' She wasn't nearly as confident in the charity of others as Nicholas apparently was.

'Here, in Liverpool. He trained at St Angelus, obviously – a few years below me – which was where I first met him. I call you my wife at the practice, you know that, and so does Bella, who loves you.' They may not have had family, but they had crumbs of affection from a limited number of people to sustain and carry them through. 'Here, I have something for you. I meant to give it to you last night. Wait there.'

He dashed out of the bedroom and across the landing to his study. She heard the click of the lock on his Gladstone bag opening and closing, and before she had finished brushing her hair he was back at her side.

'You know that emerald heart of your mother's in the dressing-table drawer? Well, look, I took it without you knowing, and I did this.'

His smile was boyish, happy, and she stretched out her hand to take the box he held out to her. Her father had brought the heart over on his one visit to Liverpool, shortly after she'd got there. It had been a gift to Sarah from Mary Kate's great-grandfather, Daedio. All Mary Kate knew about it was that it had come from America.

She opened the long box he held out to her and gasped. There was her emerald, and she had never seen it look so beautiful. It hung by a gold thread from a deep-green velvet ribbon.

'It's a choker – all the rage, so the jeweller told me. What do you think?'

Mary Kate turned back to the mirror and drew the ribbon around her neck. 'Can you fasten it?' she asked as her eyes met his in the mirror.

He stood over her, looking at her reflection as he did as she'd asked, and was overcome by a strange sense of melancholy. 'Mary Kate, will you do something for me?'

She wasn't really concentrating, she was so taken by her own image. Sometimes she was shocked at how much like her mother she looked, and at this moment, as the green velvet ribbon settled into the dip in her throat and the emerald caught the light and winked back at her, she felt as though Sarah was sitting next to her, smiling. Sarah had worn the emerald every day of Mary Kate's life. She shook her head; it was the familiarity of the stone that had made the hairs on her arms rise. Her fingers flew to her neck as she caressed the soft loveliness of the green velvet ribbon.

'Nicholas, it's so beautiful. I don't know how you thought to do this.'

'I saw it in Lewis's, when you sent me to buy the ribbons for Debbie's hair.' He laughed. 'And the idea just came to me. Will you wear it every day? Promise me?'

She nodded, her eyes full of tears. She stood and turned; her lips found his and her hands cupped the back of his neck. 'I love you so much,' she whispered as they parted.

He couldn't respond; his throat was thick with emotion and his heart was full of an overpowering, protective love.

'I can smell toast,' Mary Kate said. 'Come on. I really can't face a day of Joan's sulking, that's too much for anyone, even a fallen woman like me. You go on down. I'll pull on some clothes or Joan really will be out the door.'

She smiled at his retreating back, held her hand to her throat and felt the warmth beneath the ribbon as he ran down the stairs shouting, 'Coming, Joan!' She hoped it would be a sight she could devour every day for the rest of her life.

Down in the kitchen, Joan was in a good mood. She battled with her conscience, working for the girl from a village back home who had become her mistress under the most sinful of circumstances. 'I have to go to confession every day – imagine!' she'd confided to Deidra, the Irish girl who worked for Mrs O'Keefe, over their daily tea and natter.

''Twill all end in tears,' said Deidra. A fearful silence had fallen then, because wasn't Mary Kate sinning in the worst way imaginable, and wouldn't the price exacted be a very dark one indeed?

'I've scrambled your eggs, Dr Marcus,' said Joan, heaving the pan off the stove when he walked in.

The radio remained on loud, something both Mary Kate and Nicholas had decided wasn't worth fighting over, given how affected Joan had been by all the upset. The boys leaving had broken her heart, and Mary Kate moving into the master bedroom had seen her turning to her rosaries.

'I haven't time, Joan,' said Nicholas as he lifted his hat from the back of the door. 'Can I take a piece of toast with me to eat in the car?'

'Why haven't you time?' asked Mary Kate as she came through the door. She walked straight over to the dog, Jet, and patted his head. 'Your breakfast next,' she said, whispering in case Joan heard her. 'Looks like it's scrambled eggs.'

'Because I have to call into St Angelus to see Dr Gaskell about a patient first.'

Mary Kate followed him up the steps to the front door. They kissed again before he opened it. 'Are you going to invite William and his wife then?' she asked.

'I will, and I promise you this, if I detect even the slightest reproach, I shall rescind the invitation immediately. Is that a deal?'

She grinned and kissed him back on the tip of his nose. 'It's a deal,' she said, her stomach turning to water at the thought of entertaining in a way she was wholly unused to.

'I love you,' he whispered in her ear. 'Again and again and again. I cannot tell you enough, my love. I spend all my day dreaming about coming home to you and bed.'

She blushed furiously, her heart light and her head even lighter. 'Get away with you. I am sure there must be an Irishman somewhere in your family. Full of it, you are, and to think, I came all the way to Liverpool to hear that,' she called after him as he ran down the path to his car.

The cold wind ripped into the hallway. She wrapped her cardigan tight across her chest and shivered as she stood and waved until the car had fully turned out of the drive and disappeared from sight.

'Thank you so much for fitting me in so early,' Nicholas said as Dr Gaskell pulled out a chair for him. Instead of settling himself down behind the desk, as was his custom, Dr Gaskell then dragged his own chair around to sit next to Nicholas. Nicholas raised an eyebrow as he removed his hat and placed it on his lap. Dr Gaskell was avoiding his eye. Being a trained and sensitive doctor himself, Nicholas knew the signs; he could sense the significance. He unbuttoned his coat, too fearful to speak. Dr Gaskell was the most renowned chest doctor in the northwest of England, a man no one could imagine retiring because if and when he did, the residents of the dockside area of Liverpool would be all the poorer for it. Both he and his son, who'd been in Nicholas's year at medical school, were friends of Nicholas.

Nicholas had at first ignored the pains in his chest and the shortness of breath, believing them to be the consequences of his ongoing worries about what Lavinia might do next and his guilt about Mary Kate having to remain forever an exile from her home village because of him. It was obvious she missed Tarabeg greatly – she even spoke its name out loud in her sleep, though he'd never told her that. He had put the congestion in his lungs down to the pea-soup fogs, and the Mersey mist and dampness. The pain was often relieved by a cigarette. But when he'd coughed up blood into the basin, even he knew it was time to seek advice.

'Take a seat,' said Dr Gaskell. 'I want to show you your X-rays. How have you been feeling?'

'No different, really. In fact, I'd say possibly even a little better over the past few days.' He sounded less convincing than he thought. 'I've been too busy to notice, truth be told. The practice is becoming so busy.'

Dr Gaskell flicked on the light-box switch, then tipped up the thick buff envelope that contained the X-ray; as it slipped out, he caught it in his hand and rammed it into the clip with the efficiency of a man who had done the same thing a million times before.

Nicholas looked at the X-ray. His mouth opened and

closed, but no words came out. The overhead pendant light in its bottle-green glass shade seemed to make Dr Gaskell's white hair glow.

A nurse pushed opened the clinic door. 'Oh, sorry,' she said. 'Hello, Dr Gaskell. I didn't think anyone was here yet.'

'Not to worry. If you could make sure no one else comes in here, please, Nurse Brogan,' Dr Gaskell replied, his voice low and serious.

Nurse Brogan glanced over his shoulder at the young man staring at the light-box with tears in his eyes. 'Of course, Doctor,' she whispered.

When the latch clicked shut, all that remained was a deafening silence. Dr Gaskell stood, walked to the door, turned the key and locked it. His heart weighed heavy as he sat down next to one of the most compassionate doctors he had ever known. He placed his hand on Nicholas's shoulder. 'Is that woman still making your life a misery?' he asked.

Nicholas nodded; he didn't trust himself to speak.

'I'm going to call her myself,' Dr Gaskell said.

'No, no, please don't,' said Nicholas. 'I have to protect Mary Kate. I cannot put her in any danger.'

Dr Gaskell pushed his hands into his pockets and for a while both men were silent as they stared at the illuminated black-and-white image before them. Dr Gaskell didn't want to insult Nicholas's training or intelligence and ask him whether he fully understood what they were looking at. Heavy moments that seemed to last a lifetime passed as Dr Gaskell sat patiently, allowing the information to sink in. He waited for the inevitable question.

'How long do I have?' Nicholas said in little more than a whisper as he turned his hat over and over in his hands.

There it was: the spoken hope. Docker or doctor, the first question was always the same.

Dr Gaskell took a sharp intake of breath and held it as he once again stared at the X-ray. As if he hadn't looked at it a dozen times already. Only he knew how bad it actually was and for a brief moment he willed it to be different. How many times had he switched on the light-box and prayed for the image to show something else, something benign and harmless. But the stark truth was still there in black and white; it hadn't gone away.

'I'm afraid only months, my boy. I'm so very, very sorry, Nicholas. If there was anything at all I could do... But at this late stage...' He reached out his hand and for a moment rested it on top of the hand of the doctor he was also proud to call his friend. The first teardrop fell and hit the back of his hand. He took his handkerchief out of his pocket and thrust it between Nicholas's clenched fingers. 'Cry,' he said. 'You are safe here with me. Cry as hard and as much as you want.'

And without further encouragement or hesitation,

Nicholas did. He cried at the unfairness of it. For all that he had got wrong in his life, for his sons whom he would likely never see again, and for Mary Kate, for how could she cope with this? He didn't want to leave them, not for a minute, let alone for the rest of their lifetimes.

'Don't tell Mary Kate,' he sobbed. 'I don't want her to know.'

His tears fell like a torrent down his cheeks, but his thoughts were now racing ahead and this alone kept him in control, warding off the emotion that threatened to engulf him. 'Protect her from Lavinia for me, would you?'

He turned to face his old medical mentor, his eyes pleading, but he had nothing to fear for he was met by only understanding and kindness.

'Of course. You can depend on me. I will talk to Matron and she will insist you are nursed here in St Angelus when the time comes. I give you my word, our word, that Lavinia and Mary Kate's paths will never cross. We will break whatever rules we have to.'

Even as he spoke the words, Dr Gaskell knew this would be one of the rare occasions when he would have to pull rank with Matron, who was a stickler for standards.

Nicholas's shoulders slumped with relief. As he wrung the now soaked handkerchief between his fingers and struggled to compose himself within the safe confines of the clinical consulting room, the only sounds were those of rattling trolleys on squeaky wheels being pushed up and down the corridor, hospital porters calling out cheerfully to one another and nurses scuttling along in their crepe-soled shoes. In the midst of it all, a good man's happy-ever-after was being wept over within the comforting embrace of Dr Gaskell, who had gathered Nicholas into his arms as a father would his son.

Chapter 3

Tarabeg

The cold and quiet months had arrived as the dark, cloud-heavy skies settled into place. Up a long boreen on the top of the hill at Tarabeg Farm they were ready for the short days and long nights, having worked throughout the summer to ensure there would be enough food and drink to see them through to the other end. 'No child who lives on a hard-worked and well-managed farm should ever go hungry,' said Seamus, in a part of Ireland where children often did just that.

Of Seamus's children, only Michael had resisted the urge to leave and seek his fortune. He'd made his life in Tarabeg instead, with the help of the surprise gift of the seven acres and money from his grandfather. Daedio had presented this to Michael when he returned from the war and married Sarah, the sweetheart he'd left behind. They used the money to build a home and a business on the land next to the road, opposite Paddy and Josie Devlin's butcher's shop and bar.

Malone's General Store was positioned in the centre of the village, in front of the river at the foot of Tarabeg Hill, atop which Michael's parents, Seamus and Nola, had their farm. Sarah may have departed her mortal soul in delivering Michael's son, Finn, but according to Bridget McAndrew she was still among them in spirit. Michael knew this to be true; Sarah came to him too often for him to doubt Bridget's word.

The store had gone from strength to strength, providing everything a villager, farmer or tourist fisherman, of which there was an ever-growing number, could need. This kept Michael well rooted in the village. He lived there with his second wife, Rosie, his son Finn and their help, Peggy Kennedy. Since Mary Kate had moved to Liverpool two years earlier, Peggy now lived in as part of the family, in Mary Kate's old room.

Up on the farm, Seamus and Nola had food stored out in the old house to see them through the winter – bottled in syrup, pickled in jars, packed in straw. It gave Nola a feeling of deep satisfaction every time she placed her hands on her hips and surveyed her harvest work, just as it did every year. The sight of her wooden crates, loose tea-chests, and cardboard boxes she had requisitioned from Michael's shop all piled up, bulging at the seams and waiting for the winter to begin never failed to make her smile.

The turf shed next to the old house was packed with peat bricks that during the summer months Seamus had cut, turned, ricked and then collected to keep the fires going. This year, the shed was so full that some of the bricks had to be stored inside the old house, layered in neatly arranged stacks against the gable-end wall. This record-breaking effort was due to Joe Malone, a wealthy young man from America who had arrived, like many, in search of his roots, and had remained in Tarabeg ever since. He'd been on the trail of an old will and testament, and to his delight had found that Daedio, the youngest brother of his great-great-granddaddy, was still in residence at Tarabeg Farm and thought to be long past his hundredth birthday.

Following Daedio's death, Joe threw himself into helping out on the farm, assisting Seamus and Pete Shevlin, the farm labourer and cowman. It was the first time since the Malone children had taken off for America, years ago, that they'd managed to stack that much turf. Joe owned a business in America that made him rich without him ever having to lift a finger – something which was a mystery to them all – and Seamus and Pete were astounded to discover that he could cut the peat twice as fast as any Irishman.

'I was brought up on fresh red meat, orange juice and sunshine,' Joe told them by way of explanation, laughing as the men raised on thin stew, potatoes and rain stood back in amazement to see him slicing though the peat.

'What do you miss about America, Joe?' Seamus asked him one time as they worked.

Joe, who had taken to wearing a cap in order to fit in and had long since dispensed with the haircut that had announced he'd once been a marine, stabbed his spade into the earth, pushed back his cap and leant on the handle, taking a moment to think. 'Soda and hamburgers,' he said as his fringe flopped over his eyes. Then he pulled the spade back out of the soil as though it were the weight of a feather and continued digging.

They were none the wiser. 'That soda must be mighty powerful,' Seamus said, and Joe chuckled to himself as he cleaved away another slice of earth and wiped the rain from his dripping brow.

No one had discussed the fortune hidden behind the bricks in the fireplace wall since Daedio had died. It was Joe's inheritance by rights, sent over in secret from America long ago by Joe's great-great-granddaddy, but Joe had been keen to put Daedio's mind at rest. 'The money may have been sent here for safe-keeping,' he'd said, 'but I can tell you, Daedio, with what remained in America, I am a rich man. How much money does one man need? I have more than I can shake a stick at.'

And with that it had been decided, with Bridget in attendance, that they would know when the day came to put it to use. Bridget's spirit guide was Daedio's late wife, Annie, and she gave her assurance that this was the right thing to do. Until that day, the money would remain exactly where it was. It had never been mentioned again.

Jay Maughan hadn't been back to Tarabeg in the two years since Shona's passing. Without the protection of his gypsy grandmother's curses, he was too afraid to return. He lived as a fugitive, in the shadows, hiding away from honest, hard-working people, their priests and all that contributed to the fabric of society in the villages he roamed. So he was surprised when one of his old wartime contacts, a smuggler from Donegal, had news for him in a village many miles south of Tarabeg.

'He's back,' the smuggler announced enigmatically and out of the blue, looking Jay full in the face to note his reaction.

Jay knew instantly who he was talking about. Kevin McGuffey. But he kept his counsel, waiting for further explanation.

'You don't seem too bothered.' The smuggler handed him a case with the goods Jay was unable to buy in a shop himself. Fewer and fewer places would serve the likes of him these days.

He paid for the box of food with bits and pieces he'd stolen along the way. 'Why would I be worried?' he asked as he stored the case in the back of the caravan.

'Because he nearly fecking murdered ye before he left.' The smuggler laughed as his eyes wandered to Jay's bad leg.

'Time passes,' said Jay grumpily.

'Aye, well, just as well, because he's after seeing you. He's going to the cottage and the cave in the cliff, where he'll hide out. Told me to tell you to meet him there.'

The news that McGuffey was looking for him was more welcome than the Donegal smuggler could have known. Jay was desperate for money, and McGuffey had always been a man with a plan. If he wanted to see Jay, there'd be money in it.

McGuffey had been on the run for twenty years, since the day he'd murdered his own wife, Angela. Jay scowled at the memory: if things had turned out as they'd meant to, it would have been him, Jay Maughan, who'd married McGuffey's daughter, Sarah. But Angela had got in the way, and the girl had escaped and married Michael Malone. There was always a fecking Malone somewhere to ruin things. Jay hawked and spat at the ground in disgust. He hated the Malones a lot worse than he did McGuffey, even though McGuffey was so crazed he'd taken a shot at Jay before he'd scarpered. It was only thanks to Shona that Jay hadn't lost his leg as a result.

Everyone knew McGuffey had fled across the border and joined the IRA. His hatred of the British consumed him and the IRA would have provided a safe haven for a man with nothing to lose.

'I'd better get meself over to Tarabeg and see what he wants,' Jay said as he tied the straps on the tarpaulin.

'Don't stand too close. He's still a man with the wildness in his eyes. He's older, like the rest of us, and slower in his movements. He's thin and weak, but not in the head. A horrible wound in his own leg he has just now too – God's justice, you might say. Someone made a better job of shooting him than he did you. Got himself into trouble in the North, apparently. Upset someone, as he always does. Wouldn't go to the doctor, though – said he'd fix it himself.'

The smuggler fished out a soft parcel from his bag. 'He gave me this. Said that before you go to him, you have to let them know he's back.' The man leered toothlessly at Jay. 'I'm guessing you know who he means by "they", am I right?'

Jay nodded. He knew, all right.

'He wants to scare the living daylights out of the lot of them and let them know he means business.'

Jay took the packet and peeled away the brown paper. Underneath lay something he recognised but could not place. It was an Arran shawl and for a moment he allowed it to slip through his fingers. Then a frown furrowed his brow. 'Jesus weep,' he said.

The smuggler met his eyes and held them. 'He very likely is,' he said. 'You take care of yourself. Just because

McGuffey has a reputation, it doesn't mean you have to do his bidding the moment he clicks his fingers.'

Jay looked deeper inside the parcel and immediately threw it to the ground, repulsed. 'Ask me, what sane man would do that – keep a dead woman's clothes? A murdered woman at that. Does he have no fear whatsoever of the Divil in him? And to think he's kept it all this time.'

'Aye, well, that'll be it. I told you, he's a madman with a taste for blood. You watch your back.'

Jay tied up the brown parcel with the string he'd pulled free and threw it into the back of the caravan as though it was burning his hands. He mounted the front board, clicked the reins and without a backwards glance moved on into the night. It would take him more than a week to reach Tarabeg. He was both begrudgingly admiring and plain startled that McGuffey clearly held none of the fears that plagued him; fears of ghosts and memories. The man was even returning to the scene of his crime, to Angela's cottage.

'He kept the fecking shawl,' he muttered as he glanced over his shoulder, expecting to see Angela's ghost sitting under the tarpaulin.

He decided that on the way to Tarabeg and McGuffey he would take a risk, try and pick up as much information as he could. He would call and see the tinkers at Ballycroy. They had returned to the Bog after years of being banished by Shona. They would feed and shelter him and in exchange for whiskey would give him all the news he needed.

With every rut the wheels rolled over he heard the crackle of the brown paper in the back of the caravan. One thing he was sure of, he wanted to be rid of that parcel at the earliest possible chance.

Nola had gone about her usual day, making breakfast for the men, clearing it away, and then starting on the next meal ready for when they came in from the cows. As the temperature had dropped and there were no crops in the fields, they returned to eat well before one o'clock. Now that the days were getting shorter, Seamus and Pete spent the last hours of afternoon light down the hill in the village, sitting at a wooden table in front of the fire in Paddy's bar.

'Ah, Jesus, I need the apples,' said Nola to her friend Bridget, who was sitting on the settle next to the fire.

Bridget had called in to the farm to buy butter. Nola's reputation for churning the best butter in Mayo extended far and wide, but few were allowed to buy it. As always, Bridget, who lived in a sad house out on the edge of the peat blanket, lingered in the warm kitchen for a cup of tea and a gossip.

'There's plenty of them,' Bridget said.

'True enough.' Nola sprinkled flour over her rolled-out pastry. 'Seamus said 'twas the best year for the apples he could ever remember. I'd ask him to fetch them from the old house, if he wasn't snoring on the bed like a fecking sow.'

Seamus and Pete had arrived back from Paddy's and taken straight to their beds, and no one blamed them, not even Nola, not really. It was the pattern of life on the farm. In the summer they worked eighteen hours a day.

'Shall I go for you?' said Bridget, sensing a way to eke out her visit and put off having to return to her damp house and her miserable husband, Porick.

'Not at all. I'll go meself. They'll soon be awake and up for the milking, but not soon enough for me. I'll not be a minute. You put the kettle back on, Bridget. Don't go awhile. I'll have more than enough – if you wait, you can take a pie back home with you.'

Bridget rose from the settle to do Nola's bidding, a smile of relief spreading across her face.

Nola pushed her hair away from her eyes with the back of her hands, wiped her fingers down the front of her apron and went out into the twilight, to the old house. She shoved open the door and made her way to where she thought she'd placed the apple crate full of straw.

'Would you be admiring your handiwork down there, would you now?' called down Pete Shevlin from his bedroom, which was nothing more than a pallet in what had been the old hay loft. Nola and Seamus had tried to persuade him many times that he needed and deserved more in the way of home comforts and that he should move into the main house, but that was before Joe had arrived. Pete, born and raised and now working on a farm, had disagreed.

''Tis damp – you should be sleeping in the house, not here with the animals,' said Nola as she began to shift one of the crates to the side.

'Sure, I spend more time in there with you and Seamus than I do in here.' He gestured towards the house with his chin. 'And Joe now too, as it would seem he has no intention of moving on, not ever. Fecking loves the place, he does. If Mary Kate ever comes back, she won't be happy, I'm telling ye.'

He had a point. Nola cooked all his meals, and Pete ate and drank with them, and played cards into the night with Seamus and Joe. But when the time came, he was glad to don his cap and return with the dogs to the old house for a bit of peace and quiet.

'If you're searching for a pot of gold in amongst that lot, I can tell ye, there isn't one, I've looked already.' Pete folded his arms behind his head and lay back down on the straw pillow, which crackled under his weight.

Nola located the apples and removed them from the box one by one, dropping them into her apron's front pocket. 'Aye, well, we don't need to be worrying about Joe. Or Mary Kate, for that matter. As sure as

God is true, she is no different from all the others. She will be staying over in Liverpool and that's a fact. And doesn't Joe just have a nature for the place that she seems not to be missing nor even to care about at all. He doesn't like having to go back to America for those meetings they make him go to. Told me with his own mouth, he would much rather be here and never leave. But as for Mary Kate, we haven't seen sight of her, not a visit home once in two years and who would have thought it?'

Pete, a normally cheerful man, let out a heavy sigh. Nola craned her neck and looked up, giving him her full attention.

'She's living the feckin' high life,' he said. 'They say the craic is the best in the world in Liverpool, better than Dublin even – not that I've been there either – so who can blame her for not wanting to come back here.'

Nola tutted. 'Ah, the high life be damned. Don't we just live the high life here? No one with any sense goes looking for a high life. Sounds like the road to trouble, if you ask me. I was fierce disappointed in Mary Kate, I was, not coming home for Daedio's funeral. You know that. The whole village knows it. Most of them think she hadn't even been told he'd died and that we kept it from her, so shocked they were at her not coming to the wake.'

She patted her apron pockets, checking whether she'd got enough apples for the pie.

'Joe is welcome to stay for as long as he wants,' she said, a warm smile creeping across her face. 'He was there for Daedio. He stayed. And besides, he's family anyway. Daedio was delighted he was here, delighted to spend time with him afore he died. Said it was like having his brother back. And remember, Daedio was the youngest of the lot of them; hadn't seen his big brother since he was a little fella.'

Nola took Seamus's jug off the top of a wooden crate and began to fill it from the porter barrel. As much as she moaned and complained, she never missed an opportunity to do something that would make her husband happy, and she knew he would smile at her with pure pleasure when he saw it warming near the fire, waiting. As the liquid noisily filled the pot, the dogs both rose from their positions beside Pete's bed and rattled down the open wooden staircase to come and lie at her feet. Nola, the bringer of scraps.

'Ah, go'way with ye,' she said, flapping her free arm at them and turning back to Pete. 'Did Joe not come back from the village with ye then?'

'No, he did not.' Pete averted his eyes, rolled over onto his side and appeared to be examining a piece of straw he had pulled from his bed. 'He has gone all the way to Galway in that fancy car of his. Gone to steal the hearts of a few more women, I would imagine. He has them all under his spell and eating out of his hand in Tarabeg – bored with the women here, he is; not fancy enough for him, I reckon. Off to make them Galway girls cry.'

Nola laughed. 'What are you talking about? Like who? Who is there here in Tarabeg that he could impress or whose heart he could break? All the young women have gone off to America or Liverpool, just like our Mary Kate. There's no one for him to dazzle, unless you think he's one for the older women – he does have them eating out of his hand right enough. They fuss around him like old grannies.'

She straightened up, happy with her haul, and pulled the apron into her to protect the apples. 'If he has a liking for the older ladies, I may be in with a chance meself – what do you reckon? He's a mighty fine fella, so he is.' She laughed and gave him a wink.

Pete sulked, his face peering down, his cap still in place. 'Have ye no eyes in your head, Nola? Have ye not seen the way Peggy is when he's around? 'Tis a disgrace – she laughs all over the place like a simpleton. Julia in the fishermen's cottages can control herself better than Peggy, and she's afflicted, so she is.'

Nola glanced out of the door. The light was fading, the cattle gathering by the top gate above the house. The vegetation and dense ferns on the hill were winter dead. A single spiral of white smoke rose from the house and disappeared into the grey sky. The horse was restless in his loosebox, excited by Nola's presence. He'd been fed hot oats after his journey into the village and been rubbed down with a wad of straw, but now he threw his head over the stable door and kicked at it with some force, hoping to catch Nola's attention. There was the chance she might feed him one of the apples, or if not an extra handful of hay; he would even settle for a cupping of his velvet muzzle with her hand and a kiss on the nose, as had been Nola's way for the past twenty years.

Nola looked the horse in the eye. 'Stop that banging – you'll have the door down. Here, stop.' She walked over, extracted one of the smaller apples from her apron and held it on the flat of her palm for the cob to take. She turned back to Pete, who was watching her and appeared to be expecting an answer. 'Aye, well, we all know what it is Peggy is after – a film star. But none will be walking into Tarabeg now, of that I am absolutely sure.'

Pete didn't speak or move and as Nola looked up, she could see he was unhappy, which was unusual for such a normally self-contained man. They were not often alone, being mostly in the main house together in the company of the men. This was a rare occasion and Pete, a man of few words, appeared to have something on his mind.

'Joe is as good as any film star,' he replied. 'He has the looks and the money. He keeps taking off to America on a jet plane and then coming straight back again. How much more glamorous could he be? And he comes back flashing the dollars around and the presents for the ladies in the post office. What's there for those of us who stay and don't go off to America, or anywhere else for that matter? I've never even been to Dublin and only to Galway the twice.'

Pete rubbed his hands across his eyes, wiping away the imaginary dust. Pulling another piece of straw from his pallet, he began to chew on the end of it, but not for long, as another thought appeared to strike him. 'How long is he staying in Tarabeg for, Nola? If Mary Kate comes back, she might want to stay with you and not down in the shop, you know. She was never away from this place. Shouldn't he be finding his own bed by now? I thought he was moving into the teacher's house with Declan.'

Pete's voice had turned into a whine and Nola was taken aback at how miserable he sounded. In all the years he'd worked for them, she'd never heard him utter a cross word or a complaint.

'Pete, what is wrong with ye? Peggy has been working at Michael's shop for years and never once have you mentioned her name to me before today. Declan has his mammy to stay with him, as you know – she's old now, and he can't keep travelling back to Galway to visit her. And besides, I like having American Joe here. 'Tis no trouble to me, one more mouth to feed. Now what is it? Why is what Peggy thinks about anyone bothering ye?'

Pete flushed to the roots of his hair.

Nola pulled her hand away from the horse as he lifted the second half of the apple from her. She wiped the slobber onto her skirt, held tight onto the pocketful of apples with the other, and took a step towards Pete to see him more clearly. 'Oh, Holy Mother of God, no. Are you sweet on Peggy – after all this time? Pete Shevlin, are you a slow starter? Aren't you past thirty-five years of age? What has got into ye?'

'I didn't know. I only just... Oh, I don't know.' Pete sat up on his mattress and placed his head in his hands.

'What, you only knew you liked her when someone else began paying her attention, is that what you're telling me? Well, you deserve to lose her to American Joe if that's the case. If you can't tell Peggy you're sweet on her, don't blame her as she goes flashing her eyes at the best-looking fella around.'

Pete groaned and Nola looked shamefaced.

'Okay, second best. I've always told Seamus you're a good-looking fella and that I don't know why you've not married at all.'

'I don't know what to do, Nola. How do I tell her? She doesn't even like me.'

Nola shook her head. 'Fellas. I wonder sometimes how we all manage. I mean, how do we farm and have children and survive, because every flamin' thing you lot seem to do is wrong one way or another. Isn't there a dance coming up at the long hall? American Joe never goes to those.'

'There is,' said Pete. 'But, you know, I never go to them either.'

'Well, now's the time to start. I only know about the dance because Joe read the poster in the post office out loud to me when he took me in the car to see Mrs Doyle, and I think Josie and Keeva might be selling the tickets from behind the butcher's counter.'

A chicken began to peck at Nola's shoe. She lifted her foot and sent the chicken flapping and squawking. 'When you're there, you just have to ask her to dance and then when you get her on the dance floor, say to her, "I have a notion for you, Peggy," just like that. Look her in the eyes and smile when you say it. She will understand. And before you know it, you'll be married, in your own house, and with a babby on the way.'

Pete looked amazed. 'Are you sure?'

Nola tutted. 'Oh, here we go – now you're doubting me after I gave you the best advice anyone has ever given to you for free. Go on, help yourself to a porter. I have Bridget waiting in the kitchen – she'll be in me bed for the night if I take much longer.'

Half an hour later, with the apples stewed and the pies in the oven, Nola sat in the chair opposite Bridget at the side of the fire and held out her cup. 'Read me tea leaves then, Bridget. Tell me, do you see Pete in there, dancing with Peggy in the long hall?'

Bridget reached out and took the cup from Nola's outstretched hand. Her hat was held firmly in place with a hatpin and she still had her moth-eaten black woollen coat on, though it was unbuttoned and fell loosely down the side of the chair, revealing her faded floral apron beneath.

'Pete and Peggy, you say? Well now, I would never have put those two together, despite neither of them having settled down. Pete is too steady altogether for Peggy – 'tis a film star she's after, and saving to flit to America.' Bridget tipped the cup towards the fire and flicked it by the handle to expel the last drops of tea. The flames spat back at her as she caught the light and frowned.

'Well, do you see them?' Nola shuffled forward on the chair, her knees apart in an unladylike manner, her modesty protected by her long, unfashionable skirt and her clasped hands hanging down between. Her cheeks shone apple rosy and beads of sweat from the effort of baking and sitting too close to the fire perched on her top lip. The light from the one lamp that sat on the three-legged wooden table, carved by Daedio, cast a glow over the two of them. She picked up her glasses and placed them on the bridge of her nose, as though she were the one reading the leaves, not Bridget.

'I need them to concentrate,' she said in response to Bridget's raised eyebrow.

'I'm the one who needs to concentrate,' said Bridget.

'Well then,' she continued, 'I do not see Peggy and Pete in your cup at all.'

'Oh God in heaven.' Nola removed her glasses and almost dropped them onto the table. 'He's as miserable as sin itself up there, so he is,' she said, gesturing in the direction of the old house. 'Will you get a better reading if I make us another and drop a bit of whiskey into it this time?'

Bridget shook her head and set the cup in her lap. She looked concerned. 'The whiskey will be welcome, but it won't alter a thing. I do see something in here though.'

'What? What is it? What do you see?' Eyebrows raised, hands clasped together, voice bright with hope, Nola pushed up on the chair and eased herself to the edge of the seat, securing the arms of her spectacles over her ears.

Bridget looked up and met her friend's eye with a steady gaze. 'I see a woman coming home to Tarabeg with a heart heavier than the case she carries.'

Nola's hand flew to her mouth. 'Holy Mother of God, is... is it...?'

'Yes, it is, Nola,' said Bridget. 'It's Mary Kate.'

Chapter 4

Mary Kate was exhausted and soaked through. It was November and the days were getting shorter and colder. Frustrated at the time it had taken for a tram to arrive outside St Angelus and then the transfer to the bus, she was almost in tears as she ran down Duke's Avenue and through the back door of the house into the kitchen. Barely able to feel her fingers or toes, she saw with grateful relief that the range fire had been lit and was roaring up the chimney. And there was Jet, taking advantage of the fireside rug, far too warm and lazy to rise and greet her, but banging his big black tail to beat out his welcome home.

Mrs O'Keefe, who had proved to be more like a mother than a friend and neighbour, was laying the table. She looked up and smiled. Joan, as always, was standing at the sink, straining the boiling water from the carrots. Her face was pink from the steam and the heat of the oven, and her hair was all loose and wild, refusing to be contained.

'How is he?' Joan asked as Mary Kate banged the door shut behind her. She asked the same question of Mary Kate a dozen times a day.

'Poorly,' Mary Kate gasped, short of breath from having raced up from the bus stop.

Nicholas's fingers had clung onto hers, not wanting to let go when she'd tried to slip out of the ward while he was sleeping. His eyes had opened wide and she'd been alarmed to see they were filled with fear. 'Don't leave me. Don't go,' he'd whispered.

But Nurse Brogan was already marching up and down the centre of the ward ringing the brass hand-bell.

'I have no choice,' Mary Kate had said as her lips brushed his protruding cheekbones and hot tears ran down her face. 'I'm not allowed to stay. William's coming after surgery finishes, so he'll be here from four. And I'll be the first at the door when six o'clock visiting begins. You look to the door and you'll see me through the glass, on tiptoes, waiting to come in.'

He smiled. She always was there first, her red hair bobbing up and down in the frame of circular glass.

'I'm sorry, visiting is over.' Nurse Brogan was now at the foot of the bed, silencing the ringing of the brass bell as it rested in her hand.

Mary Kate looked down at Nicholas, his torso strikingly thin against the white of the hospital pillows.

'Don't go,' he whispered again.

He had never done that before and Mary Kate's heart beat wildly with anxiety. To gain a few more precious moments, she picked up the feeding mug from the bedside table and held it to his lips. 'I'll just give him this before I go,' she said to Nurse Brogan, who was glancing nervously towards the door.

'Nurse Brogan, have all the visitors left now, please?' said Sister pointedly from her office doorway.

'Yes, Sister. Almost.'

'Good. Shut the ward doors then, please.'

Nurse Dana Brogan looked towards Mary Kate with pleading eyes.

'I love you.' Mary Kate pressed her soft cool lips against Nicholas's own, which were hot and dry. 'I love you so, so much.' She tasted her own salty tears.

He tried to speak. He was too exhausted, but his eyes, only moments before filled with fear, had now softened with love as he lightly squeezed her hand.

'When I come back, we're going to talk about our holiday in Cornwall last summer. Do you remember? We'll plan another, just as soon as you're better.'

He nodded and his eyes never left hers.

'All those long walks along the beach and that little hotel with the smart restaurant and the waiter who told us those stories about the smugglers and the village.'

Mary Kate looked up at Nurse Brogan. 'He loves seafood and he ate it every day,' she said. 'Have a sleep now, Nicholas, and dream about those lovely waves and the seagulls and the fishing boats we watched coming in.'

His eyes were closing and his face had relaxed.

'And the sky was so blue, not a cloud anywhere – do you remember?'

He had taken her to Cornwall because he thought it might remind her of the west of Ireland, the closest thing to her homeland that he could show her. His eyes were shut now and he let out a deep and peaceful sigh.

'I'll stay with him every minute I can until you're back,' said Dana as Mary Kate carefully placed his now heavy hand on the turned-down sheet. 'If you don't want to go all the way home, Mrs Tanner will look after you in the café at the main entrance.'

Mary Kate was so choked with tears that her throat felt thick and burnt and she could barely speak. 'Thank you,' she rasped, under the stern gaze of Sister, who was tutting outside her office and closing the ward doors herself. 'I know,' Mary Kate continued, 'Mrs Tanner is so nice. She always has a cup of tea and a spare handkerchief ready. I have time though, so I'll go home.'

Dana Brogan took the warm hand that had just held Nicholas's. 'Go on now, and don't be worrying. I'm here and I won't be going anywhere until you get back. He's safe with me.'

Mary Kate looked at the nurse she had vaguely known as a girl on a farm back home and if she could have, she would have hugged her. Then she turned and fled the ward before she broke down in tears.

By the time she arrived home, what with waiting for the tram and then the bus, she had just the hour to eat and get back to the ward. The pressure of this routine was beginning to take its toll. She pulled the woollen scarf Mrs O'Keefe had knitted her last Christmas away from her throat and her fingers momentarily caressed the emerald heart and her velvet ribbon. Then she looked over at Joan and Mrs O'Keefe and managed what passed for a smile.

'I do have some good news, though. Matron has said that from tomorrow I don't have to come back home in the afternoons. She's going to move Nicholas into the side room near to the office so that I can stay between afternoon and evening visiting and I won't have to rush home and leave him at all during the day.'

Hearing that, Mrs O'Keefe's own eyes stung with tears of gratitude at the kindness of Matron.

'The nurse who is sitting with him is an angel. Dana Brogan. She does the clinics with Dr Gaskell, she told me, and she knows Nicholas, God love her.' Mary Kate removed her coat, placed it over the back of one of the kitchen chairs and dragged it closer to the fire to dry out.

'Here, let me do that,' said Mrs O'Keefe. 'You get upstairs and wash the hospital off your hands.'

Mary Kate pulled the pin out of her wet felt hat and laid it on the range shelf. 'She's from near to home, Nurse Brogan is. She's older than me, but Daddy knows the Brogans from Belmullet – we all do. We buy from him and her daddy is a farmer. I remember going in the van with Daddy to their farm and she was always there. She's just lovely. She told me that sometimes, when Nicholas is asleep and she talks to him, he thinks it's me because we sound the same, because we have the same accent! Imagine that – someone who knows my whole family being on the ward and looking after him. She said she won't leave his side until I get back tonight.'

Mrs O'Keefe circled her arm around Mary Kate's shoulders. Her words came tumbling out, as fast as her thoughts were churning. 'Right, well, that's very good news indeed, and maybe when this is all over, you two will become friends here in Liverpool. But right now our job is to look after you too, because the last thing that man needs is for you to get sick yourself. If you don't keep your strength up, you're no use whatsoever to anyone. Catch your breath, come on.'

Joan held out a cup of tea that rattled on the saucer. The past few weeks had taken it out of her too. 'Fetch it upstairs with you,' she said to Mary Kate.

Mrs O'Keefe moved to the oven, pulled out the shepherd's pie she'd made earlier and placed it on the hot plate on the range, ready to transfer to the trivet in the middle of the kitchen table. 'I have a plan,' she said. 'Don't be worrying about the buses tonight – I've ordered a taxi to take the two of us and bring us back, so that gives you an extra half an hour. I'm coming with you. But first there's a hot bath drawn and waiting for you upstairs. You go and get in it and soak your bones. You look frozen through.'

'Oh God, thank you – and you've made food too. Can we take some back to the ward to try and tempt him to eat?'

'We can. Now go, get in that hot bath before you catch your death.'

Mary Kate was desperate for the bathroom. The thought of a hot bath for her cold, aching body propelled her out of the door. She made for the stairs and didn't see the expression on Mrs O'Keefe's face.

'William is with him,' she threw over her shoulder on her way up. 'He's allowed to visit anytime, because he's a doctor. It's so mean – I've hated this having to come home in between the visiting times. I'm so glad Matron is moving him. You'd like her, Mrs O'Keefe – she reminds me of you. I don't want to be wasting the money on a taxi though, who knows how long he'll be like this? It could be that he can't return to work for years, and the state he's in, I can imagine it. He's as yellow as the mustard and there isn't a pick of fat on him.'

Mrs O'Keefe kept her tone neutral. 'Go on, up,' she said quickly. 'We can talk about all of this later.'

Moments later, Mary Kate slipped into the hot water infused with Epsom salts, her clothes discarded on the bathroom floor and her velvet ribbon laid carefully on the glass shelf alongside. She let out a deep sigh and closed her eyes as she felt the hospital washing away and the warmth seeping into her bones.

Mrs O'Keefe was accompanying Mary Kate to the hospital that evening for a reason. She wanted to catch the eye of the ward sister or have a word with William, the other doctor at Nicholas's practice, who she knew had been visiting Nicholas every day. She had suffered when her own husband had wasted away in the same manner in the same hospital. She knew what was coming and she couldn't believe that no one had told Mary Kate that Nicholas was terminally ill. Someone would have to prepare her for the fact that he would never be coming home, and with not a single member of Mary Kate's family even aware that Nicholas existed, it was going to have to be her.

The truth of Nicholas's situation had finally come home to Mrs O'Keefe a couple of days earlier, when she'd happened to answer a phone call from Dr Gaskell. He'd been wanting to speak to Mary Kate but had sounded relieved to hear Mrs O'Keefe on the other end instead. His news, however, had been distressing.

'I'm afraid I have to report that Mrs Marcus has taken to visiting the hospital each day,' Dr Gaskell had told her. 'It's a very sad state of affairs, but she is legally his wife and neither Matron nor I can prevent it. We are doing our very best to make sure that Lavinia and Mary Kate don't bump into each other.'

'Oh, no, they cannot meet!' Mrs O'Keefe had stuttered into the phone, her heart racing. 'Mary Kate is in no fit state to deal with that wicked woman.'

'We quite agree,' he'd replied. 'She appears to take a perverse pleasure in watching Nicholas's deterioration. However, Matron has come to the rescue. She has told Mrs Marcus that she must come in the mornings and for a few minutes only. Mrs Marcus is not the type of woman who would visit during normal hours anyway; she regards herself as somewhat above that, as though still being legally married to a doctor who is a patient gives her special privileges. Matron has also made sure that Nurse Brogan stands with her for the entire time she's there and keeps an eye on her. I'm afraid Mrs Marcus has displayed no compassion, and in the circumstances Matron finds that very disturbing.'

To that, Mrs O'Keefe had had no answer. She could not ask that Mrs Marcus be kept away; there was no moral high ground for her to stand on.

She'd been overcome by a feeling of gloom ever since that call, as if a dark cloud had settled over the Marcus house. A shiver ran down her spine now, as she lifted the warmed dinner plates out of the oven and stacked them on the range.

'Is Dr Marcus really going to live for years?' asked Joan. 'Because sometimes I think 'tis as plain as the nose on my face that the poor man is dying. Is he?' She began to cry, as she so often did these days, and lifted her apron to her eyes to dry her tears.

Mrs O'Keefe crossed the room and put her arms around her. 'Come on, Joan, I know this is hard, but we have a job to do here, and that's to keep Mary Kate going. Unless I've got it completely wrong, he doesn't have very long left at all, but for some reason he hasn't been able to tell her himself. I expect he tried, but maybe he just couldn't do it. Or maybe he wanted to shield her from the pain of knowing. I don't know the reason, but we are all she has and we have to be here for her.'

Joan's tears streamed down and she sat on her chair and buried her head in her arms on the table. 'Oh God, I can't believe 'tis so,' she sobbed.

Poor Joan had loved Dr Marcus; he'd been a kind and generous employer. She had her own grief to bear.

Mrs O'Keefe tilted her head, listening for any signs of movement upstairs. There were none. Mary Kate was still safely in the bath and wouldn't be able to hear. She'd made a decision and would have to act fast. 'Stay here, Joan. I won't be a moment.' She dropped a motherly kiss onto the top of Joan's head and moved into the hall to telephone her own home, a few doors further down the avenue.

'Hello, Deidra, is that you?' she whispered down the line.

Deidra wondered who else it would be she was expecting to answer the phone in her own house and had to force herself to stop grinning. 'It is, and who would that be?' she asked.

'Why, it's me of course, who else would it be?' said Mrs O'Keefe, pulling the phone from her ear and looking askance at the mouthpiece. 'Deidra, get yourself over here. The place is falling apart. No one seems to understand what's happening. I'm going to go back to the hospital tonight with Mary Kate and see if I can talk to someone. They need family here and there is none, so it'll have to be us.'

'Aye, 'tis a sad state of affairs,' said Deidra. 'Does she know that Lavinia Marcus has been at the hospital between visiting times?'

'No,' whispered Mrs O'Keefe.

'What can I do?' Deidra asked.

'I think I need you to move in here to the Marcuses' house with Joan for a few days. Mary Kate hasn't a clue, she thinks Dr Marcus is coming home, and Joan has cried so many tears, she'll be nothing but a puddle by the time the day is out.'

'God love her,' said Deidra. 'I'm on me way. I'll be

there in a few minutes. Will I get a message to Cat? She'll help.'

'You do that, Deidra, there's a good girl. Joan is wailing like a banshee, as if there isn't enough to be worrying about.'

Ten minutes later, Mary Kate was wolfing down the shepherd's pie like she had never eaten before, and it was a fact that she hadn't had anything since breakfast, a good eight hours ago. Nurse Brogan brought her endless cups of tea, offered to make her toast and placed biscuits on the saucer, but in the hospital she just couldn't eat. 'That was so delicious,' she said as she wiped her mouth and looked up in appreciation.

Joan had composed herself, helped considerably by the news that support was arriving in the form of Deidra and Cat.

Mrs O'Keefe reached out and removed the plate. 'Go on, you go and put a bit of powder and lippy on. The taxi will be here in a few minutes, and no arguments, I've already ordered it.'

The back door nudged open and in came Deidra, greeted by Jet wagging his tail and jumping up at her on his arthritic back legs. Her laughter cut through the atmosphere in the kitchen. 'Down!' she said, glancing from one to the other and immediately taking in the worry etched on Mrs O'Keefe's face, the denial on Mary Kate's and the tear stains of Joan, who was washing pots in the sink.

Mary Kate scraped her chair back. She needed no encouragement to get ready to leave the house and return to her beloved Nicholas. 'I'll be down in a minute,' she said, smiling at Deidra and heading for the stairs.

She felt riddled with guilt whenever she was away from the hospital, anxious to the bone. The shepherd's pie sat in her stomach as heavy as a brick of regret for having left him alone. Standing at the sink in their bathroom, she applied some face powder and stared at her reflection in the oval gilt mirror. In the past six weeks she'd lost at least a stone in weight. Her eyes looked sunken and hollow and they were filled with fear. She was frightened, but she had no idea why.

'He will be home soon,' she said to herself. 'Home and well.' She said it a dozen times a day, to the point where she usually managed to convince herself that he would indeed be home soon. But tonight her words had no effect.

She heard the sound of the taxi approaching the end of the drive. Folding the towel, she ran to the door. As she reached the landing, she remembered her velvet ribbon and her mother's emerald, which were still on the bathroom shelf.

'Come along, Mary Kate,' shouted Mrs O'Keefe.

'Drat!' Mary Kate glanced towards the bathroom and promised herself that she'd put it back on the second she got home.

'Mary Kate has no idea, does she?' said Deidra as she stood next to Joan at the sink and placed her arms around her shoulders.

'Neither did that one, until this afternoon,' said Mrs O'Keefe grimly, inclining her head towards Joan as she scraped the remains off her plate and into the dog's bowl. 'I'm guessing that as it's Lavinia Marcus who's the next of kin, she's the one who's been told how serious it is and poor Mary Kate has been left in the dark.'

'I sent a message to Cat. She knows the ward and is on her way to meet you,' said Deidra.

Cat had been a solid friend to Mary Kate since the day she had disembarked the Dublin to Liverpool ferry and got herself mugged. Cat had taken pity on Mary Kate and looked after her, no questions asked. That had also been the day that Mary Kate had fallen helplessly in love with the doctor who'd rescued her.

There was the crunch of wheels on the gravel outside.

'Come on now, Mary Kate,' Mrs O'Keefe shouted up the stairs. 'The taxi's here.'

Mary Kate ran down the last steps and took her thick gloves from Mrs O'Keefe's outstretched hand. Her coat was as warm as toast from having been dried by the range, and wisps of steam rose from the still slightly damp shoulders.

Just as Mrs O'Keefe opened the front door to step out, the telephone rang.

'Oh, I have to answer that,' Mary Kate said.

'No, you don't. We will lose five precious minutes off your hour if we wait a second longer. The girls can answer it. Joan, Deidra, get that phone, the meter is ticking away out here.' Pushing Mary Kate out into the now cold night air, Mrs O'Keefe slammed the front door behind them.

Joan didn't have the same degree of confidence as Deidra on the telephone and her voice was tremulous when she picked up the handset. 'Hello?' she almost whispered.

'Hello,' came the reply, in a calm, kind but authoritative tone. 'Could I speak with Miss Mary Kate Malone. It's the matron from St Angelus here.'

Joan gasped. Speaking to the matron was on a similar level to answering the phone to a call from the Pope. She looked back over her shoulder towards Deidra, who was now at her side. Her eyes were wide and frightened. 'She's gone in the taxi,' said Joan, speaking into the handset, her gaze never leaving Deidra's face.

'Oh dear. Can you tell me where she was heading? Is she on her way back here to the hospital?'

'She is, with Mrs O'Keefe. And Cat is going to meet her there – at the hospital, that is. She will have asked Pam next door to look after the children so she can come,' said Joan, not realising that Matron would not have a clue who she was referring to. 'They might sleep there at Pam's and she could come back here, if she wants too.'

'Ah, very well, I shall catch them here on the ward. So sorry to have bothered you. Goodnight.'

And with that, all Joan could hear was the dialling tone.

Matron replaced the receiver on the phone and looked over her desk to Dr Gaskell. He was sitting across from her, accepting a cup of tea from her housekeeper, Elsie O'Brien. 'She's on her way back here. I missed her. She's in a taxi already,' she said as she picked up her own cup and saucer.

Dr Gaskell sighed. 'May I ask permission for her to stay this evening? I don't think we have long. Just a few hours at the most, I'm guessing. William is sitting with him now, until she gets back here.'

'Of course. But it is very difficult. She isn't his wife and I'm treading a very thin line here.'

'Has his wife been in touch today?' Dr Gaskell raised his eyebrows. There was nothing he and Matron kept from each other.

'Has she? Only four times. It's so difficult. She doesn't want to come herself, other than for her once-a-day mawkish stare, but she keeps checking that no one else is visiting either. I don't enjoy having to lie, and I can tell you, if he hadn't trained here as one of our own doctors, my job would be so much easier. It would be his wife visiting and no one else. Having said that, Lavinia Marcus is possibly the most unpleasant woman I have met in my entire career. She challenges me every time I speak, and on the telephone she is just plain rude. Sadly, I think she is clever enough to know that the end is near. I don't trust that woman, she is up to something.'

Dr Gaskell peered at her over the rim of his cup. It was the first time he'd ever heard Matron admit that she'd found it difficult to deal with a relative.

'It's a good job Sister is more concerned about the welfare of our poor Dr Nicholas than she is about scandal on her ward. An estranged wife and a live-in mistress, both visiting... If you'd told me years ago that I'd need to tolerate this, I'd have told you you were mad. Was there ever a nicer doctor to train at this hospital or a better GP in Liverpool? It is breaking my heart, and there is no one more used to sadness than me.'

Dr Gaskell was not in the least surprised at this revelation. To everyone on the outside, Matron appeared to be all head and no heart, an austere figure who ran the best hospital in the northwest. Only he knew that there was deep compassion beneath that no-nonsense demeanour and crisply starched navy uniform, which she still wore at the longer length.

'Did the wife say if she was bringing his sons to say goodbye? I know Mary Kate has been fretting about that.'

'Oh no.' Matron leant forward in the chair and her cup and saucer clattered on her desk. 'I asked her to. I said that it would really help him in his final days, but she told me quite clearly that she had no intention of bringing them. The poor man, he asks after them every single day.'

Dr Gaskell felt a tear sting his eye; he must be getting soft in his old age. 'He knows he doesn't have long. He told me it was impossible for Mary Kate to bring his boys to see him, that Lavinia would never allow it, so he told her he didn't want to see them until he was better. That's why we're not allowed to tell her he isn't going to get better, to protect her from trying to fetch the boys from the school in Surrey and having to suffer the wrath of Lavinia Marcus. He's shielding her. If even you found Mrs Marcus a challenge, imagine what it would be like for that poor girl. Nicholas would wrap her up in cotton wool if he could.'

The phone on Matron's desk rang and as she spoke, Dr Gaskell knew without being told what was wrong. A chill ran through him and despite the fire burning high in the grate, he shivered.

'Yes, Sister. Yes, don't worry. Dr Gaskell is here with me. We will be down right away.'

If Mary Kate had been allowed to, she would have run down the hospital corridor.

Cat saw them approaching the ward doors before they saw her. She was talking to William, Nicholas's practice partner, and they were standing slightly apart from the rest of the visitors waiting to go in. 'Oh God, she's here,' she said, her feet frozen to the spot. 'Mrs O'Keefe is with her.'

'You stay here,' said William. 'I've had to do this a few times before. It comes with the job, unfortunately.'

There were just a few seconds of grace as Mary Kate, her face taut with impatience and purpose, marched towards him. Nicholas had spoken about her so often, he felt he knew her better than he actually did. 'She has turned my life around,' Nicholas used to say to him on his daily visits to the ward. 'I was only living half a life and she changed all that. I miss the boys, that's the worst part, but even that is more bearable as she's so good with them when we do have them or are allowed to visit them at school.'

William caught the eye of Mrs O'Keefe and it was apparent that no words were needed. Her jaw dropped. 'Mary Kate...' she said, putting out her hand.

But it was one minute past six and there was only one person on Mary Kate's mind. Just one man filling her thoughts as her feet strode through the now opening ward doors, the love that burnt in her heart propelling her forwards. With her gaze fixed ahead, she almost pushed past William as he reached out and grabbed her arm.

'Mary Kate…' he said, but he was too late.

She saw the curtains pulled around the bed and she stopped in her tracks as though electrified. She noted the expression on Nurse Brogan's face as she quickly walked from the opposite end of the ward towards her.

'No. No. No.' It was a whisper. A denial. 'No! Where is he? Where have you taken him?' She glanced wildly around the ward, at the approaching visitors and the beds filled with patients, as though expecting to see him in one of them. 'Where is he?' This time it was louder. Shaking free from William's hand, she ran down the ward and almost knocked Nurse Brogan to the floor as she pulled the curtains back.

'No! God, please, no!' Her wail filled the ward as her hands grabbed at the starched white sheet that covered him. She began to slide down towards the bed and a strong pair of arms hauled her to her feet. It was Dr Gaskell.

'I am so sorry, my dear,' he said. 'There was nothing we could do. He knew he was going to die and he expressly would not let me tell you. William was with him; he was not alone.'

Mary Kate was too distraught to speak as she sobbed and stifled her cries in Dr Gaskell's white coat.

Matron appeared behind the curtains and spoke to Nurse Brogan. 'Help me get her to my rooms, will you, please. Nurse Brogan, tell Porter Dessie to bring a wheelchair. This poor girl won't have the use of her legs until she is over the shock.'

Despite the warmth from the fire in Matron's sitting room and the sweet tea she was forced to drink, Mary Kate shivered violently, causing her teeth to chatter.

'It's the shock,' said Matron as she placed a rug around Mary Kate's shoulders.

Mrs O'Keefe slipped her arm over the rug and pulled Mary Kate into her side. Mary Kate laid her head on her shoulder and stared, transfixed, oblivious to the conversation taking place around her.

'I'm afraid it happened so very quickly,' Dr Gaskell said, 'as it sometimes does. His heart was as strong as an ox's yesterday, but some of his other organs were beginning to fail and cause us concern, so we knew that time was running out. It was that that made Matron take the decision that you should stay for the whole day from now on, an exception to visiting rules which she never breaks, as you know.' He glanced over to Matron. 'I am terribly sorry. Sometimes our Maker has other plans for us. I... we... we thought he had about two more weeks...' He looked to Matron again. 'But we are not God, we cannot decide the time of calling, we can only guess.'

The manner in which Dr Gaskell explained to Mary Kate what had happened, just as he would have done had Mary Kate been Nicholas's lawful wife, was a kindness they all appreciated, and the only person who was too far away in her own thoughts to understand a word he was saying was Mary Kate.

Two hours later, Mary Kate was in the back of a cab with Mrs O'Keefe and Cat. They were talking, but she couldn't hear what they were saying. Their voices were a mumble as she stared out of the rain-spattered window into the dark night. One orange sulphur street light after another lit her face as she focused on two years of precious memories, on his face when he slept, his eyes when they laughed at her, the strength of his arms as he wrapped them around her when they walked the dog along the beach at Crosby. She would shut out the world and spend forevermore dwelling in these thoughts, she decided. She would live them over and over again. They would sustain her until it was her turn to join him.

'Come on, Mary Kate, my love,' said Mrs O'Keefe, who was now standing on the gravel drive with the cab door open.

Mary Kate hadn't noticed they'd stopped. On her knee was a brown paper bag filled with Nicholas's belongings. His watch, his books, the daily letters she used to leave with him to read while she wasn't allowed on the ward. She hugged it to her. The clothes inside smelt of him and it was easy to close her eyes and imagine him there next to her. She didn't want to move.

'Mary Kate…' This time it was Cat. 'Come on, love, let me take the bag.'

Without waiting for an answer, Cat reached in, took the weight of the brown paper bag from her knee and gently guided Mary Kate out of the cab. Mrs O'Keefe took her other arm and they supported her on her feet. The two older women exchanged glances; the next few days would be counted in minutes. Both had loved and lost and knew this. Counting the hours and days of loss would be next. Then the weeks and months. Both women knew that grief was a physical pain, that it sat in the diaphragm, the worst of aches.

Cat had used the phone in Matron's office and called ahead to Joan and Deidra, who would no doubt need consoling, especially Joan, who had loved the kind Dr Nicholas in her own way. But Mrs O'Keefe knew something was wrong the second she opened the Marcuses' front door. There was no Joan or Deidra waiting, and neither of them would have been wearing the stiletto heels she could hear clacking towards them on the tiled floor of the hallway. She could smell cigarette smoke and her heart lurched. In an instant, she knew who it was.

Dry-eyed and immaculate, in a pale blue cashmere twinset and pearls, her blonde hair neatly curled and with her tweed pencil skirt swishing against the sharkskin underskirt, Lavinia Marcus stood before them.

'Returned at last,' she sneered.

It was apparent that Mary Kate couldn't take in what was happening. She blinked and Cat squeezed her arm.

'Well, you bog-jumping Irish whore, I have only one thing to say. I am legally his wife and this is my house. Here's your bag.' She bent down, lifted up Mary Kate's small tartan suitcase and threw it onto the floor before them, missing Mrs O'Keefe's foot by inches.

'For goodness' sake, can't you see she's in shock.' Mrs O'Keefe dared to front up to the woman who had made Nicholas's life a misery. 'Let her at least come in and collect some of her things.'

Lavinia turned her gaze back to Mary Kate and seemed almost amused. 'Yes, you are right. Very harsh of me. I'll give you five minutes to do that – but not her, she never sets foot inside this house again. Go on, I'm counting.' She stood back and held the door open for Mrs O'Keefe to pass. 'She leaves this house with what she came, and that's next to nothing, so it shouldn't take you long.'

She lifted her arm and looked at her watch. 'Oh dearie me, one minute down, four left. Off you go and fetch the little tart's things and then *out*!' She raised her voice as the thin veneer of a smile slipped.

Cat noticed the spittle on her lip and was hypnotised in the glare of such venom.

While Mrs O'Keefe ran up the steps as fast as a woman of her age could, Lavinia turned her attention to Mary Kate, who, dazed, stood and blinked her red and swollen eyes in the light from the hallway. 'And don't you dare ever, ever let your shadow darken this doorstep again.'

She was met by silence and it was only Cat who saw the velvet ribbon around Lavinia's neck and the emerald heart that had belonged to Mary Kate's mother nestled at her throat.

Chapter 5

They had left the house in five minutes flat. It took a further five to walk down the avenue to reach Mrs O'Keefe's. Fifteen minutes later, Mary Kate was tucked up in her old bed in the room below Deidra's. As she closed her eyes, she drifted off into a sedative-induced sleep. William had given the sedative to Mrs O'Keefe, and she'd administered it when they were in Matron's rooms. 'Valium,' he'd said. 'Two tablets. It will help her sleep tonight and then we'll give her another dose in the morning if she becomes very distressed. She seems calm now, but I have to warn you, I've seen this so many times before: the dam will break at some point. It will hit her hard.'

Once Mary Kate's eyes had flickered shut, Mrs O'Keefe turned the brown Bakelite knob on the bedroom door with precision; as the catch fell, Deidra,

Joan and Cat all let out deep sighs of relief. The four women crept back downstairs and almost fell into the sitting room.

'Thank God she's asleep. I was beginning to think tonight would never end,' said Cat.

Deidra moved to the fireplace, threw in some kindling sticks, pumped the old brass-and-leather bellows on the fire and brought the embers back to life. Silence fell while everyone watched her at work. Tongues of flame rose and licked at the kindling.

The night had been fast moving, beyond their control. They had kept their faces straight and their tears in check, stoic in the face of loss, chaos and an evil woman in heels. Mary Kate had been their first concern, but now that she was safely asleep, the events were hitting them all like a train.

The noise of crackling wood filled the room.

'That Matron, what a lovely woman,' said Mrs O'Keefe, attempting to tug their thoughts away from the desperate grief of Mary Kate and the hatred in the eyes of Lavinia Marcus, and focus on the only good thing they had experienced that night: the kindness of Matron. She had taken them all up to her own rooms and dispensed tea and sympathy with the efficiency and compassion of someone who had done it many times before. She knew the words that might bring comfort, words that they had clung to.

'Aye, and that doctor too. What was his name? Dr Gaskell? A right gentleman, he was.' Cat clicked open her handbag and shuffled around inside to find her cigarettes.

'Lavinia Marcus must have phoned the hospital herself to find out what was happening,' Mrs O'Keefe said almost to herself. 'There was no other way she could have known. While we were in with Matron and the doctor was talking to Mary Kate, she must already have been on her way up the avenue.'

Joan sniffed. Mrs O'Keefe and Cat had almost forgotten she was there and both turned to look at her as she removed a grey, crumpled and wet handkerchief from her pocket. She had barely stopped crying all evening. 'I can't believe he's dead. What about the boys? They love their daddy,' she said, for what must have been the fiftieth time. 'What am I going to do now? Where am I going to work? I can't go back there – she's that wicked, and mad with me that I stayed when she left him, she'll kill me, and all me things are in me room. I'm too scared to go back.'

Joan's sniffle became a sob and Mrs O'Keefe walked over to her and gave her shoulders a squeeze.

'Shush, Joan, don't be worrying about that. You can sleep here, in the other bed in Deidra's room, until we find you a placement, and if we don't find one, you can stay here. Deidra is always saying the place is too big for one girl to manage.'

Joan's eyes filled with fresh tears; this time they were tears of relief. 'Can I? Oh, thank you, thank God for that.' She was now on the verge of a wail. 'I just can't believe he's dead. The boys, his little boys, who is going to tell them? Imagine being told by that heartless bitch!'

Eileen O'Keefe allowed her mind to wander to that scenario. Mary Kate loved those two little boys just as if they were her own, especially sensitive little Jack. She and Nicholas used to plan their lives around the weekends they'd been allowed to see them. She shuddered. It wasn't a thought she wanted to dwell on. Some things she could change, but that wasn't one of them.

'Right,' she said, clapping her hands, 'I know what we all need.' Moving across the room, she got down on her knees by the sideboard cupboard and pulled out a bottle of whiskey. 'It was my old man's. He was given it for a Christmas present the year before he died, but I'm sure it's still got a kick.'

'God, do we need that.' Cat had finally located her cigarettes and took them out of her handbag. 'Who wants a smoke, girls?'

Mrs O'Keefe got to her feet. 'I haven't smoked for years, but I will tonight,' she said.

Cat handed her one and struck a match. She noted the tremble in Mrs O'Keefe's hand as she bent her head to the flame to accept the light. Mrs O'Keefe may have seen a lot more of life than Mary Kate, but she had clearly also been affected by all the upset. 'Gi's the whiskey here,' Cat said as she shook the match with a flick of her wrist to extinguish the flame. 'I'll pour it. Go on, your hands are shaking, you sit down. You've been a saint these past few weeks. Go on, time to do as someone else says now.'

Cat glanced round Mrs O'Keefe's smart sitting room. 'Come here, Deidra. I'll pour and you carry the glasses over to that little table in front of the fire. Joan, come on, love, stop your crying now, we can't change a thing. Push that sofa closer to the fire. I do love these big houses, but honest to God, how can you feel the heat from the fire when you're sitting a mile away from it?'

She removed the cork plug from the top of the bottle with a dull plop and began to pour the whiskey into the Waterford tumblers she had located in the opposite end of the sideboard. 'That was a strong sedative that doctor gave Mary Kate. I could feel her legs going on the way back. I reckon we got home just in time. We need a sedative of our own and this will do very nicely.'

She poured three fingers of whiskey into each glass. 'Go on, get that down your neck,' she said to Mrs O'Keefe, and they all collapsed onto the chairs and the sofa that Joan had dragged nearer the fire.

There was quiet for a few moments as the first burn of the amber liquid slipped down their throats. On the first sip, Deidra and Joan, unused to drink, began to cough. By the end of the second glass, Joan was gulping it down and letting her feelings be known.

'They was living in sin,' she half slurred. 'Deidra and I, we knew 'twould end badly, didn't we, Deidra.'

'Now, now, Joan,' said Mrs O'Keefe. 'Mary Kate is all that matters now. When that sedative wears off and the truth hits her, she is going to need looking after by her friends, and I would say that is us. God knows, there's no one else.'

Cat held up the bottle and gestured at their glasses. 'Shall I?' she asked, then began to pour them each a third shot.

When they'd all been topped up, she asked the question that had been playing on her mind for a while. 'Shall I call her da in Ireland?' she said. She had fallen badly for Mary Kate's da, Michael, during his one brief visit to Liverpool, when they had indulged in their own dangerous liaison. It had never been repeated, even though Cat wished it would be, every single day. She had met a number of men over the months since, but none had been Michael Malone, and Michael had never returned to Liverpool.

Mrs O'Keefe looked thoughtful. 'I don't know, Cat. Her family know absolutely nothing about what's been going on with her here in Liverpool. She's been living a double life: one life that she's constructed for them in her letters home, and another life, the real one, here. She has almost cut herself off from her family, for fear of them finding out about her and Nicholas living together and all. She hasn't even been to Mass for two years.'

Joan, who had never missed Mass, tutted loudly.

Cat's heart sank with the disappointment. 'Aye, well, if you ask me, it's when something like this happens that you need family the most. And besides, Mary Kate is going to have to make a big decision. What does she do now – go back to Ireland or stay here?'

'Jesus, who would want to be her up in that bed now. If she goes back, she'll be leaving with nothing to her name and her heart full of sadness.' Mrs O'Keefe knocked back the third glass of whiskey almost in one and stood. 'Leave it, Cat, it's not our decision. There's time enough for all that. She has us for now. Sleep in the spare room, Cat. Or if you're worried about the children, I can get you a taxi back.'

Cat shook her head as she drained the last drop from her glass. 'No need. My neighbour, Pam, is sleeping with them. Besides, we all need to be here tomorrow. It's going to be the hardest day of that girl's life.'

Dana Brogan sat down at her desk in the nurses' home and set about her weekly task, one she dared not miss. As she picked up her pen, there was a knock on the door. It was her good friend Pammy Tanner.

'Got any washing to go in, Dana? I'm taking mine down now.'

'No, thanks,' said Dana, looking up. 'I'm just writing my letter home. We had a lovely doctor die on the ward today – Dr Marcus – and I'm writing to tell Mammy because his wife, Mary Kate, only lives in the next village to us. Everyone knows the Malones and Mammy will want to pay her respects.'

'Fancy that,' said Pammy. 'I did hear – it was all over the hospital. Who was the smart woman who used to come in every day?'

'I think it must have been his sister. A right scold, she was. Anyway, if I don't let Mammy know so she can tell people, I'll never hear the last of it.'

'Mary Kate! Mary Kate!'

She heard her name being called through a fog; the voice pulled her up through the folds of sleep. As she opened her eyes, she saw Joan standing at the side of the bed, a steaming cup of tea in her hand.

'It's gone nine,' said Joan by way of an apology for looming over her.

Mary Kate rubbed her eyes and turned her head away from Joan, towards the window. She was disoriented. Why was she in her old room at Mrs O'Keefe's? Why was Joan bringing her tea? For a brief moment her mind raced ahead, and then, with the force of a brick landing on her chest from a great height, the realisation dawned. She had lost Nicholas.

It was as if she had indeed gone back in time, as if her life with Nicholas had never happened. She had nothing but a pain in her heart to show for the past two years. She was back to square one, back where she'd started in her first disastrous days in Liverpool, and this time she'd lost far more than just her purse and her dignity on the side of the docks; this time she'd lost her heart, too.

Tears filled her eyes but refused to spill as Joan set the cup on her bedside table and sat on the edge of the bed. She had no words for what had been the most unlikely situation: a girl from Ireland just like Joan and Deidra becoming the mistress of the doctor's house.

'How are ye feeling?' asked Joan as she placed her hand over Mary Kate's.

'I feel terrible. My head is so fuzzy.' She stared blankly at the window. 'He's gone, hasn't he? I can't believe he's gone.' She had answered her own question and she was so frozen with shock, she couldn't cry.

Joan squeezed her hand tight. 'Deidra said the other doctor has rung, the new one, at the practice. I can't remember his name – she said he sounded nice.' She looked to Mary Kate for help with the details. She'd met the new doctor, he'd been to the house and had tea in the kitchen a number of times, but she wasn't good with names.

Mary Kate nodded, her face now as white as the sheets. 'William,' she whispered. 'What did he say?'

Her eyes opened wide and she pushed herself up on the pillows as her mind played tricks. 'Oh my Lord, is Nicholas alive? Is it all a mistake? Is that what he's coming to tell me?' Her heart soared with hope, but the expression on Joan's face and the memory of the previous evening brought it crashing back down again.

Joan's mouth opened and closed. She was scared. 'He's coming here at ten, to see you. That's in half an hour.'

'He's dead. My Nicholas. Oh, Joan, how did all this happen?' Still no tears.

Joan shook her head. 'He was only thirty-five,' she whispered. She didn't dare say what she wanted to say. That she had cried all night and made herself near sick with worry about the boys and the future. If she did, she would disintegrate, and she'd only been allowed to bring Mary Kate her tea on the promise that she would be strong.

Mary Kate threw the bedclothes back, placed her bare feet on the wooden floorboards and stood, wavering slightly. Joan reached out to steady her.

'I'd better get ready. I have to see William. I have things to do for Nicholas – he still needs me. I have to arrange a wake, a funeral, and I don't know where to start, but William will. He'll help me.'

Joan descended the stairs slowly, empty tray in hand, her head full of worry for Mary Kate.

'How was she?' asked Mrs O'Keefe when Joan reached the kitchen.

Cat was sitting at the table pushing the egg and bacon Deidra had cooked around the plate. The persistent tick of the clock on the mantle shelf above the range had filled the unusually long silences of the morning as the radio had remained switched off. Nothing felt appropriate. Everything seemed trivial.

'She's mad with the grief,' said Joan, 'but she hasn't cried yet. For a minute she scared the life out of me – she thought he was still alive.'

'I can't eat this, Deidra, queen,' said Cat. 'I've got no appetite.'

'None of us have,' said Mrs O'Keefe, 'but just try and eat a bit, Cat. It's going to be a difficult day and it's a long bus ride back home for you.'

The doorbell rang and as Deidra went to answer it, she panicked at the sight of Mary Kate making her way down the stairs, looking pale and grasping the bannister to support herself. 'Mrs O'Keefe!' she shouted, and Cat and Mrs O'Keefe came thundering into the hall.

'Oh, goodness me, come here.' Mrs O'Keefe took Mary Kate's arm. 'Let's get you into the sitting room.'

But Mary Kate was looking past her, to Deidra, who was holding the door open for William.

'William, thank goodness you came,' she said. 'There are things to do for Nicholas. We have to arrange his funeral. I have to go back to the house. She can't just tell me to go – I live there. I must stand up to her for the boys' sake, and they need to be told. I can't just leave things as they are – there are things we must do, for Nicholas, and it's my home, it's where I live.'

William removed his hat and held it between his hands. He looked first to Mrs O'Keefe, his eyes pleading for help, his words coming out in a stammer. 'I'm sorry, Mary Kate... I'm sorry, but... Nicholas has already gone.'

'Gone? Gone where?' Mary Kate's voice was high-pitched and urgent. She shook off Mrs O'Keefe's hand and stood in front of William. 'How can he have gone anywhere?' She gripped his arm, as much to steady herself as to implore him for an answer.

Two housemaids walked past the bottom of the steps, pushing prams, and looked up and into the hallway. The news had already spread, via the milkman, who'd heard it from Mrs O'Keefe when she'd startled him by greeting him at six that morning.

William placed one of his hands over Mary Kate's and looked at her with such deep sympathy and care, it almost undid her. She blinked back the tears. 'Gone where, William?'

'I'm so sorry, Mary Kate. An undertaker collected him from the hospital in the early hours this morning. Lavinia wasted no time – she's taken him to Surrey. He

is to be buried in the churchyard of her parents' village.
I have a message from Lavinia, too. Shall we sit down?
You look washed-out.'

He looked entreatingly at Mrs O'Keefe. This was not
going to be easy.

'Of course, of course. Come along into the sitting
room,' Mrs O'Keefe replied hurriedly. 'Deidra, bring
the doctor some tea, and some toast as well – I bet he
hasn't eaten. And Mary Kate needs some food inside her
too.'

William took Mary Kate by the arm and led her down
the hall, her steps slow and heavy. He sat next to her on
the sofa. The fire had yet to be lit and the cold, grey
room smelt of wood-smoke and stale whiskey fumes.
In the diffused winter-morning light Mary Kate noticed
the half-empty bottle of whiskey on the table and her
eyes locked onto it to help her focus.

'Lavinia has demanded I buy out the other half of the
practice, which I am willing to do. And she, ah… She…'
He paused, glanced out the window, tried again. 'She
also told me to tell you that she's had the locks on the
house changed. She's even employed a security guard
to watch the place, and an agent is coming round this
afternoon to put the property on the market.'

'But… but… I have nothing,' said Mary Kate.

'I know, and so… She asked me to meet the estate
agent, and I agreed, because I thought in some way I
could help you, as Lavinia is already on her way to

Surrey. If there is anything I can get for you, please let me know. I could even let you in early, before the agent arrives, but then I will have to leave him with the new keys.'

Mary Kate had turned to the cold, dead fireplace. 'Did she sleep in our bed?' Her voice broke. She had wanted to return to their bedroom, to lay her head on the dent in his pillow, to close her eyes and pretend he was there next to her. To breathe in deeply and flood her senses with the smell of him. To call him back, to cry alone in their room. 'I can't... I can't even bury him. My Nicholas. That's what he'd want.' She was distraught. There was nothing left to cling to. Nothing she could do for him.

'I have offered Lavinia one hundred pounds less than the partnership is worth, because I wanted to give the money to you. It's the least I can do for Nicholas, and for you. Lavinia has accepted my offer, and I have already called into the bank.' He laid an envelope containing the money on the seat next to Mary Kate. He could tell she wasn't listening to him.

Mrs O'Keefe came and sat down on the other side of Mary Kate, bookending her. Both she and William knew the delayed reaction would filter through soon. Mary Kate was young and her heart was broken; she had no defences.

'He's going to Surrey, but... but I'm not there.' She looked from one to the other, confused.

And then it came: at first a sob that caught in her throat, then a howl, like that of an animal in pain, and then the tears that ran and ran.

Mrs O'Keefe took her into her arms. 'You poor love,' she murmured. 'Her mother died when she was a child,' she said to William over Mary Kate's head.

'Nicholas told me,' he whispered back. 'Mary Kate,' he said in a slightly louder voice, his tone gentle, 'I wanted to tell you what Nicholas said just before he died. His last words. I was with him when he went.'

Mary Kate caught her breath and, pulling away from Mrs O'Keefe, stared at him intently. 'You were... You were with him? What did he say? Did he give you a message for me?'

William looked deep into her eyes. This was important. There must be no ambiguity. As his last duty to his dear friend, he must convey absolutely correctly the words Nicholas had whispered into his ear.

'He said, "Tell Mary Kate to go home to Tarabeg. Tell her she must return to her family. Her future is there." He said he had heard you talk about it so often. He said to tell you that that was where he would look for you, and that he would finally get to see Tarabeg. "Go home, Mary Kate. Go home." Those were his last words.'

Chapter 6

Paddy Devlin stood leaning on the bar, gazing out of the windows, waiting for his first customer of the afternoon. Unless there was a wake or a death to attend to, that first customer would often be Father Jerry. Paddy's son Tig was banking up the fire with peat ready for the afternoon and evening, and Paddy could hear his wife Josie and Tig's wife Keeva chattering in the butcher's shop as they began to wipe down and close up for the day. He could smell the stew on the stove in the kitchen that his bar and the shop shared with the house and his mouth began to water.

The regulars would be in for a few hours but would hurry back up the boreens before night fell. The only time the winter routine altered was when a full moon lit up the boreens and the fern-lined paths. If his customers didn't leave for home before the light disappeared, their chances of falling down a bog hole were high. The history of Tarabeg was littered with the stories of accidents, many fatal and all of them the fault of sleeping goblins and malevolent fairies and nothing to do with the drink following a night in Paddy's bar.

Keeva called through the fly curtain to him as she made her way to the walk-in fridge with a dish of pig's trotters. 'Did you see the doctor's car coming through, Paddy?' she asked as she pulled the brightly coloured plastic ribbons aside. 'Mrs Doyle says he's away up to Captain Carter's house again. That will be every day for the past three days on the run.'

Mrs Doyle, the postmistress, had unique access to the telephone switchboard and doubled as the village oracle, a constant source of irritation to Father Jerry. Between Mrs Doyle and Bridget McAndrew, the village seer who healed people and undeniably spoke to the dead, the priest frequently found his authority challenged.

Paddy, unperturbed, clasped his hands together and sniffed in disdain. 'Well, the captain has money to burn in that case,' he said as he slipped off his white butcher's coat, replaced it with his beer-stained leather apron and began to fasten the ties behind his back.

Some people said that the only reason Paddy had turned the back of his butcher's into a bar was so that he could drink as much as he liked without Josie and the priest giving out to him. As Father Jerry was one of his best-paying customers, he had killed two birds with one stone.

'If he had any sense, he would have sent for Bridget and saved himself the money for two of those visits. Bridget would have seen him well for a fraction of the price – she's as good as any doctor.'

Keeva frowned. 'Aye, that's true, but something must be seriously wrong. He hasn't been well enough to travel to England, and him able to afford all the comforts in the world he would want, or so Mrs Doyle says anyway. And he was wanting to be back there for the shooting weeks ago, Mrs Doyle says.'

'Oh, feck Mrs Doyle, Keeva, she doesn't know everything.'

Keeva gasped. Mrs Doyle did know everything, actually, but as Paddy had been so rude, she wouldn't tell him that the doctor had called a specialist in Dublin and urged that he travel to Tarabeg at his earliest convenience. Mrs Doyle had heard that down the line only yesterday. Paddy could find out that bit of important information from someone else and wonder why he was the last to know. The fly curtain fell with a forceful swish as Keeva, never one to hide her irritation, flounced off down the passageway to the fridge.

'Ah, here's the father himself,' said Tig, glancing out the window in the direction of the presbytery. Father Jerry was striding down the road with purpose in his step, which could only mean one of two things: either his housekeeper, Teresa, was taking her afternoon nap, or he had news.

Tig threw the poker into the brass bucket and collapsed onto a chair next to the fire to warm his throbbing leg. He kicked his boot to one side, its laces dragging on the stone-flagged hearth. One of Tig's legs was markedly shorter than the other, and it was common for him to be in pain. He rubbed his back and flinched as he warmed his foot. ''Tis unusual for the father to be over here before even the school has let out,' he muttered, grimacing at the ache in his hips.

'He's just a man like the rest of us, in need of his pot,' said Paddy, always quick with an excuse for anyone who wanted to partake and pass money across his bar. He began to pour Father Jerry's pint of Guinness ready.

No sooner had the last drop hit the velvet cushion of a foaming head than the doors opened and Father Jerry stomped in, his loud footsteps echoing across the floorboards as he made his way straight to the bar and picked up his pint. 'Now there's a sight to greet me. On the slate, would you, Paddy,' he said as he lifted the pot to his lips.

Tig slipped his foot back inside his open leather boot. Unable to hide his curiosity, he got straight to the point. 'You looked like a man on a mission there, Father. Did ye have a busy day?'

Father Jerry licked his lips as he set the pot back on the bar. 'Aye, well, Mass this morning was full, not that you would know, Tig. And I have news for Michael Malone – where is he today?'

'Ah, that's an easy one to answer, Father.' Tig grabbed his stick and hauled himself onto his feet, more than used to reprimands for his slack attendance at Mass. 'He's in Galway fetching pig feed, but he always calls in on his way past and he should be here any minute now, I would be saying. Oh, and here's his daddy in through the door before him.' Tig grinned as the door opened and Seamus walked into the bar, followed by Pete and Joe.

'Joe Malone, have you called into the shop and made Peggy's day? She'll be crying into her tea if you don't. Look, would you, I can see her nose pressed against the shop window looking for you now.' Tig slapped his thigh and roared with laughter as he pointed through the bar window to Michael Malone's shop.

Keeva heard him as she came back in from the kitchen. 'Tig, why don't you shut your big mouth,' she said as she walked past, scowling at her husband.

Only she noticed the shadow that passed across Pete Shevlin's face as he hung his scarf on the coat stand. The other men erupted into laughter at the long-standing joke of the flame that burnt in Peggy's heart for Tarabeg's handsome American, Joe Malone.

Joe's American accent had not dimmed in the slightest, despite him having lived in the village for almost two years. His regular visits back to New York made sure of that. 'It's not my style to lead anyone on, Tig. Especially not a lovely lady like Peggy,' he said, the only man in the bar who ever removed his hat.

Pete's heart swelled. Despite hating the way Peggy failed to conceal her ardour for all things American, including Joe, he could hold no lasting grudge against the man himself, who had never set a foot wrong with Peggy.

'Will ye be up at the dance in the long hall on the full moon, Joe? We'll sell more tickets if I can get the word out that ye are,' asked Tig.

'Why, will you be going?' asked Seamus, laughing. 'Does Keeva know?'

Tig poked Seamus in the side with his stick. 'We will be. Keeva is looking forward to a dance. We'll be providing the refreshments – lemonade and Guinness – and Mammy and Keeva are selling the tickets over the butcher's counter. Legs Duffy and his band will be playing. Michael Malone will take the barrel up there in the afternoon to settle and I'll be up after him to lay out the tables and bring the pots and glasses. Rosie and Nola are making the sandwiches. It will be the best dance yet. Are you coming, Pete? Twill be a grand night.'

Paddy had laid the three pots on the bar and all three men were taking their first draught. Tig had to wait a prolonged moment for his reply.

'I'm going, I am,' said Pete.

Paddy had been wiping the bar down with a damp cloth, but he stopped mid sweep and stared open-mouthed at Pete, as did Seamus. Joe, unaware of the significance of Pete's statement, gulped as he downed a third of his pint in one go.

'You?' asked Paddy.

'I was only joking, Pete.' Tig came over, stood next to Pete and leant his arm on the bar. 'You have never in your life been to the dance – what's making you go now?'

The room fell silent save for the flames crackling in the hearth and Joe smacking his lips in appreciation. They waited patiently for Pete's reply.

'I thought I would just give it a go, just for a change, that's all,' said Pete. 'Nothing more to it than that.' Although he tried his hardest to look casual, he looked anything but, arousing suspicion in the others.

'Get yourself out of here,' said Seamus. 'I've known you since you were knee high, Pete Shevlin – you think I believe that? You've never danced at a ceilidh in your life.'

'I swear to God 'tis true, I'm going.' To change the subject, Pete leant forward to address Father Jerry, who was standing further down the bar. 'Will you be there, Father?'

'Aye, that I will. Someone has to keep an eye on things.'

Tig, who, although he had never danced in his life, had been to every one of the dances since he was a boy, knew that what Father Jerry meant was he would be hovering around outside, ensuring that no flirting couples were led into temptation as they sought privacy and sinfulness in nearby fields or boreens.

'Father here is looking for Michael,' said Paddy to Seamus with a raise of his eyebrow.

'What news would it be that ye have now?' asked Seamus. 'You can tell me, Father. I'll be seeing Michael tonight and I can save you the job.'

Father Jerry looked put out but knew that he could not refuse the request from Michael's own father. 'I have news from the priest in Belmullet. The Brogan mammy had a letter from their daughter in Liverpool – the nurse, Dana. She has come across a Mary Kate from Tarabeg.'

A grin crossed Seamus's face. His beloved granddaughter! Just the mention of her name brought a smile to his lips. They hadn't seen and had rarely even heard from her for over two years. He was well used to his loved ones leaving. Every one of his daughters and sons apart from Michael had left, never to return, and he and Nola had only the memories of their childhoods to sustain them through the long winter nights, when they recalled them, one day and one child at a time. But with Mary Kate it was different. He'd always known she would return. Daedio had told him so. She had no notion of the fortune that awaited her, keeping warm in dollar rolls behind the bricks in the farmhouse fireplace, but as Nola often reminded him, 'She doesn't need to know. Fate will do its work.'

'Well now, isn't that just grand,' he said as he looked about the bar. 'The Brogan mammy, and what did she say?' His smile faded and became a frown as all of a sudden his blood ran cold and his stomach dropped into his boots. 'Mary Kate, she hasn't been in hospital, has she?'

'What was that?' The curtain swished again as Keeva dashed into the room, proving beyond all doubt that she listened to every word that was spoken in the bar. Between Keeva and Mrs Doyle, there were no secrets in Tarabeg. 'Did you say there was news of Mary Kate? I'll be calling to the shop to see Rosie when the school lets out, I can tell her meself.'

Rosie was Mary Kate's stepmother, the school principal, Michael Malone's wife and Keeva's friend. Rosie had nursed a love for Michael before he had married Sarah – she had loved him first. When Sarah died, she had made herself indispensable, looking after the new baby, Finn, and young Mary Kate, helping with the shop, and running the home, until the inevitable happened, as she'd known it would, and Michael made her his wife.

Father Jerry looked far from pleased, and everyone in the bar who'd ever been given a telling-off by him could

tell by the curl of his lip and the set of his jaw that he
was out of sorts. 'Aye, well, you can tell her from me,'
he said. 'Dana wrote how sad it was that Mary Kate's
husband had died so young and so tragically and what
a wonderful doctor he had been at the hospital too, and
how much his two young sons were going to miss him.
It happened just in the last week, so she says.'

Silence fell across the room like a suffocating blanket.

Seamus blinked and swallowed before he spoke. 'It
must be a different Mary Kate. Our Mary Kate, she
isn't married. Working for a family and living in, she
is.'

'There is only one Mary Kate from Tarabeg,' said
Father Jerry with a sniff. Thinking he had now earned
his pint, he lifted it to his lips and drank deeply.

'Mary Kate?' said Keeva, almost under her breath,
her brow creased. 'It can't be. She wouldn't be married
and not tell her own family. I had a letter from her
only a few weeks ago – sure, she hasn't even got a fella
in tow.' She laughed at the absurdity of the idea. She
was as close to Mary Kate as anyone could be. Closer
than Rosie, her own stepmother, even. Keeva had been
around since the day Mary Kate was born; her mother's
best friend.

Pete joined in, having spied Declan outside the
window of the bar. 'Declan will be delighted to hear
that, so he will. I swear to God, not a day goes past
when he doesn't ask after her.'

The door opened and Declan walked in, joining the now subdued crowd. Declan Feenan was the joint schoolmaster, working with Rosie. Unbeknown to anyone, he had helped Mary Kate to escape Tarabeg two years back, giving her a lift all the way to Dublin and sending her off on the Liverpool ferry with a brief kiss and the promise of his heart waiting.

'Ah, Declan, we were just talking about Mary Kate. It seems she has herself married with two grown kids in Liverpool.'

Everyone laughed at the absurdity of it.

'What a ridiculous notion,' said Paddy. 'She loved a party, did Mary Kate. If she had been married, the fancy do would have been here and that's a fact.'

Declan didn't speak, not even to ask for his drink, which appeared on the bar before him.

The sudden change in the atmosphere was uncomfortable and no one could quite work out why.

'Mary Kate?' said Seamus again, and as he spoke her name he felt a ghostly hand on his shoulder. He could almost hear Daedio whispering in his ear, 'Hush now. Hush, leave it be, would you.'

Tig looked at his wife and at the serious expressions about him, laid his own pot back down on the bar and leant heavily onto his stick. 'Jesus, Father, there's more than one Mary Kate in Mayo. There's feckin' hundreds of them,' he roared. 'You think Mary Kate Malone would be living a married life and be a mother of two children and not one of us would know about it, eh? She's only been gone for two years, how old could the two sons be? Has there even been time for two? And didn't Michael himself go out to Liverpool to check that all was well and that she was settled. It's not our Mary Kate, not on your life. Not unless our Mary Kate became the virgin Mary Kate, and even the good Lord himself couldn't manage that in two years.'

He looked from one to the other, and the first to laugh was Seamus, and then Pete and Paddy and Keeva and Joe joined in. The only people not to laugh were Father Jerry, who picked up his pint and almost downed it in one, and Declan, who felt the flame in his heart burn until it hurt.

Out on the coast, the wind was high and wintery and the horizon was clear. The few fishing boats that had left in the morning were long returned and had been pulled up behind the large rocks to protect them from the wind. The vast cave hollowed out of the cliff hadn't been used for years, not since the night of Angela's murder, and only a local who knew of its whereabouts would have been able to locate it anyway, beneath its thick veil of vegetation. Those fishermen who did remember it believed it to be haunted. Even the occasional German tourist who had the audacity to wander along the shore was warned off. Kevin McGuffey, however, had no such qualms. It was his hideout.

The light was fading fast and he had planned to sail in under the cover of darkness, so that he wouldn't be seen. He cut in, caught the wind and wove the curragh between the rocks. With one glance up to the clifftop, he saw that there was no light burning in his old cottage. As he'd expected, it had clearly been abandoned. Even so, he thought he saw someone on the clifftop, waving a shawl. He blinked and the image disappeared. It was Angela, the wife he'd murdered. His blood ran cold; he slipped the hip flask from his pocket and finished off the last of the whiskey within. 'You have a fever, you eejit,' he muttered to himself as his hand slipped down his thigh and fingered the blood seeping through the makeshift bandage.

He had left the North on bad terms. He knew too much, had been involved in some of the worst underground operations. The IRA commanders were never going to let him escape. He had managed it, but only just. 'You need a plan. You need a plan,' he said as he felt the whiskey burn into the lining of his empty stomach.

He was sailing into his past and the only other place he knew outside of the North, but he could not stay here for long. He would meet Jay Maughan, settle some scores, find money and get away to somewhere the IRA commanders would never find him.

A turn to the left and further up along the clifftop he saw a light in Bee's cottage. 'Feck,' he hissed. Bee was Angela's sister and no friend of his. He'd been told she was living in Liverpool these days, but she was either back now or someone else was living there.

The coastline had remained unchanged for centuries and his memory of the route returned as he avoided the rocks that routinely took less experienced sailors down. He sailed in over the very spot he'd forced Bee's young husband, Rory, to sail to all those years ago. A journey from which he'd never returned. McGuffey felt a shudder below the curragh and at first thought he'd skimmed a rock he'd forgotten about. But then an icy coldness crept in on the edge of the breeze and an image of Rory's face, dead and white, lying below the surface of the water flooded into his head unbidden. It had never happened before and he would not let it happen now. 'You deserved it, you weak, British-loving bastard,' he hissed into the dark water, trying to dispel his fear. The image flew from his mind, leaving no remorse in its wake, and he took up the oars and pushed on, keeping them skimming and pumping just below the surface, clearing rocks with only inches to spare sometimes. Rory had been his first conscious act of murder, albeit not by his own hands. McGuffey had wanted to keep the best fish for himself. He'd known there was only danger awaiting Rory in his makeshift curragh that day; he understood the conditions out at sea and knew what the swell, the treacherous currents and the storm would do.

It took McGuffey a further twenty minutes to reach the beach and it was almost black as the rain began. Lumbering into the water as best he could with the gash in his leg, the salt stinging like hell, he lifted the curragh and carried it with huge effort to the mouth of the cave where he would hide it. It wasn't as easy to find the cave as he'd expected, and he had to push against the vegetation until he felt a small indentation. Clawing his fingers between the shingle and the moss, he scooped up the mass of roots, seaweed and coastal grass from the bottom and finally it lifted like a damp green curtain, revealing the cave behind. It was empty. Dank, dark, eerie and untouched since his last visit.

He let the stiff breeze enter before him, took the matches he'd brought with him out of the oilskin pouch, unhooked the pack on his back and pulled out the lantern. Only then did he begin to trace the familiar steps to his smuggling hideout down at the far end, deep inside the huge cave, where no one else ever went for fear of sudden flooding. On one of the high ledges stood a crate of whiskey he'd been unable to fit into the curragh on his last smuggling trip. He almost roared out loud with laughter. Lifting a bottle, he slipped it into the pocket of his thick black donkey jacket.

He would stay the night in the old cottage. If anyone was searching for him, that would be the last place they'd look. Only a madman would go back to the scene of his original crime. It would be the safest place to hide. He had left a message with the smuggler in Donegal for Jay to come. He would find him. The smuggler would get a message back to him with one of the gypsies travelling along the coast to Newport. In the meantime, he would find shelter, provisions and fresh water to wash his wound. And a fire. He needed that more than anything.

He was relieved to have found the whiskey. He would drink most of it, but some of it he would pour into the wound to sterilise it, and then he'd light the fire in the cottage and cauterise the wound with the cast-iron poker, assuming it was still there.

He had a granddaughter, Mary Kate. She had no idea who he was, and he had no idea where she was, but that was about to change. Michael Malone had money. Mary Kate was his daughter, and according to the smuggler in Donegal, he worshipped the ground she walked on. He would get money from Michael Malone in exchange for his peace of mind; Malone would pay for that. Jay would help – the only man on earth he knew, other than himself, who would do anything for money.

'That's the plan,' he said as he drank the old whiskey, which was none the worse for having been left for so many years. 'Feck, you taste good,' he said as he held the bottle away from his lips and tried to read the label. For the first time in weeks, he smiled.

William had rescued Jet from the Marcus house and brought him round to Mrs O'Keefe's. 'If Lavinia had been planning to take him down to live with her parents and the boys, I wouldn't have done it,' he said as he stood with Jet's lead in one hand and his wicker basket resting on the floor next to him. 'But she already told me she was calling the vet to have him put down. I hope you don't mind. I told her I would take him, but we have cats.'

No one had minded, least of all Jet, especially when Joan fell to her knees and threw her arms around his neck. She smelt of baking and bacon. Jet was happy, his future looked promising.

'Mary Kate is asleep,' said Joan, 'but she'll be so glad to see him safe and sound when she wakes up.'

'I hope there was nothing she needed from the house,' he said. 'I've handed the keys back – she insisted.' A grateful Jet licked his hand and settled down next to him. 'If I never have to speak to that woman again, it would be too soon. You don't meet many like her, even in my job.' Rather than being grateful to him for his help, Lavinia Marcus had been as unpleasant as she could possibly be. 'The agent said he would have the house sold in no time at all.'

'Don't tell Mary Kate,' said Mrs O'Keefe. 'She loved that house. It was their home. More than that, it was a sanctuary for those two.'

'It is all just so unseemly,' said William. 'Such haste. His body barely cold before he's transported to Surrey, a place he never even knew. The woman has a heart of stone, and, I hate to say, a fortune coming her way. She has the money from the practice, his doctor's pension, the house, and whatever was in his bank account.'

Mrs O'Keefe almost slammed the empty dog bowl on the kitchen table, making Jet jump. 'And that poor girl hasn't a penny to her name, even though she looked after him through every day of his sickness, and ran his home for two years. If that witch had given him a divorce, Mary Kate would be his legal wife now. I would buy the house myself for her, if I could afford it.'

Joan banged the fridge door shut and passed Mrs O'Keefe a string of sausages, which she began to chop into Jet's bowl.

'She wouldn't let you,' said William matter-of-factly. 'She's filled with such a hatred for Mary Kate, I think she would rather burn the place down first.' He took the cup of tea that a speechless Joan had poured from the pot and placed in his hand.

'Why though? Why? She was the one who had the affair with his partner, and she'd done it before – that was the reason they moved to Liverpool in the first place, to escape the havoc she created in the last practice he had.'

William was propped against the table, nursing the cup in both hands, his brow furrowed. 'I wish I knew. Do you think it's the right thing for Mary Kate, going back to Ireland where no one even knows about Nicholas?'

Mrs O'Keefe placed the bowl on the floor for an eager Jet. 'Heavens above, when did that dog last eat?' She ran her hands under the tap. 'Well, we will soon be finding out because she insists she'll be leaving in a few days, and I don't mind saying, I'm not happy about it. She is hanging onto his last words, says it's all she has to go on. Because Nicholas told you, William, that Mary Kate was to go back to Tarabeg, she's determined that that is what she'll do.'

Joan handed Mrs O'Keefe the tea towel that hung over the range.

'I really don't think it is the right thing for her to do,' Mrs O'Keefe continued, drying her hands distractedly, over and over. 'Not yet, not for a month or two, until she is over the worst of the grief. I can't think of anything worse just now, but we are going to have to let her go. I'll be worried sick, I will.'

Jet gave a hopeful bark for more sausages, breaking the tension in the room.

'What? You want more? Joan, was there anything left on that chicken carcass we are using for the soup today?'

★

The brown leather suitcase that Mrs O'Keefe had given to Mary Kate lay open on the bed. Even though it was still several days until her departure, she'd already nearly finished packing. It was a comfort somehow, like she was already putting Nicholas's last request into action. With her palm she flattened her hand-me-down linen nightdress onto the top of the pile, the latest freshly laundered and neatly folded item to arrive up the stairs, still warm from the new electric iron Deidra had gone mad with.

Mrs O'Keefe's sister, Lizzie, who was a similar size to Mary Kate, had arrived with two suitcases of clothes that were very much in place in the new Liverpool, the sort of things that women like Mrs O'Keefe were struggling to keep up with. 'I needed a good clear-out,' said Lizzie. 'There's everything in there, including a pair of red boots I love that killed when I wore them because they didn't really fit me.'

Those boots now sat polished and waiting at the foot of the bed. Even the brass corners of the suitcase had been recently polished. If it moved, Deidra ironed or polished it; she'd even eyed up Jet's wild and tangled coat after she had given him a bath.

Cat was helping Mary Kate pack and was sitting on the bed next to the case. Mrs O'Keefe was perched uncomfortably on the wooden chair next to the washstand. She had booked Mary Kate a berth on the night ferry to Dublin later in the week, but she was far from happy about it.

Mary Kate's hand flew to her throat. 'My ribbon, my heart!'

Both women's eyes darted to her neck, where the emerald heart had lived, on the velvet ribbon that Nicholas had given her.

'Where is it?' asked Mrs O'Keefe. 'When did you last wear it?'

She had worn it every day since Nicholas had given it to her and only ever took it off to bathe. She didn't have to think for long; she remembered exactly where she'd left it. The days since his passing had been spent in a fog of tears and Valium, days dogged by bad headaches, a heavy heart and a pain deep in her belly that nothing would shift.

'It's by the bath. I left it there on the night he died, before we went to the hospital.' She sobbed at the thought of it lying there abandoned, unworn, her most precious gift from Nicholas. She'd promised him she'd wear it every day, and now it wasn't even in her possession. 'I've got to get it back. It's not staying in that house and there's no way I'm going to Ireland without it. It's all I have…' She broke off, her voice choked.

'You might have to leave it, Mary Kate,' Cat said as gently as she could. 'That house is a fortress now – I can't see the estate agent handing over the keys to you, not after all the fuss Mrs Marcus has been making. And as for the evil witch itself, you've obviously got no chance there. Can you not just forget about it?'

'I can't leave Liverpool without it,' Mary Kate said. And with that she raced out of the bedroom and flew down the stairs.

Cat hurried after her, intercepting her in the front hall. 'You can't go round there on your own, you've no key.'

'True, but I know the house.' Mary Kate was already thrusting her arms into the sleeves of her coat. She shouted up the stairs for Joan, oblivious to everyone and everything. 'Joan, get your coat!' she yelled.

Joan didn't have to be asked twice.

'For goodness' sake, let me come with you,' said Cat as she pulled on her own coat. 'I wouldn't let me own kids do this and I'm not letting you go on your own.'

'Be careful!' shouted Mrs O'Keefe from the landing at the top of the stairs. She was holding the bannisters and stooped down, her body folding into her hand-knitted cable cardigan, to get a better view of them in the hall. Under the overhead light, her white hair cast a halo; her expression was one of great concern.

Mary Kate felt a pang of guilt, the first emotion to pierce through her deep sadness. 'I will. I'll be back in ten minutes. I'm not leaving my ribbon in that house a moment longer.'

The three women hurried down the avenue and stopped at the end of the Marcuses' drive, taking in the large Victorian house. The moon shone above the chimney and flooded the driveway with a silvery light.

'Why are the lights on?' asked Cat.

'Maybe the agent did it?' said Mary Kate, no longer in such a fighting mood.

'I doubt it. What, he comes out here each night to switch them on and returns each morning to put them off again?'

'Let's go around the back,' said Mary Kate, 'and take a look in though the kitchen window.'

The three women crept forwards, aware of every leaf that crunched and twig that snapped. In seconds they were standing to the side of the window.

'I can hear voices,' said Joan, her eyes wide in alarm.

'I don't think this is a good idea,' said Cat nervously. 'Let's go back.'

'There's obviously someone in there, someone in my house. I can't leave without knowing who it is. I'm going to look,' said Mary Kate, and before Cat could stop her, she had snuck to the edge of the window.

Both Cat and Joan held their breath as she gripped the deep sandstone windowsill and lifted herself onto her tiptoes. The light briefly illuminated her face and then she dropped back down to the ground. Her eyes glistened and her face was as white as a ghost. 'It's her, with Robin, the doctor from the practice she had the affair with,' she hissed. 'I thought William said she'd gone back to Surrey.'

'Well, just like she lies to everyone, she obviously lied to him,' said Cat. 'She must have had the funeral pretty quick. Where's Joan?'

Joan had disappeared from her side.

'Oh, for God's sake, where is she?' Cat began to creep away towards the drive. 'Let's get out of this garden. At least we can do a runner on the drive if we get caught. My heels keep sinking into the grass. Joan! Joan, where are you?' she hissed.

There was no reply.

'You know the house, Mary Kate – where will she be?'

Mary Kate looked around her; she had no idea. 'Well, the back door leads into the kitchen, the front door will be fastened on the snip, and there's the side door, to the washroom.'

The two women looked at each other.

'Where's that?' said Cat.

Mary Kate didn't answer but headed off into the darkness around the side of the cypress tree, with Cat following close behind. They both gasped at the sight of the washroom door standing wide open, but there was no sign of Joan.

Joan knew every step on every stair and every floorboard that creaked. She glanced towards the kitchen. The radio was on and she heard the giggles of Lavinia Marcus and the deep, rumbling laughter of a man. It made her blood boil. Glasses chinked and there was the loud glug of liquid being poured out of a bottle; these were sounds all too familiar to Joan from when Lavinia had lived there and would take full advantage of Dr Marcus being out at his surgery until late.

If the angel sitting on her shoulder hadn't restrained her, she would have marched into the kitchen and given Lavinia Marcus a piece of her mind. Instead, Joan took a deep breath, entirely unaware of where her courage had sprung from. But she was on familiar ground, in the house she had lived in for twice as long as Mary Kate.

She had felt at the bottom of the pile in all of the grieving for the man whose washing she had done and meals she had prepared. She'd never got a word of thanks from Lavinia Marcus, but he had always popped his head into the kitchen of a night. 'That was delicious, Joan, thank you. Have you heard from your mother this week?' He always had time for her, the housemaid from Ireland, and she wanted to prove that she had loved him too, her lovely Dr Marcus who would sometimes sit in the kitchen with her while she fed the boys.

He always spoke to her as though she were a proper grown-up, someone who had opinions and knew things, and he was genuinely interested in what she had to say. No one else in her life had ever treated her like that, and that was why she was doing this. For him; to say thank you.

I need to get back out as quick as I can, she thought, and began her ascent of the stairs.

'I left it in the bathroom on the glass shelf next to the sink,' Mary Kate had said on the way down the avenue. 'I know exactly where it is. I just need to get in there. I will break a window if I have to. It was my home – that can't be classed as burglary.'

Joan had not responded but had thought to herself that it had been her home too, long before Mary Kate had arrived.

She was at the bathroom door in no time. The door was shut fast, but the handle turned easily. She could tell by the steam and the misted-up mirror that reflected her own ghostly image that it had just recently been used. She didn't dare put the light on but crept over to the sink and began sweeping her hands along the shelves. Nothing. She felt her way down the brackets that held the shelves and located the bottom one, sliding her hand along, but she was in too much of a hurry and a glass jar of bath salts crashed onto the black-and-white tiled floor.

Her mouth dried, her heart beat so wildly, it hurt, and she had a sudden need for the toilet that was standing right there to the side of her. She froze and remained that way for what seemed like an eternity, until she felt she was safe. They hadn't heard her. There was not a sound from the stairs.

Letting out the breath she'd been holding, and releasing her grip on the sink she was using to steady herself, she resumed her quest with trembling hands. She didn't feel quite as confident now. Her bravery had dissolved as fast as the bath salts scattered across the damp floor. Her ribs were painful and her hands shook even harder, but there was no point in turning back now. She would have to finish what she'd started and so wished she hadn't.

It had been Deidra's idea. 'You get the ribbon,' she'd said. 'Don't be letting Mary Kate in there – she will be a wreck and go mad with the grief.'

'I will. I want to. I'll do it for him,' Joan had replied. 'If he could speak, he would tell me to. He trusted me, did the doctor.'

She'd begun her search of the shelves to the side of the sink nearest the bath and decided that maybe she needed to move across to the other side now, even though it didn't make sense to her for Mary Kate to have placed the velvet ribbon that far away from the bath, because those shelves had been on Nicholas's side of the bathroom.

She glanced out of the window, but she could only see the moonlit driveway; there was no sign of Mary Kate or Cat and she hoped they'd not followed her into the house. She took a step, crunching broken glass and salt crystals as she went, and started at the bottom of the other shelves. She traced her finger along the lowest one, steadily and carefully this time, and then froze as light flooded the bathroom.

She turned on her heel and gasped. 'Oh God in heaven,' she whispered, for in the doorway stood Lavinia Marcus and behind her the man she recognised as Dr Robin.

'Oh, so it's you,' said Lavinia. She inhaled on her cigarette and exhaled into the air for dramatic effect.

Robin leant against the door jamb and folded his arms. 'Forgotten something, have you?' he sneered. 'Joan, isn't it? Had you down as a skivvy, not a cat burglar.'

'Seems like she has a new job, darling. And here was me thinking she'd run off with the tart.'

Joan's blood boiled and, as she recalled later to Deidra with a degree of pride, she lost her senses. 'Tart? You're the one who's the tart, missus. I know what you were up to all the time when Dr Marcus was hard at work, so don't you be calling Mary Kate a tart – that's you all right. And you, Dr Robin, you should be ashamed of yourself. Your poor wife, God love her.'

They both stood and stared at her, open-mouthed, Lavinia's cigarette in mid air. And then, as if on cue, they both burst out laughing at the same time.

'Get you, spikey miss,' said Lavinia.

'I asked you a question, you cheeky skivvy. Have you forgotten something?' said Dr Robin.

Joan noticed that at the mention of his wife's name his expression had altered considerably and his self-satisfied sneering smile was now nowhere to be seen.

'Oh no, she hasn't forgotten anything in here,' said Lavinia. 'She wouldn't have left something in my bathroom – it wasn't hers to use, was it, Joan? Not unless it was a tin of Vim and a cloth she was short of.'

Joan couldn't speak; her voice had deserted her. It appeared that bravery was a very short-lived commodity. Her knees began to tremble.

'She must have come back for something the Irish tart left. Now, I wonder what that could be?' Lavinia Marcus placed her fingers at her throat and Joan gulped as she recognised the emerald on the green velvet ribbon. 'Was it this? This trinket, by any chance? You need to go back to wherever your Mary Kate is and tell her that this is my house and that anything in it is mine too.' Without warning, her expression shifted from mocking to angry and her normally pale complexion turned puce. 'Now get out of my house,' she shouted and, stepping forward, slapped Joan right across her face.

It wasn't the first time she'd done that to Joan. Over the years, she'd hit her with increasing frequency, every time things didn't quite go her way, although never in front of Dr Marcus. Joan's hand rushed to her face and tears welled in her eyes. There was no point trying to reason with a woman like Lavinia Marcus. Summoning up as much pride as she could muster, she shoved past them both, knocking Dr Robin so hard that he wobbled over the edge of the bath, screamed out and grabbed the shower curtain.

Without looking back, she ran down the landing. Halfway down the first set of stairs, she shouted back up, 'And as for you, Dr Robin, don't think I won't be telling your wife that I saw you here, and all that I saw, because I bloody will.' She took one last glance up, blessed herself for swearing and then belted down the rest of the stairs before one or the other of them came after her.

Mary Kate had begged Cat and Mrs O'Keefe not to call her father or the post office in Tarabeg or tell anyone she was returning home. 'I don't want anyone to know,' she'd said. 'I have to think what I'm going to be saying to them. How do I keep such a big secret from everyone I know? You don't understand – Tarabeg isn't Liverpool. If they knew the truth, I wouldn't be able to go back home, and I need that more than anything. Please, don't be saying a word to anyone because, really, you have no idea.'

Mrs O'Keefe and Cat had caught each other's eye and frowned, but nothing more had been said. Now though, with Joan's account of Lavinia's crazed behaviour still fresh in her head, Cat had hatched a plan. She waited until Mary Kate was back in bed, then shared her thoughts with Mrs O'Keefe.

'Oh, no. You can't be doing that,' Mrs O'Keefe protested.

'Why in God's name not? Her daddy has a right to know. I know what to do – I just call the post office or the shop and say what time I'll call back and they fetch him to speak to me.'

Mrs O'Keefe felt an unexpected anger rise within her. 'Cat, it was as obvious as the nose on your face that you were carrying on, or trying to, with Mary Kate's father when he came to Liverpool that time two years back. Now ask yourself, why are you calling him – for Mary Kate's sake or for yours?'

Cat bristled and wasted not a second replying. 'They have a right to know if she is coming home, and what is she going to do when she gets there – act like nothing has happened? She's out of her mind with grief. Of course they need to know what's been going on.'

Mrs O'Keefe closed the sitting room door just as she heard Joan's footsteps on the stairs and hissed back, 'None of us know what's going on in her head. She has lost Nicholas, the boys, her money, the clothes off her back. And now Lavinia Marcus has taken his last present to her, her precious choker. You cannot add to her troubles by doing something which carries a risk and, added to that, something she hasn't agreed to. You cannot let Michael know. She is determined to get back to Tarabeg as fast as she can and nothing we can do or say will stop her. They are her people, she will know what to say when she gets there and it really is none of our business.'

Mrs O'Keefe felt like she had just made the speech of her life and she hoped it had worked. She sighed with relief as Cat looked suitably chastened, but it was short-lived as Cat's eyes flashed right back at her.

'Right, well then, her Great-Aunt Bee is my friend. I'll let you have your way over Michael, but I don't care what anyone says, someone has to know. She can't just turn up there pretending nothing has happened – she's no actress. I am writing to Bee. You have to agree to that. I can trust Bee – she was my neighbour for ten years. I know she'll do the right thing, and apart from anything else, she would expect me to tell her.'

'That's up to you, Cat, if you think she can be trusted. I have to say, I am worried about Mary Kate. If she goes home and doesn't tell a living soul about what she's been through and is reduced to telling lies about her life here, she could end up going truly mad.'

Cat didn't need any further prompting and didn't want to lose the moment while she had Mrs O'Keefe onside. 'Well, there's not a minute to waste then. Do you have an airmail letter?' She pulled out a chair at the table and glanced at the sideboard.

'I do.' Mrs O'Keefe hurried to the drawer and removed her writing case. 'I hope we know what we're doing, Cat?' she said as she placed it in front of her.

'So do I. Surely they will understand that they had to live together because that witch of a wife wouldn't give him a divorce. I mean, how backwards can they be over there? It's not like anyone will blame her. They weren't living in sin, Mrs O'Keefe, they were living in love. Anyway, I know Bee and I think she had her own secrets, although I never got to know them. She can hold a secret, can Bee, and she is definitely the best person to write to. I promise you that.'

Grateful to have redeemed herself in Mrs O'Keefe's eyes and ashamed that she'd been exposed in her search for a reason to have contact with Michael Malone, Cat lowered her head and bit her lip in concentration as the pen scratched across the paper.

Mrs O'Keefe felt a sudden weight in her chest. She and Mary Kate had become as close as mother and daughter. With no children of her own, she had treasured and secretly enjoyed the fact that their bond had strengthened as each day passed. It was a bond built on trust in the face of adversity and even though this letter would bear Cat's signature, she felt strongly that in writing it without consulting Mary Kate they were betraying her. Her biggest fear was that when

Mary Kate returned to Tarabeg and discovered this, she might lose her forever.

'I'll tell you this Cat,' she said as she pulled out a chair and sat next to her at the table. 'You spelt "saddest" wrong – it's two ds not one.'

Cat cursed and inserted another d.

'I don't think Nicholas was right, sending her home. I feel it in my bones, I do. I know she has to go, but I don't think she's any safer there than she is here. It's running right through me. Maybe it's because she's such a trusting and innocent girl, I don't know, but I always feel as though there's something around the corner with Mary Kate. Like when she first arrived in Liverpool – remember? – and she was mugged.'

'I can't forget, can I?' said Cat. 'She ended up at my door. That's how we both got to know her.' Cat chewed on the end of the pen and looked thoughtful. 'She's a liability, you're right, because she's one of those people. Not ordinary like me and you. Nothing ever happens to me from one month end to the next, but Mary Kate, she's just different. You know what I mean, don't you?' She looked up at Mrs O'Keefe.

'Aye, you're right, she is different. It's not just that she is the prettiest girl to have ever lived in this avenue, and Lord knows, that's enough to bring its own fair measure of trouble, but there is something about Mary Kate and it makes me worry too. You're right, that's a good word to describe her – a liability. Mind you, it's a liability I'm happy to know.'

'And that,' said Cat, 'is the reason why I have to write this letter to Bee and get it in the post right away.'

Chapter 7

Peggy hauled a sack of flour from inside Malone's General Store onto the wooden pallet under the shop window and waved to Keeva as she stepped out onto the wide road at just the same moment, to watch her five boys make their way to school.

Despite it being November, a weak and watery sun had made a reluctant appearance, but that was doing nothing to take the chill off the breeze blowing in from the coast a mile away. One by one, Keeva tucked hand-knitted woollen scarves deep inside the jumpers of each of her sons, before dropping a kiss on the upturned brow of the youngest only. She loved motherhood and took immense pride in making a good job of it.

Scrubbed clean and pink faced, each one of her sons was the image of their father, Tig, and of each other, with hair the colour of ripe carrots and piercing bright blue eyes. It was only their age and height that enabled the villagers to tell them apart. ''Tis like watching five little Tigs set off for school,' Grandad Paddy had said with pride as they filed past him in an orderly line, under Keeva's instruction.

The line had disintegrated into a tussle and scrum by the time they reached the opposite side of the road, all five of them calling out their hellos to Peggy as they passed.

'Has Finn left already, Peggy?' Aedan, the eldest, asked her.

'He has that,' said Peggy as, disappointed, Aedan caught up with his less-than-well-behaved brothers.

The sack of flour dropped from Peggy's hands onto the pile stacked against the window. Wiping her fingers on her apron, she pushed back her hair to watch and enjoy the tableau of domesticity play out before her. 'Don't they just brighten up a dull day,' she shouted across to Keeva, who, crossing her arms to ward off the bitter wind, ran across the road to speak to her.

'How can I not watch them leave every flamin' morning,' she said. 'The second I turn my back, they will start fighting. All except Aedan. I did something right with him.'

Peggy tucked her hands into her apron pocket and turned to watch the boys walking up the road towards the school. 'Finn left with Rosie at eight o'clock. He's on fire-lighting duty in the classrooms, and none too pleased about it either. I swear to God, being the son of the headmistress is a curse for that poor lad.'

She laughed at her own analysis, a laugh that hid her sadness. Thirty, single and childless, it had only recently dawned on her that her fertile years had slipped away while she'd been busy hankering after the truly unobtainable, her all-American dream. Her life to date had been lived vicariously through the film stars whose careers she'd documented in the ever-growing pile of scrapbooks stored under her bed. She had spent years reading every word that was written about every film and film star, devouring with fervour the American magazines that very occasionally arrived in the post office. She'd even persuaded Michael to take her to Dublin on a couple of his buying trips in the past year, so that she could see a film, no matter that it had been released a long time ago. Her obsession had started when she was a girl, with Rita Hayworth, Ginger Rogers and Fred Astaire, and had finished with Marilyn Monroe and Montgomery Clift. It had come to an abrupt halt only recently, when she'd realised that no matter how many films she watched, her jar of savings was never going to grow as fast as her aspirations.

She was known as 'poor Peggy' to everyone in Tarabeg, and on her thirtieth birthday Rosie had taken pity on her, folding a brown ten-shilling note around her gift of a tub of lily-of-the-valley talcum powder. Peggy had almost cried with gratitude. Rosie had helped her count the pennies and silver shillings in her stone jar and had made a quick calculation. 'Well, Peggy, at this rate you'll have enough for the fare to America when you're fifty-two. You've a better chance of catching the eye of American Joe up at the farm and persuading him to take you over there as his wife.'

Michael, who'd been sitting by the fire with Finn, reading a book, had laughed. 'Well, Peggy, 'tis our fortune,' he said. 'You'll have to put up with us, I'm thinking.'

Poor Peggy was also known as 'raggedy Peggy', due to the shabbiness of her clothes. To Michael, Rosie's suggestion that Peggy could catch the eye of Joe Malone was as fanciful as Bridget's stories about the faeries. Bridget claimed that he'd built his house and shop on the faerie path from the river to the village and that the only way to placate them would be to plant a hawthorn bush, their favourite, for them to play under. Despite his scepticism, Michael had acquiesced, and Bridget had duly planted the bush at the side of the shop.

'It looks that way, Michael, does it not?' Peggy replied. 'Fancy me, all this time – imagine! I was wondering why I wasn't gone to America already and living the high life.'

They laughed. She laughed. They all laughed, even Finn, his comic book dropping from his knee onto the hearth. And she was grateful, as the laughter hid her turmoil. Fifty-two before she had a chance to escape, and who would want her then? Where had her head been? As the youngest child of ten on a hill farm, living a miserable life, she'd been smitten and in a dream from the moment she'd seen her first glossy magazine. She thought she could do it, escape, just like all the others, but she was the poorest girl in Tarabeg and as a consequence she was left behind. It was only since she'd moved in to live with Michael and Rosie, after Mary Kate had left for Liverpool and at Rosie's gentle insistence, that she'd begun to see herself as others did. The night Rosie helped her count the pennies in her jar, she watched the life she'd dreamt of disappearing out the door, laughing at her as it went. Weeks later, she was doing just as she always had, day after day, lugging the bags of flour and potatoes out onto the shop display at the front and chatting to Keeva.

As the last of the boys filed in through the school gate, Keeva broke into Peggy's thoughts. 'Are you off to the dance, Peggy?' she asked. 'Only you haven't bought a ticket and they are selling over the butcher's counter faster than the rashers. It's the talk of Erris. Tig reckons 'twill be the best yet. Bridget was telling Nola that the great thing about this one is that everyone is going. There'll be food – Josie and Nola are making the pies. It's a full moon that night, so plenty of light home, and Legs Duffy will be playing. Imagine! It'll be fantastic.'

Peggy looked at Keeva and bit her lip. She wanted to say yes – she always went to the dance. 'What's the point, Keeva? The fella I want to dance with won't be going. This lot will, though, and who wants to dance with them?' She shook her head at the group of farmhands walking past the Malones' seven acres and towards the boreen up to Captain Carter's land.

The lads almost drowned out her words, whistling and shouting indecencies at Peggy. 'Is your bed cold, Peggy? Will you be wanting me to slip down this evening when I'm done at Paddy's bar? Don't be telling the missus on me now, I'll be over later.'

'You'll have Michael's gun at your back and Rosie will be straight down to see your missus, TJ, if you even try it,' shouted Keeva in response, to guffaws of fading laughter.

'See – the very state of them! Why would I be wanting to buy a ticket to be in the same room as that lot. Did you see the cut of that one? I feel sorry for his wife, she must have been drunk or desperate on the day she took her vows.' Peggy nodded towards the back of the man who'd shouted.

'She was definitely both, if I remember right,' said Keeva thoughtfully, rubbing her hands together for warmth.

'And has been ever since, so she has,' said Peggy. 'The last time I went to the dance, when his wife couldn't go because she'd just had the last of the babbies and hadn't yet been churched, he only jumped out at me when I tried to ride my bicycle back home. Put his hands on the handlebars, he did, and one leg either side of the front wheel, and tried to shove his filthy tongue down my throat.'

Keeva placed her hand over her mouth in disgust. 'And him a married man. What did you do to get away, Peggy?'

Peggy grinned. 'I bit it,' she said proudly, crossing her arms. 'And then I pushed one of my feet on the pedal so hard, I rammed the front wheel right where it hurt him the most. He screamed so loud, half of the people still dancing in the long hall came running out. He would have had a job explaining that to his missus when he got home too, and he hasn't had another babby since, so he hasn't. He'll not be coming over here tonight – he wouldn't dare.'

Keeva began to laugh. 'Peggy, I wouldn't dare to cross you, you scare the life out of me.'

Peggy looked pleased with herself. It was not often that someone paid her a compliment and Keeva's words counted as just that.

'Well, Tig is going and I am too, and Michael and Rosie have bought tickets.'

'Have they?' They hadn't told her or even mentioned it to her.

Keeva noticed the brief look of hurt that swept across her face.

Peggy, the single one who no one ever thought to include in anything. It had been easy enough when she was in her teens and early twenties and had hung about with the crowd of other single village girls, picking off their husbands from the village boys one by one. But after a while, dreamer Peggy, head-in-the-clouds, film-mad Peggy, was the only one left. Now, past her thirtieth year, she was an old maid and largely forgotten. It wouldn't be long before they added a new insult and started calling her 'old Peggy from the shop', and no one was more aware of that than Peggy herself.

Keeva had realised her mistake as soon as she'd spoken and almost bit her own tongue. 'Tell you what,' she said, 'I know of two good-looking single fellas who are going and they are both a cut above the rest.'

'Oh aye, who would that be then?' Peggy dragged a hessian sack of carrots out from the shop doorway and began emptying it into the straw basket, lifting up the 'Halfpence a pound' sign she'd written herself to prevent it from being buried. 'And don't be saying Declan. He's not my type. I don't like the clever ones – not that I've met many. They make me feel so stupid, they do.'

'I wasn't counting Declan. I was talking about Joe Malone and Pete Shevlin, from up on the farm,' said Keeva with more than a little triumph in her voice.

It worked. Peggy's head swivelled sharply round. 'Joe and Pete? But neither of them ever go to the dance. Joe is always heading out to Galway for his entertainment, or so Mrs Doyle told Father Jerry, who told Teresa Gallagher, who told Rosie, who told me.'

Keeva smiled. 'Well, that's not a crime, Peggy. He is from America and used to a bit more by way of entertainment than he can find here in Tarabeg, and that's a fact. But they are both looking forward to the dance this time, they said so themselves to Tig over in the bar yesterday, and Joe even bought two tickets for them both. Pete gave him the money with no objection.'

Keeva peered hard at Peggy's face; she was giving nothing away, but she saw the light flash in her eyes. Keeva had long guessed it and now she knew it: Peggy was thrilled at the thought that Joe and Pete were going to the dance, but she was proud, hurt from having been passed over, and felt foolish for having held such high hopes for her life.

'I'll think about it,' Peggy replied. 'I have to get behind the counter now. Michael is in the back with Father Jerry and he looks none too pleased. He'll be giving out if he sees me gassing out here.'

Keeva made her way across the road, back to the butcher's and bar, but before she reached the other side, Peggy called out, 'Keeva, keep me a ticket. I'll bring the money over later. I'll come.' She thrust both of her hands into her front apron pocket and grinned.

Keeva, delighted, waved and grinned back. 'I'll do it right now, before they all go,' she shouted, 'and we can walk together, me and you. Come over here before and I'll do your hair.'

Keeva's words made Peggy feel warm inside, but she knew that was Keeva's gift, she did it to everyone she spoke to. She bent over and heaved up a sack of potatoes that Michael had left for her to put outside, a sack that Michael had carried on his shoulders with ease. She lifted up a hank of hair that hung over her shoulder and examined it despairingly. She couldn't remember when she'd last washed it. Her hair had once defined her. She wore clothes close to rags, but her hair had shone like polished mahogany. Now it felt thick and coarse, filled with peat and potato dust. She flicked it back over her shoulder and huffed and puffed to the door, dragging the weight of a dead man in potatoes and muttering to herself.

'I'm going to that dance and I'm going to bloody change my life,' she whispered. And there and then she decided that whatever else happened, she would use that dance and that night to turn her life around and to let him know she was waiting for him. She would make him notice her and she would tell him that there were no games to play and that she was willing to be his wife if only he would have her.

In the kitchen behind the shop, Michael picked up a clay pipe from the jar on the hearth, pulled free a wad of tobacco and used the diversion of stuffing and puffing to think about what he had just been told.

''Tis a mystery to us all, Michael,' said Father Jerry, 'but there cannot possibly be a mistake. There is only one Mary Kate from Tarabeg.'

Michael's cheeks burnt as he drew on the dudeen. He swallowed down his anger. He wanted to roar at Father Jerry, tell him to get the hell out of his home, but he was his friend as well as the priest, so that was impossible. He surprised himself as a thin voice left him in an even tone. 'Well, Mrs Brogan's daughter has made a mistake. My Mary Kate has not got married – would not, indeed could not, without my permission. And, Jesus, for feck's sake, you think my daughter would have a husband who died and I wouldn't even know about it?'

What Father Jerry had told him was preposterous. And yet the girl who loved Tarabeg was elusive, barely ever got in touch. He couldn't help himself, he ended on the roar he had tried to avoid. But Father Jerry, a man who had witnessed every human emotion in his years as a priest, did not flinch.

'See now, I know Dana well, she is a very bright girl, and sure, she's a great nurse, she's not likely to have made a mistake. Would you like me to be ringing the hospital for you to see if it is your Mary Kate?'

'No,' Michael snapped, leaving Father Jerry in no doubt that it was time for him to leave.

If there were any enquiries to be made, Michael would call the pub in Liverpool and speak to Cat. If anyone would know what was going on, she would. He watched Father Jerry's back as he retreated from the kitchen, deflated, shoulders slumped. It occurred to Michael that if it was Mary Kate, which it obviously could not be, he would be even more angry if the father had been given that information and had not passed it on to him. He had done the right thing.

'Father,' he said in a gentler tone, 'I will call Liverpool myself, and when I do, I will tell you what's what and then you can tell Mrs Brogan that her Dana has made a mistake.'

'Ah, do you have a telephone number for her, Michael? Can you make contact with Mary Kate herself?'

'I do that, Father. As you know, she herself works for the family of a doctor of some repute in Liverpool and I have the numbers for a wonderful woman by the name of Mrs O'Keefe, her friend and neighbour, and Cat, who lived next door to Bee when she was in Liverpool. You see, there's no end of people I can talk to who can tell me themselves that this story is a crock of the fairies' shite.' That sentence finished on a roar too.

Father Jerry smiled at Michael, attempting to dispel the animosity. He failed.

As the door closed, Michael threw the dudeen into the hearth and it shattered, sending splinters of clay across the floor. He went to the desk in the corner of his sitting room and pulled open the drawer. It had been made by his grandfather, Daedio, for Michael and his first wife, Sarah, what now seemed an age ago. The top was strewn with orders and invoices, bills, IOUs and notes of payment. Rummaging beneath, he found his address book and, opening it, the numbers he was looking for under L for Liverpool.

The first number was Cat's and his heart beat a little faster, but the photographs on the desk of his wife Rosie and son Finn forced him take a deep breath. He'd surprised himself that he felt no shame for his passionate two-day affair in Liverpool with funny, irreverent Cat. She and her quirky accent had made him laugh every time she spoke, but he was firm in his resolve: it must never happen again. What had felt like a pleasure in Liverpool was most definitely a sin back at home. And it was two years in the past now.

As Father Jerry reached the doors of the church, he fingered the thin blue airmail paper he was still holding in his hand and flicked open the letter Mrs Brogan had given him so hard, the flimsy paper almost ripped. He read it once more.

She loved him like no woman I have ever known to love a man. It was like something from the films. Dr

William told me they were totally devoted to each other.

Every nurse on the ward cried the day he died, even Sister closed the door of her office for a while and bit the tea lady's head off when she wheeled her trolley in. It wasn't just because he was a marvellous doctor – Sister used to tell us every single day how great he was and how lovely to his patients – he'd been a big favourite with all the ward sisters when he was a houseman at the hospital. Dr Gaskell, he's the big-boss-man doctor in this hospital, said we were all upset about it not only because the doctor had been a part of the hospital family, but also because he was as devoted to Mary Kate as she was to him and it was a sadness that they had so little time together.

And get this, Mammy – the day Dr Marcus died, he said to me the one place on earth he wanted to visit before he passed was his Mary Kate's precious Tarabeg. Imagine that – he wanted to visit Mayo, Mammy.

Father Jerry carefully folded the letter then clasped his hands in prayer and sighed, drawing his thoughts inwards and waiting for the Holy Ghost to find him and help him deepen his meaningful prayer for the family he was devoted to. As he closed his eyes, it was Daedio who came to him as clear as though he were in his regular seat in the pew before him. Despite the lingering smell of the holy smoke from the swinging thurible at Mass, he thought he could sense the old man, long dead though he was now. He could feel his warmth before him, and one of their last conversations came to him, as though Daedio were whispering the words into the empty church.

He closed his eyes tight and pressed his palms together as the letter crackled in the sleeve of his vestments, dragging his thoughts back to Mary Kate and her predicament. She had been through so much in her short life; Father Jerry had been there long before she was born and had witnessed it all. He had held her mother, Sarah, in his arms as she took her last breath, and Sarah's mother, Angela, before her. His most ardent daily prayers had always been for the Malones and he lived in fear for Mary Kate; he did not want her to die in his arms as her mother had. He prayed day and night against the curse that had haunted the family and which, despite his best efforts, he'd been unable to dispel.

He'd made her great-grandfather, Daedio, a promise during a visit to his bedside up at the farm just days before he'd died, and it was that day which was now at the front of his thoughts.

'Look out for Mary Kate, Father,' Daedio had whispered. 'Shona cursed her – do you remember the night?'

Father Jerry had held a drink to Daedio's lips and had taken great pleasure in being able to pass on news that had allowed the old man to finally die in peace. Shona the gypsy, who was older than anyone could guess, had cursed the Malones for many years. 'Shona is dead, Daedio. I heard it from the priest at Newport. She died only last week. You did it, Daedio, you outlived her.'

He had never seen the gaze of a dying man shine so bright with relief. Rheumy and red with age, Daedio's eyes had stared deeply into Father Jerry's. 'Is that a fact, Father? Do you know that for sure?'

Father Jerry had smiled down at him. 'Daedio, I'm a man of God, would I lie to you? I spoke to the man who buried her himself.'

Daedio had slipped from his hands back onto the pillow and to Father Jerry's utter surprise had turned his head to the fire and said, 'Annie, do you hear that? You can come and get me now.' He was talking to his long-dead wife.

'Now, now, Daedio, 'twill be the angels the good Lord sends for you when the time comes. Annie has been gone for a very long time.'

'Father...' The whisper was faint and hoarse. Father Jerry sat down on the side of the bed in front of the fire and leant closer. 'Mary Kate, she will be back – she has a nature for the place. Look out for her, will you. Not everyone understands about Shona, but you do, Father. You know. I don't trust that old witch. She'll have done something on her deathbed, used the last of her strength to cast another curse. She never stopped blaming me for taking the seven acres out from under her.'

Father Jerry did understand only too well. He fought off the evil spirits that floated into Tarabeg from time to time by marching around the village late at night, chanting, protecting it with a band of prayer. Since Shona had died, he had felt the urge less; he'd thought they were safe. But now he was sure that, even far away in Liverpool, misfortune had befallen Mary Kate. She was beyond his protection. It would appear Daedio had known what he himself could not countenance: Shona may have cast a final curse.

If the letter from Mrs Brogan's daughter was right, Mary Kate was in desperate trouble again. How had that happened? Had he let the Malones down? He closed his eyes and prayed out loud for her to return safely home to Tarabeg, where he knew he would have more chance of protecting her than in Liverpool. A wind of discontent was blowing through the village. He prayed hard, knowing he would need all the help that God could afford him. He was the priest in a village of ghosts and not all of them meant well.

Mrs Doyle in the post office had connected Michael to the number in Liverpool. 'Oh, 'tis you, Michael. Well, isn't this just the thing. Is it a number in Liverpool you will be after?'

Michael gave her the number and then took a deep breath as a familiar irritation rose within him. 'It is, Mrs

Doyle. If you could connect me as soon as possible, I would be very grateful.'

He read out the number again to Mrs Doyle, who he could hear writing it down on the other end of the line. He wondered if it would be quicker just to walk to the end of the main street and shout it through the post office door to her.

'And who does that number belong to? You've never called it before.' Mrs Doyle's line of questioning was not unusual in a village where the inhabitants were strangers to secrets.

Mrs Doyle could get no answer at the Marcus household, so Michael had her try Dr Marcus's surgery instead. Finally, to his relief, the phone rang out and was quickly answered by a male voice.

'Hello, Doctor, would that be you? I apologise for calling, but I was wondering, would it be too much trouble to have a quick word with my Mary Kate?'

His request was met with silence and then a soft voice replied, 'This is Dr William here. Were you looking for Dr Marcus?'

'I am that,' Michael replied cheerfully. 'Although I don't want to be disturbing the good man, or yourself, 'tis just Mary Kate I needed a quick word with.'

Two minutes later, Michael replaced the receiver and stood stock still as he stared at the phone. Mrs Doyle had heard every word. Thank God the man calling himself Dr William had not revealed the intimate contents of Mrs

Brogan's letter, but he had confirmed that Dr Marcus had died and that his only daughter, Mary Kate, was on her way home to Tarabeg. Decency and propriety had been preserved, and with it the reputation of the family name, their place in the social pecking order of the village and the future of his business. If the contents of Mrs Brogan's letter were proved to be true, theirs would be seen as a house of doubtful virtue and sinful happenings. They could never recover from a scandal such as that. It would be the end of the Malones in Tarabeg.

When finally Michael was able to gather his thoughts, he decided he would not yet share with Rosie the news of the Brogan letter, nor indeed would he tell her about his phone call to Liverpool. He needed time to decide what it was he should do other than simply wait and see would Mary Kate show up. Instead, his thoughts turned to Mary Kate's mother, his long-dead, beloved first wife. The past cast long, dark shadows and Sarah had never left him. Their enduring love bound her to Tarabeg; she wanted to stay, and when his day came, they would leave together.

'Sarah, did ye hear that?' he hissed, still staring at the phone beside him.

He held his breath, he waited, he looked about him, he willed her to reply. He yearned to hear her whisper, feel the faint cool touch of her fingers brushing against the dark hair on his strong arm – anything to let him know she was still there with him. But nothing came. It had been that way for weeks and he took a deep breath as he wondered where it was she had gone.

Chapter 8

The ink on the death certificate was barely dry before the news had flown from one end of the village to the other. The biggest landowner in the area, the British master of the great estate, Captain Carter, was dead.

Father Jerry ran into the church and jumped on the ropes, and the bells began to peal loud and clear, calling people from their homes and down into the village to hear the news.

Peggy burst in through the school doors and raced into the girls' classroom, down the side of the rows of long benches, her heels hammering on the wooden floor, seeking out Rosie, who turned from the blackboard where she was in the process of writing a sentence of composition. Narrowing her eyes, she looked past Peggy to the windows, as if expecting to see the reason for the commotion written in the condensation.

'He's dead,' whispered Peggy.

Rosie wiped the chalk from her hands on the dusty rag on the ledge below the blackboard. 'Who is?' she hissed back, taking Peggy by the sleeve and leading her to the back of the class.

Thirty-five heads rose from their books and turned as one.

'Back to your work, please, girls,' said Rosie in the authoritative tone she'd acquired over the years, a tone the children dared not disobey.

The classroom smelt of chalk powder, old textbooks, floor wax, burning peat from the fire in the grate, and grubby children. Peggy waited for the shuffling of feet and paper to die away and for the thirty-five sets of curious eyes to turn away before she answered.

'Captain Carter, 'tis him who's dead. It was the chest that took him. The doctor could do nothing and they sent for Bridget too late.'

Rosie looked thoughtful. 'Shall I close the school out of respect, or what?'

Before Peggy could respond, Declan stepped into the room. 'What is it?' he asked, looking from one to the other. 'Why are the bells ringing?'

His question was answered by Teresa Gallagher, who just at that moment hobbled in through the main door, banging her stick on the floor as she walked. 'Captain Carter is dead. Father Jerry says to send the children home at once.'

There was a sense of air leaving the room as the children all inhaled at once, pencils held mid flight. Had they heard right?

A small voice echoed Rosie's. 'Captain Carter from the manor house, he's dead?'

'Home it is then,' said Rosie to Declan, and the words had barely left her mouth before the classroom filled with the sound of chairs scraping and books being closed. 'No playing in the yard, no noise, straight back up to the farms, and keep your eyes down and your hands at your sides all the way home. Show respect and pray for the soul of Captain Carter on your way,' she said, blessing herself as she spoke.

Declan returned to the boys' classroom and issued the same order, then stood by the main door to check there was no joviality in the cinder yard outside.

'Can we play football?' asked one brave boy.

'I'm afraid not,' Declan replied. 'Away home now and tell your mammy the news. There will be no football until after the wake.'

Those who dared groaned in dismay as they shuffled down the path, out of the gate, and, more importantly, out of sight of the school.

'Well, that is it now. God himself knows what's in store for us all,' said Peggy.

'Why, what difference does it make to us?' asked Declan.

'It will make a great deal of difference to the Malone shop, I would be saying, Rosie,' said Teresa. 'Goodbye now, Declan, and you too, Peggy,' she added as she limped back to the door, stick in hand. 'I'm away to the post office and to see Mrs Doyle. She will have all the news, so she will. The poor man, God rest his soul.' She blessed herself, cast an overly mournful expression their way, one she kept especially for deaths and wakes, outdoing those of any other woman in the village, and was out of the door before Peggy could reply.

'The Carters have been on the land forever – they've never had any luck at all,' said Peggy.

'Help me with these, would you, Peggy,' said Rosie as she began to gather up the discarded books from one end of the row of desks.

Peggy, never missing an opportunity to help, began at the other end. 'What will become of the place I'm sure I don't know,' she said.

Declan leant against the door jamb that led to the central hallway. 'What did that man ever do for the village?' he said, shaking his head. 'He gave a few people jobs and paid them a subsistence wage. Nothing more. They were trapped between working for him or having to leave for Liverpool or some other place. He had money spilling out of his coffers and yet the people who worked for him had to work themselves sick six days a week just to scrape by, begging him for their five days' holiday a year, unpaid, of course. The man was a money-grabbing scoundrel. He lived the high life off the backs of people who had no choice. I won't be crying any tears over his loss.'

'Declan, hush now,' said Rosie. 'We can talk about all that after the wake, but for now, set the example expected of you as the teacher and keep those opinions to yourself. God knows, I agree with every word you say, but let's just see what happens now, shall we? Because it could be that many of those people will have no job at all tomorrow and we might be having to find ways to help.'

Declan huffed and strode down to his classroom to clear away the day. Rosie had nothing more to add as she wiped the blackboard clean and riddled the peat in the hearth. Twenty minutes later, she left the school with her basket over her arm, accompanied by Peggy and Declan. As she closed the front door and the latch dropped, she had a sense of foreboding. Teresa was right. Michael depended on Captain Carter's land for a good deal of the shop's income. They couldn't survive on selling their wares to the villagers and the farms alone. A portion of their money came from selling fishing licences to tourists, along with the tackle and everything else a fisherman might need, including the sandwiches Peggy made to order each morning. Captain Carter and the Malones' business were inextricably linked. The death of the captain might indeed have a negative outcome for their family.

'There won't be anyone coming to the shop just now. Shall we go to the post office for a cup of tea?' said Peggy. 'Will you be coming with us, Declan?'

Declan, who lived under the thumb of his mother, frowned. 'I had better get home. Mammy will be wanting to know why the bells are ringing.'

Rosie put her hand on his arm; she felt so sorry for him. The perfect son, he'd brought his invalid and demanding mother from Galway to live in the teacher's house with him and was paying a high price for his kindness. 'Why the post office, Peggy? We have a perfectly good kettle in the shop.' Rosie had never been a gossip.

'Because if there are any phone calls coming in from England for the manor, they will have to go through the exchange there. And we will find out what's going on.'

Rosie shook her head as an image of half of the women in the village crowding around the post office counter trying to hear the news from Mrs Doyle's Bakelite earpiece flew into her mind. 'No, you go, Peggy. I'll look after the shop and call in and see Keeva. Michael will be back from the deliveries soon. I'll get his dinner ready.'

Rosie didn't want to say, but she was secretly enjoying the thought of the unexpected free afternoon ahead. She supressed the spring in her step as she saw Bee and her husband walking down from the coast road towards her. Bee gave her a muted wave and pointed at the shop as she and Captain Bob parted, him heading for Paddy's bar and her for the Malones'.

As Captain Bob stepped into the bar, he was not the least surprised to find it was full already. Unbeknown to Rosie, Michael had heard the bells and turned the van around and come straight back down to the village.

'God love him,' said Paddy. 'Sure, the captain was no trouble. We never so much as saw him walk through the village once, right from when he was a young man. Always in his carriage or on a horse, and just lately in that fancy car of his.'

Michael reached out his hand for the pint of Guinness that had already been poured for him. No one would be leaving for some time. The demise of Captain Carter would fill the Devlin till to overflowing before the night was out. Death and drink went hand in hand and always brought Paddy his biggest profits. 'Well, they say his family were grand during the famine. Took a few families in and sent out food, and did it all in secret because some of the landowners and the army were giving out to those who so much as gave away the crumbs from their table.'

There was a moment's silence, as there always was when the famine was mentioned, each one of them the offspring of a survivor and all of them having heard first-hand stories from relatives not long dead.

'Aye, 'tis a pity that generosity doesn't run in the blood,' said one of the farmhands. 'He was always late with the pay and I haven't had a rise for years, and neither has anyone else. I don't want to speak ill of the dead, but he had enough money for a doctor from Dublin but not enough to pay the cook. The place has been falling down around his ears.'

Before Michael had taken his second gulp, the door opened and in strode Seamus, Pete and Joe. Conversation quickly moved on to the future of the estate.

'How many rooms has the manor house?' asked Joe in an almost absent-minded fashion. He'd been aware that the manor house existed, had heard the talk of the declining health of its owner, but, not being from the village, he had no prior knowledge of its inhabitants and, until now, no interest either.

'Well now,' said Josie, 'half the girls from the village work up there cleaning and half the men on the land. I'd be saying maybe thirty or forty upstairs rooms, not that I've ever been in. We deliver the meat around the back to the old scold of a cook in the kitchens. They send all the laundry out to the convent on the road to Castlebar.'

Joe nearly choked on his pint. 'Forty rooms! Holy moly, that's the size of a hotel.'

No one in the bar had ever stayed in a hotel and they nodded, losing interest in his line of enquiry, and turned their attention to the wake and the prospect of free drinks.

'Will his body be sent off to England?' asked Seamus.

'Sure, I've no idea,' said Paddy. 'I would imagine so. The Carters, they have houses over there too, loads of them. It was only the fishing and the sport that kept him here, and then he got too ill to travel. I'm sure he'd have preferred to have died in England, with his own sort around him. All he had here with him was you, Father, the doctor, and Bridget, but none of his family.'

'That was all he needed,' said Father Jerry, slightly wounded.

'Now, who would this be?' said Paddy, staring out the window at the man standing on the doorstep dressed in a dusty coat and formal hat and carrying a briefcase.

Father Jerry took pleasure in being able to pass on the information with authority. 'Ah, now, that's the—' He looked stunned as Joe interrupted him and stole his moment of glory.

'The lawyer,' said Joe. 'Or I'm losing my marbles.'

Father Jerry would have asked him how he knew that, and Joe would have told him that he'd mixed a great deal with lawyers of late, having become the biggest shareholder in one of the largest law firms in New York as a result of the generations-old Malone will. He could spot one a mile off. But the father had no chance to put the question because the man had already stepped into the bar.

The room fell deathly quiet as everyone in it appraised the stranger and everything about him, from the cut of his coat to the leather of his case.

The silence was only broken by Paddy rushing forward from behind the bar. 'Sorry for your troubles,' he said. 'Is it a drink ye are after, or a meal maybe?'

'All of those,' said the man in a crisp English accent. 'And do you have a clean room for the night, landlord?'

Within seconds, the stranger was surrounded. He was the entertainment for the evening and the source of news that even Mrs Doyle had no access to.

Joe remained at the back. He was only two years in the village, still considered to be a guest, a visitor. He would have to put down roots, become a member of the village and marry into it before he was fully considered to be a part of Tarabeg, even if he was Joe Malone the fourth and a direct descendant of Daedio's brother. The word 'hotel' was flying round and round his brain. Wasn't that just what the village needed to breathe life into it? To bring money in and lift the living standards? Maybe scraping a hand-to-mouth existence from the inhospitable land didn't have to be the only way to survive around there. Ideas were tumbling into his thoughts as fast as he could process them. He had the money... He would buy the estate, turn the land into a golf course, sell the fishing rights and market holidays to the wealthier members of the Irish diaspora back in New York and Brooklyn. The flights from Shannon to

New York with American Airlines were becoming more frequent by the day.

His eyes were bright with excitement. As he downed his drink, he determined that as the lawyer left the bar, he would catch his arm and ask him who was dealing with the will. For the first time since he'd inherited his great-grandfather's money, he felt its worth and understood why he had remained in Tarabeg for so long. It was fate. His moment had come. He had more money than even he knew, because the pot was added to every week with the profits from the law firm in New York.

As the solicitor finished his whiskey and the bacon and eggs Josie had brought out to him, for which she'd accepted no money in return, Joe hovered by the door and waited for his chance. First, though, they were all distracted by Declan.

'You made it,' said Michael as Declan entered the bar. They all felt sorry for him, for they all knew he would never be able to marry. There wasn't a woman on earth who would saddle herself with the care of his mother. The house could be made of gold and even Peggy wouldn't step over the threshold.

'Mammy's sleeping,' said Declan. 'I thought I'd just pop down for a quick one, before I go back to make her tea.'

Michael put his arm around his shoulders and guided him towards the bar. 'There is a place waiting for you in heaven, Declan. You will get your reward – won't he, Father?'

Father Jerry turned to Declan, his eyes full of sympathy. Declan's path was not one he ran down. 'You will that, Declan,' he said. 'How is yer mammy this afternoon, is she well?'

As the chatter moved from the demise of Captain Carter to the trials of Declan's mammy, no one noticed Joe standing outside the bar, deep in conversation with Mr Keene, the solicitor from Galway, nor the look of mutual pleasure on the faces of both men as they shook hands.

Bee and Rosie had more important things to talk about than the death of the richest man in Mayo. Cat's letter to Bee had arrived and rather than tell Rosie what was in it, or read it to her, Bee had given it directly to Rosie to read herself.

She is beside herself with grief, Bee. She loved him so much and, God knows, she didn't half go through it to be with him. I'm afraid she's coming back to you with her heart broken in two.

We're not happy about her travelling on her own, and the grief just makes it worse. She's that innocent, you could write 'mug' on her forehead and it wouldn't make it any clearer. She's one of those people, your

Mary Kate, who would tip up her purse and give a
beggar her last penny. And God love her, she is trying
so hard to be brave.

Mrs O'Keefe is packing up her food for the journey
and has sorted the tickets. I swear to God, if it wasn't
for the kids, I'd bring her back to you meself, but me
and Mrs O'Keefe have said we will be over to see her
really soon, if you will have us.

Rosie read the letter without a flicker of emotion
crossing her face and then carefully, having scanned it
a second time to make sure she had read every word,
slipped it back into the envelope and placed it on the
table. 'God love her, indeed,' she said. 'Do we know
when she'll be here?'

'No. As you can see, Cat doesn't say, but I imagine it
will be any day now. The letter was posted several days
ago.'

'I don't know what you are thinking, but this is a
women's thing, I'd say. Should we keep this just to us,
Bee? No one else needs to know and it'd be the best
way of making sure no one ever does.'

They both knew that the opinion of the village
would be that the flames of hell would be roaring up in
readiness for the day Mary Kate arrived, so unspeakable
was her sin.

Bee tutted. 'Sure, she won't be wanting anyone to
know her business, Rosie. When the poor girl arrives

here, she needs to be dealing with her grief, not the opinions of the people in this village. That's what we need to concern ourselves with. She will have made her own peace with God and herself, and if I know Mary Kate, she will not be troubled by guilt. She must have loved him a great deal.'

Rosie stared at the envelope on the table as the words swam. She knew the pain of love. The worst kind of love. Unrequited love, or in her case a love that had been acknowledged but never truly returned. Michael tried to hide it from her, but Rosie knew he still longed for Sarah, still talked to her even, the one true love of his life. She sighed. 'We can manage between us,' she said. 'I will tell Michael, and I don't expect you to keep a secret from Captain Bob. Couples shouldn't keep secrets from one another, but that will be as far as it goes.'

There was no time to discuss the matter further. Peggy shouted through from the shop that she was back from the post office and had brought Nola and Bridget with her. They all bustled into the kitchen and Bee said her goodbyes and headed home. Unusually for Rosie, a woman who had spent the greater part of her life concealing her feelings, she blurted out, 'Mary Kate is coming home.'

Nola glanced at Bridget as they both pulled out the pine chairs from around the table and sat down. 'Well, sure, we know that, it was in the tea leaves. We came here to learn something we didn't know.'

If the situation hadn't been so serious, Rosie possibly would have smiled. She should have known. Bridget, the village seer, reader of teacups and fortunes, the thorn in the side of Father Jerry, always knew everything there was to know in Tarabeg before anyone else. 'I'll tell Michael tonight,' she said, unaware, even after all these years, that in the Malone family she was always the last to know. 'Right now, we can all have a cup of tea and the cake I made yesterday. I used your jam, Nola, and your butter too.'

'It was the cake that brought me back from the post office,' Nola said. 'And there's been no news coming through from England yet anyway. Mrs Doyle was very disappointed. She thought she might be getting to answer a call from royalty about the death of Captain Carter, and all she got was the mother superior from up at the convent wanting to know who would be paying the laundry bill when the delivery was made tomorrow.'

Peggy grinned as she looked over at the press, hungry for a slice of Rosie's cake. 'She's all heart and godliness, that woman is. 'Tis the last convent where any novice willingly takes the veil.' She did a guilty tiptoe over and with a stealthy hand lifted the cloche from the slate board on the press. Her face dropped. 'God in heaven!' she exclaimed, looking round at the others, her mouth open, the cloche hanging in mid air. 'The flaming cake, it's gone.'

'It can't have,' said Rosie. 'I only made it last night and no one touched it at breakfast.' She sprang to her feet and joined Peggy at the press, peering at the empty plate.

Nola and Bridget were at her side in seconds.

'Could it have been Finn?' asked Peggy.

'What, the whole cake? Are you mad? It's more than his life's worth and he knows it,' said Nola.

'There's only one other answer,' said Bridget. ''Tis the faeries, and I don't like it. They only steal food when they've been crossed or something they don't like is occurring.'

The three women looked at Bridget. They all believed every word she said. But Bridget was hiding the truth. She looked about the kitchen as if searching for evidence – a trail of crumbs to the back door or some other clue – but, as she'd expected, there was nothing; he was smarter than that. She'd been waiting for him to appear. Had dreamt it, had heard the whispers from the other side as she half woke, had seen his face in her crystal ball. He was back: McGuffey, Angela's murderer. He was in trouble and she'd been dreading it.

The spirits had told her there was danger ahead, but they hadn't told her what, only that McGuffey was not alone. The warning had been brought to her by Sarah, who'd become a restless ghost, crowding out Bridget's thoughts, waking her, filling her with anxiety. Sarah would not rest and Bridget knew she would have to find a way to warn the Malones. But not tonight; she needed more time. Despite the heat in the kitchen a cold shiver ran down her spine.

'Honest to God,' said Peggy, 'I would put money on it being one of Keeva's lot. A right handful, they are.'

'Right, well, I'm off to have a word,' said Rosie.

'Now, now,' said Nola. 'Be careful. We don't want no falling out.'

'Nola, those boys are out of control. Poor Keeva is run ragged with them,' said Peggy.

'That's as maybe, but it's not our business and you don't have any proof, Rosie,' said Nola. ''Tis a difficult thing to complain to a mother when you haven't had a child yourself. You wouldn't understand, and Keeva might take offence. Leave it be for now and let me have a word with Granny Josie. 'Tis only a cake.'

An angry heat spread through Rosie. She'd stood and made the cake the previous evening, exhausted after having marked thirty-five composition assignments. She had been Finn's mother practically since the day he was born, the day Sarah had died, and yet her mother-in-law always managed to make her feel as though she was on trial, and for one reason only: because she had never actually given birth herself and therefore did not have the wisdom that was apparently miraculously bestowed upon women in childbirth.

She banged the kettle down on the range. 'See you do, Nola,' she said in the sharpest tone she had ever used with her mother-in-law.

Nola sighed and raised her eyebrows to Bridget.

'Don't bother,' Bridget said in reply. ''Twas definitely the faeries, and have I ever been wrong?'

A murmur of agreement rumbled around the kitchen. Now was not the time for Bridget to tell them who she thought it was. It would only cause alarm. She knew it was no coincidence that the night she'd seen in the tea leaves that Mary Kate was coming home was also the first night she'd dreamt about McGuffey. This could be her biggest challenge, and yet she felt her powers were ebbing away.

Rosie almost slammed Nola's cup and saucer on the table in front of her and the women finished their tea in an uncomfortable silence.

Chapter 9

The final departure of Captain Carter from Tarabeg was a grand affair such as the village had never seen before. A few days after his passing, a Mass was held at the Scared Heart. The roads were filled with the cars of mourners who'd travelled over from London. They followed behind the captain's body, which was transported from the church in a shiny black carriage pulled by horses brought in from Galway. Later, the coffin would be taken by car to the airport and returned to London and the family tomb.

Tarabeg's main street was lined with families watching the cortège and paying their respects. The sight of the coffin perched precariously on the back of the carriage made the villagers gasp as it rolled past. They were less impressed by the mourners in the fancy cars, who, for all their finery, looked as if they couldn't wait to get out of rural Ireland and back to England.

'Would you look at that,' said Nola as a car filled with women wearing black, their faces hidden behind veils, crept past at a snail's pace.

'Is it the car you are pointing at, Nola?' asked Joe.

'No, not the car, the women. Not one of them ever visited here before, of that I am sure. Although that one there' – she half pointed to an old woman in the front of a passing car – 'she's the living image of the old woman, his mother.'

Joe didn't ask who that was as he surreptitiously raised his hand to Mr Keene. The solicitor was in the front car, sitting alongside a young woman who at least had the good grace to clutch at a tightly wound handkerchief and dab at her dry eyes. Mr Keene acknowledged Joe with a sombre nod of the head, a silent confirmation that the two men would be meeting later at a hotel in Galway and that present at the discussion would be one Lady Georgina Carter, the niece and direct beneficiary of Captain Carter's will.

'They say up at the manor that in the last five years not one member of the family came to visit him when he was here. Who are they all?' said Nola.

'He was in his bed more of the time than he was out of it,' said Seamus. 'I don't suppose he was up to visitors. Loved the fishing back in the day, he did. They say he never got over the death of his wife. Didn't stop the ghillie though. The bastard never let up, not for a minute. We had the worst summer poaching ever – he became so lazy, he barely moved along the river and was right in our eye every night.'

'He has no respect for tradition, that man,' said Michael. 'He will not have it that the Malones have always poached on the Taramore because it runs through our land.'

Joe looked thoughtful as he listened to the chatter and watched the mourners pass. They looked more bored than sad and he guessed they wouldn't be staying long.

Paddy, Josie, Keeva and Tig had crossed the road to join them just as Rosie and Michael had stepped out of the shop. They all walked over to Declan, who was standing with his hat in his hands. Recalcitrant children had been banished indoors, to hide inside darkened rooms whose curtains had been drawn as a mark of respect.

'Who will inherit?' asked Joe of Seamus and Michael, even though he knew he'd find out all he wanted later.

'He had a son,' said Seamus. 'The little fella died not long after the mother. 'Tis my guess the house will be knocked down and the estate land sold now. No Carter will want to live here any more. And to think, the parties they used to have there and the money they used to spend in the shop when it first opened – do you remember that, Michael?'

Seamus leant forward and looked down the row to

Michael, who, like all the men, had reluctantly removed his cap as the procession rolled past.

'I do. And the licences he sold to the Germans for the fishing. If it hadn't been for that, we would have struggled, having to depend on the village alone.'

'How big is the estate?' asked Joe again.

'Feck, enormous,' said Paddy. 'Why, are you interested in buying it?' He laughed. He was joking.

Joe didn't respond. If he'd replied with the truth, Paddy wouldn't have been laughing.

Father Jerry walked towards the villagers and stopped in front of Mrs Doyle, looking unhappy. He had hoped to persuade Captain Carter to make the village churchyard his final resting place. He felt cheated, as though he'd failed to deliver the good Lord a prize.

'The family request the attendance of the villagers up at the manor house,' he announced with more than a hint of self-importance. 'They are away to Galway, but the housekeeper and the ghillie are expecting us and he says you are all welcome but that you are all to behave now.'

'What in the name of God does that mean, Father?' asked Nola, looking very put out. 'Is it because he was an English policeman before he came here that he thinks we'll all be stealing the captain's whiskey or maybe the silver? Does he not know we are all God-fearing folk?'

Nola was about to continue, but Josie dived in with a complaint of her own. 'Are they sending the cars back for us?' she asked.

Father Jerry looked embarrassed.

'No, of course they aren't,' said Philomena O'Donnell. 'We are expected to walk the dusty road there and back again and be grateful for the privilege.'

'Will you not be going then, Philomena?' shouted Michael.

'Of course I will, you eejit,' she said as she fixed her hat and strode out into the road. 'I haven't been in that house since I helped my mammy when she did the washing there, before they began to send it up to the convent laundry. I won't miss a chance of a free glass. Besides, it wouldn't be right if we didn't fully pay our respects, would it.'

She looked surprised as Joe Malone fell into step alongside her. 'Let me escort you, ma'am,' he said, and Philomena blushed to the white hairs on her chin as she felt the eyes of Peggy and the women of the village burning into her back.

'He's up to something, he is,' whispered Nola to Rosie.

'I think you might be right, Nola. He seems mighty curious about the manor and Captain Carter, and look at him, he can't get there quick enough. What he might be up to, however, is anyone's guess. Are you coming, Michael?' Rosie turned to Michael, who was closing the shop door.

There was no need to lock the shop door. Not a soul for miles around harboured a dishonest bone in their body. There was no such thing as crime in Tarabeg. Unless you counted the children who scrumped apples from the trees on the Carter estate and mysteriously removed a cake. Or the adults who occasionally, on a black, cloudy night with no moon or stars to spoil their cover, poached salmon from the Carter river. But as Seamus often said, 'The Carters are British, it doesn't count, so 'tis not a crime as such. The good Lord will turn a blind eye, and if he does notice, he will call it retribution for past wrongs by the British. We don't even need to go to confession for poaching the fish – Father Jerry has said so himself on many an occasion.'

'Aye, especially after he's spent a night out with us himself,' Michael would reply.

Michael looked up at Rosie in surprise. 'Why would I not be coming to the manor with you?' he asked. 'There won't be any customers until the wake is over, so I may as well. We won't get another chance to see inside the manor if it's to be knocked down, as some are saying.'

He looked up the road past the church to the school. The village was eerily still and quiet. Only he knew who he was looking for, or so he thought, but there had been no word from Mary Kate herself, no sign. He turned on his heel and fell into step alongside his father.

'I hope they have fecking Guinness and it isn't all that sherry shite the English drink,' Seamus said.

Michael, knowing that mirth on such an occasion was sinful, couldn't help himself as he roared with laughter.

Daylight had almost disappeared by the time the bus turned into the main street. The familiar landmarks in the distance she had known since childhood were fading one by one, and the green grass on the hills had blurred into grey.

The bus pulled away, leaving its lone passenger standing on the roadside, clasping her case with both hands and holding it against her shins before her. Her hat was tugged low over her eyes and she'd turned the collar of her coat up against her neck to ward off the chill. She suddenly felt conspicuous as she stood there in her tweed coat, fur collar and red leather boots with leopardskin lining peeping over the top. This was fashion such as the women in Tarabeg would never have seen before and Mary Kate felt it was significant, symbolic even. Her clothes didn't belong in Tarabeg and maybe she didn't either. She had changed, and possibly it had taken setting foot on Tarabeg soil again, with her grief packed in her suitcase alongside all that she now owned, to realise that. Maybe there actually was no going back.

'Remember,' Mrs O'Keefe had said, 'there won't be any answers to your questions. The pain of losing Nicholas will be no less intense just because you've taken it to a different shore. You can't just remove yourself from how you feel – you are carrying your loss with you and it will be a heavier load because of it. And although you don't know it, being there, with people you can't talk to about all that has gone on here in Liverpool, may make it that much harder to deal with. Being in Tarabeg cannot change the past. As my poor husband found out every time he visited Dublin, going back is always a disappointment. You understand that, don't you?'

Mary Kate had thrown her arms around Mrs O'Keefe's shoulders. 'I do, but at least I will be in my own room, my own house, my own bed. Being with Daddy and Rosie and Finn, I need that to help me, and I want to be close to Bee – I can talk to her. Tarabeg was where Nicholas wanted me to be. "Go home," he said, and that's all that matters.'

Mrs O'Keefe said nothing. Secretly, though, she had given thanks that at least there'd been no child. If there had, there'd have been no possibility of Mary Kate returning home to her small Irish village, not ever in her lifetime. There were no second chances then.

Now, in the darkening twilight, Mary Kate's eyes were drawn across to the white walls of the Church of the Sacred Heart. A memory snagged on her mother's looming gravestone. Sarah was there, always would be, had never left, and Mary Kate felt a new wave of grief wash over her. It was as though the death of

Nicholas was making her suffer the loss of her mother afresh.

She saw herself as a little girl kneeling at her mother's grave, laying lady's-tresses watered with endless tears. She thought of the night she'd run away from Tarabeg and left her mother. She'd not visited the grave to say goodbye, so full of herself had she been.

She turned to look up at the school. Was Declan still in Tarabeg? She had barely given him a thought in the past two years and was filled with sudden shame. He had put his job on the line by helping her to run away, taking her all the way to the port in Dublin and seeing her onto the boat for Liverpool. He had kissed her, told her he would wait for her. Her friends, she'd lost contact with them all, too ashamed to tell them about the life she was leading: a mistress in another woman's house, a part-time mother to a married woman's children.

She'd spent the last two years with a man she'd loved with all her heart, but it had by necessity also been a life full of pretence, a half-life. Only now did she feel the weight of the secrets she'd kept slipping from her shoulders, to be replaced by remorse for all the people she'd let down. She gazed up at the church spire. She could never take confession again. Her love had not been a sin and she would never recant it for as long as she lived.

She took deep breaths and filled her lungs with the damp air, relishing the familiar sounds of her childhood.

The raw smell of the fields almost stung the insides of her nostrils and she closed her eyes for a moment to lose herself in the thunder of the Taramore river as it crashed down over the rocks.

It took her a while to realise that something about the village was very different. The lights were on in the butcher's and bar, but there was no sign of Paddy, Josie, Keeva or Tig, nor any of the children. The meeting place on the main street where the young men and women of the village gathered at dusk, huddled against walls to ward off the cold, flirting and talking noisily, stealing first kisses and promises of more to follow, was also empty and silent. Bemused, she turned towards the shop. Her heart was banging in anticipation of meeting her father and having to explain herself, having to lie. But the lights there were off too.

The only sign of life in the fog of the evening gloom was a colourless shape walking up the incline towards her. The shadowy figure made a lonely vision against the empty windows of the village street and it took Mary Kate a few seconds to work out who it was.

Tears filled her eyes, she dropped her case and ran. 'Bee! Bee!' she shouted to the woman she'd not seen in many years, the woman she'd originally travelled to Liverpool to meet. Within moments she'd thrown herself into her arms, her mother's nearest living relative. Bee, her great-aunt.

For what seemed like the first time, Mary Kate felt her heart breaking as Bee whispered into her hair, 'Not to worry. I know. I know all about everything. About your lovely man, God rest his soul. Cat wrote to me. Rosie and me, we are the only ones who know, and God knows, we are glad to see you. You're all right now. Unburden yourself, your secret is safe, Mary Kate – you are home in Tarabeg.'

Dr Gaskell walked beneath the bright lights of the ward, closely followed by the retinue of doctors known as his firm, and a gaggle of medical students. 'And what have we here?' he said, stopping at the foot of a patient's bed, lifting the clipboard and examining the chart.

The patient's complexion was tinged with yellow, and he seemed very nervous; Dr Gaskell noticed his hand was trembling. He turned to his retinue of white coats. 'Go to the ward kitchen, all of you,' he said. 'Tell the auxiliary nurse and the kitchen orderly that I've said you all need some tea and toast before I can get any sense out of you. And ask Sister to give me five minutes alone with this new patient before she brings me his case notes.'

The silent pack spontaneously burst into exclamations of thanks and hurried back down the ward before he could change his mind.

Dr Gaskell sighed and smiled at the patient. 'Do you mind if I sit here in the visitors' chair and rest my feet for a moment?'

The patient stammered his reply. 'Er, no,' he mumbled, not sure what else he should say to the doctor who was a legend on the Dock Road.

'Ask if you can see Dr Gaskell,' his wife had insisted when she'd left him in casualty earlier that afternoon. 'They say he's the best man in the country for chests, they do.'

'I can't ask that,' he'd replied through the rubber oxygen mask as he'd gasped for his breath on the trolley.

'Yes, you can,' his wife had insisted, folding her arms and leaning over him. She was a woman used to getting her own way. 'If you don't ask, our Bert, you don't get.'

Bert now looked up at the kindly face of the white-haired doctor. No one in his life had ever asked him whether he minded if they sat down in his company, let alone a doctor who was also a legend in his own right.

Dr Gaskell pulled the chair close to the bed. 'Sister will bring me your notes in a minute,' he said, 'but I can see you're a bit worried, so I thought that as you've been assigned to me as my patient, we should get to know each other a little first. Now, tell me, what brought you in here to my ward? And if you can just take a moment to think, when did the problems start?'

The patient rubbed his chin and furrowed his brow. 'I'm not sure really – the missus, she knows. I just got weak and went off me food, you know. I just didn't fancy anything, and when I did eat, I got that full, I didn't enjoy it. The gaffer sent me home, said I was no use to man or beast if I couldn't catch a rope, and that's how I ended up in casualty. The missus is worried about the rent, so she brought me straight here. I'm not due to retire for another five years, got no pension until then, you see, Doctor. I need to get back to work.'

Dr Gaskell's heart sank. He'd heard every story of hardship there was and not one had failed to touch him. 'Tell you what, do you fancy a cuppa and a custard cream? I think I'll follow that lot to the kitchen and bring us both back a nice pot of tea. Don't you go anywhere, I'll be five minutes.'

Half an hour later, Dr Gaskell was sitting at the doctor's desk in Sister's office, filling out a request form for the pathology lab, when Nurse Brogan bustled in. 'Oh, sorry, Dr Gaskell,' she said. 'I thought the ward round was over, I didn't mean to disturb you.'

Dr Gaskell looked over the rim of his glasses. 'Nurse Brogan, isn't it?' he asked.

'Yes, 'tis me. I'm the easy one to remember. If you can't do it on the red hair, you can get me on the accent.'

They both laughed. Dr Gaskell was the consultant every nurse at St Angelus adored. Many of the doctors, such as the surgeon Mr Mabbutt, were aloof and would only speak to a nurse if they were either shouting at her or barking out a command. But Dr Gaskell was different. Every nurse said the same: he spoke to each of them as a father would to a child, and he was like that with all of his patients too.

'I will always remember you,' Dr Gaskell said. 'You nursed Dr Marcus with such kindness.'

She could practically see the idea forming in his head.

'Nurse Brogan, we have another case, almost the same. The patient admitted this afternoon into bed five, he's almost a carbon-copy diagnosis, as the X-ray taken in casualty shows. Only I'm afraid this patient has just days, a week at the most. Do you have much longer on male medical?'

Dana looked towards the light-box and the X-ray that glared the obvious out at them both. 'I do, Dr Gaskell, why?'

'Would you mind if I asked Sister if you can be allocated to this patient for his end-of-life care, as you were so good with Dr Marcus?'

Dana looked stunned. 'Do I mind? Not at all. It's an honour to be asked.' She looked out of the window and down the ward. 'He looks a lot older than Dr Marcus was though.'

'Yes, he is, by thirty years.' Dr Gaskell sat back in the chair and thrust his hands into the pockets of his white coat. The brown rubber tubes of his stethoscope quivered about his neck. 'I often think about him,' he said, and then, looking up, 'Have you seen the girl – Mary Kate? You know her, don't you?'

'Oh, I don't know her, not really, she just comes from a village not far from mine back home in Ireland. Did you go to the funeral, Dr Gaskell? I wanted to go, but it wasn't in Liverpool, so Dr William told me when he came by the hospital the other day. That was a bit of a surprise.'

'It wasn't a surprise to me, I'm afraid. That was Mrs Marcus's doing.' Dr Gaskell flicked distractedly through the papers in front of him. 'I tell you what, I know where Mary Kate is staying, at Mrs O'Keefe's, Dr Marcus's neighbour. I have the address, so I think I'll call in later tonight and see how she is. It's only five minutes out of my way as it is. I did promise Nicholas I'd keep an eye out for her and make sure that wicked wife of his didn't make any trouble.'

Dana dropped the case notes she was carrying onto the desk. 'Oh, Dr Gaskell, was Mary Kate not his wife?'

Dr Gaskell flushed. 'Er, no, I'm afraid, my dear, that she wasn't. It was a very complicated story. Love in the most adverse of circumstances.' He patted his white coat nervously. 'I, ah, trust you will keep that to yourself.'

Dana swallowed hard and thought about the letter she had already sent home to her mammy. No one knew the villages better than Dana. Her letter could change Mary Kate's life. If her own family didn't know the truth, Dana's news would be explosive. 'I think that's a really good idea,' she stammered. 'Will you let me know how she is? I, er, might go to see her myself.'

'That's very kind of you.' Dr Gaskell looked up at her with admiration in his eyes. 'I will call into Mrs O'Keefe's this evening. You know, I often laugh at Matron's mantra that St Angelus is just one big family, but you, Nurse Brogan, you have just proved Matron right. You are a huge addition to this family.'

Dana looked down the ward to her new patient, who was sitting with his head in his hands. 'Does he know?' she asked.

'I'm afraid he does, yes. I've left him to be on his own for ten minutes, but I'll go back and see him now before I head off to outpatients.'

'Poor man.' Dana glanced down at his notes. 'The CA strikes again.'

'Yes, but one day soon, you know, there'll be a drug that will stop that hideous disease in its tracks.'

Dana smiled. She couldn't blame Dr Gaskell for wishful thinking, but she doubted he was right.

Chapter 10

Mary Kate sat at the table and watched as Bee placed the kettle on the old range. They were the only two people in the kitchen at the rear of the shop. 'Where is everyone?' she asked. 'If I was hoping for a welcome committee, I would have been very disappointed, would I not?' She managed a smile, and it occurred to her how easy it had been. Just days ago she'd thought she would never smile again.

'They are all down at the wake,' said Bee. 'It's Captain Carter,' she added quickly, realising that Mary Kate would have no idea who the wake was for. 'He died.'

'Oh, that's sad news. How old was he?' She'd met him a number of times with her father when she'd been just a girl. He was a distant figure in more ways than one as he used to spend most of his year in England and she would only see him when the salmon were running.

'You know, I've no idea. Just old, you know.' The words, 'And your man, he was young, was he not?' hung in the air behind her, unsaid.

Bee busied about getting mugs from the press, grateful to have the niece she'd not seen in far too long all to herself.

'Was it a surprise?' said Mary Kate.

'Aye, to everyone. You won't remember, but his father and Daedio were sort of friends. It was a mutual respect they had for one another in as much as they shared the same enemies. It was his father Daedio bought this land from, and then much later your daddy built the shop and the house here.'

This was news to Mary Kate. It was not a subject that had ever been discussed in her presence and she had never thought to enquire how her father had come to own the shop and the house. 'I never knew that,' she said as she gripped the tea.

'Aye, it was a bad business, so. The gypsy Shona Maughan and her family were driven off the land – she was a wicked scold, that one.' Bee quickly blessed herself before she continued. 'Anyway, the Carters never had any luck and they thought the Maughans were the ones to blame and that's a fact. One day I will tell you all, but I'm thinking that now is not the right time. I haven't seen you for so long and look at you, you've troubles of your own to be dealing with, Mary Kate, would I be right in saying?'

Mary Kate cast down her eyes, avoiding Bee's, and took a sip of the scalding liquid. It burnt the lining of her stomach. It occurred to her that she'd not eaten since she'd had breakfast in Dublin. 'Is Daddy at the wake? And Rosie? What about Finn?'

'Aye, they are running riot at the manor. The Carter family have all left, there's no one there. The housekeeper and the ghillie were already as drunk as lords when I came away, and everyone was having the dance of their lives. They've taken the captain's body back to England on a jet plane, and while he climbs high in the sky, everyone else is pissing his wine cellar into the Taramore.' She laughed.

'Captain Bob, he came up from the coast with me and has gone into Paddy's to set up a few extra barrels for when they get back. There will be no sleep in this village tonight and no work done tomorrow, I'll bet.'

Mary Kate smiled again. That was twice in as many minutes. She remembered enough wakes and enough harvest parties to know exactly what Bee meant, and as Bee spoke, she felt a further lightening of the weight. She took a deep breath and sighed. 'Nothing has changed then, since I left?'

'Mother of God, no. I was gone for ten years and 'twas just the same when I got back. You would think I'd been up to Galway for a bit of fancy shopping for all the fuss anyone made.'

'That's good to hear. Do you think it will be the same for me?'

Bee looked Mary Kate in the eyes and held her gaze for a moment. 'No, Mary Kate, not at all. For one thing, you left a girl and you have returned a woman.'

Mary Kate blushed. They both knew exactly what Bee meant.

'And another is that you are Mary Kate Malone and no matter how much you try and slip back into the ways of Tarabeg, you won't be able to. Jesus wept in heaven, Mary Kate, would you just look at you. Those boots you are wearing, they will attract more admirers than Father Jerry can get through the door into Mass on a Palm Sunday. There's no heather in your hair or holes in your frock. You won't be running up the boreens with your shoe leather falling off and your knickers tied up with string and bits of wool you've cut out of your cardie. You are nothing like the people you left behind. I understand it, I lived in Liverpool, although I was glad to get back with all that was going on there, what with the modern ways and the boots like yours. I was a fish out of water – I was too old to be changing anything. But you, you are young, it's different for you. I'm not going to lie to you, Mary Kate, your return will be the talk of the west, from here to Clew Bay.'

This was not what Mary Kate wanted to hear.

Bee pulled out a chair, sat down at the table next to her and slipped her hand over Mary Kate's. 'Look, no harm will come of it. You know what the place is like. You will settle back in just fine. It might take a bit of time, that's all.' She glanced up. 'Have you eaten?' she asked – the second question to fall from the lips of every woman in Tarabeg, after the first, which was always the offer of a cup of tea.

Mary Kate shook her head. 'I haven't. I'm starving.' She hadn't felt hunger since the day Nicholas had died. A deep, dull ache had lodged in her belly, supressing all thoughts of food.

A beam spread across Bee's face. 'Well now, listen, isn't that a good sign. I want you to tell me all about it, I know it must have been an awful time you've had, but I don't think after a long journey is the right time to be going over everything. You need to get your bearings first, and besides, who can talk sense on an empty belly?' She squeezed Mary Kate's hand. 'I'll go and slice a few rashers in the shop for you. I'll be just a minute.'

Mary Kate finished her tea and heard the bacon slicer grind into life. She rose and picked up her case. While Bee was frying the rashers, she would go upstairs and unpack some of her things into her room. She wanted to sit on her bed, look out of her window, feel and see the familiar things that she could tell were already weaving their magic. For the first time in many months she felt as though her heart was beating at a normal and steady rhythm.

Her feet echoed on the wooden stairs and for a fleeting second she was reminded of the plush wall-to-wall Axminster carpet on the stairs in Duke's Avenue. Carpet, along with a million other modern necessities that were routine in Liverpool homes, was yet to reach Tarabeg, and that felt good to her. Change was not something she wanted Tarabeg to be tainted with.

The image fled from her mind as she caught sight of her bedroom door. She breathed a deep sigh of contentment. This would be her safe place. Even within her own home, there was a further sanctuary, the bedroom of her childhood. The suitcase banged against the side of her leg as she clattered along the wooden floor of the landing. She pushed at the door and was about to walk in, but gasped and remained frozen on the threshold, unable to move.

The wardrobe door stood open and in it hung clothes that weren't hers. The bed was messy and had a dress flung across it, and a pair of worn slippers had been shoved against the wall.

'Mary Kate! Mary Kate!'

She could barely breathe.

Within seconds, a panting Bee was at the door beside her. ''Tis Peggy,' she said. 'You won't be able to stay here. Peggy moved in when you moved out two years ago.'

The tears arrived with only the faintest tremble of her bottom lip as a warning and there was no time, as had so often been the case since Nicholas had died, to hold them in check. The home she had held onto in her mind during every moment of the journey from Liverpool was no longer hers. Someone had taken her place. She didn't even have that to call her own.

The last shreds of reserve she'd maintained through the worst days of her life dissolved in the salty torrent that gushed as fiercely as the river outside the window. Her hands reached out to the wall to steady herself as she swayed, unable to see, aware of a moan escaping from her mouth that sounded like an animal in pain.

Bee, out of breath from running up the stairs, threw her arms around her. As she clung on to her, she felt Mary Kate's knees buckle. 'Let it out,' she whispered into her hair. 'Let it all out. You needed to be here to let it go.' She hugged her niece tightly to her breast, wanting to absorb some of her pain, knowing it was futile. She remembered what she herself had been through when her own husband had died out at sea and she'd known he was never coming back. She could share some of what Mary Kate was feeling. This would be her safe place, in Bee's arms.

'Shh, shh,' she murmured as the sobs reached a heart-rending crescendo. 'There now, there now,' she whispered, stroking her hair.

This was the refuge and the comfort Mary Kate had been searching for. Mrs O'Keefe, Cat and everyone in Liverpool had been so kind, but their words had not eased her pain the way Bee's were doing right now.

Sarah's blood ran through both their veins and even though they'd not seen each other for years, the invisible ties of family bound them together.

'Shush now, don't you be worrying any more. The journey is over. You are home and it will all be fine, we will sort everything.'

Mary Kate pulled back and gulped at the air. 'Who will?' she said.

Bee extracted a handkerchief from her front apron pocket and began to wipe at Mary Kate's eyes and the strings of mucous dripping from her nose, just as she had when Mary Kate was a child. 'Mary Kate, this is where you belong and everything will get a little easier now, I promise.'

It was only minutes they'd been standing there, but it felt like hours as Bee waited for the sobs to end and the shaking to subside. She didn't speak until the last of the tears were spent.

'Now listen here, I know you're going to tell me you feel sick after all of that, but come on back down and I'll make you another cuppa and fry those rashers. You have no strength, God love you.'

Mary Kate looked over her shoulder and into her bedroom, the room she had imagined was still waiting for her and missing her. 'It looks like Peggy has taken my place.'

Bee shook her head and clasped Mary Kate's fingers in one hand and her case in the other. 'Sure, if we had known you were coming here today, we could have moved Peggy out, and who in God's name could take your place anyway?'

She guided her down into the kitchen, took her by the shoulders and pressed her back down into her seat.

Mary Kate blew her nose. 'I'll go up to the farm,' she said. 'To Granny Nola and Granddad Seamus. I'll stay with them, in Daddy's old room.'

Bee's heart sank. How could she tell her that an American relative had taken up residence at the farm and was himself sleeping in Michael's old room? The farm, with Pete and Joe there, was not a place for her right now. Bee instinctively knew that some of the changes in Tarabeg would not be to Mary Kate's liking. Change was slow, but it was definitely happening.

She was spared the explanation as they both heard the front door crash open. Michael, slightly the worse for drink, half stumbled into the room with Rosie hot on his heels.

'Captain Bob said he thought he saw you at the bus stop,' were his only words as he looked at his daughter. 'Why didn't you call and let me know? I would have come to Galway to meet you off the train.' His mind was racing. This would be a fresh start for the Malones. It had to be. Hadn't he and his daughter now experienced the same pain? She had suffered enough.

Rosie didn't speak but instead, in complete silence, pulled one of the painted pine chairs around the table next to Mary Kate and slipped her hand into her stepdaughter's. 'The words will never fall from our lips,' she said. 'We will tell no one, we will protect you. Michael and you had better go to see Father Jerry and tell him to call on Mrs Brogan and say she was entirely wrong and that Dana must have some fanciful nature to be coming up with stories like that.'

Mary Kate's hand flew to her mouth. 'You know?'

'Aye, we do.' Rosie pushed the hair away from Mary Kate's wet cheeks. 'Your one, Dana, she wrote home to her mammy. She meant well.'

Mary Kate's cheeks flushed red. She had never imagined such a thing might happen, but how could she have? She had thought of nothing else but Nicholas. 'I loved him, Rosie, with all my heart.'

It was as if Michael wasn't in the room as she looked into the eyes of another woman, her stepmother, and met understanding and compassion.

Mary Kate's face was streaming with fresh tears and Rosie's heart folded in sympathy for her. How could she tell her that she would love again, when enough time had passed. She couldn't; now was not the moment.

'If people know, will I have to... leave the village?' Mary Kate sobbed and stared dejectedly at the table, her head low. 'I can't bring shame on you all. I'll go back to Liverpool.'

'No, you will not.' Rosie spoke in a tone that brooked no challenge. 'If we never confirm that the story is true, it won't be. No one will be any the wiser apart from us, and haven't we all been through enough in the past to know how to protect you from this. Jesus, this is nothing. Your own grandmother was murdered in cold blood. The Malones have dealt with worse than a bit of unholy scandal. This is a village where everyone talks, but not here, not now, with this. Not one of us ever says a word to anyone. Now' – she looked up at her husband and her eyes were hard – 'we must be united as one and speak to no one. Michael, do you understand? What we know stays in this house and doesn't go any further. It's family business. You will have to be a better actress than Debbie Reynolds herself, but I know you, Mary Kate, you have great spirit. And if you don't know who Debbie Reynolds is, ask Peggy. There isn't nothing that has been written about any actress that Peggy doesn't know.'

Mary Kate felt weak with relief. She wouldn't have to lie to her family and, despite her chequered history with her stepmother, when it came down to it, Rosie had her back.

'Welcome home, Mary Kate,' Rosie said and for the first time ever, there was a connection between the two women. The old animosity, the lack of eye contact, the avoidance of conversation that had dogged their relationship since the death of Sarah, it was all gone. 'All that matters is you and that you are here.'

Mary Kate looked to her father. 'Da, how did you know?' she asked quietly.

He put his hand on her back and squeezed her shoulder. 'I tried to phone you in Liverpool and I ended up speaking to a Dr William, who told me your man had died and that you were very upset.'

'Does Granny Nola…?' Her words tailed off.

'No.' Michael's response was swift. 'They don't need to know and it's better that they don't.'

The burden of shame and guilt Mary Kate had been carrying began to lighten. Nola and Seamus would never be able to understand. Her eyes were still wet and bright as she looked at Rosie. Her stepmother knew she'd been living in sin with another woman's husband and yet here she was, holding her hand and not judging her or wanting the priest to run her out of the village.

'You will be all right, you will,' said Rosie. 'Nothing can make time pass any faster than it does, but all you can do is wait for the days to go by, and as they do, each one will get easier to bear. You are such a young woman, with your whole life ahead of you.'

'I loved him Rosie, with all my heart.'

Rosie was close to tears herself; Mary Kate's grief was so raw. 'I know,' she whispered, then changed the subject. 'Wait until Finn knows you're here. I'll keep him at Keeva and Tig's tonight so that you can have his bed and then we'll sort things in the morning.'

'I won't be able to stay on here, though, will I? Peggy's in my room.' Despite trying not to, Mary Kate did sound affronted.

Michael smacked his hand to his forehead. 'I'd clean forgot. You are staying here – I'll sleep on the floor if I have to.'

'No. I'll stay tonight, but then tomorrow I'll go up to the farm.'

'You can't,' said Michael, looking stricken. 'Joe lives there now. Nola wouldn't be comfortable with you staying in the house with a single man.'

Before Mary Kate could take it all in, Bee piped up. 'Michael, she can have Angela's cottage if she wants it. If that's all right with you? It is hers, after all, and it's clean and waiting there with no one in it. It just needs a fresh pair of sheets on the bed and a good airing. It will give Mary Kate the privacy she probably needs just now, and a bit of distance from the village. Besides, the sea air will be good for her. It won't take us long to get it right.'

The image of Angela's cottage flew into Mary Kate's mind, the cottage where her mother had been born and had lived as a child. It was close to Bee's house, on the cliff edge, looking out over the Atlantic towards America, and with nothing but the sound of the ocean below and the vast expanse of sky and ever-circling terns above. She had never met Angela, her maternal grandmother, but she loved her anyway, felt close to her.

She smiled. 'I can't think of anything better,' she said as Bee set the rashers and egg down in front of her. 'Angela's cottage.' This time she whispered the words, but in a voice that didn't sound like hers. Everyone noticed it, but only Michael knew whose voice it was. It was the voice of her mother, Sarah.

He came and stood behind her, placed his hands on her shoulders, dropped a kiss on the top of her head and rubbed her back with his large calloused hands as though warming her, easing the strain.

Rosie sliced and buttered the bread she had fetched from the press and laid it on the side of Mary Kate's plate, while Bee, seated opposite her great-niece and smiling at her, poured her tea. They had surrounded Mary Kate with love and care. 'Angela's cottage it is then,' Bee said. 'You really have come home, Mary Kate, and all the way back to the cottage your mammy was born in.'

Mary Kate didn't know if it was the effect of her father's hands, the reassurance of Bee's words or just being back in the heart of her family, but it was as though a balm had been rubbed onto the pain of being without Nicholas. She already felt less alone and less desperate than she had for many days.

The number of villagers at the wake had begun to dwindle as those with lanterns led the way back into Tarabeg and to Paddy's bar. The moon was shrouded in cloud and without the lanterns the path would have been dangerous. Everyone knew of someone who, the worse for drink, had lost their life down a bog hole on the side of a boreen, trying to find their way home in the dark.

In the manor house itself, some lay where they had fallen, but one thing was sure, the ghillie had come over more difficult in drink than he was without. Once the third barrel had been rolled out, he'd locked the cellar, refusing to allow them any more. He sprawled in front of the door, guarding the place and staggering to his feet whenever anyone came near, shotgun dangling by his side, pot in hand and managing not to spill a drop, as he shouted, 'Away with you all or I'll be calling for the guard and using the gun.' Having finally dispelled the bonhomie and brought the wake to an abrupt end, he slid back down onto his backside.

Peggy had joined a train of people who'd found lanterns in the stables and were lighting the way home, leaving others to sleep it off in the straw, away from the ghillie. Peggy saw Pete at the rear and slowed her pace to match his. The weary revellers walked slowly, someone at the front singing a haunting wake song and others joining in one by one until the night air filled with their melancholy melodies.

'Paddy will be waiting up for us to get back, so he will. He won't be expecting us to carry on up to the farms,' one of the farmhands shouted out as the singing stopped.

'God bless Paddy,' said another, and, despite the hour, their pace quickened at the thought of a drink and a warm welcome in the village bar.

Pete had his cap pulled down low over his eyes and his hands thrust deep into his pockets as, once more, the singing began.

'Did you enjoy that, Pete?' Peggy asked.

'Aye, it was good enough,' he said, not raising his head or looking at her. 'It would have been better without the ghillie. He was fierce protective about the drink. I don't know why, 'tis not as if the man himself needs it where he's gone.'

He stole a glance at her, the lantern illuminating her profile, her eyes shining as she looked ahead and smiled at the singing. It was so dark and he was so quick, she didn't see him look, but his heart pounded in his chest at nothing more than the closeness of her body to his. Her shawl brushed against him and his breath caught in his throat as she placed her hand on his arm and squeezed it. He looked down in shock, at her hand and then to her face, as, smiling, she sang along with the others.

'If you will bend and tell me that you love me,
Then I shall sleep in peace until you come to me.'

She smiled again, her eyes scanning his face.
He stared, not knowing what to say or do.

The rest of the party continued singing and, embarrassed, Peggy abruptly removed her hand from Pete's forearm, tore her eyes away and stared down at her feet. Pete looked straight ahead. She had no idea what to say or do next. She waited for him to ask her a question, feeling increasingly foolish. Her face burnt hot and she wanted the earth to open up and swallow her.

Their steps crunched on the road. Pete was silent. No words were forthcoming. She scrambled for something to say, wondering what she could do to cover her embarrassment, how to change the subject and keep the conversation going. 'Did Joe not come to the wake?' she blurted out.

Her words were like a knife slicing deep into his heart. He knew it – Joe was the only man she had any interest in. She was just being the usual overly friendly Peggy. What an eejit was he to have thought even for a moment that she'd been singing those words to him. If he could have punched himself he would have. It had been that way ever since Joe had arrived in Tarabeg and tonight was no different. Peggy was mad about the American man. He shook his head. 'No, he walked Philomena up and then headed straight off again. Had business in Galway. He's not much interested in what goes on in the village or the people in it. And he's no interest in the Carters or the wake – he never knew the captain,' he said, more sharply than he'd intended. 'He's in Galway every chance he has now. Some think he has a woman there.'

He'd slipped the knife from his own heart and thrust it into Peggy's, or so he thought, and he felt even worse now for having done so. Hastening his step and without another word, ashamed of himself, he moved away from Peggy and caught up with one of the farmhands, leaving her alone and bewildered at the rear. He could have kicked himself, bitten off his tongue, run into the Taramore and drowned himself a hundred times over. He'd seen the look of hurt and confusion on her face as he glanced at her from under the brim of his cap and had immediately regretted his words.

He liked Joe, and he loved Peggy – it was the thought of the two of them together that made him so miserable. He groaned with the pain of it every morning when he woke and had to spend another day asking God in his prayers why, if he'd made his own heart desire Peggy so awfully much, he had made Peggy's heart fall for Joe. 'Have you made a mistake there, Father?' he asked every night, and when there was no answer forthcoming, he knew that a lifetime of pain was to be his lot because with few single women in Tarabeg of a suitable age, them all having departed for Liverpool or America the second they left school, it would only be a matter of time before Joe took Peggy to be his wife.

★

Bridget and Nola had left the wake long before anyone else. Seamus had remained with Bridget's husband Porick and had put Nola and Bridget in the horse and cart. Nola was not used to this. 'Will we be all right? We won't fall out, will we?' she said to him.

'What's that in your pocket?' Seamus asked her as he patted the rug down over her knee.

'What pocket?' she said. 'Nothing at all. Now help Bridget up, will ye. I don't like this, Seamus, I think I'd rather walk.'

'Nola, you know what this old nag is like on the way home. You don't have to do anything, he would know the way if he was blind. You just hold on for the last stretch at the top of the boreen, once the old house comes into sight, as he will go at a fierce pace and have you out of the seat then, so he will.'

Seamus had been right. Nola had no need to do anything other than rest the reins lightly in her hands as the old nag took them safely home.

Once they were inside the house and the fire had been encouraged to roar and the kettle to sing, Nola stuck her hand into the oversized pocket of her coat and began easing out a huge bottle of Powers whiskey. She grinned.

Bridget looked shocked. 'Nola, what are you doing? Did you take that from the manor?'

'Holy Mother of God, Bridget, don't you be pulling your face at me. 'Tis not a sin – you can't steal from a man who is already dead. He won't be wanting it where he is and it was only going down the ghillie's neck. I'm sure a dead man can't take his Powers to heaven with him, can he now.'

'Aye, not even an Irish one can do that, and he was never one of us, anyway,' said Bridget.

Nola set the bottle triumphantly on the kitchen table.

'You bring nothing with you into this world and you can own as many manor houses and estates as you like, but you can't be taking a single one out with you and isn't that the truth,' Bridget declared.

Both women began to giggle as they imagined what Seamus and Porick would say if they knew what it was they had brought back with them.

'Seamus only nearly went and caught me,' said Nola. 'The bottle is that large, I had to slip the sleeve of me coat over the neck to stop the ghillie catching sight of it. I've never seen one that big before.'

'Is that the whiskey you're talking about, Nola, or your wedding night?'

Both women roared with laughter and sloshed as much whiskey into their cups as they did tea.

Never one to let a moment alone with Bridget be wasted, Nola gulped down the warm tea and whiskey and held out her cup. 'Read my tea leaves, would you?' she said.

Bridget peered over the rim and wrinkled her nose. 'You need more sugar in it and you need to spin it around a couple more times.'

Nola did as she was told and, after the next serving, tipped the cup over onto the saucer with great speed and dexterity, handed it to Bridget and sat back in the rocking chair. Feeling like she lived the best life on earth, Nola rocked to and fro in the chair that had once belonged to her mother-in-law, Annie. On occasion, it rocked all by itself in the middle of the night, and they all knew that was Annie, back to check that they were all doing just what they should.

Nola didn't have to wait long for Bridget to give her the news. 'She's here,' she said.

'Who is?' Nola rocked forwards and, swivelling around in the chair, looked towards the front door.

'Not here, you daft old cow. Mary Kate, she's in the village.'

Nola's eyes filled with tears. 'Holy Mother of God, is she? Well, isn't that the best news. No matter what has happened, if she's here, she's safe.'

Bridget was smiling, but her expression quickly darkened. She picked up the bottle of Powers, poured some more into her cup and took a gulp. 'Feck,' she said, with so much feeling that Nola rocked forwards again.

'What? What is it, Bridget? Tell me.'

'No, I might be wrong. It can't be. Go and make more tea and give me a fresh cup and I'll give it another go.'

Nola made the tea in silence and with a growing sense of dread. She did not like this one little bit. Bridget looked serious; she was whispering to herself, which was always a bad sign.

While Nola busied about the range, Bridget rocked and stared into the fire, waiting, hoping it was a fluke and that the next cup would tell her something altogether different. She leant back as she called upon Annie for help. 'Are ye there, Annie?' she whispered. 'Is anyone there?'

Nola knew better than to disturb her when she was communing with the spirits. This time when she made her tea, she put extra sugar in without having to be told, to make sure the leaves stuck to the side of the cup. Her eyes never left Bridget's face, but she knew. 'It's Shona, isn't it?'

Bridget looked up and met Nola's gaze. 'She hasn't been here since the day she died. I don't know what's going on, but I see her here, in your cup. She's outside Angela's cottage and there's someone with her – I can't see who, but I think I can have a guess.'

The air became still and cold and both women felt it; something or someone neither of them wanted was standing in Nola's kitchen. Bridget had called up Annie, but it was Shona who'd answered; the wicked gypsy whose curses had blighted the Malones for generations.

'Angela's cottage?' whispered Nola, not liking to mention out loud the home of Sarah's mother, the home of the woman who'd been murdered in cold blood in one of the wildest storms known to the Atlantic coast by a gunshot fired by her own madman of a husband. McGuffey, Mary Kate's paternal grandfather.

Bridget swallowed hard, stared unflinchingly at the ghost of Shona and hissed under her breath, 'You don't scare me.'

'Who doesn't?' asked Nola, pouring out more whiskey, which they both downed in one gulp.

There was a vibration in the air, a shifting of dimensions, and then she was gone. Both women breathed a sigh of relief. Shona had come, had hovered near the fire and had left. Bridget had seen her clearly, but she kept that to herself.

'Angela's cottage? Why would Shona be there?'

Bridget shook her head. 'I've no idea, but she's brought me the sight of it. Hush a minute, Annie's coming now – she's here. Sit back and close your eyes.'

There was no need to tell Nola twice; she did exactly as she was bid. She didn't have to wait long. She felt it as keenly as if she'd stuck her hand in the fire, as the air turned from chilled to warm in a heartbeat.

Bridget let out a long sigh. 'Pour me another cup of that Powers, would you? Calling up Annie was hard work. She's restored the balance, seen Shona on her way.'

Nola filled Bridget's cup almost to the rim. 'Why did Shona come to you?'

'I wish I knew, but one thing's for sure – she's back for a reason. The dead don't go making all that effort to take in the view or warm their arses on the fire. We are going to need eyes in the backs of our heads. It's no coincidence she's returned on the same day as Mary Kate and that's a fact.'

Both women blessed themselves. Ghosts were everywhere in Tarabeg and no one was surprised at the mention of a dead villager returning to the place they had once lived. But Shona had never even visited the farm, had never been welcome; she had hated the Malones and blamed them every day of her life for her family's eviction from the seven acres all those years ago.

Nola grasped the rosaries in her apron pocket and let them slide through her fingers. 'When will it end?' she whispered, even though she half knew the answer. It was Mary Kate. Mary Kate held the key to breaking the years-old curse on the family.

'I don't know, but we will have to find a way. It can't go on now that Shona and Daedio are both dead. There has to be an end to it,' said Bridget. 'A way to end the Malone curse once and for all.'

Chapter 11

Michael was complaining about his parched throat and aching limbs. It was early and he'd come out as usual to milk their lone cow in its byre at the back of the shop. Today, though, he had company. Mary Kate had slipped out of the house to help him, just like she used to as a child. It brought a lump to his throat, but he didn't want her to see his upset. As he stood there, he saw not the new Mary Kate, the grown-up, but the little girl who used to chatter away to him as he worked. She'd done the same with her mother before she died.

Mary Kate stroked the cow's flank and smiled as she snorted. 'Hello, old girl,' she said, breathing in the comforting aroma of warm cow, straw and fresh milk.

'How was your woman, Cat, when you left Liverpool? Did she see you off?'

Mary Kate knew that something fleeting had taken place between Cat and her father when he'd come over to Liverpool. She herself had seen them in an embrace the day he left and the number of times Cat had casually enquired about him every time a letter arrived from home had left her in little doubt. 'She's still a widow, Daddy.'

Michael glanced up from under the brim of his cap. 'Sure, she's a fine woman, she should be married. What's up with the men in Liverpool? They must be all pansies, the lot of them.'

Mary Kate had no idea what he was talking about and wondered would he say any more, to explain himself.

For a moment the only sound was of the rhythmic squirting of the milk as it hit the sides of the metal pail.

'I know how you feel, Mary Kate,' he said. ''Tis a terrible thing to have happened to you so young, to have lost the man who would have been your husband. I know it won't be easy to carry that secret around in your heart. But wouldn't every one of them here in Tarabeg be just delighted to know you've come back for no other reason than you missed the place   that will satisfy them enough, so it will. There isn't a man or woman who lives here who doesn't think it's the last stop on the ladder to heaven. Why wouldn't you miss it and be desperate to be coming home? The other story, you know... it might be bad for business.'

Mary Kate felt like she'd been slapped. The shame of her sin, spoken out loud by her father. Heat rose in her face, but she swallowed it down hard. He was right. There were consequences to her actions and wasn't he putting into words the very reason she could never have brought Nicholas home, no matter how much in love she was. Tarabeg could have been a hundred years behind modern Liverpool. Everywhere was moving with the times, but in Tarabeg it was still as it had been in 1930; nothing had changed.

Despite his words, Michael was so delighted to have his daughter home that at breakfast he dug around for any excuse he could not to drive Mary Kate to Angela's cottage, even though it was only a mile away on the coast.

'Can you not wait until tonight? I really have to go into Galway first, even with this banging head. I've feed to collect and stock for the shop. There'll be nothing on the shelves for Peggy to sell if I don't get to the warehouse quick.'

He was standing with his back to the range, drinking his tea out of a pint-sized pot, washing down the enormous breakfast Rosie had cooked for them all, along with two aspirins.

'Is your head not feeling any better?' asked Rosie, who was packing sandwiches wrapped in greaseproof paper into the wicker basket on the table. Her hair had lost its youthful auburn lustre and the first flecks of grey could be seen at the sides of her schoolmarm bun on the nape of her neck. She wore her customary mid-calf skirt and the caramel-coloured cardigan she had knitted herself.

'No, my head is doing well, all things considered. You won't be able to say the same for that lot over the road though. I reckon Josie will be in the bar with the broom soon enough, sweeping some of those bodies out onto the street. She hasn't changed one iota since you left, Mary Kate.'

They all laughed, including Mary Kate, who was sitting on the chair by the fire, with Finn at her feet. They were all familiar with the words Josie used when she kicked drunken farmhands out of the bar door. They were welcome when they had money to spend, not so much when they were begging for a breakfast.

It occurred to Mary Kate that it was as if she'd left Tarabeg only yesterday, as if Liverpool had been a dream. She had to admit that the trauma of her loss felt different here. The ache in her diaphragm felt softer. Here there was nothing to anchor her to the life she'd lived with Nicholas, none of the people, objects, sounds or smells that had coloured the last two years; there was a strange dissonance between her recent past and her present. It was almost as if Mrs O'Keefe, Cat, Joan, Deidra, the people she'd spent every day with, didn't really exist. This was not something she wanted to happen. She needed them as the bridge to her Nicholas.

But as she laughed at the thought of Josie sweeping out the over-stayers from her bar, a sight she had seen many times during her childhood, she realised with a flashing certainty that letting go a little might be what was needed. Maybe Nicholas, in his dying words, had known better than she did what was best for her.

She placed the book Finn had been showing her onto her lap and ruffled his hair. 'I'll go on the bike and put what I need in the basket if you can't take me this morning, Daddy.'

Michael bristled, pushed himself away from the fender and stood upright, blinking as he searched for a response, anything to keep her there a little longer.

Rosie pulled the cover over her basket and tied her headscarf under her chin in a knot. 'Come on, Finn, Mary Kate can see your book tonight.' She smiled at her stepdaughter. 'He's a great one for the reading,' she said with a flush of pride on her face. She looked at her husband and felt her heart ache a little. He wanted more time with his daughter. He wanted to protect her from her pain, but he didn't realise that was what he was trying to do, in his own clumsy way. Rosie had other plans; she would help.

'Listen, Mary Kate, it will take a little time to get Angela's cottage sorted, even with Bee's help. Tonight, I'll get everyone here – Nola, Seamus, Bee and Captain Bob. Peggy will put a big pan of stew on the stove. We can all go over to Paddy and Josie's first to see Keeva and Tig and the boys – what do you think? Your daddy will fetch you all in the car and take you back after. In fact, why don't we just have a big welcome home party. They will all be expecting it anyway. Can you face it, Mary Kate?'

It was more of a challenge than a question, and Mary Kate rose to it. Even as Rosie spoke, she knew she could and she should, because if she didn't take herself out into the village, the village would come to her. And it wouldn't be long before too many people began to ask awkward questions if she acted anything other than delighted to be back in the heart of Tarabeg.

'Go on – will you?' Finn jumped to his feet and hurled himself at her, throwing his arms around her neck.

'Aye, I will,' she said as she hugged him tight.

'That's grand. You can meet Joe, too,' said Michael. 'Pete will bring them down with the horse and cart. I'll go and bring the car around the front if you're sure you're ready to go now.' The prospect of driving her to the coast was suddenly not as daunting now he knew she would be back the same evening.

The door opened and a blast of cold air filled the kitchen.

Peggy walked in just as Michael was lifting the keys from the hook on the wall. 'Where are you off to this early?' she asked.

Rosie could tell Peggy was subdued, sad almost, and both Rosie and Mary Kate immediately assumed it was because she was sleeping in Mary Kate's room and felt awkward.

'Look at you. Did ye not have the best time last night then, Peggy?' Rosie had hoped that maybe last night would have been the night Peggy and Pete finally realised what was occurring between the two of them. The dance in the long hall was still days away. 'Was Pete Shevlin not there?'

Peggy flushed and flopped down at the table with a huge sigh. 'I'll move out of your room, Mary Kate,' she said absently. 'I'm sure Mrs Doyle will let me sleep in her house at the post office. She's offered before, she doesn't like being alone much.'

Mary Kate stood next to her and placed her hand over Peggy's. 'Not at all. You stay. I'm going to my Granny Angela's cottage.'

No one spoke – no one ever did when Angela's name was mentioned. Murder was an evil and not to be talked about. No one ever spoke of the night of Angela's murder, for fear of beckoning back to Tarabeg the evil spirits that had caused the tragedy. It was as if the worst night any of them had known had never happened. As if Mary Kate's grandfather had never lived. 'It will take only one careless whisper to summon evil,' Bridget had warned them, and they had heeded her ever since.

Peggy was relieved at the news that she didn't have to leave and she found it hard to hide the fact. She loved living with the Malones. Having to move in with old Mrs Doyle was not an enticing prospect. 'Oh, thank God for that. Something is going my way.' She threw her folded arms onto the table in a dramatic gesture and rested her head upon them.

'Is anyone there?' a voice called out from the front of the shop.

Peggy groaned and, laying both hands flat on the table, pushed herself back up. 'Aye, I'm coming, Philomena,' she shouted and pulled a face at Rosie and Mary Kate.

Philomena O'Donnell, despite having a son in the priesthood, was the biggest gossip in the village and they all knew why she was there.

Rosie placed her finger on her lips. 'Shh,' she whispered. 'Come on, Finn, Mary Kate, let's go out the back door.'

Peggy, who knew nothing, looked confused. 'Why?' she asked.

'Mary Kate is still tired from the journey and she isn't up to answering fifty questions from the likes of Philomena,' said Rosie. Finn had run on ahead out of the back and had climbed onto the wall of the cow byre. 'Get a stew on, Peggy. There'll be a few of us here tonight – the usual crowd. A welcome home for Mary Kate – they'll be expecting it. I'll ask them down from the farm, and Pete too. Make it a big one. You know what they say, the way to a man's heart is through his trousers.'

Peggy let out a squeal and Mary Kate blushed. Not everything was the same – this was a very different Rosie. 'Rosie Malone, no they do not.'

'Aye, well, maybe try his stomach first then.' Rosie laughed. The sound of a car engine filled the kitchen. 'Here's your daddy with the car – run before the priest comes looking for you, Mary Kate. And, Finn,' she shouted, 'get down off that wall before you fall in.'

The morning was cold, sharp and bright, but Bee knew it wouldn't last. By three in the afternoon it would be dark and miserable and she wanted Mary Kate to feel at home before that happened. She pulled her coat around her and picked up her basket from the floor. Captain Bob had long since left to take out a trawler from Blacksod Bay and she had been busy with her own cleaning jobs, ensuring that she was finished early so she could get straight round to Angela's cottage and prepare it for Mary Kate's arrival. She could dry the sheets on the line and could not have been more grateful for the good weather if Captain Bob had arrived home with a diamond ring.

Angela's cottage stood on the escarpment looking out over the ocean. It wasn't visible from Bee's cottage, which was tucked away up a boreen, protected from the worst of the gales. Having to live so close to her sister's empty cottage, a continual reminder of the night she was murdered on that very escarpment, had been part of the reason she had fled to Liverpool. The image of Michael with Angela dead in his arms would never fade. Sarah, on her knees, half drowned in the rain of the awful storm, was there too, burnt into her memory, always waiting for her as she turned the corner.

Bee dropped the latch on her own front door and felt the familiar hammering in her heart as she made her way up towards the cottage of the sister she'd loved, the sister who'd endured a life of violence and fear at the hands of her truly evil husband, Kevin McGuffey. Bee had always suspected but never been able to prove that he had also been responsible for the death of her own first husband, Rory.

The bed sheets were bundled in the basket she had strapped to her back and she felt like a mule as she half walked and half ran up to the cottage. She pushed open the door and stopped in her tracks. Someone had been in. It smelt of wood-smoke and body heat. She walked over to the fireplace, kicked the turf with her toe and felt the warmth through her shoe leather.

Her skin crawled with fear as she looked around the cottage. 'It cannot be him,' she whispered, her head refusing to accept the fact that McGuffey could have returned after so many years in exile. He was still a wanted man. His crime of murder still stood.

She shook her head. He was mad, but not that mad. Even he wouldn't be so stupid as to return to the scene of his crime. Then she noticed the blood on the rush mat and squatted down onto her knees to look at it. It must have been a tramp; that's who it was. Maybe he'd fallen and hurt himself and, desperate, had called into the house for cover. He'd probably just stayed the night and moved on.

She had already swept the cottage, raked out the ashes from the fire, had the sheets blowing on the line and put the cast-iron kettle on to simmer when she heard the car pulling up at the bottom of the rise. There was no way the car could get all the way to the door. She ran down to greet Mary Kate and help her carry her case.

Michael was lifting a cardboard box out of the boot by the time she reached them and in his hand swung a small metal churn of milk.

'I helped milk this,' said Mary Kate as she took the pail from Michael and handed it to Bee. 'I thought I might have forgotten how, but not a bit of it. She even knew it was me, I swear.'

Bee grinned. 'Get you – straight back into the country ways. And how do ye know that? Did she say, "Good morning, Mary Kate" when you walked in?'

'No.' Mary Kate smiled. 'She said, "Thank God 'tis you with your silky-soft hands and not him – the milk will be sweeter for it."'

Bee laughed, relieved to see a spark of Sarah coming through in Mary Kate. 'Well, that's true enough,' she said as she put out her arms to take the box from Michael. 'I'm just about to bring those sheets in from airing—'

Mary Kate wasn't listening to Bee. She had taken a few steps forward and, cupping her hand over her brow, was surveying the cottage. It stood side on to the ocean to protect the door and the window from the worst of the gales, and there was something about the limewashed walls, the heather thatch, the stone buttress one end that she had no idea who had erected since she was last here. She had rarely been to the cottage. Angela had died long before she was born, but it was as if she knew every nook and cranny. This view of the cottage from the side, silhouetted against the cloud-heavy sky with the gulls circling high above... It suddenly struck her that this view had been in her dreams every night she'd been away from home.

'Come on, let's go inside,' said Bee, who almost jolted as the shifting sands of time moved beneath her feet. She took Mary Kate's hand and for a shard of a second was thrown into the past. She was taking the hand of Sarah, Mary Kate's mother, and they were running up the escarpment together. Only this time there would be no Angela waiting inside to greet them.

McGuffey had got out only just in time. He stood behind a rock from where he could see the side of the cottage and ducked down before hobbling back towards the cave.

Despite his pain, he smiled to himself. The young woman looked too much like Sarah not to be his granddaughter, Mary Kate. A plan formed in his mind in moments. She was his means to the money he desperately needed. If she was going to stay at the cottage, it would be easy to kidnap her, make the Malones pay to get her back, and then get himself away as far and as fast as possible. Jay Maughan would help and McGuffey would split the ransom with him.

They couldn't have made it any easier for him if they'd tried. She could scream all she liked from the cave and not a soul would hear her. He and Jay would find a way to collect the money and he would be off, leaving a note with the tinkers in Ballycroy to let the Malones know where to find her.

He glanced over his shoulder and saw Mary Kate, her hands on her hips, looking up at the cottage. *Feast your eyes*, he thought. *You won't be there for long.*

Nola banged on Joe's bedroom door when he failed to surface. Pete was sitting at the kitchen table with Seamus, wiping the last of the egg yolk from his plate with a piece of fried bread. ''Tis not like him to sleep in,' said Nola.

Joe had made a surprise appearance at the bar on his way home from Galway and had stopped for an hour before bringing himself and Seamus back up the hill in the car. Pete, once he'd delivered everyone safely to Paddy's bar, had kept the lantern and made his own way back up to the farm in the early hours, refusing to stay. Despite having been the first to bed, his eyes were red from lack of sleep; he'd been tossing and turning for half of the night.

'Why did ye not stay, Pete?' asked Seamus at the table. 'The craic was grand, so it was. They were all there, the whole village, and the girls too from across the road. Peggy and Keeva, you should have seen them dancing, Nola – I thought the floor would collapse.'

Nola laughed. 'I bet Josie was cursing the lot of ye. She loves her sleep, that one.'

'Not a bit of it. Joe gave the colleens a dance, so he did, and when he stopped dancing with Peggy he gave Josie half a turn and she loved it. I never heard a word of complaint and, God in heaven, Peggy looked like she was going to keel over when he asked her to dance. I said to him, be careful, you'll never get rid of that one once she's got her claws into you. She would have him up the aisle of the Sacred Heart before he had time to sober up.'

Seamus flinched as the corner of the tea towel hit him square across his shoulder blades. 'Feck, woman,' he wailed, 'what did ye do that for?'

'Shut your loose lips,' said Nola as she cast a glance at Pete. 'Any man would be lucky to have Peggy. Joe has an eye for no woman in Tarabeg and I do not believe Peggy has an eye for him either.'

She rolled the tea towel, ready to flick him again should he answer her back. He knew it and decided instead to sulk into his tea. Nola went back to peeling potatoes, tucking the towel into her belt. Being related to the best-looking and richest American to ever return to Mayo's shores gave her a notoriety she relished. Now it seemed she was having to adopt the role of referee between the men in her house.

'Are you sure you don't have an eye for him yourself,' said Seamus moodily, not looking up from his cup, which he held in two hands just under his nose.

Nola roared with laughter. 'Seamus, sometimes you really are an eejit. I am old enough to be his granny and just because he has tried to foist all manner of mod cons on me to make life easier, none of which I have wanted, doesn't mean I turn to mush. God in heaven, I am past all of that nonsense, and besides' – her voice softened – 'haven't I the best man in Tarabeg in you?'

Despite himself, a grin spread across Seamus's face. 'Do you remember the day he came back from one of his trips to America and brought you that bloody great big Kenwood Chef food mixer?'

Nola began to chuckle at the memory. After a drink or five, if it was mentioned, she would laugh until the tears ran. 'Oh God, I remember his face when I said, "And what do I do with this?" as I held the plug in the air. It was his expression, when he looked at the wall for somewhere to stick it, knowing full well there wasn't anywhere! Never mind, it looks nice on the top of the press, it's a lovely ornament.'

She rapped her knuckles on Joe's door harder still. 'What time did he get back into the village from Galway?'

'About one in the morning, I'm guessing. He saw the lights in Paddy's and stopped. Maybe Peggy sneaked into the boot of the car and she's in there with him.'

Nola rapped again and was pulled up short by the sound of the enamel plates clattering in the sink and then the door slamming as Pete walked out.

'Feck,' said Seamus, 'what's up with him?'

For a moment Nola looked at the slammed door with a frown. 'Seamus, is there any chance that when it comes to Peggy's name in this house, you could keep your mouth shut and your opinions to yourself?'

'Why, what have I done now?'

Nola had no time to reply as the door to the room that had once been Michael's swung open and Joe stood there in his vest and long johns. 'There's a lot of doors banging around here,' he said with a grin, and then, spotting Seamus, stepped into the room. 'My head is killing me,' he said.

Seamus grinned back. 'Well, you turned some heads

in Paddy's last night with your dancing. I imagine there's a few of them still spinning in the village. Did you hear Josie giving out to Paddy, telling him if she was forty years younger, 'twould be you she'd be marrying with her butcher's shop, not Paddy.'

Joe laughed. 'Was that the dowry of the day, the butcher's shop?' He reached out to the teapot. 'Or did Paddy marry for love?' Nola flicked his hands with a tea towel. 'Ouch,' he yelped and looked up, hurt.

'That's what I'm here for,' she said, and she meant it.

'She's a bit handy with the towel this morning.' Seamus gave him a knowing raise of the eyebrows and a nod in the direction of the tea towel.

Nola liked to serve Joe his tea. He wasn't allowed to lift a finger. It had broken her heart that all of her children other than Michael had left the farm for America and never returned, but then Joe had arrived. Nola had made her peace with the Holy Mother while she was on her knees at the shrine in the Church of the Sacred Heart. 'I know what ye are doing,' she'd whispered as she knelt. 'You've sent me the nearest you had available. I understand, and I promise I will look after him as if he were me own. But if you see our Mary – you will find her in Brooklyn, so you will – if she is praying for a visit home one day to see her Mammy before I die, I would love to see her, Holy Mother, just once more. She was my firstborn, you see, and I haven't laid eyes on her since the day she left. She was just seventeen, she was, and oh God, I would love to see her sweet face and hear her voice before the good Lord calls me. She was such a good child and she writes home every week. If it's not too much to be asking, like.'

Seamus, sitting on the pew beside her, had heard Nola's words. They fell on his heart like a heavy hand on a fresh bruise and no matter how hard he'd rubbed his eyes, the tears would not go away.

Now though, sitting at the breakfast table, he was smarting from the sharp side of Nola's tongue. 'I can't speak for saying something wrong,' he grumbled to Joe, just before he stuffed the last of his fried bread in his mouth.

'What do ye want for ye breakfast, Joe? Will I do ye a bit of everything?' Nola asked as she poured his tea.

'He's missed his breakfast now – it's out to fix the fence, so it is,' said Seamus and instantly regretted it.

'Shut your mouth, you,' she said. 'He'll be going nowhere until he's eaten.'

Seamus was saved by the door opening. It was Michael.

'I have news,' he said before the door was even closed behind him.

Nola, unused to moments of glory, blurted out, 'Is it Mary Kate? Is she at Angela's cottage?' and blessed herself as Michael's mouth dropped open.

'Was that letter from the Brogan mammy a crock of shite then?' asked Seamus.

'Of course it was,' said Michael. 'Not even our Mary Kate, as clever as she is, could get herself married and have two grown-up sons in two short years.'

Seamus laughed. 'The very notion. But the Brogans have known the Malones forever – how could Dana have made a mistake? I'll tell you this, that woman, she's too fond of the bottle.'

Joe slipped into the scullery to wash himself down before going back into his room to dress. He would help Pete fix the fence just as soon as Nola had finished cooking his breakfast. He had deliberately left the family to have a few minutes' privacy to talk. It was the fact that Nola had cried, although he recognised them to be tears of happiness, and that Seamus had blessed himself and said a little prayer, that confirmed to him that this was good news and news they should be able to appreciate alone.

When he'd finished dressing, he slid the papers that the solicitor had given him the previous evening into his drawer, pushing to the back the sheet of paper upon which was printed the deed of sale. He had bought the manor house there and then and now it was his.

While in Galway, he'd also set another plan in motion, something that had been on his mind for some time. It had not been possible to call his own firm in New York, so he had roped in Mr Keene instead. 'If you could phone New York at your earliest convenience and tell Mr Browne to make every effort to comply with every detail of the telex I've just sent. Ask him to put Miss Carroll onto it. I have no doubt she will have one hundred per cent success. Miss Carroll will never give up and lets nothing defeat her.'

Mr Keene had been amused. 'You want her to find all of them? They could be all over America.'

Joe had to admit that what he was asking for was very unusual indeed. 'Yes, everyone. All of them. Leave no one out. I cannot be the only Malone who comes home.'

'Good luck with your new venture, Mr Malone,' Mr Keene had said at the conclusion of their meeting. 'I am sure every single villager in Tarabeg will be delighted with your plans. You will transform the place.'

'Let's hope so,' Joe had replied. 'It could be that I am run out of the village, and if I am, it will have been a very expensive mistake.' On his drive back to the village through the dark night, the first niggles of doubt had settled in his belly. Had he gone mad? He didn't even know how to run a hotel.

With the deeds now safely hidden away, he sat on the edge of his bed, taking in the muffled sound of chatter in the kitchen and the sizzle and aroma of frying rashers seeping under his door. He would invite Mr Browne from Messrs Collins, Browne and Malone out soon enough to see the manor. He heard the laughter in the kitchen and the back door opening and closing. He wanted – no, he needed – a wife, and that was all the fault of the Malones of Tarabeg. He wanted all of this for himself: the family, the comradeship, the laughter and the love; the togetherness and the work. He lived among them, but the sheer closeness of them often made him feel alone. He loved the hand-to-mouth existence and the graft, but he had better for himself whenever he wanted. He had a way out if he chose to leave.

His ambition to convert the manor into a hotel would bring Tarabeg into the same century as America, give many villagers a choice and an opportunity. And as for his other momentous task, the one he had charged Miss Carroll at the firm in New York with, he would need to confer with Mrs Doyle and Teresa Gallagher on that. Seamus and Nola could not get to hear about it; it had all to be kept well away from them or the surprise would be ruined.

As he stood and pulled his braces over his shoulders, he thought of the milky white skin of the barmaid in Galway whom he'd enticed to a hotel room for an hour. He needed to find himself a wife. Peggy? Maybe, but she was a bit too country. He would easily become bored, although he loved the impetuous, mad drama of Peggy and that was a fact. There was nothing for it – he would have to travel over to New York and bring back an American wife. His heart sank. He couldn't think of a single woman he had ever known who wouldn't run a mile from Tarabeg. A village that would laugh at the very idea of a hairdressing salon. He decided that he would ask Miss Carroll to come out and visit when she'd completed her first impossible task and then he would set her a second one, equally impossible, that of finding him a wife.

He closed the drawer, fastened the braces and joined the others.

'Ah, Joe.' Michael was sitting at the table and Nola was dishing out breakfast onto two plates, one for Joe and one for Michael.

'I can't believe Rosie sends you out with nothing in your insides,' she tutted.

Michael felt guilty, but not enough to put Nola right. 'Morning, Joe. Your presence is required again tonight. A repeat performance of last night will be in order down at the house. 'Twill be a test of your manhood, or you can call it training for the dance at the long hall.'

Joe half grinned as he recalled how his manhood had been very much tested the evening before. The barmaid had turned out to be neither as shy nor as holy as she'd made out and had in fact had a voracious appetite.

'Peggy has a big pan of stew on. My daughter, Mary Kate, she's home. Home for good. We thought we would all eat together in the kitchen and invite everyone over.'

'We have to stay in the house,' said Seamus. 'As God is true, if we spend much more time in Paddy's, he'll be charging us the rent.'

They all laughed. All except for Pete, who was lying on his bed in the old house outside. Peggy had been dancing in Joe's arms. He'd seen the grin on Joe Malone's face – she would be in his bed next. He rolled onto his belly and groaned into the pillow; his heart was surely going to break in two.

Chapter 12

Dana had spent her entire morning in the sluice room. The first-year nurse who had started her first day on the ward had fainted twice. She had survived the first faint unscathed. The second, however, had required two stitches in her chin due to a collision with a trolley, and after a spell in casualty and much wailing for her mother, she had been sent back to the nurses' home and its housekeeper, Mrs Duffy, leaving Dana to finish her chores.

Dana had left the high sash windows open, despite the cold damp weather, to dilute the smell in the room – a tip she wished she'd passed on to the first-year nurse at report earlier in the morning. In addition to ensuring there was plenty of air circulating, Dana wore her mask tight around her face and made sure she breathed through her mouth. She'd also borrowed a few drops of aftershave from one of the patients, which she'd dabbed on to the mask.

Despite all of the precautions, she still felt nauseous. Three faints on the ward in one morning would probably be a record.

Pammy Tanner called into Dana's ward on her way to morning coffee and found her leaning against the wall, taking deep breaths. 'Are you okay?' she asked as she popped her head around the sluice door.

'Oh God, it's been a bad morning for the bedpans,' said Dana. 'The worst ever. They've taken one nurse down and I'm only just about still standing. I'm not lying when I say it's much worse on men's medical than on women's.'

Pammy wrinkled her nose. 'Come on, let's go for coffee. Have a milky coffee and a bacon barm to settle your stomach. You do look peaky.'

Dana slotted the last bedpan into the warming rack and unfastened her rubber apron. She began to wash her hands and arms and flicked off the taps with her elbows to shut off the constant flow of cold running water, which for some strange reason also helped with the smell. 'Pass me my cuffs, would you. They're on the clean trolley outside the door.'

Five minutes later they were walking towards the greasy spoon. After filling her lungs with fresh air and the pungent aroma of clean-smelling Lysol, Dana felt restored. 'Do you know what, Pammy, I don't think I have had a holiday… well… since I last went home. I think I might ask Matron can she spare me for a couple of weeks. That last patient of mine who died, so soon on top of nursing Dr Marcus, it's taken it out of me. He was a lovely man, he was. We thought he was in for weeks, but he gave up all hope almost as soon as he was admitted. He told me that his wife was a battleaxe and that he was the mouse, but he missed her so much he just gave up. I feel so tired out – it's such hard work on men's medical.'

'A holiday in Ireland, at this time of the year? Won't the weather be awful? You said yourself that it rains every day. Why don't you go at Christmas?'

Dana looked thoughtful and trotted along in Pammy's wake. 'You know, I think I might do both and split it. I know it's a long journey, but I need to be in my own bed for a week. I won't notice the weather. I just won't get out of bed.'

'Don't you always end up working on the farm when you go back?'

'I do. I used to call it work – until I was put on male medical. Now I'd call it a bloomin' holiday.'

Both girls were laughing as they entered the greasy spoon. They found the other nurses from the Lovely Lane nurses' home and took their places at the table. Within minutes, they were deep in conversation. A little while after they'd sat down, Pammy interrupted the chatter. 'Oh look, here's Dr Gaskell. You never see him

in here, he usually has his coffee with Matron. Looks like he's heading our way.'

As Dana turned, he smiled at her and inclined his head. He was looking for her. She pushed back her chair. 'He is, and I think I know what it's about.' She walked over and met him by the coffee urn, before he got to within earshot of her table. 'Are you looking for me, Dr Gaskell?' she said.

'I am indeed. Thank you very much for coming over. Best to keep this to ourselves. You know what Matron's like about standards – she's been very accommodating, but she wouldn't want the Marcus situation to become common knowledge.' He raised one eyebrow and smiled.

'I do,' said Dana. 'Don't worry, I haven't even told Pammy what you told me. It doesn't feel right – they were so much in love, those two, and it feels like I'd be intruding, even now after he's dead. Do you know what I mean?'

Dr Gaskell nodded slowly and surveyed her face, satisfied that she was as sincere and trustworthy as he'd thought. 'I wanted to let you know that I called to see Mary Kate, as I said I would, and was rather surprised to discover that she has left Liverpool already.'

Dana swallowed hard. She thought about the letter she'd written home and prayed her mother had not told a living soul; and yet, even as she did so, she knew the chance of that was as good as zero. She hadn't told anyone in Liverpool, but she'd told her mother everything, if only to fill up the large sheet of flimsy pale blue paper that folded over into its own envelope when you licked the sticky edges and pressed them down. Dana liked to fill the sheet; it made her feel like she was getting her money's worth.

She knew that every letter she sent home travelled halfway around Mayo before the next one arrived, but she hadn't thought it mattered that much because she never normally mentioned any names and no one back home knew who she was writing about anyway. But this was different. She'd broken a golden rule. Dread began to flood through her veins. Liverpool was a million miles away in both culture and attitudes from the villages of Ireland. Over there, unmarried women who fell pregnant went missing virtually overnight.

'She's left Liverpool?' she said. 'Do you know where she's gone?'

Dr Gaskell helped himself to a mint-green national-issue cup and saucer from the pile on the wooden tray and began to pour himself a milky coffee from the urn. 'I haven't had one of these for a long time,' he said as he flicked the handle on the urn back to upright and spooned three sugars into the cup. 'Here's another secret for you to keep: don't tell either my wife or Matron that you saw me doing that. Those two are in cahoots.' He winked.

Although his eyes were so kind and mischievous, he didn't manage to dispel Dana's fear that she might have unwittingly helped make Mary Kate's situation worse. She felt like running home herself, just because she was tired. She knew exactly what he was going to say next.

'She's gone home to Ireland,' he said as he stirred, 'or so I was told by her neighbour.'

Dana swallowed again. She felt sick and this time it wasn't because of the bedpans.

'It's such a shame,' Dr Gaskell continued. 'She reminds me of you such a lot. I do remember your interview. You were as young as Mary Kate is now, and I saw a similar spark in her. She would have made an excellent nurse, and having known loss herself, well, as you know, compassion for a patient is something that can't be taught in the school of nursing. That young lady has sadly learnt it the hard way, at a very young age. Never mind. Our loss. I just thought I would let you know, as I promised I would.'

Dana remembered to close her mouth and respond just in time as an idea flashed through her mind. 'I have an idea, Dr Gaskell. I was just saying to Nurse Tanner that I fancy a trip home for a holiday. Why don't I call in and see Mary Kate? Tarabeg is such a small village – it's all farms, like in our village – and I would find her in a minute. I could see how she is for you myself and if the conversation moves that way, I shall tell her what you said. It might give her something to look forward to for the future. I'm sure she has never thought of nursing, but you never know, it could give her hope and help her, maybe?'

Dr Gaskell sipped at his coffee and smiled over the brim of the cup. 'What an excellent idea. Matron thinks she'd have made a marvellous nurse too. She liked her very much. It was Matron who first gave me the idea. We have new wards opening soon. There is no sign of the new hospital being built in my lifetime, I can tell you. Matron has even been talking about moving away from Liverpool to find potential nursing staff for the hospital.'

'Well, I can't guarantee anything, but I can keep your promise to Dr Marcus for you and check that Mary Kate is doing all right. And I will tell her you were asking about her and that was why I called.' Her fingers were crossed behind her back. Knowing all the time that she would have to go home and lie through her teeth.

Minutes later, she joined the others back at the table. 'Right, that's it,' she said. 'I'm going to see Matron this afternoon and ask will she let me have a little holiday.'

'That's great,' said Pammy, 'but are you going to tell me why you had your fingers crossed behind your back when Dr Gaskell was speaking to you, because it looked to me like you was lying, and being a good Irish Catholic girl, you aren't supposed to do that.'

Dana flushed bright red. She knew that Pammy and all the nurses on the ward had assumed that Mary Kate and Dr Marcus were married. 'I can't tell you, Pammy,' she said. 'I just need to go and put right something I think I might have done wrong. I've said something I shouldn't have, or rather written something I shouldn't have, and so I need to go and put it right.'

'Oh, get you, the mysterious one,' said Pammy. 'Honest to God, it's like reading a book, knowing you. Every day's a different story. Tell you what, I'll help you pack when we get back to the nurses' home tonight. I'm sure if you explain to Matron she won't mind a bit.'

'I hope not, Pammy. I really need to go, I've done something terrible.'

Bee and Mary Kate had worked all morning long without any kind of a break and Mary Kate had been surprised to discover that as she scrubbed the walls and dry-ironed the sheets, the pain she carried in her heart for Nicholas was numbed by the sustained effort. She had even caught herself almost singing as she lit the fire while Bee finished limewashing the back walls in that part of the cottage that Sarah had slept when she was a girl.

It was only when they stopped working and sat at the kitchen table to eat the lunch Bee had brought with her that Mary Kate felt the weight of sadness fall across her shoulders like an invisible cloak, pressing her down onto the chair. Sensing the sudden change, Bee strode across the cottage floor and flung the wooden door open. 'We can catch the last of this sunshine before it disappears,' she said.

Despite the wintery sun, the ocean before them remained grey and the white breakers looked as angry as the seagulls that screeched and hovered above them. The mountain was just in view to the side and its slopes, caught by the sun, reflected back a deep emerald green.

Mary Kate's eyes filled with tears and her throat constricted. Unable to put the bread and cheese into her mouth, she nursed the mug of tea in her hands. How Nicholas would have loved to have sat there and viewed that perfect, unspoilt scene.

Bee placed her arms around her shoulders. 'It will happen like this,' she said as she dropped a kiss on her head. 'Hours will pass and you'll be amazed at how you forget, especially when you're busy, and then you'll be filled with the guilt, haunted by it, you will be, just because you've momentarily forgotten. But it happens the way God meant it to.'

She pulled out the chair next to Mary Kate and drew her hands inside her own. 'Don't feel guilty. Cry if you want to in these early days. Don't try and do anything other than you do. Let it all out, because this is the way it has happened for every woman who has lost the man she loved, since the beginning of time, and nothing you try and do and nothing anyone says will make one bit of difference. The only thing that will help is the passage of time.'

Mary Kate flinched as she looked into her great-aunt's eyes. Bee's husband had drowned at sea when little Ciaran was just a baby. 'Oh God, I am so sorry,' she said. 'You lost your husband too.'

Even so, Mary Kate didn't think she could quite understand how she was feeling, because the love that she and Nicholas had shared had been all the deeper on account of their circumstances. In her heart she was sure that no one else could truly understand what she was going through.

Bee echoed her thoughts. 'Aye, but that will mean nothing to you. Everyone's grief is different. Your father has felt it too, but not one of us can help you through it. We can just be here to keep you company, make sure you're fed. We will walk along the road with you and stay at your side until you're ready to go on ahead alone and meet someone else. I know' – she raised her hand – 'you don't think that will ever happen, but that's something else I know too. It will. And if you asked Bridget to tell your fortune, she would say that too and no doubt give you his name and describe to you what he looks like.'

Mary Kate had taken the handkerchief Bee had

held out for her and was blowing her nose. Between sniffs, Bee heard her say, 'Thank you. You're just like a mammy.'

Bee's heart contracted. Would she ever tell this girl all that had passed? Would she describe to her the life Sarah had led in that very cottage, tell her about her monster of a maternal grandfather, Kevin McGuffey? How he had almost married her mother off to the gypsies before Michael had come and spirited her away. How if it hadn't been for Father Jerry taking the wedding with little notice, McGuffey would have got his way. She doubted she would tell her. No one wanted to invoke the spirits of the past. But lately Bee had wondered if she might have the sight herself; she heard whisperings on the wind she'd never heard before. She pulled her cardigan tight around her as she banished the thought and changed the subject. 'Why did you throw away the curtain at the end of the room? Angela made that. I thought it would be useful if you put the bed behind it.'

'I didn't,' said Mary Kate. 'I haven't seen a curtain.'

Bee rose from the chair and ran her fingers along the wall where the willow pole that held the curtain had once slotted in. She was confused. Why would a tramp have removed the curtain?

Mary Kate, distracted, her emotions churning, turned and looked once more out at the ocean.

'Maybe it was Captain Bob,' said Bee doubtfully as

she made her way back to the table. She made a mental note to ask him before they left for Michael's.

★

Father Jerry called into Belmullet with a list in his vestments, given to him by Teresa Gallagher the moment he told her where he was heading.

'Since I took the keys to the car off you, I sometimes feel like I spend half my waking life running errands,' he'd grumbled.

'Well, if you give me the keys back, I'll be away to buy my own wool,' she'd replied, putting her hand out in readiness to receive them.

'Not on my life, woman,' he'd answered, snapping up the keys from the table. 'I'd be busy taking funerals if I gave these to you. I'd rather be shopping.'

Now, as he approached the wool shop, he wondered if he had actually meant what he said. 'Blush-pink, two-ply, baby wool, three ounces,' the list said. As he opened the door, the bell above it rang to announce his arrival. As usual, there were a number of women in the shop, gathered around and talking.

''Tis a wonder any bread is ever baked,' he had once said to Teresa Gallagher. 'Women talk that much, so they do. For hours on end, I mean. How do they manage it?' He came to regret that comment as Teresa never spoke a word to him for over a week afterwards, and nor did she bake any bread, claiming that the range had gone temperamental.

'Good morning, Father,' the women trilled in chorus as he stepped in.

His heart sank. He would now be the news bearer for all that had happened in Tarabeg and would face a thousand questions before he was allowed to leave. He turned and looked out of the shop window to the small café that had recently opened across the road. His stomach grumbled. The owner made better cakes than Teresa. His sweet tooth was his sin. He had seen as he passed the window that there was one slice of a Victoria jam sandwich cake and he wanted it very badly, with a nice cup of tea.

'Has Miss Gallagher sent you with a list, Father?' asked the shop owner.

'She has indeed,' he said gratefully, handing over his piece of paper.

The owner read it with as much interest as if he had passed her a personal note from the Pope. She bustled out from around the counter. 'Baby blush! Well, she must have the second sight, your Miss Gallagher, it only came in this morning,' she said.

He had no idea what to say and decided to look grumpy in order to limit the chatter. The group of women were staring at him and, even worse, he saw that Mrs Brogan was among them. She pushed through to stand next to him, her eyes beaming up at him, holding a cup and saucer in her hand. One day he would ask someone, maybe Paddy or Josie, why did they make cups of tea for their customers?

'Did you get my letter, Father?' she asked him.

Of course she was going to ask you, he thought to himself. He sounded irritated as he responded. 'Aye, I did. Thank you very much for that.' He tried to move on. 'Mrs Douglas, I hear you have one more daughter to add to the nine others,' he said. 'Father Joseph was telling me.'

Mrs Brogan was not to be deterred. 'And did you pass on the news to the Malones, about their daughter, Father? So sad.' She turned and said to the women behind her, 'Her husband only went and died, leaving her a widow with two young children.'

'Who – Mary Kate?' one of the women asked, looking confused. 'My God, when did she get married?'

Father Jerry jumped in, hoping to stop the conversation before it ran away with itself. 'I did get your letter, Mrs Brogan. I'm afraid you've got the wrong Mary Kate, or at least your daughter did. Mary Kate Malone, she is home in Tarabeg with Michael and Rosie, and she was not married in Liverpool at all.'

Mrs Brogan looked hurt and bemused. 'Oh, I know that, Father. Dana rang me. She's coming home and she said to me very clearly, "You know Mary Kate from Tarabeg, Mammy, she's gone back home, so I might pay her a visit when I'm there."' Gathering her confidence, she announced, 'I am afraid it's you that is wrong, Father. Mary Kate was married, although the poor girl is a widow now.'

Just at that moment the shop owner pushed something soft and pink into his hands. 'There you go, Father – blush pink.'

By the time he reached the small café, the cake had been sold. Father Jerry swallowed down his annoyance as he sat at the table and comforted himself with tea and the ubiquitous brack. His annoyance was more with the Malones than the woman on the next table, obviously a tourist, going by her red lips and nails and the size of the camera around her neck, who was finishing off the last bit of his cake. The Malones were keeping something from him. He had protected the village from so much since the day Sarah had died; he could not allow sin to just walk right in unchallenged. He took his first unsatisfying bite of the enormous piece of buttered brack the waitress had placed on the table, mortified that she'd sold the last slice of Victoria sandwich only a moment before, possibly thereby losing one or two of her brownie points on the stairway to heaven. Staring sullenly out of the window, he was all too aware that the battle was raging, and for the first time in many years, he was losing.

*

'Nola, did you bring some extra knives and forks with you?' Peggy was laying the table and greeted Nola as she walked into the steam-filled kitchen.

'I did that. How many are we expecting?' Nola undid her headscarf and with a flick of her wrist shook off a film of raindrops and hung it on the back of the door.

Peggy used her fingers to count. 'Well, with Declan and Keeva and Tig, I make that eighteen altogether. It'll be a bit of a squeeze, but we've done twice as many often enough. Then of course there'll be all the others from the village who'll come in to see Mary Kate and drink to her health.'

Nola noted the huge cauldron of stew perched over the dying embers at one end of the fire, and the two vats in which the potatoes were cooking. The new electric cooker hadn't even been switched on.

Peggy, noticing, looked over her shoulder and said, 'That fancy cooker is all right for a bit of toast, but you can't beat the old range and the fire for a big dinner, can you? And it certainly can't manage a pot of stew for twenty on it.'

Seamus came in behind Nola, rubbing his hands together.

'Is Joe not with you?' Peggy said, not wanting to ask after Pete in case she made it too obvious. But she caught the tut of the tongue and the sharp look Nola gave her from the corner of her eye.

'No, he's kept Pete with him and they are off to fetch Bridget and Porick in that fancy new car of his while Michael does the coast run for Mary Kate and the others, in the van full of potatoes and cabbages. Two modes of transport more different you could not imagine.' Seamus laughed as he placed a wooden box filled with bread on the table.

A grin spread across Peggy's face at the prospect of a second evening in the company of Pete Shevlin.

'I'm off to Paddy's to fetch some drinks.' Smiling in anticipation of the first drink of the day, Seamus headed towards the door.

'Seamus Malone!' shouted Nola.

He stopped dead in his tracks and turned.

'Rosie and Finn will be back from Mass in five minutes. You can go over to Paddy's bar, but only to bring the drink back here. I've no doubt Paddy and Josie will come back with you. Tig and Keeva will bring themselves when the boys are in bed. Don't you for one minute think you are staying over there. The cushion on the chair over there is still warm from the last time your fat backside was sat on it.'

Nola began unpacking loaves of floury, freshly baked bread from the box onto a shelf on the range to keep them warm, followed by three large fruit pies on enamel plates.

A look of disappointment crossed Seamus's face as he hurried out of the door. He would have killed for a drink and would have liked nothing more than to stand and have one in Paddy's bar, but he was well aware that his wife would kill him first if he disobeyed her.

Ten minutes later, Paddy and Seamus rolled a barrel of Murphy's across the road, just as the congregation began filing through the gates after Mass. There appeared to be an unusual amount of excited chatter amongst the normally reflective villagers. The ghillie from Captain Carter's estate was standing with a small crowd gathered around him.

'After the news, so they are,' said Paddy as he nodded towards them. 'No one has a notion what will become of it all now he's dead and there's no one in the family with any interest in living here.'

Seamus had other things on his mind. 'How long will we need to leave this to settle before we can tap it, Paddy?'

'An hour. So we'll go straight back and pull a few from the barrel in the bar, to keep us going.'

Seamus could not have been happier and called out to Mrs Doyle as she hurried past them, 'Did you make your confession then, Mrs Doyle? I hope you didn't confess to the burning passion you have in your loins for Paddy here. If the father tells Teresa Gallagher, she will be that jealous, she'll run down here and belt you one with her shillelagh.'

He roared with laughter and she would normally have given Seamus back as good as he gave out, but not this evening. Instead, she mumbled, 'You are getting as bad as your father was, it must be in the blood,' and without any further word of greeting, she was gone. She was a woman on a mission.

Seamus removed his cap and scratched his head. 'Well, what was all that about? She didn't even crack a smile.'

Paddy had his hands on his hips and was also staring in surprise at Mrs Doyle's retreating back. 'I reckon someone has taken bad and she needs to open the post office and call the doctor's house,' he said.

And both men, satisfied with that as an explanation and without another thought, continued rolling the barrel.

Almost everyone was gathered in the Malones' kitchen as Michael tucked the van in around the rear and his passengers spilled out. Captain Bob was up front and with some difficulty turned to Mary Kate in the back seat. 'Are you all right now – this won't be too much for ye?'

Michael bristled; he was, after all, her father. 'She'll be fine. It's just what she needs. Peggy says there have been people in and out of the shop all day long asking after her. This way, it doesn't look like she's in hiding, does it. It's a proper welcome home with nothing to conceal. We don't want any suspicions raised.'

Mary Kate was now the one to bristle. But what did she expect, she asked herself. She knew her father was right. If the villagers had any notion of the life she had led in Liverpool, there would be no one calling into the shop to enquire about her, no one calling into the shop for anything at all. Michael's business would be sorely affected. No one would pass their money over the counter of a place of sin. She dragged herself out of the van and felt Bee's arms around her shoulders.

'Are you up for this?' asked Bee. 'We can say you have a headache and are exhausted from the journey home and the work up at Angela's cottage if you like. 'Twould be no trouble at all. You wouldn't be the first or the last person not to attend a party thrown in their honour.'

Mary Kate looked over to Michael, who came and stood by her other side. 'Bee's right. You can go straight upstairs if you want to.'

'No, let's do it. And besides, I want to see Granny Nola and Aunty Bridget. I've missed them.' And, smiling weakly, Mary Kate was the first to step in through the door.

Michael bent his head to Bee. 'You go on in now too, Bee. I just need a word with Captain Bob here.'

With the women safely out of earshot, he handed Captain Bob the keys to his car. 'Does Mary Kate have any idea about the surprise visitors?' he asked.

'Not a clue,' said Captain Bob. 'And nor even does Bee.'

'Be as quick as you can,' Michael said, 'before anyone starts asking after ye.'

Captain Bob winked at Michael as they shared a conspiratorial smile. No one heard the car start up as Michael followed the others into the warmth and light of the kitchen. Only he heard the gears change as the tyres crunched and the car pulled out onto the main street.

Mary Kate entered a room filled with excited chatter and the clinking of glasses. The first person she saw was Peggy, fussing over Pete Shevlin, forcing a cup of tea into his hand as his cheeks flushed as red as the fire. Next her eyes alighted on Seamus and Nola, and even she wasn't prepared for the rush of emotion as they fought to be the first to fold her into their arms.

'For the love of God, would you look at her! Isn't she the image of her poor dead mother,' said Nola, and for a second the room fell quiet.

Rosie didn't flinch. Before Mary Kate had left Tarabeg, she used to hear someone make that same comment at least once a day. Rosie may have been Michael's wife and the stepmother to Sarah's children, but no one would ever let her forget that Michael had chosen Sarah first.

Bridget and Porick were standing against the range with Paddy and Josie, who was stirring the stew over the fire. It felt like it took forever for Mary Kate to meet and greet everyone, and then Keeva and Tig arrived. Neighbours had been invited to call in for a glass and there wasn't one that didn't take up the chance of a free drink.

Keeva joined Mary Kate and prevented the questions from becoming too deep with frequent interventions of her own. She dragged her away, over to Tig. 'Keep your eye on this one, Tig,' she said. 'As nosey as crows, the lot of them. They ask her that many questions, they'll be wanting to know when she last went to the toilet. Something is wrong,' she whispered. 'I don't know what it is, they aren't telling me anything, but she's not right. Keep an eye on her and don't leave her alone while I dish out the food.'

Tig's expression turned from cheerful to concerned.

Mary Kate wasn't even listening. With eyes glazed, she was watching her Nanny Nola keep her promise and dish her up the biggest bowl of stew. 'Jesus, there's not a pick on you. Is it still the rations over in Liverpool?'

Mary Kate had no need to answer. People talked at her, with so many questions, and so fast, she only needed to provide the occasional answer of a few words to satisfy them. She felt a glass being pressed into her hand and looked up as Tig winked at her.

'Get it down you – it helps,' he said. 'I don't know why you've come back and I'm not going to ask, but as God is true, you are a sight for sore eyes. I'm as happy as anyone that you've come home, not least because something tells me 'tis where you need to be.'

Mary Kate felt the first tears prick her eyes. Uncle Tig, her godfather, her father's best friend, had been a part of her life since the day she was born. She remembered him from before her mother died and his own boys were born, carrying her on his shoulders up the boreen to Nola and Seamus's farm to see Daedio, her mother and father walking ahead in the sunshine, her father's arm lovingly placed around her mother's waist. In a village like Tarabeg, you didn't need to be related by blood to feel the bonds of family love.

She was about to answer him when the chatter in the room rose an octave and the air seemed to shift as a man she had never seen before in her life walked into the room with Father Jerry and Teresa Gallagher. The kitchen was hot and filled with the smell of stew and stout and the breeze as the door opened and closed was a welcome one. She looked up and instantly met his gaze.

The man was the tallest person in the room and he stood out, not just because he was head and shoulders above everyone else but because his bones were better padded. His dark hair was brushed back, slick and gleaming. His skin was pinker and more clean-shaven than Mary Kate had seen on any man. His teeth were white and dazzled when he smiled, and yet there was something about him that was familiar. And then it struck her: he had the look of a Malone. Of Daedio, her late great-grandfather, to be precise.

His shirt was pressed and tucked into the waistband of his equally crisp trousers, which were held up by a smart leather belt, not string like Pete Shevlin's. It was all she could do not to stare. He looked completely out of place, and yet he seemed entirely comfortable as the people she had known all her life flocked to his side.

Her eyes met his and they were the same, almond-shaped and twinkling. With a start, she realised he had noticed her close inspection. His expression was inquisitive, mocking almost, as he lifted one eyebrow and raised the glass someone had placed in his hand in her direction. Mary Kate flushed and turned quickly back to Tig, but he was gone.

Walking towards the tall man was her father. 'Joe, come here, would ye,' Michael said. 'Come and meet my daughter, Mary Kate.'

Meanwhile, Peggy fussed about him, placing a plate of food in his free hand before she'd even served Father Jerry. It occurred to Mary Kate that Father Jerry didn't look in the least put out that this man the villagers appeared to be enthralled by was taking precedence over himself.

Keeva had returned to her side. 'Would you look at him,' she said. 'Rich as Croesus, he is, and yet he lives here. Would you imagine it? Turned this village and every woman in it on its head, he has. Even Father Jerry doesn't complain and thinks he's a saint. I'm sure it has nothing to do with the money he's spent on the church or indeed on increasing Father Jerry's stipend.'

Mary Kate stared at her and couldn't quite believe what she was hearing. 'What, he is giving Father Jerry money? For what?' She looked back at Joe. She had seen the occasional man in Liverpool that looked like him, and certainly on the television. But no one had a television in Tarabeg.

'He's just gorgeous, isn't he?' Keeva sipped on her drink and giggled. 'There's no man for me other than my Tig, God love him, but even I can see why he turns heads. Is he turning yours, Mary Kate?'

Mary Kate opened and closed her mouth, but nothing came out. She wanted to tell Keeva, as close to her as any sister, about her Nicholas and her broken heart and that if he were to walk into the room right now, it wouldn't be Joe they were all looking at and fawning over. She felt a sharp pain in her heart. Grief had returned with a vengeance, having been stilled for much of the day. Keeva was comparing Joe to the villagers, but Mary Kate had known better. She had known a man people adored for his kindness to others, his healing skills, his compassion, the way he spoke to the poorest of his poor patients with such respect that an eavesdropper would have thought they were royalty.

'But where does he live?' she asked.

Keeva's head swivelled around as she laughed. 'Where does he live? What do you mean – has no one told ye anything yet? Up on the farm, with Nola, Seamus and Pete.'

Mary Kate's mouth fell open. 'Is he the visitor?'

'Oh, aye. The visitor who's been here for as long as you've been away. He's not a visitor any more, he isn't. He came and never left and nor will he, by the looks of it, and I'm sure nobody minds that one little bit. Least of all Peggy. She's been waiting for a rich American to turn up all her life. Mind you, she needs to buy herself a bottle of perfume or something because he doesn't seem to have noticed her, lying there across his feet every time he steps into the village.'

She laughed but had no time to say any more as Peggy shouted, 'Keeva, help me to dish up, would you.'

Mary Kate stood on her own watching Joe surrounded by people demanding his attention. She felt stupidly neglected and out of place in her own home. She was the person the party was supposed to be in aid of, but she had been all but forgotten. Keeva was wrong: someone did mind him being here – Mary Kate minded. She disliked him on sight and hoped that his spell as a visitor would soon come to an end. She felt a strange and growing hostility towards the man who appeared to attract the women in the room like bees to honey.

She had already discovered that the best way to deal with grief was to keep busy, so she went about the room collecting the enamel bowls as people finished eating. She could feel Joe's eyes boring into her back, but she refused to look his way. *I'm sorry to disappoint you*, she thought to herself, *but we haven't all spent our entire lives in Tarabeg. I won't be falling at your feet like the rest of them.*

She was only halfway through clearing up when Father Jerry scraped back the chair he was sitting on and rose to his feet. 'I have an announcement to make, on this special night,' he said.

The room fell quiet and Mary Kate stopped in her tracks. 'Oh God, this is it,' she said to Keeva, who took the dishes from her. 'The official welcome home.'

Keeva frowned and hugged the bowls to her as she fixed her eyes on Father Jerry.

Mary Kate was surprised that Father Jerry had barely acknowledged her. She had thrown him a watery smile as he'd walked in through the door, but that had been met with a steely gaze and a frown. He'd ignored her since and appeared to be deep in conversation with the shiny-faced, rich-as-Croesus visitor from America.

As Keeva laid the plates on the table, Mary Kate clasped her hands in front of her, convinced that Father Jerry was now going to give an embarrassing eulogy on how he had known her since birth, how she used to sit behind the counter of the shop and serve him, and how

happy they were to see her, a prodigal daughter returned
to the heart of the village. She smiled, composed herself,
and banished thoughts of Nicholas and her friends in
Liverpool from her mind, promising them that as soon
as her head touched the pillow, they could return.

'Well now, we have news,' said Father Jerry.

Captain Bob suddenly appeared from nowhere and
it occurred to Mary Kate that she hadn't seen sight nor
sound of him all evening. He smiled sheepishly at her,
and she gave him a small and curious smile back just as
Tig raised his pot to her from alongside the new visitor.

Imagine, she thought, *I've been away all this time
and it's as if I never left. I could have been gone for
ten years and it would be the same. Bee was so right.*
This Tarabeg, her Tarabeg, it was special. It had not
altered in appearance or missed a beat in its own slow
and steady rhythm of life for as long as anyone could
remember – apart from the annoying visitor, but he
wouldn't last long, she was sure. Tarabeg was a haven
for pained souls and that was the point of home, wasn't
it? A place to turn to, a refuge in times of trouble. She
felt overwhelmed with gratefulness for the solid rock
that was her village, unchanging beneath her feet. Her
safest space and the only place on earth she could heal.
She felt a surge of gratitude to Nicholas too, for having
sent her home with his final breath. In his last hour, he
had thought of her, had known what was best for her,
and who was she to argue with that.

She looked back at Father Jerry, but he wasn't looking at her, his gaze was firmly fixed on Joe, and she was perturbed by the adoration and respect in his eyes. *For pity's sake*, she thought, mildly irritated, *is that what money does to people? Has Father Jerry never met a man who knows how to use a razor before? He should have met Nicholas.* The pain returned to her heart. She needed to stop thinking, but she couldn't. If Nicholas had been a free man, if they had been able to marry, if she had brought him to Tarabeg, it would be him they were all fawning over, not the man in the fancy shirt.

She wanted Father Jerry to get on with his welcome home speech so she could talk to Nola and find out more about why this so-called cousin was living up at the farm and what his real intentions were. She didn't have to wait for very long.

Father Jerry cleared his throat. 'It is always a joy when a lost sheep returns to the fold. Didn't the Lord Jesus preach the very same to his followers and don't we all know how that feels, here in Tarabeg.'

'Amen. We do indeed,' said Teresa Gallagher in a well-timed chorus.

Mary Kate looked over, a smile ready and waiting on her face, but Teresa was not looking at her either. She folded her arms in front of her and a shiver ran down her spine, even though it was warm in the kitchen.

'But isn't it a fact that when a lost sheep returns to the fold and brings a whole new world to our door to learn from, well, that has to be a blessing now.'

Keeva circled an arm around Mary Kate's waist. 'Are you okay?' she whispered.

'Aye, I just wish he would get on with it,' Mary Kate whispered back.

Bridget slipped in next to her, on the other side. 'I have a message for you, Mary Kate.'

Mary Kate almost jumped out of her skin. 'A message?' she whispered. 'From the other side?' Her heart began to beat wildly as the words she could not say stuck in her throat. *From Nicholas?*

'Come on, Father, get on with it,' Michael called from beside the barrel, where Paddy was filling his pot.

'Don't be rushing me, Michael. 'Tis a special thing to celebrate. So many leave Tarabeg and never return, not in a lifetime. Always meaning to, but, as we all know, time slips away and with it the hopes and dreams. You know, everyone thinks the grass is always greener, but how can it be – don't we have the greenest right here on our very doorstep? I have always thought how blessed we are here in Tarabeg and wouldn't it be the Lord's own work if we could share what we have.'

Mary Kate shuffled from one foot to the next. Father Jerry was heading off in a very strange direction.

He paused, lifted his whiskey glass and took a sip. No sooner had he put it back down on the scrubbed pine table than Nola had filled it again.

'And now I have news,' he said with a flourish. 'An announcement to make that will please every one of you. Joe here has informed me tonight, just before Mass, that he has bought the Carter estate. He is going to turn it into a hotel that everyone in the village can benefit from. He's going to make it into a... What did you call it, Joe?'

'A tourist destination,' said Joe as he raised his glass to the room.

Mary Kate's heart thumped and her cheeks flushed. How could she have been so stupid. The speech wasn't to welcome her home but rather to announce how this annoying visitor was about to change everything about the place she loved. 'What if we don't want Tarabeg to become a tourist destination?' she blurted out.

'What in God's name is that?' Teresa Gallagher asked Bridget.

'I have no idea at all,' Bridget replied, 'but it sounds smashing to me.'

'Smashing?' Mary Kate leant her hands on the table and was aware that everyone had turned to look at her. 'There will be cars and people up and down the village road, Miss Gallagher. The place won't be the same. It will change beyond all recognition. It won't be Tarabeg,' she whispered.

Tig frowned at her and muttered to Keeva, 'She's fierce mad.' He raised his voice. 'Will they be wanting to buy beer at the bar?' he asked, trying to dispel the silence that had descended on the room.

'I would imagine they would enjoy a bit of authentic local beer. I do.' Joe laughed and looked relieved.

'And will there be jobs so that people don't have to leave Tarabeg if they don't want to? Wouldn't that be grand,' said Nola as she refilled her own glass.

Mary Kate could barely speak as she stared, openmouthed, at her grandmother.

'What about the fishing?' asked Michael. 'I sold the licences for the captain and he gave me five shillings for each one.'

'The river runs through your land,' said Joe. 'I think we can come to a fairer and more beneficial arrangement than the one in place now. The stretch that runs through your land should be yours, together with whatever spawns or swims there.'

Michael looked as though he was about to faint with delight.

'After all, we both know how the land was bought. If my great-grandfather Joe Malone the first had still been alive, he would maybe have been able to support Daedio at the time, who was, after all, the youngest brother, and perhaps they would have struck a harder bargain with the Carters.'

Michael removed his cap, something he never did,

and Mary Kate wondered for a moment was he going to fall at the feet of St Joe and kiss them?

'We can all drink to this,' shouted Paddy. 'Send your pots over here.'

'Aye and then we can all raise them to Joe Malone. Our prodigal son returned, and a man bringing great prosperity to Tarabeg. When the news gets out, everyone will be wanting to live here.'

The room filled with laughter and Mary Kate looked about her, amazed. 'Have they all gone mad?' she hissed to Keeva. 'A man who claims to be related to us – *claims*, mind; does anyone have any actual proof? – turns up here with a few pounds in his pocket and they all go gaga.'

'Dollars,' whispered Keeva. 'And for pity's sake, look at him. Even I can see he looks just like a much younger version of Daedio. He's a Malone all right.'

Mary Kate turned and stormed out of the back door, quickly followed by Rosie. Sensing her stepmother behind her, she spun on her heel. 'Rosie, did you hear him? He comes here from nowhere and wants to turn the place on its head. If it isn't good enough for him as it is, why doesn't he go back to America, where he came from.' Hot tears sprang to her eyes. No longer tears of grief but of anger.

Rosie was careful to lace her voice with kindness when she replied. 'If it was good enough for you, why did you run away and leave for so long without so much as a visit?'

Her words hit their mark. Mary Kate's hand flew to her throat. She had no answer. Tarabeg hadn't been good enough for her once. But now, when she was at rock bottom, it was the only place she could heal and she wanted above all else for everything to stay just the same.

'Look, never mind. This is news to all of us and who knows what will happen. The Carter manor may become a hotel, but your family aren't going anywhere. We will all still be here and isn't it the people who matter, not the place? Couldn't you be in hell itself, but if we were all there, it wouldn't be so bad now, would it?' Rosie smiled.

Mary Kate wiped her eyes and nose on her sleeve. 'Rosie, I feel stupid. I thought Father Jerry was going to be making a speech for me, but it was for that American.' She jabbed her finger towards the kitchen. 'Why is he doing this, why is he changing everything? Why won't he go home like all the visitors from America do? Why does he even want to stay here?'

'Ah well now, that's a lot of questions to be asking all at once and there's a story there,' said Rosie. 'His great-great-granddaddy was Daedio's big brother – the man who sent a deal of money to Daedio.'

'Who cares?' Mary Kate almost shouted. 'That doesn't make him related, it's that far back. There's people all over America who are closer to us that we never see.'

'Joe the first, our Joe's great-granddaddy, apparently he always meant to come back but never made it. So I think our Joe is just doing what he thought his ancestor would have done. There was unfinished business between Daedio and his brother. Mary Kate, the man's worth a mint. Owns a law firm in New York, so he does. Honestly, there is nothing to be gained from getting on the wrong side of him, and, anyway, give him a chance. I haven't heard anyone say a bad word about him.'

'Well I can be the first.' Mary Kate searched her pocket for a handkerchief, then gratefully took the one Rosie held out and blew her nose, hard. 'The man's obviously obscene. He's all money and no brain. Look at that car...' She flicked her head towards the Bentley at the end of the back pathway. 'Why would anyone drive a car like that around here? He's just showing off. My Nicholas, he would never have been that vulgar. He healed the sick – people loved him because he did it with his hands, not his wallet. Rosie, he was the kindest man you could ever meet. You would have liked him so much more than that show-off.'

Rosie stroked her arm. 'Aye, I'm sure, but they do things differently in America and that doesn't make anyone the worse for any of it. Come on, dry your eyes, let's get back inside in the warm before they all come out here looking for you.'

'I doubt that will happen with flash Harry in the kitchen,' snapped Mary Kate as she allowed Rosie to lead her back in.

They were stopped in their tracks by the sight of Declan in the doorway. He was wearing a new green Fair Isle jumper his mother had knitted, and his customary cap.

'Hello, how are ye?' he said, and Rosie, without another word, hurried around the side of him and disappeared into the kitchen.

Mary Kate hadn't seen him since he'd risked his job to help her run away from Tarabeg in the dead of night. For the briefest moment, she just looked at him, remembering his kiss and his request that she think of him as someone other than just the man who worked with her stepmother and taught at the school. She felt a brief flash of shame. 'Hello, Declan. I'm all right, I suppose. How are you?' She blew her nose and patted her eyes, then took a deep breath. 'I'm sorry,' she mumbled, thrusting the handkerchief into her pocket.

Declan was carrying a pint pot in one hand, but he slipped the other into his trouser pocket so that Mary Kate wouldn't see it trembling. 'You don't have to apologise to me,' he said. 'I'm grand. That was big news in there and you didn't seem too happy about it, if I might say so. There's no need to be too upset about it though. You know this place – the people will stay the same.' He'd seen every thought as it crossed her mind.

'That's what Rosie said. What's Mr Big Pockets like, Declan?' Mary Kate asked, thinking she might have found an ally in him.

'Oh, he's a good man, right enough. Spends a lot of his time in Galway. Asked me to go with him once, but Mammy wasn't well again, so I couldn't. He told me all about it when he got back, mind – he's good like that.'

'Oh, Declan, I am sorry. Bee told me your mammy lives here now...' Her voice trailed off. Bee had also told her what a tyrant his mother was, the most unreasonable mother in the west, and how she never gave him a moment's peace.

'Aye, well, it was too difficult for her on her own.' He looked at his feet, scuffed his toe against the cinder path to cover his embarrassment. 'I was wondering, would you be wanting the outside of the cottage painting, only I've just done me own and I could come anytime to paint it for you. You know, as well as algebra, I'm a dab hand with the brush – I'd be happy to do it an' all.' He glanced up and smiled to see that her eyes were smiling now too, looking a bit less sad.

The exterior of Angela's cottage hadn't been limewashed in years and the dark green paint was peeling off the windowsill. 'Well, if you don't mind?' she said tentatively. She hesitated, wondering how to bring up their last meeting, when he'd told her he'd wait for her. 'Declan—'

He stopped her almost before she'd started. 'Mary Kate, don't. You don't have to explain. I knew you must have found someone when you didn't write to me. I'm not going to say the first year wasn't hard or that I didn't mope around like a lovesick puppy, but I'm a grown man now and all is good. I'm offering to paint the cottage as your friend.'

Relief washed through her. What she needed more than anything was a friend. She was missing Cat and Mrs O'Keefe, and Joan and Deidra more than she had imagined she would; she felt a pang in her heart just at the thought of them.

She and Declan stepped back into the kitchen just as Michael began to bang his pint pot with a fork. 'Right, everyone, as if Joe's news wasn't enough, let me tell you, 'tis a night for excitement. The fiddler has arrived' – a cheer went up around the room – 'and what is more—'

His speech was cut dead as two of Keeva's sons ran in through the shop and hurtled into the kitchen, the eldest, Aedan, at the front, yelling, 'Mammy, there's a man in the house.'

'God in heaven, where are your brothers?' Keeva tried to keep her voice steady, but her words still came out almost as a scream.

Aedan rubbed his eyes with the back of his hands and stammered, 'They wouldn't wake up, Mammy. They're asleep in their bed.'

'Sure, 'twill be just a dream,' his Granny Josie said, looking anxious and putting her arm around Aedan's shoulders.

'No, Nanny, it wasn't. He was at the bottom of the bed, and when I woke up, he ran down the stairs. He kicked the pot over, Mammy. 'Twasn't me.'

Despite how much he usually enjoyed leading her a merry dance with his hijinks, Keeva instinctively knew that this time her son was telling the truth.

Out in the street, Mrs O'Keefe and Cat stood in the doorway of the tailor's shop, waiting for the sign from Captain Bob that they could walk in to the Malones' house and make their surprise entrance.

'Do you think they've forgotten about us?' said Cat as she lit a cigarette.

Mrs O'Keefe watched in amazement as a mass of people came racing out of the shop at full pelt and across the road into the butcher's. They were like a pack of wild animals, shouting and with their arms flailing, led by an athletic young man and a figure she recognised as Michael Malone. 'Would you look at that, Cat,' she said, waving away her offer of a cigarette.

Cat peered out of the doorway and into the darkness, squinting to try and see better. The lights of the butcher's shop flared into life and lit the patch of road outside it. 'Blimey, they have funny parties out here,' she said.

'There must be a late-night offer on the trotters, or they've ran out of butties or something. Who goes to the butcher at nine o'clock at night? Oh God, what is that smell? I need the smoke from the ciggie to hide it.'

Mrs O'Keefe smiled. 'It's just the raw country air, Cat. Nothing fresher than that.'

'Jesus wept, the chimneys in Liverpool smell better. To think we sent Mary Kate back to this stink, and people charging across the street screaming like madmen. There's not even any street lights or a proper pavement. What were we thinking of? What in God's name have we done, sending the poor girl back here?'

'I'm not sure,' said Mrs O'Keefe. 'I'll tell you what, though, not one of them is running as fast as that fella with the sack who just legged it over the church wall.'

Chapter 13

The men pushed past each other as, one by one, with Joe Malone leading the way, they raced out of the shop and across the road into Paddy's bar. Tig struggled behind on his stick, but Keeva was up at the front with Joe, screaming the names of her three youngest sons as she ran.

Joe thought he saw a fleeting light, the burning end of a cigarette, in the tailor's shop doorway. 'You go up and check on the boys,' he said to Keeva as they entered the bar. He flicked on the light switch as the door banged against the wall. 'If there's anything amiss, come straight back down and tell me.' He wanted to run to the tailor's shop and see who it was who was in the doorway, but his marines training kicked in: *secure the immediate area* was his first instinct. He grabbed Keeva by the arm and held her eyes with his. 'You can do your crying later

– the priority is to tell me immediately what you find, or don't find.'

His words ran like ice down Keeva's spine. She bounded up the stairs to the room where she'd left her sleeping boys, her heart beating madly, her throat so tight she could barely breathe.

The men followed Joe in a pack, falling in through the door, puffing and gasping.

Joe took control immediately, pointing to each of them, putting his training to good use as one man after the other appeared to be going round in circles, wondering what to do next. 'Paddy, take the back of the bar and the fridge. You go with him, Seamus. I'll search the shop at the front. Everyone else, get outside and surround the bar and shop in case he's still around and hasn't got away. Michael, go and check the doorway of the tailor's shop – I think I saw something up there – and then the top by the crossroads and the church.'

Relieved that someone else was in charge, Michael followed Joe's orders without question, straightaway running back out of the door and up towards the crossroads and the tailor's.

'Paddy, do you have a gun?'

Tig heard Joe's words and flinched. Fists and boots were the village way, but he knew Joe was right. They were lucky to have him with them, Tig thought, cursing his leg as he hobbled up the stairs behind Keeva, shouting, 'Are they there? Are they there?'

Keeva burst into the bedroom. Despite the commotion, her three youngest were sleeping peacefully exactly where she'd left them, exhausted from a day of playing down on the football pitch and by the river's edge, their faces flushed pink and their cupid lips parted. The youngest was sucking his thumb loudly.

'Thank you, thank you, Holy Mother of God,' she gasped as she collapsed to her knees at the side of the bed and sobbed with relief, her arms spread out across the covers.

Tig waited a second for his beating heart to calm and his lungs to fill. 'Keeva, steady on, would you. The lads must have been dreaming, to be sure, and you know Aedan, he would imagine any excuse to get up from his bed and take himself over to the Malones' to join in a party. He would have brought Iain to give him cover.' He shook his head in disbelief. 'Would you look at the trouble they've caused. Everyone running around like madmen downstairs. Feck, they've done it this time, so they have. Mammy will skin them alive. And Father Jerry will have them serving at the altar for first Mass every day this week for lying again.'

There was some truth in what Tig said. Five boys who did not have red hair for nothing ran Keeva ragged most days and tied their father in knots; the only person they behaved for was Granny Josie, who brooked no nonsense and loved them as much as she scolded them. Tig's words began to penetrate Keeva's distress. She rose from the bed, lifted the covers high over the younger boy's shoulders and tucked them in protectively around all three.

The crochet throw she had made herself had been kicked to the bottom and she straightened it out, appearing to Tig quite calm now. But then she spoke, through almost clenched teeth. 'The little feckers,' she hissed, her equilibrium restored. 'I'll kill them, if your mother doesn't get to them first.'

Tig, who normally did nothing but admire his sons' high spirits, tried as hard as he could, but he couldn't keep the grin off his face as he negotiated his way back down the wooden stairs with his stick in one hand and his torch in the other. The only time he and Keeva argued was when she chastised him for being too easy on the boys. He had never once so much as raised his hands to one of them, unlike his mother, who always managed to make contact with at least one backside out of five when she took her slipper off and hobbled after one of them.

Halfway down, he turned back to Keeva. 'Come on, leave them. This will be the talk of the place in the morning, so it will. They are all fine, and since when has it been that they aren't? And besides, Keeva, we should have caught on when the drama queens came into Michael's. What fecking man? Those who can walk, talk and drink are all over the road with us. We should have known.' Tig was whispering, so that the others couldn't hear, and trying not to laugh out loud at the same time. 'There's not a man in the village who can walk who isn't half cut already. I'm the one with the gammy leg and even I could keep up with that lot as they ran over the road.'

Keeva let out a long breath. She looked at her husband and a smile lifted the corner of her mouth. 'Oh, Tig, I will not be responsible for what I do to those boys when I get back over there.'

He reached for her hand, the hand of the woman who had never cared a jot about his disability and had loved him just the same, even though he often had less puff than she did and couldn't get about as fast. She never chastised him, or became irritable or despaired of their lot. She simply accepted him for the kind man he was. Whenever he made it to Mass, he gave thanks for whatever it was he'd done that had made God think he deserved to have the most wonderful woman in Tarabeg as his wife.

As they made their way down the stairs, they heard the men in the bar and the butcher's shop. The place was flooded with bright light, courtesy of the newly installed overhead electricity cables, which also allowed Paddy to operate his fridges without a generator. Doors were being opened and closed and raised voices called out to one another.

'Nothing in the shop has been touched, Paddy,' shouted Joe as he marched through to the back.

Keeva could hear Paddy in the walk-in fridge, which was never locked. He slammed its door with force and stormed to the rear of the bar.

'There was no man, Da,' Tig shouted to him. 'Keeva and I reckon Aedan was making it up to get himself over the road and in on the party. He was probably jealous that Finn was staying up later than he was.'

'Fecking bastard. Fecking, fecking, motherless bastard,' they heard Paddy shout in response.

'God in heaven, that's a bit strong. I don't think he's that bad, Daddy, he's just high-spirited,' said Tig apologetically, flushing with uncustomary anger at the strength of his father's response.

But Keeva sensed that all was not right. 'What is it?' she yelled as she hastened her pace. She hurried through the bar to where the men were standing in a huddle, navigating her way between the tables and the stacks of chairs and stools piled precariously on top, where she'd left them a few hours earlier as she'd cleaned the floor. She knocked one to the ground with a clatter as she rushed past.

'Jesus, Keeva!' shouted Tig as the chair landed at his feet.

'Are the boys in their bed?' shouted Paddy in such a way that it seemed to Keeva he half expected the answer to be no.

She could hear the fear in his voice and she knew something was very wrong. Her skin prickled with fear at what might have been if Aedan hadn't had the presence of mind to run away and over the road. Twenty years ago, the villages had been rife with stories of children that went missing, but that was a rarity now, since the Garda had built new barracks and then a police station. And since the death of Shona, the tales of missing children and heartbroken mothers had stopped altogether.

'The boys are sleeping – all of them,' shouted Tig. 'Is there anything taken, Daddy?'

'Aye, there is.' Paddy slammed the bar door as hard as he had the fridge door and walked into the bar. 'Two bottles of whiskey and as much pig as one man could carry – cooked and ready to eat, it was. Aedan was imagining nothing. There was someone here and the boy may have stopped more from being taken.'

As the men moved back into the bar, they gathered around Paddy, caps lifted, heads scratched.

'Who the hell could it be?' asked Seamus. 'There's not a car passed through the village tonight.'

'Well, if it was only as much bacon as one man could carry, that tells us something,' said Michael. 'It was someone acting alone.'

'A genius you are, Michael,' snapped Paddy.

'Sorry, Paddy.' Michael wondered how he would feel if his shop was broken into and goods taken. It had never happened, but he could still feel the anger rising from somewhere in his belly. He tried to make amends.

'But I'm thinking who would it be that knew where the walk-in fridge was and that everyone was over at my place?'

'And,' interjected Father Jerry, who had joined them, 'it cannot be a stranger. Any other night and the bar would have been busy, so this was someone who knew there was a party on over the road. And whoever it was had assumed the back door would be left open.'

They all looked from one to the other, stumped. Father Jerry was right. This was a village where no door had ever been locked, not ever. Honesty was a virtue preached from the pulpit and practised in the homes and on the streets.

'Well, whoever it was, he left us a souvenir.' Paddy held up a woman's shawl and as he did so, Michael's blood ran cold.

Michael had seen it before, on that most tragic of nights, a wild and windy night that changed his life forever; the night of Angela's murder. He had just returned from the war and had ridden out to the coast to collect his Sarah. The shawl was Angela's: she'd made it herself, as all the fishing wives did, with wool from the Aran Islands off the coast that was thick and coated in natural lanolin, protection against the coastal rain and storms. She'd knitted it in a distinctive pattern and she used to wear it as any man would a coat.

The last time Michael had seen that shawl was when it was pulled from her shoulders and carried off by the wind, only moments before McGuffey's bullet hit her. Seeing it again now, twenty years later, he tried to speak, but the words stuck in his throat. He looked to Seamus, who had comforted him and Sarah as Angela lay dead in his arms. His heart hammered in his chest.

Michael remembered searching the clifftop for the shawl while Angela was being laid out on her kitchen table in the cottage. He'd been sent to find it by Bridget, so that it could be placed over Angela's body. But it was nowhere to be found. Everyone had assumed the fierce wind had carried it off – the storm had smashed the boats down on the shore and would have made short work of a shawl. No more had been said or thought about it, until now.

'You don't see many shawls like that,' said Joe, reaching out and lifting a corner. 'Could the thief be a woman?'

Paddy's eyes met Michael's. Paddy knew. Paddy used to travel to the coast and exchange meat for fish. He'd seen Angela wearing the shawl on many a day.

Seamus laid his hand on his son's arm and squeezed lightly. Seamus knew. He said nothing.

Father Jerry pushed to the front, raised the shawl to his face and smelt it. Father Jerry knew.

All the men who'd been there on the night of Angela's death knew who the shawl had belonged to, but no one dare speak her name out loud or talk of the worst night in Tarabeg in living memory.

'A woman? No, Aedan saw him – 'twas a man,' said Tig.

'Aedan may be a young terror, but as his teacher, I can vouch for him being no liar,' said Declan.

'I'll save this for the guard in the morning,' said Paddy, shoving the shawl out of sight, under the bar. 'I'll call him first thing. Maybe one of the other villages has had something similar happen, someone on the road through to Belmullet, chancing his luck.'

Michael removed his cap and pushed back his hair. His life had been blighted by the tinker Shona and her curse, and he always had one eye on the road, watching for the caravan carrying the woman he called the witch – even now, although he knew she was dead and buried. The shawl on the bar perturbed him as much as if it had been the ghost of Angela lying there. Someone was trying to frighten them.

'We all know what and who we are talking about,' he said. 'The only other person to have been there on that night was McGuffey himself.'

'Who? What are you talking about?' asked Joe, glancing around. 'Do you think you know who it was? Because if you do, we can go after him.'

'No,' said Paddy, who, as owner of the bar, picked up as much of the news and the gossip as Mrs Doyle. 'He was over the border on the boat and joined the IRA years ago, since the night of...' The men shot each other furtive glances. 'He's not been back across since he left, and why would he? Holy Mother of God, he's a wanted man. He wouldn't last five minutes if he stepped foot near Tarabeg. If anyone knows that we have our own magistrate and guard, he does.'

'I wouldn't be surprised if he's changed his name, is not even a McGuffey any more,' said Seamus. 'Keep your eye on Mary Kate, Michael, would you? 'Tis a funny thing altogether that this turns up when she comes home.'

Michael's face flushed with anger. ''Tis hard to believe a woman like Sarah was ever spawned from that evil man. God rest her soul.'

Each man blessed himself at the mention of Sarah's name.

'If he thinks we're all eejits and he can scare us half to death, he's about to find out he can't,' said Paddy. 'And anyway, the man is older than me. If he's around here, the guard will find him and that's a fact.'

Joe looked at Declan and shrugged his shoulders. Declan appeared equally bemused, both of them having arrived in Tarabeg long after its worst days. Alienated from the conversation, the two men moved closer to each other. The room fell silent. Father Jerry felt for the rosaries in his pocket that Mrs Doyle had brought him back from one of her recent trips to Rome and they all heard the click as they slipped through his fingers.

Joe looked about him at the strange expressions on the faces of the men he had come to know and, in the case of Seamus, love. He wanted to ask again who and what they were talking about, who had wiped the joy from their faces and instilled the fear of God in all of them. Who the shawl had belonged to. But he thought better of it.

'Things are changing around here, all right,' said Tig. 'We won't be leaving the lads asleep upstairs on their own again and that's a fact.' He put his arm around Keeva.

'Keeva,' said Paddy, 'you go back over the road to the women. We men need to talk and we want to do it alone.'

'I'll stay here now,' said Tig, squeezing her hand. 'I won't be leaving the boys. Put the other two in bed with Finn.'

Keeva didn't answer him but gave her husband a look and a weak smile that spoke for itself. As always, they were united in both intention and deed. She was relieved he was staying. She was suddenly keen to praise her boys for having woken up and had the sense to get the hell out of the house and raise the alarm. She was proud of them; they both were. As she opened the door, her hand on the knob, she turned back to the room.

'You can talk all you like, you lot, and you will, into your pots too, but my boys saw who it was and had the sense to run across the road to find us. In the morning, make sure you tell that to the guard so that he can get a sense at least of what the fella looked like. The guard may even recognise him from their description. There might have been something about him that was unusual, distinctive, like.'

They all stared at her, open-mouthed. She had spoken the truth and it was not something even one of them had thought of.

'We will that,' said Paddy, equally as proud of his grandsons. 'You never know, one of our boys could be a key witness. Who knows what this fella is up to. 'Tis a strange affair, it is.'

Tig grinned. The Devlin boys had been transformed from village villains to heroes in the blink of an eye. His chest swelled with pride.

Jay left his caravan and exhausted horse tucked away half a mile from the coast and headed to the escarpment, where he could avoid the coast road and slide down the cliff to the beach. He had strapped a wicker lobster pot to his back containing food. There was always water in the streams, but he knew that if McGuffey was on the run from someone, he wouldn't risk searching for food. Jay had already eaten half of the stolen cake, still surprisingly good, even though it was a few days old now, but he'd only taken a couple of nips from one of the whiskey bottles.

His heart was pounding against the walls of his chest and his mouth dried when he reached the clifftop as the fear of ghosts crept deep into his bones. He knew McGuffey would be in the cave. That was where he'd last seen him, years back, before McGuffey had taken a shot at him. Jay's thigh throbbed at the memory of that parting gift. But it sounded like McGuffey might finally be paying the price. Jay had to keep reminding himself of what the smuggler in Donegal had said. 'He doesn't look in a good way to me. Those fighters, they get old, and once they can't fight any more, they don't know what they're here for. He must be sixty, but he looks ninety. You can't stay on the run from the IRA for long – they'll always get you in the end. He needs your help.'

It was those last four words that had pushed Jay to come all the way back to Tarabeg. That and morbid curiosity. Although he wouldn't admit it to himself, Jay was lonely with Shona gone and was actually looking forward to seeing his former friend and enemy again. But not here, not on this cliff, where Angela McGuffey had been murdered in cold blood.

His eyes darted across the top of the escarpment, out to the ocean and back to the cottages. 'Why here?' he asked himself again as he began to shake with fear. This small fishing village, this coastline – everyone knew Angela's ghost haunted it. She'd been seen by many a fisherman over the years, pacing the clifftop, her shawl billowing in the wind, in exactly the spot Jay had to pass on his way down to the cave. The locals said she stood there looking out across the ocean, searching for her daughter, Sarah, who had tried that night to escape with Captain Bob in a fishing boat, fleeing her father and his vow that he would marry her off to Jay. That made him, Jay, indirectly responsible for the awful things that had happened and for the haunting of the coastal village. Never before had he felt that as keenly as he did right now. He had travelled for days to get here and had worn out his horse in the process, but now that he was here, he wanted to be somewhere else.

As he slid down the escarpment towards the beach, he thought he heard a scream. He stopped partway, clung to the gorse and let out his own weedy wail; it was carried on the wind as the prickles pierced his skin, his face pressed into the cliff, terrified. The night was dark and the wind off the ocean was strong. He had no protection from the elements and although it was less than a hundred yards to the bottom and the promise of shelter behind a rock, fear froze him to the cliffside. He could barely move.

There was an answering cry. He recognised the voice – was it Angela's ghost? It came again, closer, and the blood drained from his face into his boots. He was sick and dizzy with fear. It wasn't Angela, it was her daughter, the girl McGuffey had once promised to him, almost twenty years ago. Sarah's ghost. Jay lost control, clung on, blubbering and now wailing to himself. 'Please leave me alone.'

He turned to look at the ocean instead, but there was no escape. He could see her face in the clouds of the night sky; she was coming towards him, forbidding, terrifying, turning the blood in his veins to ice, and she was threatening him. His fingers began to lose their grip and his feet pushed and scrambled against the slippery, scaly cliffside. His legs flailed, desperately trying to secure a foothold, but it was no good. As he grunted and gasped, his eyes bulging with the effort, his fingers, locked and unresponsive, failed him. The gorse ripped through his hands and, calling out like a baby, he tumbled all the way down.

'About fecking time.'

McGuffey was standing at the bottom, leaning on a blackthorn stick and swaying as he stretched one hand out onto a rock. 'You just missed that rock. Dead, you would have been, if you'd hit it.' His voice was flat and far weaker than Jay remembered.

Jay looked up from the ground, nursing his head, and gasped, 'Did you hear her? Did you hear that noise?' He raised himself to his knees, then pushed himself up with his hands and scrambled onto his feet. He had never known McGuffey not to carry a gun and you never left yourself in a vulnerable position with a madman like him. His cap had landed a few feet away and he grabbed at it and pushed it back onto his head.

'Come into the cave, we can't be seen there,' McGuffey said.

'No one's in the cottages,' Jay hissed. 'They're all at Malone's.'

Miraculously, the wicker lobster pot was still in place and he shrugged it from his shoulders. He felt braver now that he had company. 'I brought you food. Cake, and meat too.'

McGuffey could smell it and his stomach began to rumble. 'Did you bring water? I can't get up to the well.'

'I did.' Jay was feeling pleased with himself and was almost grinning now.

He was amazed to see that the opening to the cave, after years of not being used, was now completely hidden by hanging vegetation. McGuffey fumbled along the shingle shore, using nothing but his hands to guide him, and then, lifting the tangle of grasses like a curtain, and with a small yelp of pain, crouched and crawled inside. In silence, they moved deep inside, towards the rear wall.

'You don't want to be this far in,' said Jay into the damp air. 'When it rains heavily, the water pours straight in from the cliff above and this part floods.'

'You think I don't know that?' snapped McGuffey. 'Do you forget, it was me who used to decide who fished off this coast and where they fished.'

Jay remembered Rory's drowning; that had been McGuffey's doing too. He was in the presence of a man who'd murdered who knew how many people since he'd been in the North. But Jay played it cool. Being with McGuffey was a lot less frightening than facing the ghost of Angela or her Sarah. He couldn't imagine even a dead woman wanting to trespass into the far reaches of this dank, dark cave.

McGuffey lit a candle in a lantern on the rock, taken from his own rucksack. His time in the IRA had taught him how to survive out on the land. 'Give me the food,' he said. He grimaced as he bent down and grabbed his thigh.

'How did you get hurt?'

McGuffey refused to answer as, with what was left of his teeth, he ripped into the slice of bacon joint. With each bite, his humour was restored, little by little. Finally, he collapsed onto the sandy patch he had made his bed, the lantern beside him in case the pain kept him down for the night; it often came on without warning.

Jay perched on a rock ledge. The cave was warmer than he'd imagined it would be at night and was surprisingly dry underfoot. There'd been high winds but little rain in the west for weeks.

'Did you get the parcel from the smuggler?' McGuffey asked.

'I did.'

'Did you do exactly as I instructed with the shawl? Have you left it where it'll put the fear of God into them? They'll know I mean business when the time comes.'

'How else do you think I got the meat? What was the point of that shawl – do you want them to know you're back?'

McGuffey gave a sneering laugh. The effort of it creased his face. 'I want them to know I'm a free man. None of them will sleep well in their beds tonight and they will never find me here. Where's everyone gone? The place is deserted, most of the cottages are empty.' And then, with a hint of impatience, 'I need money.'

Jay nodded thoughtfully. 'How about, "Thank you for the food and drink, Jay, and how are ye, by the way? Did you hurt yourself on the way down?"' He smirked. McGuffey no longer frightened him as much as he once had. Jay was a good ten years younger and whereas before, he'd been the worse for wear, living on the road as he did, it was now McGuffey who was showing his age. The Donegal smuggler had been generous in his analysis. 'Jesus, you look a hundred,' Jay said. 'What do they make you do in the IRA – drink vinegar? And why are ye on the run? Who did ye fall out with?'

'None of your business,' said McGuffey. 'I need money. My granddaughter, she's here, isn't she? My flesh and blood. We need to take her, and when we do, we'll make them pay for her.'

Jay snorted. 'What the feck are you talking about? Have you lost your head? She's a grown woman.'

'I'm talking about a way to make us rich. I only have one granddaughter and she can get us money.

Kidnapping is something we did a lot over the border. I know what to do. Have you brought tobacco?'

Jay removed the tin from his pack and thrust it into McGuffey's grasping hand. McGuffey seemed to be having trouble talking. 'Does it hurt ye much, that leg?' Jay asked, gesturing at the dark brown bloodstain on the thigh of his trousers.

Again, McGuffey didn't answer, just pushed a pipe towards Jay. 'Light that for me,' he said.

Out of habit, Jay did as he was asked without question, his eyes never leaving McGuffey. He might not be as scared of this sick man as he'd once been, but he would still never trust him or take his eyes off him. The gun was strapped to his belt, as always. He might look older, unrecognisable almost, but some things appeared not to have changed at all; he was still mad.

'I thought she was in Liverpool,' said Jay. 'Been there more than two years, she has.' A stunned look crossed McGuffey's face. 'But as luck would have it, she's back. I saw her with my own eyes, tonight, from the Sacred Heart. She was stood out the back of Malone's, talking to the teacher, Declan. The tinkers in Ballycroy told me she was back. Come home, she has. It was her, all right.'

'I've seen her too, before you.' McGuffey grunted. 'I was up at the cottage until she arrived with that witch Bee. They've been up there all day – I can't even get into my own house. But I'm invisible down here. Only yards away from them, and they have no idea.'

Jay wanted to tell him that he couldn't get into any house because the moment he was seen, the guards would be hot on his tail. McGuffey the murderer was still spoken about into the cups of men who drank too much in every bar along the west coast. But he appeared to be oblivious to his notoriety, even in a county where the news was still handed down by the storytellers. 'There's a rich American staying up at the farm too,' he said. 'The tinkers at Ballycroy said he's related to Daedio through the Malones who went out to America. They say it was his family money that Daedio bought the seven acres with.'

McGuffey pushed himself up against the cave wall and shoved his rucksack behind his back for support.

'Shona knew the money must have come from somewhere.' Jay picked up the tobacco tin from the ground and stuffed a pipe for himself. 'He's a big fella, though. A giant of a man, he is. You wouldn't want to be kidnapping him.'

McGuffey shook his head in impatience, the pain in his leg robbing him of words.

'You are playing with fire, living down here, close to the ghosts you yourself made.'

'I don't believe in ghosts.' McGuffey snorted. 'If I did, I wouldn't be down here, now would I? Just think, it was just up there...' He looked up to the roof of the cave. 'Her blood would have dripped through that soil and down into this cave.' He laughed but stopped abruptly, and they both looked over at the same time as a cold breeze blew into the cave and the light of the lantern flickered and sputtered and almost went out.

As Jay nervously lit the match and held it to the pipe he was very much in need of, the face of Shona appeared in the flame. He was so startled, he almost fell off the rock. He jumped to his feet and his pipe fell to the floor. 'Feck,' he hissed, pulling down his cap and then scrambling to retrieve the pipe.

'What is it?'

Jay's heart was pounding. He had seen the magic in Shona's eyes when she was alive, had witnessed first hand her curses and her powers at work, and now she was back. ''Twas Shona,' he said. 'Ghosts do exist. She just came in here, right in front of my own eyes. On the night she died, she said something to me about the Malone farm on the hill. Something about money, a fire, an American... Jesus, I don't know, maybe the American has money.' He sat back down and pulled on his pipe.

'What fecking American doesn't have money.' McGuffey spat out the words. 'The poor ones stay in America. They have to be rich to get here.'

Jay looked about him uneasily. He wasn't sure what frightened him more: the fearful vision of Sarah in the clouds or the hatred in McGuffey's eyes. 'They're all at the Malones' place for a party – all drinking, they are. And the big American, he's in there, lording it about. I heard him from the back.'

'Find out more about him,' said McGuffey. 'I need money to get away. You don't want me to die here, do you? If I do, I will haunt your bones forever – there's no heaven waiting for me.' A shrill laugh filled the cave. 'If he has money, he will pay to get her back. You need to go to the tinkers in Ballycroy, ask for a potion.'

'A potion – what for? She's not a kid any more – she's as tall as me. Have you lost your mind?'

McGuffey tried to laugh, but all he could do was grimace in pain. Kidnap and torture had been a part of his life for more than twenty years. He had learnt much over the border that would curdle the blood of the people who lived in the backwater of Tarabeg. Jay obviously knew nothing and understood even less.

'Find out more. Go now. I need to think how to get money. You will benefit from half – you'll be a rich man. I have the brains and the ideas, you just carry them out. You did well leaving the shawl. I wanted to scare the fecking life out of the lot of them. Like you, the eejits believe in the ghosts and the fairy stories of Bridget McAndrew. If you do as I say, and if there is a rich American Malone in Tarabeg, we will find a way to get money from him. We will plan her kidnap and you will never want for money again. Neither of us will. Can you do that?' He flinched again.

'I can,' said Jay. 'How much money will it be?'

'I don't know.' McGuffey gasped and waited for the pain to subside. The exertion of walking from the cave to get Jay had made his wound bleed afresh. 'It will be plenty enough for the two of us.'

Jay grinned. 'What shall I do now?' he asked, eager at the prospect of escaping a life of wandering the lanes and fields.

'Find out if she's staying at the cottage. Watch it closely. When Bee goes and leaves her alone, come and tell me. We'll do it in the dead of night, when she's sleeping. You'll need to gag her and then drag her down here, to me.'

Jay was a thief and a sneak, he was poor and wretched, but what he was not was brave. An idea came to him and his face lit up. 'I'll tie her hands too, that'll make it easier.'

McGuffey smiled back. 'Now you understand. Just do what you have to, but get her down here into the cave, to me. Then we'll need to get a ransom letter to Michael Malone and the American and arrange a drop – they will want her back and will pay up. Once you've collected the money, you'll leave another note telling them where she is, and by that time we'll be long gone, out there, at sea, where they won't think of following us. Now go and find me an outboard motor for the boat and bring it here. It all needs to be planned first.'

Jay was filled with a new respect. 'Anyone would think you'd done this before.'

'I have. Many times, for the IRA.'

A chill ran through Jay's body. 'Did all the people pay the money?'

'Not all.' McGuffey shuffled his weight onto his good leg.

'What happened to them?' Jay's eyes were wide.

McGuffey picked up the knife he kept by his side, grinned and made a slicing gesture across his neck. 'Now feck off,' he said.

'Right.' Jay jumped from the rock. 'I'm off to get a motor. And then I'll watch the cottage and come and tell you when she's there alone.' He was looking for praise, but he got none.

'Make sure there's plenty of petrol in it.' McGuffey closed his eyes and leant back against the wall of the cave.

'McGuffey,' whispered Jay. He had one more question. He had no money; he needed money now. But there was no reply. The pain had finally beaten the whiskey and McGuffey was unconscious.

Chapter 14

Keeva arrived back in the Malone kitchen and was bombarded by a hundred quick-fire questions. Mary Kate stood next to her, running her hand up and down her arm to comfort her. 'Everyone is safe,' Mary Kate said. 'You can stop worrying now.' Forgetting her own sadness, she smiled into the face of someone who needed her help. 'Will I get you a cup of tea?'

'God, please, Mary Kate, and I think I need a drop of whatever Nola's been dishing out before I can stop shaking.'

'A burglar, did you say? But that only happens in Dublin,' said Nola.

'The whiskey he took – well, he's a man with taste,' said Mrs Doyle. 'Paddy only has the best.'

'The place is falling apart.' Philomena blessed herself.

'The wickedness of Dublin is spreading as far as here – who would ever have guessed it.'

'We should all say a prayer and as the father isn't here, I'll be the one to lead us,' said Teresa Gallagher.

'No, you will not. Shut up, woman,' said Bridget.

Teresa looked stunned. The only teetotaller in the room, she rose as if to take her leave from such indignity. Mary Kate was crestfallen. The housekeeper of the presbytery was never spoken to like that.

'Oh sit down, Teresa,' said Nola. 'It's drink we need, to settle our nerves. Here, give me that cup and I'll give you a glass – you need one as much as the rest of us. That's if the fecker hasn't taken the crate from outside the back door.' She stood up to go and collect a fresh bottle, and Teresa was quickly pacified. 'Pass me the rolling pin, Mary Kate, in case he's still there,' Nola added.

'She will not,' said Rosie. 'I'll come with you.' And she grabbed the rolling pin from Mary Kate, who'd taken it from the range and was holding it out to her.

'Don't use it,' said Mary Kate, only just about adjusting to this new, bolder Rosie.

'Peggy, make sure everyone has a glass ready,' shouted Nola over her shoulder. 'I swear to God, with all this going on there'll be someone falling down with the shock and needing a doctor if we don't get a drink down them. Best to be on the safe side.'

Peggy had already started removing fresh glasses from the press, aided by Teresa, who began handing them around. 'Get you, Teresa,' she said. 'And I always thought you never touched a drop.'

'Aye, well, that was before Father took the keys to the car from me. I've only had the odd one. Joe brought me a bottle for my birthday and he had a glass with me. What a man he is, God love him. And do you know what I thought to meself, Peggy, when Joe poured me one?'

Peggy gave Teresa her full attention. 'No, what?' she asked, amused at the strength in the old woman's voice.

'I thought to meself, what a lot of fun I had missed, only ever drinking the tea and giving out to everyone.' She dropped her voice. 'Especially Nola.'

Peggy stared after Nola. 'Aye, she loves a drop and she's spent most of her life laughing. There's something in that, I'll be bound. Don't have any regrets, Teresa.' She reached out and squeezed the old woman's hand. 'Take your hat off, go on.'

Teresa's hand flew to her hat. 'Take my hat off?' she repeated. 'I can't do that.'

Peggy grinned. 'Yes, you can. Let your hair down.'

A smile crept across Teresa's face as she pulled out her hatpin and removed her hat.

'There you go,' said Peggy. 'That wasn't too difficult, was it?'

While Nola dispensed the amber medicine, Bridget pulled Bee to one side. With glasses in hand, the two of them sat together on the settle by the fire. The others, meanwhile, were extracting every last drop of information from Keeva. Nola, who had as good as poured her drink down her neck, held her glass out to Peggy for another.

Bee grinned. 'She loves a good excuse for a tipple, does Nola.'

'Aye, and she's doing well on it.' Bridget was now well into her seventies herself and she smiled as she watched Nola being eased down into the chair by Rosie. 'I remember the day Nola married,' she said. 'Her mother and Seamus's mother, Annie, began toasting the happy couple before we'd even reached the church. That was quite a wedding, Seamus and Nola – went on for days, it did. That was also the day I found out for sure I had the sight.'

'How was that?' asked Bee, curious and fearful at the same time. Everyone knew it was Bridget's powers that had kept the village safe from Shona, but they also knew that there'd been times when Shona's powers had been stronger, like the night she'd cursed Sarah as she stood there with Mary Kate in her arms.

'It was Annie who told me. She said, "I will leave before my time and I have to pass my powers on and I've chosen you, Bridget." But, really, I already knew. I'd been given signs from the other side. I knew.'

Both women stared into the fire and sipped on their drinks.

'Did you see that coming?' asked Bee as she inclined her head towards the large kitchen table where the other women were sitting.

Bridget didn't hesitate in her response. 'No, I did not, but I did see Mary Kate, and the two things are connected, I can see that. I just can't see how. I'm struggling now. My powers are weak and the sight, it's failing me.'

Bee had only known Annie when she was a child, and as far as she was concerned Bridget had been the village seer for all of her life. To learn that Bridget could no longer tell fortunes, commune with the spirits, heal the sick or cast spells should have caused alarm, but Bee knew already what Bridget was about to say.

'I have had a message from the other side,' said Bridget. 'They tell me to ask you to be ready. It's time for me to hand over to you. Are you ready, Bee?' She turned to Bee and placed her calloused hand over hers. 'Bee, you need to come and start spending time with me. I have to show you the herbs. It will take some learning. Which ones to use and how. We have herbs here in Tarabeg and out on the Nephin Beg that grow nowhere else. It's a mystery to many why the people in Tarabeg live so long, but not to me. One of us in Tarabeg was always going to be chosen and the spirits have good reason for choosing you.'

Bee felt almost faint, not only at the news, but because of the added weight of responsibility.

'It's you, Bee, and that means my time here must be coming to an end.'

Bee's eyes welled with tears and she turned to face Bridget, whose own eyes had also filled. She squeezed Bridget's hand tight and held on. 'I already know,' she said. 'I hear voices on the wind. I heard Angela this morning. She was calling my name and I looked to see had Mary Kate heard it too, but she hadn't. I heard Rory's voice too – that was stronger and he was trying to tell me something, but I couldn't tell what it was.'

'That is just the beginning. They are helping you from the other side. You have to find ways to sit and listen and let them in. It takes total quiet, and time, but don't worry, I will teach you just like Annie taught me. We'll start with the first herbs tomorrow.'

Bridget swivelled in her seat to look at Mary Kate, who was leading Keeva's sons and Finn up the stairs to bed. It was as if she had never been away. 'I brought Finn into the world, Bee, but I've been under attack from bad spirits ever since. As soon as I left Sarah that day, she slipped away from us – in this very house. They all blamed me around here, I could hear them, but it wasn't me. I've never lost a single child or mother, and that's more than can be said for the doctor. It was Shona's work. She waited for me to leave and then she got her spell in and did her worst. Shona may be dead now, but I can feel her still. She is here, no longer in body, but here nonetheless, still haunting this village.

There is something she wants and she won't settle until she's got it, she never has.'

'What do you think it can be?' asked Bee.

'There was one thing that kept Shona as strong as she was, Bee – revenge. My guess is she won't rest until she's had it. Listen hard to Rory and Angela. They'll only bring messages that you need to hear and there's no doubt they're warning you. Listen to them. Be still, concentrate and let them in. And come to my house tomorrow morning, we need to start work.'

Both women turned at the sound of a commotion out in the shop. 'God in heaven, what's going on now?' said Bridget.

Bee smiled as she saw Captain Bob walking into the room. But then her mouth fell open in astonishment. Behind him stood Cat, their old neighbour from Liverpool. What was she doing there? Bee almost pinched herself, seeing her old friend from Waterloo Street standing right there, in the Malones' kitchen in Tarabeg. She'd had a letter from her about Mary Kate only a few days ago, but there'd been no mention of a visit. What was going on? And who was the older lady with her – white-haired, smartly dressed, with the gentle smile?

Remembering her manners and finally closing her mouth, Bee rose to greet them.

All the other women in the room had fallen silent at the sight of the strangers.

'Hello, everyone,' said Cat. 'I'm Cat and this is—'

Before she could continue, there was the sound of footsteps on the wooden stairs and Mary Kate burst back into the room. To the amazement of everyone, she shouted, 'Mrs O'Keefe! Cat!' and ran across the room and threw herself into Mrs O'Keefe's arms.

'Are they the robbers?' Nola whispered to Rosie, extracting the rolling pin from Rosie's hand.

'No, they're not,' said Rosie, wrestling it back.

'They're Mary Kate's very good friends from Liverpool,' said Captain Bob from behind. 'They wanted to surprise her with a visit.'

'They've done that all right,' said Nola. 'Peggy, two more glasses from the press, please. Ladies from Liverpool, you are very welcome, 'tis a drink you need.'

'Aye, it is. I have them here.' They all turned to see a hatless and flushed Teresa standing with two glasses in her hand. 'Can I have another one too?' she asked.

'God in heaven, what a night this is,' said Nola. 'Get Teresa a chair someone, quick,' she added as she refilled her glass.

Cat had found their arrival in Tarabeg bewildering: so many questions, meeting Rosie, Mary Kate being so distracted, all the chatter about the break-in. The men had come back across to the house as soon as they'd heard there were visitors. There were so many people, all of them talking to her as though they'd known her all of their lives, and there was Rosie too, Michael's wife, the wife of the man she had slept with, being as kind as though she was her own sister.

Cat hadn't seen the man jumping over the church wall, but Mrs O'Keefe had, which instantly made her the centre of attention. Cat needed fresh air and a cigarette, so she took herself out onto the cinder path at the front of the shop. She had a ciggie lit in one hand and was nursing a mug of Guinness in the other, her first ever. 'No better barrel to get your first Guinness from than here in Tarabeg,' Paddy had said as he'd served her in the kitchen. As she drew on her cigarette, she gazed up at the sky, her eye caught by the brightness and closeness of the stars.

She was so engrossed in the wonder of the night sky that she almost jumped out of her skin when Michael came around the corner of the shop and spoke to her. 'That was a shock indeed, to see you standing there, Cat,' he said.

She recovered and was about to reply rather tartly, along the lines of 'I bet it was', but she stopped herself. It wasn't his fault she'd fallen in love with him. She'd known he was married and they'd both known what they were doing. It had been just one glorious night. And he'd been so kind when he left, giving her money to pay the rent for a year, which had changed everything for her and the kids, ensuring they had two safe

Christmases when she hadn't been totally dependent on the club money.

'I hope you don't mind me coming,' she said instead. 'It was Mrs O'Keefe's idea. We couldn't settle and we just wanted to see for ourselves how Mary Kate was faring. She's been through a terrible time and we missed her when she left. It was very last-minute, but Captain Bob said he thought it was a smashing idea, and so we came.'

She flicked the ash of her cigarette onto the cinder path and took a sip from the mug. She had to keep her hands busy, and, more importantly, her eyes as well, because she was in danger of staring at him. He might have noticed that her hands were ever so slightly trembling. 'Aren't the stars close to the ground here?' she said as a means of distraction. 'I've never seen them look so bright or twinkle so much in the sky. Honest to God, it's like they aren't real.'

Michael gazed up at the sky he looked up at every night of his life. 'The ghillie says it's because we have no real buildings or street lights, so you see them in all their glory. I didn't notice it meself until I came to Liverpool. It's one of the reasons I love this place, the night sky. 'Tis like a show, it is. A performance up there, when you're lucky and there's no clouds, like tonight.'

He was rambling and she thought she knew what he was leading up to. He took his pipe from his top pocket, lit it and puffed hard. He was playing for time, thinking out his next lines.

From inside the house at the back of the shop the nervous chatter about the break-in had turned to laughter. There was the sound of clinking glasses and a harmonica flared into life. She smiled, and in the glow of the moonlight he thought how soft and pretty she looked. In a flash he remembered their lovemaking. The joy of the smell and the feel of her and her abandonment, which was not something that featured in his lovemaking with Rosie, less frequent as it now was. He sighed. Rosie was his wife and there was nothing to be done to change any of that. He was getting older and he felt it creeping up on him.

'How are the children?' he asked.

'Oh, they're all good. They're staying in Mrs O'Keefe's house while we're here. Joan and Deidra are in charge.'

Michael laughed and kicked a cinder with his foot. 'Jesus, I hope they both have eyes in the backs of their heads. Imagine!'

Their eyes met and they both laughed at the thought of Cat's unruly children. He'd got to know them well in the short time he'd spent at Cat's house and it brought a closeness between them. She felt warm inside that he remembered the children, that the memory of them made his eyes light up.

'I almost shudder to think,' she said. 'God alone knows what I'll be going home to.'

'Cat—'

'Michael—'

They both spoke at the same time.

'I was just going to say—' It was Cat speaking first. Michael stopped her. 'No, please, let me.'

'Are you sure, because—' She wanted to save him from having to put it into words. To save them both. As much as she had thought about him and wanted to be back in his arms, she would do nothing to hurt this family or that lovely woman, Rosie, who was being so kind to her and had made her feel so welcome.

'Cat, I wanted you to know… You can see for yourself, I am not a free man and I never will be. It's not the way over here. There's not a man in this village who has ever left his wife or been divorced. It's not like Liverpool.'

Cat threw her cigarette to the ground and stubbed it out with the toe of her shoe. 'Michael, please, you don't have to explain.'

'No, I do. I should have behaved better than I did. You looked after me and, God alone knows, Mary Kate too. I took advantage of the situation and it was unforgivable of me.'

'Michael, that was me – I took advantage of you.'

Their eyes locked and they both laughed together. Only one was lying; the other was relieved.

'You don't have to worry,' said Cat. 'Not a word will be spoken to anyone, it's just between us.'

The weight slipped from his shoulders. 'You are a grand woman, Cat.'

'And you're a good man, Michael. Rosie is a very lucky woman.'

He leant forward and placed a gentle kiss on her lips – not something a married man in Tarabeg did to anyone but his wife.

Cat smiled. Her heart hadn't broken.

Michael looked up to the night sky and scanned the stars. 'Do you know, Cat, sometimes I look up at that sky and I feel so small and insignificant. Don't you? Do you ever wonder which one is your poor husband or ask yourself why, if we are such little people in the whole scheme of things, did God need to take our loved ones from us?'

Cat looked up. She had never shared such thoughts. Her life since her husband had died had been about bringing up her children alone and surviving from one day to the next.

Cat took a cigarette packet out her pocket and removed one. 'On the night Sarah died, I felt like the world had ended, and if it hadn't been for Rosie, I don't know what would have happened to us. It's all thanks to Rosie that I didn't kill myself because I felt like doing that often enough. And you know...' He struck a match and raised it to the cigarette that was perched between Cat's lips and held between her fingers. As the flame reached the end of the cigarette, their eyes met and for a brief moment his voice faltered. He pulled his eyes away, shook the match, threw it to the ground and then looked back up to the stars. 'I think for every star there is up there for someone who's been taken, there's also an angel down here, on earth. My angel is Rosie, and you, Cat, you're a good woman, you will meet your angel soon.'

Rosie had moved from the kitchen to the inside of the shop to get a packet of Woodbines off the shelf for Seamus. As she turned to go back into the house, she noticed the two shadows on the other side of the shop window. She hadn't seen either Cat or Michael leave the party; she'd been too busy refilling drinks and clearing away plates of food. For the past half hour, she and Peggy had been washing dishes and her hands felt red raw.

In the morning, while everyone else slept off the spoils of the night, she would be up and on her way to the school. There'd be no child missing out on their studies because the teacher had a hangover. Rosie wouldn't mind or care that her limbs ached with exhaustion and her eyes stung with tiredness. What had mattered was putting on a welcome for Mary Kate and an appearance for Michael. Even if a rumour escaped from Belmullet and reached Tarabeg, no one would believe it. Mary Kate was not in hiding, she had nothing to be ashamed of. She and her family were celebrating her return home and that was the most important task in hand.

She moved closer to the window, heard the whispered voices, saw the flare of the match and the reflection of Cat's face. Her heart pounded in her chest with the fear of what she would see. Then came Michael's words: 'My angel is Rosie.' He had never said that to her, but it didn't matter. It was what he thought, and that was all she needed to know. It had all been worth it; she was his angel.

Chapter 15

Bee awoke to darkness and nudged Captain Bob in the side. 'What time is it?' she asked. He was already awake, lying on his back, his arms folded, fingers intertwined and tapping out a beat on his chest. She could tell he'd been lying there for some time, keeping still, trying not to move or disturb her. It was the way with him: always thoughtful, always looking to make her life easier.

The bed creaked as he turned to face her. 'It's time you got up and lit the fire and made me a cup of tea, woman,' he said as he dug her in the ribs and kissed her on the forehead.

She could sense his grin before she saw it. 'Is that an order there, is it? Because if it is, you can make your own flamin' tea,' she said, stretching her arms above her head.

'Well, I might as well,' he said as he flung his legs out of the bed, 'because there'll not be any work for me today, not with that storm brewing. We won't be seeing daylight today.'

She heard the match strike as he lit the oil lamp. The cottages on the coast had no electricity and it was thought they never would. As more and more residents either left to travel to America or England or simply grew old and died, the cottages stood there uninhabited and were eventually abandoned altogether. Times were changing. The young didn't want to cook over fires and read by candlelight. They wanted electric ovens and lights. Bee was more than aware that her having returned after ten years away was unusual. The fishing community was all but disappearing. The odd small boat and the lobsterman still went out early each morning, but most of the fishing was now done by the trawlers out at Belmullet, away from the head.

The kettle clanged as Captain Bob placed it on the hearth. He riddled the peat ash in the fire and threw the kindling on the top. Last thing each night, the kettle was filled and rested on the dying embers, to warm the water ready for the next morning. As the flames flared and sparked the fire back into life, an orange glow filled the cottage and she instantly felt warmer.

'Let's take a look, shall we.' Captain Bob pulled back the curtain by the door and let in the day's dishwater-grey light.

She watched him as he lumbered about the cottage, her heart filled with affection at the sight of his belly stretching his string vest and protruding over the top of his flannelette pyjama bottoms, and his wild white hair, now wispy thin at the front, curling at the back and too long, always too long. She plumped the pillow and shuffled up the bed to await the return of her husband and the arrival of her tea. She hated the bad weather but loved that it meant her Bob didn't have to set out in the trawler. Having lost one husband at sea, she lived in fear every single day of losing another.

'Do you think Mary Kate enjoyed last night?' he asked as he fanned the flames and threw on a handful of peat bricks underneath the fire dogs on which the cast-iron kettle was perched.

'She did once Cat and Mrs O'Keefe arrived. How in God's name did you manage to keep that from me? I still can't believe they're here. And how long is that tea going to take? I'm near dead with thirst.'

She picked up her dressing gown from the end of the bed – black, quilted, and patterned with bouquets of pink roses; a purchase from Liverpool that had been examined and exclaimed over by every village woman who had visited her in the cottage – and slipped her arms in, then fastened the belt across her middle against the cold, damp ocean air.

'It wasn't as hard as you might think,' he said. 'Cat

phoned Mrs Doyle's and I was there when the call came through. The rest was easy.'

'Trust you to keep a good secret, and thank God you did. If they hadn't arrived and the highlight of the night had been a villain stealing from Paddy, scaring the life out of the boys, or Joe announcing that he'd bought the estate, we would all have been bored to death, with nothing to talk about.' Bee began to laugh. 'Holy Mother, it's only all just sinking in – all that in one night! A year of news all in an hour. Nothing will ever be the same again. Imagine, the next time we're all at Michael and Rosie's, we'll be expecting the Pope himself to pop in, or the Queen of England to knock on the door, otherwise it will be a very dull party.'

Captain Bob straightened up and frowned. 'That news of Joe's about the hotel was news that Mary Kate didn't seem to like one little bit. If I hadn't brought in my surprise visitors, it would have been a terrible night for her altogether.'

'Yes, but as it was, you, my lovely man, saved the day with your ingenious plan. Was it you that arranged with Seamus for them to stay at the farm?'

'It was.' Captain Bob was by now looking very smug indeed; nothing brought him more pleasure than pleasing his wife.

'Mary Kate top-and-bottomed with Peggy last night so she can get up to the farm this morning, and do you know, when I went up to say goodbye to her before we left, she was already sleeping and there was a smile on her face. She was beside herself with the pleasure of seeing them.' Bee reached her arms around his waist and he hugged her into him, resting his chin on top of her head and rocking her from side to side as if she were a fractious child.

'That break-in was a funny thing altogether,' he said. 'Look...' He held her slightly away from him and looked down into her face. 'I wasn't going to tell you, I didn't see the point, but a few days ago, as I got back home, you were at Mass, I saw a boat I didn't recognise coming into shore down below the cliff. When I went down to check who it was, the boat was gone. It wasn't tied up against any of the rocks – it had disappeared altogether. I've never seen such a thing.'

'Who could it have been?'

'I have no idea, but it wasn't right at all. Whoever it was wasn't from around here, and why would they be dragging a boat up across the beach onto the head? It doesn't make any sense. Where is there to go from here if you've no business here, other than up the cliff? It's not the easiest way to get into the village.'

They both thought over what he'd said.

'He could have gone to Paddy's, I suppose, but he'd be the first person to take his curragh down there on his back, and there are hardly any fishermen left here as it is, let alone ones who drink in there.' Captain Bob had his suspicions, but he wouldn't voice them. There was only one man who would have been mad enough to sail in from that angle, across the rocks. A man who'd disappeared a very long time ago and hadn't been seen since.

'I have news of me own,' said Bee with a sigh as she detached herself from his arms and pulled out one of the chairs. 'Bridget wants me to call at her house today. She wants to teach me about the herbs and the things she uses to make people well.'

Bob poured the boiling water over the tea leaves in the pot. 'That's not a bad thing, is it? Are you happy to do that?'

'I am.' She rubbed away at an imaginary pattern on the table with her finger. 'There's more to it than that though.'

He placed her enamel mug of tea before her and his own in front of the chair next to her and sat down. 'What could that be – she wants you to start telling the fortunes and communing with the dead?' He tilted his head back and roared with laughter.

Bee looked up at him through her fringe, which had flopped over her brow. Her beauty in the glow of the firelight took him by surprise, as it sometimes did. 'Yes,' she said. 'Exactly that.'

His laughter stopped abruptly and he leant forward in the chair. 'How do you feel about that then?' he said, knowing better than to call into question Bridget's powers.

'Last night I was dubious, scared even, but this morning not so much. I've heard voices, Bob. Out there.' She pointed towards the window. 'At first I thought it was the wind, but then I knew it wasn't – it was Angela, and Rory. And I've heard other things. I think Bridget's right. They're calling me, and it seems it doesn't matter what I think because I don't have any choice – it's happening.'

He picked up his mug. 'What will Bridget do then?'

A sadness came into Bee's eyes. 'That's the worst of it. Bridget knows her time is coming. She says that when you have the sight and the spirit world works through you, you just know. She was very insistent we start today. I think I'm going to have to learn to drive that car of yours. It'll take me half the morning to walk there and if I have to go every day, I'm going to need it.'

She expected him to find a hundred reasons why she couldn't. Besides Michael and a handful of others, Captain Bob was one of the few in the village to have a car, and it was his new toy. Instead, he jumped to his feet.

'Right, well, get my breakfast ready, woman.' He grinned. 'And then let's get you behind that wheel. You can have your first lesson on the way to Bridget's, starting today.'

*

Mary Kate woke in a cold sweat, with Peggy's toes stuck in her ear. The cock crowed and she could hear him scratching about below her window. Her brow and top lip were covered in perspiration, and her hair was wet and clinging to her cheeks and the back of her neck. Her heart beat wildly as she wiped her mouth with her hand; pushing her hair away, she fought the urge to call out. It was the same nightmare she'd had the previous evening, and even though she was almost too afraid to, she attempted to recall its vivid details as already it was fading away.

'Are you all right? Only you're breathing funny.' Peggy's face loomed over her as she sat up in the bed. 'A bad dream, was it?'

Mary Kate nodded, not trusting herself to speak as she committed the details of the nightmare to memory, knowing she would never share them with anyone.

'Do you know, I've never had one of those in me whole life and I feel sorry for those that do. I asked Bridget about it once, and she told me no one in Tarabeg has nightmares. Sure, what does anyone have to worry about?' Peggy swung her feet over the side of the bed. 'I need a pee,' she said by way of explanation. 'Isn't it grand, living in a house with a bathroom.' She padded out of the room, her long nightdress trailing on the wooden floorboards, her dark hair hanging loose down her back, almost reaching her waist.

Mary Kate guessed that the over-large nightdress had been a donation, probably from the likes of Teresa, who always had an eye out for Peggy. The wintery light filtered in from below the curtains and cast a haze over the room so that looking towards the door after Peggy was like trying to peer through a piece of grey chiffon. The nightmare came back to her: her mother, a cave, a man in black, being unable to breathe; it felt real in the silence of the room, but the one thing she couldn't recall was her mother's words.

An hour later, Mary Kate had found her old bicycle from behind the shop and was ready to head off up to the farm to see her visitors.

'You have a grand day,' Peggy shouted from the shop doorway before getting on with stacking the new delivery of cigarettes onto the shelf.

Michael, Rosie and Finn left soon after Mary Kate.

'Will I be seeing you for lunch, Michael?' asked Peggy as she lifted the counter to let them through, her hand in the small of her back. 'Is there anything you want me to do in the house, Rosie?'

Finn, grinning, leapt back and pinched a piece of Bubbly gum from a box.

'Oi, put that back,' said Rosie as she held onto his collar to stop him leaving the shop.

''Twill be mighty busy in this shop soon if Joe gets his way,' Peggy said, addressing Michael. She had a plan to live another life, and as soon as it was possible,

Michael would need to find a new Peggy. Despite her recent setback with Pete, she was still determined that the night of the dance was going to change her life.

'Don't you be worrying about that,' said Michael. 'Now that Mary Kate is home, you will have plenty of help in the shop.'

Even Finn looked surprised. Rosie almost laughed out loud. 'What, you think Mary Kate is going to spend her days working behind this counter? Oh, sorry, Peggy.' Rosie instantly looked shamefaced. 'Come on, Finn, out.' She pushed him in front of her, towards the calls of Keeva's sons.

'Oh aye,' said Michael to Peggy, as she was now the only one left in the shop. 'What else is she going to do? And isn't that why she's come home? She missed the place. I'll give her a few more days to find her feet. She'll settle into Angela's cottage and then, as God is my judge, she'll be down here every morning to work. She's a Malone after all and this is a Malone business. That's what she came home for, Peggy.'

Through the window, Peggy watched Michael speaking to Keeva and the boys. Then he jumped into his van and Keeva came into the shop. 'Has Mary Kate gone already?' she asked.

'Aye, she's gone to the farm to see her visitors – she couldn't get there fast enough. And get this, Michael only thinks that once she's taken a few days to settle in, she's going to be working here in the shop with me. Just as I plan to get away, he thinks Mary Kate is going to tie herself to this counter.'

'He must be mad,' said Keeva. 'Mary Kate isn't going to stay here long enough to need her washing done, never mind work in the shop.'

Mary Kate, meanwhile, had cycled to the bottom of the boreen and run all the way up to the farmhouse. The house was empty when she raced through the door and for a moment she was glad of it, as she took in the familiar sight and smell of the kitchen. Nothing had changed, everything was as it had always been. The room smelt of warm bodies and freshly baked bread. She had no need to shout for anyone as she heard voices approaching the back door and rushed to meet them.

Cat and Mrs O'Keefe were walking up from the creamery towards the house. Seeing her, they waved. 'A real cow and milk,' exclaimed Cat as she hugged Mary Kate. 'They used to have a dairy down on the end of George Street when I was a kid, but it took a direct hit during the war. The street smelt of roast beef for a week.'

'How are you, love?' asked Mrs O'Keefe. 'Nola is making the butter, said she'll be an hour yet. We offered to help, but she wouldn't hear of it.'

Cat looked a little nervous. 'You don't mind us coming, do you, love?'

She looked her friends in the eye and with a smattering of the old Mary Kate in her voice said, 'Well, actually, Cat, I'm all the better for seeing you two. I was feeling like a fish out of water in my own home until you both arrived. Let's go inside. I know I haven't been gone for long, but there must be some news. Is Jet missing me? Did Debbie get over her bad chest? I've been so wrapped up in my own grief, I feel as though I've forgotten everyone else.'

'Well, talk about a Spanish inquisition,' said Cat. 'Come on, Nola said she'd be very grateful for a cuppa, so we'll take one down.'

Mary Kate looked over towards the old house. 'Has he gone?' she asked.

'Who – Pete or Joe? They both left while we were having our breakfast. Joe said he had to go to Galway in the car to meet someone. He is just gorgeous, Joe, isn't he?' Cat didn't wait for an answer. Giving Mary Kate a pat on the hand, she squeezed past.

Mary Kate felt a twinge of something she simply could not recognise. She wanted to scream. Joe was nothing more than a loathsome intruder – why hadn't Cat said that? But Cat was already back in the kitchen.

'Like I said, he's gone to Galway, but on his way back he's going to call into the village to get us tickets for the dance. How about that? And your da, he's coming up here later to take us to see Bee and your cottage. Fancy you having your own place. And he said he's going to show us around the village. He's taking us to Bridget's to have our fortunes told. We feel like royalty. Do you know what, I can really see why you wanted to come back here. I totally understand it now. I don't think I'd have ever left, meself.'

'Can you? Really?' asked Mary Kate, amazed. 'I'm not sure I have done the right thing. I just keep wishing I was back in my own house on the avenue. I miss Nicholas so much, and our home too. It's like I've lost everything.' She fell onto the chair and buried her face in her arms as she cried.

'See, I knew it was the right thing for us to come.' Cat sat down next to her and wrapped her arms about her shoulders.

Mrs O'Keefe busied herself as she watched. Things were not as they should be for Mary Kate.

Bee got out of the car, slammed the door and marched up the boreen to Bridget's house. By the time she reached the sod house on the edge of the Nephin Beg she'd regained just about enough composure to enable her to speak.

Bridget appeared to be aware of her arrival before she got to the door, but the smile on her face disappeared when she saw the expression on Bee's. 'I take it you aren't as happy about coming here this morning as you once were?' she said, her heart sinking.

'Oh God, no, that's not it,' said Bee. 'If the truth be known, I'm delighted to be here. Anything to get away from that big lump of an eejit.'

Bridget was horrified. Bee and Captain Bob were known to be inseparable. They functioned as one, not two. When you asked him a question, she would often answer, and the same in reverse, or quite often they would answer together. 'You can't be talking about Captain Bob?'

Bee almost pushed past Bridget as she walked through the door. She began unbuttoning her coat so vigorously that one of the buttons flew across the room. 'Can't I? Why would that be then? Because to the whole world he's Mr Wonderful and Marvellous, until of course his wife asks the big man can she learn how to drive the car.'

She untied her scarf and threw it over the back of the settle with such force, it fell down the back. 'Oh, let me tell you, the face of the Mr Nice Fella totally falls away then, so it does, and do you know what it leaves behind, Breege? A beast, that's what he is. A beast and an eejit who hasn't the manners, the good sense or the patience to teach his wife how to drive without losing his temper. That's who Mr Nice Fella Captain Snarky-Mouth really is, a great big bloody beast.'

Bridget couldn't help herself, she roared with laughter until the tears threatened to pour down her cheeks. A more unlikely beast she had never met. 'Oh Holy Mother of God,' she said, almost crying into the handkerchief she'd removed from the sleeve of her cardigan. 'Have you heard yourself?' She blew her nose hard, dabbed at

her eyes and shuffled in Porick's slippers over to the fire
to shift the kettle across onto the hot embers.

Bee had removed her coat and flopped down onto
the settle next to the fire, folding her arms firmly across
her chest, her face set.

'Why did you want to learn to drive anyway? I
didn't even know women could do that. Isn't there a
law against it in Tarabeg, or something along those
lines, since Teresa Gallagher drove the father's car
straight through the church wall and landed upside
down on a grave? Lying on top of mad Mick Feenan
all night, she was, before anyone found her. You should
have heard Paddy. He said that was the closest she'd
ever got to being on top of a man, and she chose one
who'd been dead for fifteen years.' Bridget giggled at
the memory. 'Mind you, 'twas lucky she was alive. Not
a scratch on her, there wasn't. She was just filthy; filthy
and shaken up a bit, you know. Father Jerry wouldn't
let her near the car after that. What a scold she was
for weeks. Blamed everyone except herself for the
accident.'

Bee gave Bridget a sharp look from the corner of
her eye. She was still seething, that much was obvious,
and she glared at the fire as though it might dare to
answer her back. A lump of burning turf spat at her and
she folded her arms tighter. She was in no mood to be
amused. But the thought of Teresa Gallagher, renowned
teetotaller and a woman who wouldn't be seen dead

without her hair done and a hat on, lying on top of mad Mick Feenan's grave, a man who had never been seen sober since the day he was allowed into Paddy's bar, was her undoing. It began with a smile, which she tried her hardest to stop, but one look at Bridget and she was lost as her shoulders heaved and the laughter escaped in full-throated flow.

A cup of tea and a slice of brack later and Bee had regained her usual good humour. 'You know, I wouldn't be surprised if there actually was a law to stop women driving here in Ireland, never mind Tarabeg.'

Bridget leant over and slopped a drop of whiskey into Bee's tea. 'Always handy for restoring a good temper, and you will need that today.' She winked and tipped a splash into her own. She'd always been abstemious, but with her fate now laid out before her and her time left on earth limited, she had other plans.

'Even the Queen can drive in England, Breege. That's what she did in the war, you know, drove jeeps and things. We had a television in Liverpool, not long before we left, and I saw her driving meself. Here they'll use anything they can to control us women, and that's always been the way. The Church, the government, the Law, not to mention the men in the family with their fists and their rules. I think it's because they know. In Liverpool, women drive, go to work, earn money, get divorced. The married women, even the Catholic ones, take the birth-control pill so they don't have a dozen kids like we do here in Ireland. Women over there, they're free. It's only here we're still wrapped in chains.'

'Because men know what? What do they think they know?' asked Bridget.

'That if we women were ever to have our own jobs, money and houses and be in charge of our own destiny, we would rule the bloody world, that's what. I bet I can drive ten times better than Captain Bob, and I'm not even kidding you. When he's had a drink, he's all over the road.' Bee let out a big sigh, the tension easing from her shoulders.

'Is that why you and Captain Bob haven't any of your own? Were you taking that pill?'

Bee shifted in her seat. The pill was available on prescription for married women only. She and Captain Bob hadn't been able to marry until his wife had died, just two years ago – one of the many secrets of Tarabeg. She'd been careful to use the ugly rubber cap and to go through the uncomfortable ordeal of religiously inserting it every night. 'Of course I used it,' she lied. 'Not all the doctors will prescribe it, although it's perfectly legal over there. Our doctor did. He was good like that. He worried about the women, not the Pope. It's only in this backwards country that it's bloody illegal to take it.'

She changed the subject, keen to move on to safer ground. 'I just thought if I need to be here every day, it would help if I could use the car sometimes, and in this weather there's no fun to be had on the bike. I don't see why it is he tried to open the car door and jump out once I got going. I could have stopped it, once I'd remembered which was the pedal for the brake. I could see meself the car was going faster, I'm not blind, I just needed a second to lift the foot off, but you know what it's like – when someone's shouting, I go all to pieces. He shouldn't have shouted.'

Bridget buried her face in her hands. 'Bee, I need you here, not six foot under. Please, just use the bike. You can't be complaining about Captain Bob – didn't he just give you the chance to drive? Wasn't he the one who agreed to teach you and isn't he a great man for that? Me, I'd rather die than get behind the wheel of one of those things. I'm a bag of nerves, I am, whenever Bob or Michael gives me a lift home. Takes two large pots of Porick's poteen before the shaking stops.'

Both women stopped talking at the sound of footsteps approaching the cottage. There was a tentative knock on the door. Bee had begun to feel dreadful. A knot in her chest had appeared from nowhere. She and Captain Bob never argued and now that her anger was subsiding, it was replaced by remorse and a strong desire to find her husband and make up.

Bridget got to her feet. 'That will be the two ladies from Liverpool.' She popped the cork back into the whiskey bottle and hid it in the press. 'They're coming to have their fortunes told. Here begins your first lesson, Bee.'

'What, you mean Cat, my old next-door neighbour?' Bee jumped up and flung open the door. She'd hardly had time to talk to Cat the evening before, finding herself in competition with every man in the village who wanted to know the price of everything in Liverpool and get a running commentary on the going rate for every job, from labouring to working on the pick 'n' mix in Woolworth. Bee had smiled as she'd heard Cat being asked by one of them, 'Do you know the O'Haras from Killala? He went out there in forty-six, just after the war, and the others followed a year later. You must have met them?'

She grinned as Cat stood before her in Bridget's doorway. 'Would you get a look at you! You're a sight for sore eyes.' She opened her arms and Cat fell into them.

Mrs O'Keefe was right behind her. 'I never knew you in Liverpool, Bee, but what a funny thing that I met Mary Kate on her way to visit you – and it turned out you'd already left, just the day before. What a thing. And she ended up staying with me and we became the best of friends and now would you look at this, we're all here.'

Bridget took the coats from the visitors while the women chatted. She knew very well what Mary Kate was suffering from and why she was home, even though no one had told her. It was something serious enough for these ladies to have left Liverpool and travelled all the way to Tarabeg to see her for themselves. Every family needed to keep its own secrets safe and even though she'd been there at the moment of Mary Kate's birth, was close to all the Malones and had been all her life, she was not strictly family.

She'd been asked for more potions and cures for grief than she could count, and when she met it, she knew it for what it was. Mary Kate was grieving, and if Bridget could, she would find a way to let her know that there was only one cure. She had potions to fix everything from a hangover to a baby refusing to leave the womb, but the one thing she didn't have was a cure for a broken heart. Only time could heal that, and no matter how many herbs she brewed, they didn't make a jot of difference; she could not compete with Mother Time, who had the best cure of all.

When it was time for Bridget to read the women's fortunes, Cat was open-mouthed with amazement. Bridget used a crystal ball first and then finished off by looking at Cat's used tea leaves. 'You have lived a hard life, that much is true. 'Tis all here,' she said. 'But you've had a bit of luck along the way.'

Cat remembered to nod. 'Not lucky enough,' she wanted to reply. She'd not confessed to anyone that there were other reasons she'd jumped at the chance to come and visit Mary Kate, and she wasn't about to open up now.

'Swill the cup around, Cat, and then quickly turn it upside down onto the saucer.'

'She's had enough practice at drinking the tea,' said Mrs O'Keefe. 'Who would have known that you could tell your future from it?'

'Welcome to Tarabeg,' said Bee with a smile. 'Were you both comfortable last night, up at the farm?'

'We were,' said Mrs O'Keefe. 'So comfortable. Nola's asked us to stay for a week and we've said yes, haven't we, Cat?'

Cat grinned. 'I've never been away from our kids for more than a day before, never mind a week. I can't believe that I don't actually know what they're up to right at this minute.'

'They've got Mrs Doyle's number, and Michael's, if they need us,' said Mrs O'Keefe. 'And my sister Lizzie is going to be dropping in every day. But if you ask me, those kids will be having their own holiday with Deidra and Joan – they won't want to go home.'

Cat smiled as she handed over her cup. Every word was true. Not one of the children had run back to her for a kiss when they left; she'd had to demand that they did. 'A whole week ahead of me, and to think I've never even been out of Liverpool before.'

Bridget looked into her cup. 'Did you say you've never travelled, Cat?'

Cat shook her head vehemently. 'Not unless you call walking to the offie for a packet of cigs travelling. Or going into town. I take the kids to the Pier Head every now and then, and once a year we have a big day out in the park – that's all the travelling I do.'

Bridget looked serious. 'All that is about to change,' she said. The air between them suddenly felt heavy. 'I see you making a journey over deep water. Very deep water, very often, and then it stops. I see you moving house and settling. The chance to move is unexpected, sudden, and you are in a quandary, you don't know what to do.'

'That could be us going home next week, the deep water,' said Mrs O'Keefe.

Bridget rested the cup on the table. 'Well, it could be, but it isn't being made once, it's a number of journeys.'

There was a gasp in the room.

'Well I never. I wonder what that could be about?' said Mrs O'Keefe.

'Can I have a look?' asked Bee.

'Yes, go on, let's see how much you can see already,' said Bridget.

Bee picked up the cup and rolled it around in her hands, examining one side and then the other, and then doing the same thing over again. 'I see a very tall man,' she said. 'He has dark hair and he is looking for you now. He's a man with a nature for children; he won't be bothered by yours one little bit. He's been thinking about you and he knows you are here in Ireland. I think all will be revealed to you very soon, in a moment of joint acknowledgement.'

'Oh my giddy aunt,' said Cat, 'I can't believe it. Is there a hairdresser's in Tarabeg? I better get me hair done quick.'

'How are you getting back?' asked Bridget. She liked both of these ladies, and they liked her.

Mrs O'Keefe answered. 'Seamus is collecting us with the horse and cart any minute now.'

Bridget laughed. 'Well now, I think I've just answered your question about a hairdresser's, Cat.'

At the door, while Bee and Mrs O'Keefe discussed the latest news in Liverpool, Bridget handed Cat her scarf. 'That was a good decision you made,' she said.

Cat flicked the headscarf into the air and, holding the corners, waited for it to land like a parachute on her head before she tied it under her chin. 'What decision?' she said, confused.

'I think you know what I mean. I don't reveal everything I see. Rosie hasn't had the easiest life. After the worst of times, she held that family together and brought them out the other side. Her and Michael, it's not a match made in heaven, I'll give you that, but it works.'

Cat was speechless. Her mouth opened and closed like a fish, and her eyes blinked rapidly.

'You don't have to say anything. Men are fickle creatures, and no one knows that more than Rosie.

Your future is a good one, it was a pleasure to see it. You have much to look forward to, Cat, just make sure Rosie has too.'

'Right, are we ready for that walk down the boreen, then – isn't that what you call it here?' asked Mrs O'Keefe.

'It is that,' said Bee, standing next to Bridget in the doorway and crossing her arms. 'There's no streets or avenues up in these hills.' They waved Mrs O'Keefe and Cat off down the fern-lined footpath.

'Did you really see a tall dark man in the leaves?' asked Bridget.

'I really did,' said Bee. 'And what's more, I saw his name, but I wasn't sure, am I supposed to reveal that?'

Bridget closed the door and began to clear away the cups. 'Ah, now you're learning,' she said. 'Always best not to involve the name of another person, just in case. I sometimes do, mind. You can give someone the courage to take a little step they might not otherwise have thought of taking.' She carefully placed the cups in the enamel washing-up bowl. She wouldn't tell Bee all she had seen herself, or the ladies. But as soon as they were finished at the cottage, she would seek out Mary Kate.

Bee appeared at her side with the plate from the brack. 'He's not a man I thought was in search of a wife.'

'Ah well now, he wasn't, isn't it funny. But last night at the party something happened and I know for sure he is now. Right, we have to start on the potions.' She lifted her basket from the floor by the press. 'I picked these fresh this morning, pennyroyal and mugwort. We might not have the contraceptive pill in Ireland, but we do our best.'

Chapter 16

Matron was late for her afternoon tea with Dr Gaskell but had so far just about adhered to her own no-running rule by walking at a swift heel–toe pace. Tucked under her arm was a folder containing the plans for the two new wards. She checked to see that no one was looking, then sprinted up the stairs to her flat and in via the small kitchen at the rear.

Elsie, the housekeeper, was buttering the crumpets, and Blackie, her cantankerous Scottie dog, was sitting obediently at her feet, waiting to catch the stray crumbs. 'It's not like you to be late, Matron,' she said. 'Dr Gaskell has just sat down in front of the fire. Wiped out, the poor man is. I reckon he'll be catching forty winks by now.'

Matron hung her long scarlet-lined cape on the back of the door. 'Yes, and when I wake him, he'll say, "I wasn't asleep, I was just resting my eyes, that's all," and he'll be grumpy for all of two minutes, or until he's eaten his first crumpet and drunk his first cup of your lovely tea.'

Elsie preened herself as she placed the tea cosy over the pot on the trolley and lit the small candle beneath. 'Do you know how old Dr Gaskell is, Matron?' she asked.

'He's as old as me, Elsie, and that means you'll never know.' Matron pushed open the green baize door with force and entered her sitting room noisily. It didn't work. Dr Gaskell had entered his rumbling-snore mode. She smiled down at him with great affection in her eyes. She had lied to Elsie. He was older than her, but she knew he would never retire. He would leave St Angelus in a coffin. She coughed, loudly, and he jumped in the seat.

'Oh, it's you, returned at last,' he said as he rubbed his face. 'I was just resting my eyes.'

Elsie had followed Matron with the trolley and they smiled at each other.

'Good, well, that means your eyes will be fresh and ready to take in these plans I've just been given by the architect.'

Elsie handed Dr Gaskell his tea and he winked at her. 'Indeed. We're going to need lots of new staff. I was thinking to myself, er, while I was resting my eyes, do we have enough room in the doctors' accommodation and in the nurses' home, to take in the extras? We need a whole new firm of doctors and you would need to add a further ten nurses on to the next intake.'

'You know I love a challenge,' Matron said, unable to hide her excitement. 'Thank you, Elsie, I'll serve myself,' she added, aware that the hospital had its own ears and that news travelled fast. She waited for the baize door to swing shut and then, her eyes bright, said, 'I have had what I think is another one of my excellent ideas.'

Dr Gaskell bit into his buttered crumpet and with his mouth half full asked, 'Is it one of your more modest ones, too?'

'Stop,' she said, pouring her tea. 'Now, I have a question for you. If we had a Nurse of the Year award, who would you say should win it? Oh, and by the way, I am thinking of introducing such a thing.' She pointed to her chin with her napkin. 'You have butter on your chin,' she said.

He wiped his chin distractedly. 'Well, you know' – he leant forward and put his plate on the trolley – 'we had a special intake in Nurse Tanner's year. They were all so enthusiastic, not as stuffy as others, and one of those nurses has shone out to me – the nurse who specialed Dr Marcus.'

'Exactly.' Matron jabbed her teaspoon at him as she finished stirring her tea. 'You mean Nurse Brogan.'

'I do indeed. Why?'

'Because I have had a marvellous idea.' She looked sheepish. 'Even though I say so myself. I think we should try to repeat the success with Nurse Brogan times ten. Liverpool is an Irish Catholic city, as you know, and many of our patients come from the rural west. It has only just occurred to me what a huge bonus it would be if they could be looked after by nurses who shared their roots. I see that almost as a healing advantage – what do you think?'

'Well, I don't know how you intend to make that happen,' he replied. 'I don't think I have seen one application for a post from the west of Ireland since we interviewed Nurse Brogan.'

'I know, and isn't that a shame. You won't be surprised to hear that I have an answer for that.' She paused to make sure he was paying attention. He was. 'Let's go ourselves to check the place out. Make contact with a local employment agency and set up an exclusive arrangement whereby they send girls to us. What do you think?'

Dr Gaskell held out his cup for more tea, his brow furrowed. 'Well, I can't think of a reason why not. I have already told Nurse Brogan what an excellent nurse you thought Dr Marcus's young lady would make.'

Matron frowned. 'I did say that, and I meant it at the time, but I'm afraid moral standards are equally as important. I'm not sure we could have someone living in the nurses' home who had... well, you know.'

Dr Gaskell shook his head at her.

'Don't you give me that look,' she said. 'You know what I mean. Where would it end if I dropped my standards that far?'

'Matron' – he put on the voice he used when he was about to win an argument with her or get his own way – 'we both know that if a widow applied for a job and she was suitable, you'd take her on in a flash, because that's what you're like.'

'Yes, but—'

'There are no "yes, buts" about it. Now, I'm not saying this is something you should encourage, but in the case of Mary Kate, I think it's an exception to the rule that you could overlook.' He had won with very little effort and he knew it. Matron appeared chastened, but as he was only too well aware, there would be a price to pay.

'Well, I am going to go to Ireland and I insist you come with me. We leave this week.'

He almost spluttered his reply. 'I can't do that, I'm operating tomorrow.'

'Yes, I know,' she cut in, 'and by the evening you'll know if all has gone well. Assuming there haven't been any complications, your registrar can take over and deal with the list. After all, you're always saying that you should hand over more responsibility. I thought we could get the boat over early the following morning. I'm sure you'll be excited to know that I have already arranged accommodation and set up a meeting with a solicitor in Galway who will help me with introductions to an agency. If it goes well, you and I can report back to the board the following week.'

She began to pour herself more tea and he noted the look of triumph on her face.

'I can tell there's no point in my resisting this, is there? You want me there so that at the board meeting I can back you up.'

'Exactly. And now that you've had your nap and your tea, you can take a look at these plans with me. We'll need more than ten new nurses, I think. With the new clinic extension, it's going to be more like thirty. We have a great deal of work to do.'

Cat and Mrs O'Keefe had been in the village for a couple of days, but they still felt like royalty whenever they sat in the back of Michael's car. Right now he was driving them to the post office. Mary Kate was in the front next to her father.

'So, is it a custom around here then, Michael, that you have to call on everyone when you visit Tarabeg? Because, honest to God, if I have to drink another glass of whiskey, I don't think I'll be able to stand up.'

They'd just left Philomena O'Donnell's, and before that they'd spent half an hour sitting on the wooden chairs at the front of the butcher's, being plied with generous-sized glasses of whiskey from Paddy's bar at the rear.

Michael turned out onto the main street and laughed at Cat's question. 'Of course. If I don't introduce you to everyone before the dance, I'll be in fierce trouble. Isn't that right, Mary Kate?'

Mary Kate turned in her seat, smiled at Cat and reached across to squeeze Mrs O'Keefe's hand. 'I can't tell you how pleased I am that you came,' she said, for what must have been the fifth time in the last two days.

Mrs O'Keefe noticed that her eyes were misty. 'Oh, that's all right, my love. As I've said, it just didn't feel right, sending you back like that. And if the truth be known, we missed you the minute you left, didn't we, Cat?'

'Not half, and you should have heard Joan and Deidra. We've got a list of instructions, and my suitcase was half full of those parcels in the boot to post.' Cat gestured at the parcel shelf in the rear, which was piled high with packets from Joan and Deidra to be posted to their own families in the west. 'At least I've got a job to do when I'm in the post office. You can give me a hand, Mary Kate – the money's a bit funny over here.'

The car pulled up outside the post office, where a crowd had gathered. Women clutching shawls and baskets grinned aimlessly at the car as it came to a halt.

'Holy Mother of God, who are they all waiting for?'

'For you ladies,' Mary Kate said.

'The last time there was a crowd that big outside the post office was the day Joe arrived,' said Michael. 'Teresa Gallagher – she was still allowed to drive at that point – brought him down to show him off. That's Teresa on the sticks at the front. She's Father Jerry's housekeeper, you met her at the party. She'll be the one wanting to do the introductions. I should warn you, they will all be giving you messages to take back to Liverpool. They've no idea how big the place is. If I were you, I'd just write it all down and say you'll do your best.'

Cat opened her handbag in search of a pencil.

'I have to say,' said Mrs O'Keefe, 'Joe is a very nice young man. I had no idea he was so wealthy until Nola told me.'

'Aye, he's wealthy and he's just bought the Carter place to make him even wealthier.'

Mary Kate's head shot up as she turned to her father. 'And that is a disgrace,' she said.

Mrs O'Keefe was more pleased than alarmed at Mary Kate's reaction. It was a sign of passion, proof that Mary Kate was coming back to life, and what was more, it was raw anger, which she knew from experience was a phase she would have to pass through.

'Well, there's nothing to be done to stop him,' said Michael, taken aback by the venom in her words. 'A man is entitled to do as he wishes with his own money, and meself, I have no objection to his plan. He will bring more jobs and tourists to Tarabeg and that means more money. There's nothing wrong with that, Mary Kate.'

'Yes, there is,' Mary Kate fired back. 'The whole place will change. It won't be like Tarabeg any more. He's an oaf. A loud-mouthed show-off. He's despicable.'

'Oh no, Mary Kate, you have him all wrong. He is not. Nola and Seamus love him, as does everyone around here.'

'We don't need him or his money or his bloody tourists.' Mary Kate turned in the seat, folded her arms and glared at her father.

This was not the daughter that Michael knew. He stared ahead through the windscreen and raised his hand to Teresa and the woman standing next to her, and to Declan, who had called into the post office for his tobacco. The children were in the playground at the front of the school and Rosie was standing there with her tea in her hand, watching. Declan stopped and nodded at Michael and Mary Kate.

'That's Declan,' said Mary Kate over her shoulder to Cat and Mrs O'Keefe. 'He's my friend. A good man, not like big-mouth Joe.' She waved to him and he came over to the car.

'Good afternoon, ladies,' he said as he poked his head through the passenger window. 'We will be needing a hotel at this rate.'

Mary Kate looked horrified. 'Oh no, not you as well.'

She pressed the handle down on the door and almost pushed Declan over.

'Jesus, Mary Kate,' said Michael, struggling to contain his temper. 'You see Mrs McGinty there, next to Teresa, in the shawl with the big hole on the shoulder and the shoes with a rag tied over the front to hold them together? I think she might disagree with you. And the children who come down the hills from the farms and walk into school with no shoes on their feet – their mammies might have something to say too. There has to be more to life than scratching a meagre living from the land in the pouring rain, Mary Kate. Everyone should have the opportunity to work where they've grown up, close to their families, and not have to travel thousands of miles to earn a crust, do you not think?'

If Mary Kate agreed with a single word of her father's lecture, she did not show it. 'No, I do not,' she answered, her jaw set. 'I've told you what I think. 'Tis a disgrace and so is he. Who does he think he is – Lord Malone?'

Without waiting for a reply, she walked forward and was greeted by a rush of women around the car, all of them delighted to see her safely back home and keen to meet and talk to her visitors from Liverpool.

'I've no idea what's got into her,' said Michael apologetically to his passengers.

'I think we do,' said Mrs O'Keefe. 'I think she's come back too soon. It might not be the right thing for her, Michael.'

She placed her hand on the back of his seat, expecting a rebuke. But he simple stared at his daughter's retreating back. 'I'll do everything I can to keep her here – she's all I have of her mother,' he said. 'But I fear you may be wiser than me.'

When they finally made it to the post office door, Mrs Doyle sent Michael on his way as fast as she could. 'Keeva and Tig are waiting for you. They need for you to go and get your van and give them a lift to the long hall so they can take up one of the barrels ready for the dance at the end of the week.'

'Right, ladies, I'm off. Mary Kate, could you look after Cat and Mrs O'Keefe and walk them back to the shop. They're having tea with us, Rosie has it all sorted, and then I will run them back up to the farm.'

'Well, didn't you just pick a grand week to visit,' said Mrs Doyle as she clasped her hands together. 'And was it the dance in the long hall that brought you? Is it the talk of Liverpool now, is it?'

Cat looked confused. Mary Kate came to her rescue. 'Sure, I couldn't have picked a better time to come home, could I? Mrs Doyle, do you still make the best tea in Tarabeg?'

'Well now, why don't you come inside and try it and tell me for yourself,' she said.

They all turned as they heard a car horn beep and everyone began waving like a group of cheerleaders as Joe drove past in his car.

'Hello, Miss Gallagher,' he shouted out of the window as he slowed down. Joe had a soft spot for Teresa. She was the one who'd told him about his heritage and taken him to Daedio. If it hadn't been for her, he might have left Ireland without even making contact before the old man died. Teresa was his favourite and everyone knew it.

'Hello, Joe,' she shouted back.

'Will I be seeing you at the dance, Miss Gallagher?'

'No, Joe, you will not. I am long past the dance,' she said with a twinkling smile. 'I will be sat by my fireside with a cup of cocoa.'

'Now that sounds like a very inviting proposition,' he said.

'Have you met the new visitors?' she asked. 'You aren't the only one now, Joe. There are visitors all over. It seems Tarabeg is the place everyone wants to come to.' She took a few tentative steps towards the car.

'That's a fact. I don't think they'll stay as long as me though. Teresa, I want the first dance of the evening with yourself down at the long hall and no arguments. I'll take you in the car meself and I'll pick you up at seven. You've still a few days to look out your best frock and your high heels.'

Miss Gallagher blushed like a seventeen-year-old. 'Joe Malone, you are a card,' she said. 'May the good Lord forgive you.'

'Don't forget your glad rags now, or I'll be very disappointed.' He caught sight of Mary Kate glowering at him from the post office steps. 'Good afternoon to you too, Mary Kate,' he shouted.

Mary Kate narrowed her eyes. 'Good afternoon, Mr Malone. Have you bought any new hotels today? How about Paddy's shop and bar? I reckon he would sell it to you for a good price, and then you could turn it into one of those big American diners or something similar. Something else that will make Tarabeg unrecognisable and life here intolerable for everyone, and then we'll all move out. Isn't that what you want?'

Joe frowned, his feelings hurt. He chose not to reply. 'Stuck-up madam,' he hissed as he revved the engine, pulled out the choke and rolled away down the main street.

Mary Kate turned on her heel and marched into the post office, aware that her red boots were causing a stir all of their own.

'Now, now,' said Mrs O'Keefe as they walked in together. 'I can see that anger is bubbling up inside you, but it isn't Mr Malone's fault that your Nicholas died or that life is moving on. You must remember that.'

Mary Kate felt chastened and for a ha'penny would have run back down the steps. To where, she had no idea, but Tarabeg was not doing what she'd hoped it would. She felt far from settled, and Mrs O'Keefe was right, her grief was turning to anger – with God, and the world, but mostly towards Lavinia Marcus, the woman who'd caused her Nicholas so much pain. The woman plagued her nightmares, which had been all too frequent recently. She made Mary Kate feel emotions she didn't know she had.

Cat walked over to Teresa Gallagher. 'Get you, you have a date for the dance,' she said, grinning. She took Miss Gallagher by the arm and began helping her into the shop. Declan looked on, pausing in admiration as he watched Cat's easy charm with Father Jerry's housekeeper. He flashed Cat a big smile before he hurried back to the schoolyard. Cat caught it and threw her own smile back at him, over her shoulder.

The chatter in the post office was non-stop, the volley of questions thrown Cat's way unremitting.

'Did ye ever meet Father Doherty? He went out to Liverpool. From Ballycroy, he was.'

The questions came one after the other and Cat was dismayed that she had never met even one of the people she was asked about. Even so, she made a good job of giving the impression that she had. Mrs O'Keefe laughed when she heard her say, 'Oh, everyone knows the O'Sheays. They deliver our coal, and the milk, one of them runs the *Echo,* and they have the corner shop on the end of the Dock Road.'

'Go'way, they don't. Well, haven't they done well,' Mrs McGinty said.

Mrs O'Keefe dabbed at her eyes with a handkerchief, hiding her laughter. She had a much easier time of it as she was sitting next to Mrs Doyle herself, and after an hour there wasn't a thing she didn't know about Tarabeg and everyone who lived or had lived there, going back fifty years or more. She felt almost sorry when Mary Kate told them it was time to leave.

'We can't be late for Rosie,' said Mary Kate.

'Indeed not,' said Mrs O'Keefe, who was a paragon of good manners.

'And then we will see you up at the long hall, ladies, in a few days' time, will we?' asked Mrs Doyle.

'It would seem so,' said Mrs O'Keefe. 'It would be rude not to go. I'm not much good at the Irish dancing though.'

'Oh, don't you be worrying about that,' said Mrs McGinty. 'I can show you a dance or two, if me hip doesn't give in while I'm at it.'

One by one the voices stopped chattering as the women turned to see who had sent the bell jangling above the door.

'Hello,' the young woman said.

'Hello,' they replied as one.

'Would you be another visitor as well?' said Mrs Doyle. 'We'll be needing that hotel of Joe's sooner than he thinks. Are you looking for someone, dear?'

'I am. I'm looking for Mary Kate Marcus. I'm Dana, Dana Brogan, from Belmullet.'

No sooner had she blurted it out than Dana could have kicked herself for putting her foot in it and getting it wrong all over again. Mary Kate hadn't actually been married to that nice Dr Marcus, had she, so she wouldn't be Mary Kate Marcus, she'd still be plain old Mary Kate Malone. But it was too late now.

'Ah, the Brogan girl. You're the nurse, aren't you?' said Mrs Doyle. 'There's no one here by that name – Marcus is not a name from around these parts.'

Before Dana had time to correct herself, Mary Kate walked in from the back of the shop. The first person she saw was Dana. A look of delight crossed her face, to be quickly replaced by one of horror. 'No one knows,' she hissed into Dana's ear as she pulled her to one side.

'I'm afraid some of them do,' said Dana, 'and it's all my fault.'

Hunger had almost driven him out of the cave, and the pain in his leg, out of his mind. He had shuffled to the edge of the cave to catch the daylight and see if there were any boats leaving or returning, perhaps even the trawler heading out from Blacksod Bay into the deeper waters of the Atlantic. He had no idea of the time, felt disoriented and weak. He was close to the edge of despair.

When he heard footsteps sliding down the shingle towards him, however, he hid his relief well. It had to be Jay. No one else would have reason to descend the cliff at that point.

'Jesus, you look even worse than you did before,' said Jay. 'Do you want a drink? I only have cold tea.' He took a bottle out of his basket, unscrewed the top and held it to McGuffey's lips.

McGuffey pulled in long draughts of the welcome liquid and when he was sated pushed the bottle away and wiped his lips with the back of his hand. 'Did you bring food?'

Jay shrugged his backpack from his shoulders and let it slide to the ground with a thud. 'I did. I took some from Bee's cottage, up at the top. Here.' He passed McGuffey the bread and ham he'd taken; it was wrapped in one of Bee's cloths. 'I took the whole plateful, and the plate as well.' He grinned.

McGuffey couldn't manage to raise a smile. 'You should never leave any sign that you were there,' he said. 'Always cover your tracks. Be invisible. Let no one know you're about.'

'I'm as invisible as that feckin' ham is in her cottage now,' Jay replied. 'I've been thieving stuff all my life. Do you think I don't know that?'

'Do you have news?'

'I do.' Jay squatted down onto his haunches and grinned, displaying an uneven set of dark brown teeth interspersed with large gaps. He was keen to tell McGuffey his plan. 'There's a dance up at the long hall in a few days' time – on the full moon. I reckon that'll be the night I can get her, before she sets off. Everyone will be busy. If someone's collecting her, they might think she's already left.'

'Full moon's no good for us, you eejit.' McGuffey hawked and spat. 'Makes it too easy to spot us. And anyway, I need to get away soon – I can't survive here much longer. Did you get anything from the gypsies in Ballycroy for this?' He clutched at his thigh, as though to stop the pain in its tracks. It was so swollen, he'd had to rip his trouser leg up the side to free it.

'I did. Here.' Jay pulled a jar of murky-coloured liquid out of his pack and handed it over. 'But even they said you should go to Bridget McAndrew. She has the right spells for sickness in these parts and the best potions too.'

'I can't fecking do that, she would call the guard,' McGuffey replied through clenched teeth. The spasms had become more frequent and were lasting much longer. He rolled onto his side and groaned out loud, which sent a shiver through Jay. 'It's a doctor I need. They may have to take the leg off, which is why I have to get away. Did you get a motor and petrol?'

'I did. I took one from the back of a boat at Blacksod Bay. 'Tis on the top. I'll go back up and bring it here and then I'll be off and get the boat.'

Jay was relieved to get out of the dank, putrid-smelling cave. He clambered back up to the dip on the clifftop where he'd hidden the outboard motor, manoeuvred it into the crook of his arm and began the slow descent down the cliff-face once more. 'Feck this,' he muttered, repeatedly wiping the sloshes of petrol from his forearms as he half carried, half dragged the motor with him. 'I'm getting too old for this sort of malarkey.' He ignored the stink of petrol that trailed in his wake, pleased only to find that the engine felt lighter at the bottom than it had at the top. 'Must be fitter than I thought,' he muttered with a curl of his lip. Not that McGuffey would appreciate it.

He heaved the motor on to the floor of the cave, next to McGuffey. The air filled with the smell of petrol. He couldn't wait to be out of there again. 'I'll be back,' he said as he slung his bag across his shoulders. 'Where will ye be going in the boat? Maybe I'll be coming with you.'

'One of the islands off Scotland. I know people from when I fished over there. If I have the money, there are places I can hide and a doctor I can see.'

Jay mulled this over in his mind. He didn't much care for the Scottish. They had no truck with the Irish tinkers. 'I'll be the first person they come after when they notice the girl's gone. I'll have to come with you,' he said. 'We could buy our own bleeding island if we get enough money out of that rich American for the girl. Don't be going anywhere. I'll be back.'

McGuffey lay still. Even though he was in the cave, eventually, through a parting in the curtain of vegetation, he could see night falling. The sound of a car engine thundered on the unmade road above. Life was moving on, but down there in the cave he felt as though it was slowly slipping away from him.

'I've never seen you use this china before,' Peggy said to Rosie as they laid the table. Rosie had rushed back from school and got Peggy to help her lift down the wooden box of best china from the scullery shelf.

'I've not used it, Peggy, because we never have visitors. It's like a breath of fresh air has swept through this village with the ladies from Liverpool.'

'I think so too.' Peggy beamed. 'Mind you, 'twas the same when Joe arrived from America.'

'No, it wasn't really. He never came for tea, and wherever he went, the ladies went flocking, which was never in my kitchen.' She finished placing the side plates on the fresh cloth and stopped dead. 'Peggy, do you have a soft spot for Joe?'

Peggy flushed deep red. 'No, I do not. It's bloody Pete Shevlin who has my heart, but the bugger won't take it and he won't give me his back.' Tears welled up in her eyes as she folded her arms.

'Oh, Peggy, does he know?'

'Does he know? Could I have made it any more obvious?'

Rosie knew the entire village believed it was Joe that Peggy had a soft spot for.

'I'm going to give it one last go at the dance. I mean, what do I have to do, throw myself at him? If I have to be the one to ask him to dance, then so be it. I'll make a show of myself, but if it works, it will be worth it.'

Rosie walked to the other side of the table and put her arm around Peggy. She could remember only too well how it felt to love someone and not have that love returned. 'Ask him to dance if you have to, but when you do say something to him, you need to be completely unambiguous. You need to say, "Pete, I have a notion for you," and then see what he says. You will at least know one way or the other. Some men are terrible at this, you know.' She lifted a cake plate out of the wooden crate. 'I don't think Pete likes being a single man. I think he would love to have a wife and I wouldn't be surprised if he's been worshipping you from afar. I've seen the way he looks at you.'

Peggy's eyes lit up. 'Have you?'

'I certainly have and that's no word of a lie. The night Mary Kate came home, I watched him and he never took his eyes off you for a moment. Do as I say and let him know, Peggy. What have you got to lose?'

They both heard the chattering voices as Mary Kate approached the shop with her visitors.

'I'll do just that,' said Peggy. 'And if he says no, I'll throw myself in the Taramore and be done with it.'

Rosie had no time to reply as the door to the shop opened. At the front was Mary Kate and next to her a pretty young woman with short red curly hair and the brightest blue eyes. It was as easy as blinking to recognise a visitor who didn't live in Tarabeg, by their clothes alone. This young woman wore a smart camel coat, tied at the waist, a felt hat of the same colour, and black boots that looked crinkled and shone so brightly it was as if she'd walked through the deepest puddle on the way in.

'Holy Mother of God, another visitor?' said Peggy. 'We have none my entire lifetime and now they're coming so thick and fast, I can't keep up.'

Cat smiled. She liked Peggy and her impetuousness, the way every thought tumbled out of her mouth unchecked.

'Rosie, this is Dana Brogan,' said Mary Kate. 'Nurse Dana Brogan, I should say. She looked after Nicholas at the hospital and she's come to see me – isn't that just lovely. Her family are the Brogans from Belmullet.'

Rosie was surprised that Mary Kate had spoken about Nicholas in front of Peggy, who knew nothing about Mary Kate's real life in Liverpool, but she quickly recovered herself, ignoring the look of confusion on

Peggy's face and her blurted-out comment, 'Who is Nicholas? Nicholas who?'

To save Mary Kate from having to answer that, she said, 'Well, isn't it just grand to see you. Let me take your coat, Dana. Mary Kate, pull out a chair, would you. And, Peggy, set up for an extra guest, please.'

Rosie began to bustle about, excited and delighted to have a new visitor and yet more fresh things to talk about.

Dana began to untie the belt on her coat, looking slightly nervous. 'I am so sorry,' she said. 'I have the most awful confession to make.'

'You don't have anything to confess,' said Mary Kate. 'You are kindness itself, coming all this way.' Her lips wobbled and her eyes filled with tears. 'How did I ever think I could come here and not be able to talk about him?'

'You came because it was his dying wish,' said Mrs O'Keefe, who'd come and stood behind her. She stroked her hair as she placed a handkerchief in her hand. 'And that was why Cat and I took the decision to follow you, so that you could have someone to talk to. It was only when you left that we realised it was too much for you to bear alone.'

'I thought we were barking mad, just letting you leave like that,' said Cat.

'We just had to get out here after you, didn't we, Cat?' said Mrs O'Keefe.

Cat, who was standing next to Rosie, placed an arm around Rosie's shoulders and gave her a squeeze. 'We did, although, to be fair, we didn't know what a fantastic person Rosie was, did we?'

Rosie couldn't help herself as a spontaneous smile reached her eyes. 'I've tried my best,' she said. 'We all know the pain of losing someone, or the fear of it, which is almost as bad.'

'I bloody don't,' said Peggy, feeling rather grumpy and left out. 'Is someone going to tell me what's going on?'

Mary Kate couldn't resist a smile herself as she blew her nose. 'Yes, I am, Peggy. I was in love with the most wonderful man, who died. I lived with him as though he were my husband, because his wicked wife wouldn't divorce him, and I don't care who knows.' With her voice now firmer and stronger, she repeated her announcement. 'I really don't care who bloody knows and I have a mind to go straight to the presbytery and tell Father Jerry myself. He can do his worst. I don't care if the doors slam shut in my face when I enter the church. I don't care if no one in the village ever speaks to me again. My Nicholas will not be kept a secret. He was a good man and I am bloody proud of the love we had for each other, and if taking him from me was God's punishment for our being together, then I am bloody done with God. Dana, I am so glad you came today and said what you did.'

Peggy gasped and her hand flew to her mouth. 'Holy Mother of God,' she exclaimed. 'You lived with a man – *alone*? *As his wife*? But you haven't any children?'

Mary Kate sighed, feeling better than she had for days. 'I was a sinner not an idiot, Peggy.'

Peggy grabbed at the nearest chair and sat down. 'Does anyone know, apart from us?'

'Well, I think that's where I come in,' said Dana. 'I was such an eejit. I walked into the post office and asked for Mrs Marcus.'

The blood drained from Rosie's face. 'God in heaven. Did Nola leave any whiskey here the other night?' She blessed herself and made for the back door. 'Wait until your father hears about this. He may as well close the shop. I think we all need a drink now.'

Chapter 17

Mary Kate lit the lamp in the cottage and stood listening to the sound of Captain Bob's car as it drove along the cliff road towards Bee's, less than half a mile away. The cottage felt warm from the smouldering fire and smelt of peat smoke and memories. There was a hint in the air of another life having been coaxed from the walls; it was almost as if she had been there herself, during another time.

Captain Bob had opened the door for her. 'It's late,' he'd said. 'The excitement of the day has been enough for anyone.' The unspoken words 'especially someone recently bereaved' hung in the air.

'Daddy said he would call into Paddy's when he gets back from taking Dana to Belmullet,' said Mary Kate. 'Will you too?'

'Me, no. I'm away to collect Bee from Bridget's.

Bridget is teaching Bee all she needs to know to take over, should anything happen to her.'

Mary Kate was confused. 'But Bridget's always been here. I don't suppose she's likely to be going anywhere, is she? She's as fit as a fiddle.'

'Aye, true enough. Anyway, it's bed for me after Bridget's or it'll be my ghost out at sea tomorrow. I'm dead on my feet, so I am.' He slapped his hand to his head. 'Aargh, I'm so sorry.'

Mary Kate hadn't even noticed his slip. 'Oh, that's all right. Don't watch what you say on my account.'

'Don't worry about your da,' said Captain Bob. 'Rosie can more than handle him. She'll tell him that the secret is out, once she has him alone. She's always been able to cope with your father. She loved him even before your mammy did, you know. In all fairness to Rosie, she had no idea he was seeing Sarah at the time – your mammy was living here in this cottage, and Rosie was in the schoolteacher's house in the village. When Michael went off to war, Rosie waited for him to return, and he did, but not to her.'

Mary Kate looked at him for a long hard moment. 'I had no idea.'

'Aye, well, we don't speak of such things. 'Twas a bad business, all of it, but I can tell you this, the reason Rosie can manage your father when she tells him that the whole flaming village is alight with the gossip is because he loved Sarah just as you loved your Nicholas.

I can promise you this: he will understand. You have nothing to fear.'

Mary Kate looked out towards the dark ocean. The breaking of the waves on the shore provided the background to their conversation. 'Captain Bob, when you came back to Tarabeg from Liverpool, did you find it hard? As in, was it like you'd expected it to be?'

He studied her face, noted the bags beneath her eyes from not sleeping, and the loss reflected from them. 'If I'm honest, no. But then it doesn't matter to me where in the world I live, as long as Bee is with me. It's people not places that matter.'

His words hit home as realisation dawned. 'I feel so stupid,' she said. 'I raced back here to Tarabeg thinking that because it was what Nicholas had said he wanted, his last wishes, I should comply. I thought I had to be here because... oh I don't know, it sounds too stupid now, but I thought I would be healed from the pain of losing him and that maybe that was what he meant.'

'Mary Kate, there is nothing and nowhere in the world that can do that. I hope you don't mind me saying this, but the important thing is people, and those people may not be family. You can always come and see us, as often as you like, but the things you want from your life might not be available here in Tarabeg.'

Mary Kate looked into the face of the kindly Captain Bob and she understood why her Aunty Bee loved him so much.

He made his way to the car and before he climbed in he shouted back at her, 'I'm off out of Blacksod Bay tomorrow and over towards Scotland. I'll be gone a night or two but back in time for the dance. If I don't see you beforehand, I'll pick you up for the long hall at seven and then we are up to the farm to collect your ladies. Have you plans for the rest of the week?'

Mary Kate leant against the doorjamb and slipped her hands into her pockets. 'No, just more visiting and sitting in kitchens being plied with tea. Off to visit Ellen Carey tomorrow and then the usual round of the village. I would imagine that after today I'll be asked a million questions. Maybe Ellen won't even let me in.'

'Don't be daft.' Captain Bob laughed. 'She'll let you in just for the gossip – she won't be barring you from the tailor's shop until after she has it. Mind, she'll probably ask Father Jerry to step in and bless the place after you've left and wash the chair you sat on in holy water. Now get some sleep, will you.'

After waving him off, she'd stepped back inside and closed the door. The cottage was flooded with a warm glow from the now fiercely burning lamp and, just as every Irishwoman did on returning home, she went straight to the fire and made sure the embers were alight. Now that she'd moved in, she couldn't let them go out; if she did, the damp from the sea air would take hold and it would take another week to drive it out from the stone walls.

She looked around the cottage and her heart sank, but before she had a chance to dwell on thoughts of Nicholas, or Liverpool, there came the sound of a car driving along the cliff road. She flung open the door, thinking it was Captain Bob returned, but it wasn't Captain Bob, it was Declan.

Declan stepped out of the car, removed his cap and stood and looked at her, waiting for an acknowledgement from her in order that he would feel comfortable approaching. She raised her hand and waved him up.

'How are ye?' he asked as he reached her. 'I have the paint and I thought I would call up tomorrow, if that's all right with you?'

She stood back and opened the door wider. 'It is, and come in, I'll be glad of the company, Declan. I was about to put the kettle on the fire – will you stay for a drink?' It was obvious Declan hadn't called just to ask about the painting of the cottage; there was something on his mind and she could read him like an open book.

'Are you all right here?' he said as he stepped towards the pine table and pulled out a chair. 'They say it was where your grandmother was... well, where she passed away.'

'You mean where she was murdered?' Mary Kate sighed. 'I am. You know, I never knew her. I don't feel scared at all. If I had known her, I suppose it might have been different.'

'You've made a grand job turning the place around, so you have. It looks like it's always been lived in.' Declan cast his eyes around the cottage and admired the scrubbed and polished press and dresser, and the freshly beaten rug in front of the fire. But the wind howled through a gap in the roof and whistled around the room and the place didn't feel good to him. It was not somewhere he could live with any ease.

'To what do I owe the honour?' asked Mary Kate as she placed the mug down in front of him. 'I've no milk, sorry. Not until Daddy comes up tomorrow with a pail. If he does come, that is. I might not be in his good books once Rosie has spoken to him tonight.'

Declan, always a man of few words, nodded. 'You seem to have half of Liverpool following you to Tarabeg,' he said. 'I met the two ladies and they are grand people.'

Mary Kate blew the steam away from the top of her cup. 'They are, and they're staying until after the dance. They love the place. It's funny, Declan, you see, I'm the one who missed Tarabeg and wanted to come back, but... I'm not so sure any more.'

Declan didn't appear surprised to hear this.

Mary Kate peered into her cup of dark tea and lost herself in her thoughts.

'Your one, Cat, she's a nice lady,' said Declan. 'I saw her talking to Josie in the butcher's. She was telling me she has never been away from her children before, and I told her, "There's a classful across the road I can let you sit with if you're missing them that much."'

Mary Kate laughed out loud. 'I can tell you, your classful would be a lot easier for Cat to handle – all except for Debbie, that is, she's just a dote. Deidra and Joan will have aged ten years by the time she and Mrs O'Keefe get back, but it's nice they're staying for the dance anyway. Are you going to the dance, Declan?'

'I am now. I wasn't going to…'

He looked up at Mary Kate and, thinking she knew what he meant, her words rushed out.

'Declan, I'm not free. I love someone else, even though… he's no longer here…'

Declan nodded. 'I know, 'tis all over the village. Has been for days. There's not a one who's not convinced you were married and lost your husband, although no one knows why you kept it such a secret. When Dana Brogan came into the post office, she just confirmed it. It's nothing to me, Mary Kate. I'm sorry for your loss, but you're my friend and I hope I can count on you to help me.'

Mary Kate let out a sigh of relief. If the worst the village thought was that she had married and lost, it wasn't so bad. Being a widow was infinitely preferable to being a harlot.

'It's, er, Cat I'm here to ask about.' He kept his eyes fixed on his mug as his face flushed scarlet. The rest of his little speech tumbled out in a hurry. 'Do you think she'd be interested in a simple man like me, Mary Kate? And what would she make of my mammy? She's a one to handle and, God knows, I've been living the life of a priest thanks to her. Or is she used to much more sophistication over in Liverpool? I teach kids, kick a ball, fish and have the odd pint in Paddy's, but I'm true and fair and honest and I would be a good father to her children, a father they haven't got.'

Mary Kate placed her arm on his. 'Steady on, Declan, you don't even know her.'

He looked up at her, finally, and there was a new intensity in his gaze. 'I don't need to,' he said. 'I knew the second I laid eyes on her, and I think she knows too. There was like... oh, I don't know...a feeling, I suppose. I just know, Mary Kate. Is that possible?'

Mary Kate gave him a sad smile as the memories of the day she'd met Nicholas came flooding back. She remembered feeling exactly that, as she'd lain on the ground after she'd been mugged in Liverpool and opened her eyes to see Nicholas leaning over her. She knew precisely what Declan was talking about.

'Yes, that is possible. It happened to me with Nicholas.'

Declan wrung his cap in his hands and immediately seemed encouraged. He moved to the edge of his seat. 'But will you help me, Mary Kate? Could you see if she would be interested?'

Mary Kate sat back in her chair and surveyed him.

He could have been hers. Simple, he was; deep, some said. Bookish and kind. Cat could do a lot worse. 'Tell you what,' she said, 'why don't you just ask her for a dance at the long hall and take it from there. I'm sure she'll be delighted. And then if that fails, I'll have a word – if I'm still around.'

'What does that mean? You're not going anywhere now you're home, are you?'

Mary Kate sighed. 'Declan, Tarabeg is not for me. It was a mistake coming back. I can't live here.'

'Oh my – do Michael and Rosie know?'

'No, I'll tell them soon enough, maybe after the dance. I've only just decided, while I was talking to Captain Bob a bit earlier. I'm going to go back with Mrs O'Keefe and Cat. Coming home was a mistake. I wanted to step back in time, but no one can do that, it's not possible. Too much is changing, and I cannot stand Joe Malone and his hotel. I hate it. He has stolen Tarabeg from me.'

Declan looked surprised. 'That's a bit harsh, Mary Kate. He's going to be bringing jobs here for everyone.'

'Oh, not you as well! Everyone in the village is smitten with him. I thought you at least might be on my side.' She got up and went over to the fire. 'Declan, I hope Cat is for you, and I will help, but right now I have to go to my bed. I'm exhausted.'

Sleep, however, proved elusive. Mary Kate tossed and turned for a long while. At one point she thought she heard a noise outside the window. She knelt on the bed and looked out through the gap in the curtains. She remembered her mother telling her stories of smugglers during the war, working from this part of the coast. On the clifftop she thought she saw a shadowy figure, but then it was gone, as though it had fallen over the edge. Maybe the smuggling was still happening, she thought, and that made her feel safer, knowing there were others around, albeit under the cover of darkness.

Jay pushed the toe of his boot into McGuffey's side to wake him. McGuffey's hand flew to his gun as he shuffled up against the wall of the cave. Jay settled down on a sandy patch of floor. There was a ghastly smell – he'd noticed it as soon as he'd arrived – and it was coming from McGuffey's wound. His leg was even redder and more swollen than before, and there was some sort of discharge bubbling out of the wound. It stank and almost made Jay gag. 'Here,' he said, handing McGuffey a ribbed brown glass bottle. 'For the pain. One swig at a time.'

McGuffey only just managed to unscrew the top, then took a deep pull from the bottle. 'Where is she?' he asked.

'She's up there, in the cottage. She was brought back by Captain Bob. Then Declan from the school called in, but he's just left.'

'Do it now,' said McGuffey.

'What, take her now?'

'Yes. Do you have the twine?'

'I do. And I have this too.' He pulled another bottle out of his bag.

'What is that?'

'I don't know, but if I put it on a rag and hold it over her mouth, she'll pass out and it'll be as easy as stealing a baby.'

McGuffey almost laughed. 'Shona did enough of that,' he said.

'Shall I go back up now then?'

'Yes.' McGuffey was barely audible. 'I might not make it if we wait.'

'I've pulled the boat just inside. The motor's next to it and I have supplies in the boat.' Without another word, Jay grabbed the bottle, pulled a rag out of his bag, took one last look at McGuffey and ran out of the cave.

Michael and Dana chatted happily all the way back to Belmullet. 'So, how do you find living in Liverpool?' he asked. 'And a nurse, you are? Will you be coming back to Belmullet or staying over there?'

'Oh, I'll always come home to Belmullet,' said Dana. 'It's easy enough on the boat, and besides, it's a holiday for me, but I will never leave Liverpool now. I love nursing, I can't imagine ever giving it up.'

The road was straight and the night clear. Dana had stayed to eat with the Malones, at Rosie's insistence, and not another word had been mentioned about her faux pas in the post office. It was clear to Dana, however, that Michael had not been informed that Mary Kate's secret was out of the bag.

'You'll be wanting to come home at some point though, to marry a good Irish boy. That's a big farm your daddy has and he's not getting any younger.'

Dana averted her gaze and looked out of the window as she replied, keeping her tone even. 'Ah well, that won't be for me, I'm afraid, Mr Malone. If I marry at all, I will definitely settle in England.' And then she bit the bullet. 'Mary Kate would make a grand nurse, you know. Matron and Dr Gaskell, from the hospital, they were both impressed with her, and Dr Gaskell said that they would be very lucky indeed to have someone like Mary Kate training as a nurse at St Angelus.'

Michael laughed out loud. 'Mary Kate? She came home, Dana. In another week or so she will probably be wanting to help out in the store, and I'd be grateful for that. Like your daddy, I'm not getting any younger.'

She could hear his voice in her sleep, see his face, and his smile reached her heart. They were walking along the Cornish beach where they'd spent their idyllic holiday, she carrying her sandals as the wash of the waves lapped over her toes. He was calling her name, 'Mary Kate! Mary Kate!', but as she looked at his face it was full of horror and now he was shouting her name, running across the sand towards her, his arms outstretched. But he couldn't reach her and she couldn't move.

She sat bolt upright in bed, awoken from her dream, the nape of her neck damp, her heart beating rapidly. She shouted out his name, 'Nicholas! Nicholas!', but as she opened her eyes in the darkness it wasn't Nicholas in front of her and there was no time to scream for help. A hand was clamped over her mouth and the smell was unbearable, the panic wild as she fought and pushed and tried with all her might to yell out, but it was no use, the adrenaline coursing through her veins and the fight that had come from nowhere had now left her. Her last memories were of a gagging in her throat, an inability to breathe, a blackness descending, and her mother's face appearing over her, with tears running down her cheeks.

Chapter 18

Dr Gaskell and Matron were seated across the desk from the solicitor in Galway. Mr Keene had very quickly been made aware that, in Matron, he had met his match.

'And who would vet the applications?' Matron asked. 'Would that be yourself? Or would it be the agent who asks the girls to fill in the forms and gives them the necessary information about St Angelus and the role of a nurse and the duties expected of her?'

'Well, Matron—'

She had only stopped to draw breath, as he soon realised.

'And who will provide the girls with the details about the nurses' home and their rooms? And there are the exams too.' She turned to Dr Gaskell. 'We need to make sure they are all very much aware of what they are coming to. We don't want anyone arriving in Liverpool with the idea that training as a nurse at St Angelus is a holiday, now do we?'

'Oh, are you asking my opinion?' Dr Gaskell said with raised eyebrows.

Mr Keene gave him a rueful smile.

'You see, the problem is, Mr Keene, there is a shortage of nurses all over England, the hospital is expanding and we were so impressed with the last girl we took in from these parts, we thought this would be a good idea. But I am very concerned that we do get the right sort of girl. We maintain very high standards at St Angelus. Without standards there is only chaos.' Matron picked up the glass of water Mr Keene had poured for her and took a sip.

Mr Keene seized his opportunity. 'Matron, let me explain exactly how it will work,' he said, in a very firm tone. 'The agent will tour the villages along the Atlantic coast, further west than here, and he will display in the post office of each one an advertisement announcing his arrival. It will say that he will return on such a day between certain times. The postmistress or master will lay out a table and two chairs on the said day. Before him he will have all the details, as furnished by you, and then, when he has spoken to whoever has expressed an interest, he will ask the girl if she would like to submit an application form.'

'What are these villages like?' Matron asked. 'We can only take girls who have had a good schooling.'

Mr Keene thought of Rosie over at Tarabeg. Now there was an impressive schoolmistress, and someone Matron would have difficulty bossing around. 'Look, I'm about to visit a property a client of mine has bought over in that direction. It was a manor house and he's to convert it into a hotel. Why don't you join me? That way, I can introduce you to one of the schoolmistresses and you can see for yourself the sort of villages and homes the girls are coming from.'

Matron clapped her hands together. 'Gosh, I think that sounds like a very good idea, don't you, Dr Gaskell?' It had been a long time since she'd felt this excited about the future of the hospital. The shortage of applicants for nursing positions had begun to worry her and she'd lost count of the times she'd begun her day dreading the possibility that one or more nurses might be off sick. When they were short-staffed, standards were compromised.

Dr Gaskell had slipped so far down in his leather chair that if he'd sat there for very much longer, he'd have ended up on the floor. But now he straightened up. 'Are there any golf courses out here?' he asked, and was given a scolding look by Matron for his trouble. He had agreed to accompany her for the forty-eight hours she reckoned it would take to end her biggest administrative headache, but he didn't really want it to take any longer.

'Funny you should ask that,' said Mr Keene, rising to take his hat off the wooden hat stand, 'because that is exactly what my client intends to do with the old property he's bought. He would like to turn it into a hotel and golf course. However, I'm afraid you're a couple of years too early. Matron, shall we drop by your hotel first?'

Half an hour later, Matron and Dr Gaskell were sitting in Mr Keene's car, whizzing through the countryside on their way to Tarabeg, about to pay a surprise visit to Rosie.

Bee opened the cottage door to the smell of oatcakes cooking on the skillet and placed the basket of herbs she'd been collecting on the floor.

'I see you've started already,' Captain Bob said, nodding towards the basket.

'I'm under strict instructions,' said Bee. 'I have to collect them while they're still wet with the dew or they don't work as well. When are you leaving?'

'As soon as I've eaten these together with a good spread of Nola's butter.'

'Make sure you check the weather,' said Bee, 'and get back in plenty of time for the dance. We are on the sandwiches, you and I, and I don't know why but I have this funny feeling it's going to be eventful.'

Captain Bob placed his flat seaman's cap on his head with one hand, and with the other popped a hot oatcake into his mouth. 'Are you hearing things again?' he asked, grinning.

Bee walked over to the press and took down a cup. 'Not hearing as such, but, honestly, I was on the clifftop looking for mugwort and I felt very weird indeed. Someone was trying to say something, and if you asked me who, I would have said Sarah, but I couldn't tell what it was. I just don't feel good. You know, I'm not sure I like this, taking over from Bridget. Being the seer is a huge responsibility and I'm not seeing well enough to take it on anytime soon.'

Captain Bob did what he always did when he wasn't sure what words to use. He enfolded her in his arms and gave her a hug. They stood there together until she felt better.

'Right, Blacksod Bay here I come.' He tapped the top of his cap and shuffled his coat up his arms.

Bee walked over to the skillet and flipped a hot oatcake onto a plate. 'I called into Angela's cottage for Mary Kate to come here for her breakfast. We are off into the village this morning to take the Liverpool ladies to Ellen Carey's for tea.'

'So I hear,' he replied.

'The funny thing is, she's gone already, without me.'

'Really? That's not like her. Are you sure? Was the bike there?'

Bee poured herself some tea. 'It was. She must have set off fierce early for me to miss her.' She placed her hands on her hips as a thought struck her. 'Bob, did you remove the willow pole that Angela used for the curtain at Sarah's end of the cottage?'

'No. Why would I?'

Bee sat down at the table with her plate and cup. 'Oh, I don't know. You probably think I'm going mad, but someone's taken it. Along with Paddy's whiskey and Rosie's cake. I just think it's all a bit funny.'

'Aye, and you're forgetting the shawl on the night Aedan thought he saw someone, and the boat I saw down at the cove.'

'That was Angela's shawl,' said Bee. 'I've brought it here, it's in the chest. I thought that maybe it was one just like it, from over on the islands, one that someone had dropped.'

There was silence for a moment, and then they both spoke together. 'It was Angela's.'

Their eyes met and they both felt the change of atmosphere in the cottage. Only Bee knew it was because Angela had joined them.

'What shall we do?' said Captain Bob. 'What do you think it all means?'

Bee looked up at him and the fear in her own eyes was reflected in his. 'I think it can only mean one thing

– McGuffey's back.' Her eyes filled with tears and her hands began to shake. 'God in heaven, he can't be, not after all this time, can he? I'm so scared, Bob, scared that if I lay eyes on him, I'll kill him meself.'

She was back in his arms before she could say another word.

'I suggest you ask Bridget, when she arrives. If anyone knows, she will, and if anyone can do something about it, it's you two, and Father Jerry. Between you, you're stronger than him. How old is he now anyway? He must be into his sixties, and besides, the rumours are that he was working with the IRA. He won't be back over here.'

It didn't matter how much he tried to reassure her, they were both aware that this time his words didn't work. They knew he was wrong and in their hearts they could both sense there was trouble ahead.

Nola had already turfed the men out of the house to work and was left with Cat and Mrs O'Keefe, who insisted on helping her clear up after breakfast. 'Stop, would you, I have all day to be doing this once you've gone off on your visits.'

'You don't fool me,' said Mrs O'Keefe. 'The bread doesn't bake itself nor the butter churn if you shout instructions to it down the path, and I've seen the mound of washing waiting to be done in the tin bath on the back step. Why don't we stay here and help you for a day? We can meet Ellen Carey later this afternoon. I would love to just stay here on the hill with you. To be brutally honest, Nola, there's only so much whiskey I can drink in a morning – although I'm getting better at it and that's a fact.'

Nola looked confused. 'But you are on your holidays, and Michael's on his way here for ye.'

'Well, we will tell him when he gets here that he doesn't have to be our chauffeur. Let us stay and then you can get your jobs done in half the time and if Michael wants to come back for us later when Paddy opens, he can take us all down the hill for a little tipple. That way, we can see Rosie when she finishes school, and if I know Mary Kate, she'll be coming up here to join us.'

Nola sat back down in her seat and dabbed at her eyes with her apron. 'It's so nice having you here,' she said. 'I miss the company during the day. It can be lonely around here since Daedio died – not that he was any help, the useless eejit.'

Mrs O'Keefe laughed. 'Good, that's settled. I'm going to fetch myself one of your aprons out of the scullery.' As she passed through the scullery door, she bumped into Cat, who was having a cigarette on the back step, taking in the view.

'Fill your lungs with that,' said Cat. 'Isn't it marvellous.'

'You've changed your tune,' said Mrs O'Keefe. 'At the beginning of the week you were complaining about it hurting your nose and missing the smell of the gasworks. I've rearranged our plans for today – me and you, we don't have to answer a hundred questions this morning, we can stay here and help Nola, and to be honest, I'm looking forward to it.' She reached up onto the shelf in the scullery and pulled down two aprons. 'Catch,' she said as she threw one to Cat.

Cat grinned from ear to ear. 'Oh thank God.' She ground out the cigarette with the toe of her shoe. 'That's more like it. Let's get stuck in.'

Bridget arrived at Bee's on her bicycle, carrying her own basket of herbs on the handlebars. 'Are you ready to start work?' she shouted as she walked through the door.

Bee was sitting at the table looking solemn. 'Have you seen Mary Kate?' she asked. 'Only she's not in Angela's cottage, no car has been up here yet and Michael said he would be collecting her, and the cottage door was wide open. Bridget, I have a very bad feeling. Something's wrong. Is it him, is he back? It hasn't felt like this around here since last time he was here.'

'Feck, I haven't even got my headscarf off yet,' said Bridget as she untied the knot. 'Bee, look into your own heart – are the spirits trying to speak to you? What are they saying?'

Bee's eyes filled with tears.

Bridget knew the answer was there, but she had to coax Bee into acknowledging it. She took Bee's cold hand in her own. 'Yes, he's been back in these parts for a few days. I saw Shona's caravan coming into Tarabeg, with Jay driving, in my crystal ball. Of course, Father Jerry thought he was telling me great things when he heard the news from one of the tramps a few days later – I didn't bother to enlighten him. There is only one reason why Jay would be back and that would be if McGuffey told him to be here.'

'What are we going to do?' asked Bee. 'Is Mary Kate safe in Angela's cottage?'

'I don't know. There's only one person who'd know the answer to that question. We need to call up Annie. Angela has never come to me, but now that you're in training to be a seer she may come to you, as she's your sister. Between them, we'll find out the answers.'

Teresa Gallagher opened her front door to the sound of the bells calling her to Mass. She pulled on her gloves and secured her hatpin, then made to retrieve her sticks, which would be leaning against the wall, left there for her by Father Jerry on his way down to early Mass. In recent years, she'd not been able to make first Mass herself, finding the mornings harder; so she attended the second Mass, after school had started, along with the young mothers, something she secretly enjoyed.

'Shall I walk with you, Teresa?' Keeva's voice called out from the bottom of the drive.

Unbeknown to Teresa, Father Jerry had asked Keeva to call for her and walk her down. He'd become more worried about her of late and had noticed her wobbling as she crossed the road the previous day.

'Good morning, Keeva. I'm quite capable of walking myself, thank you.'

Despite the frosty greeting, Keeva remained exactly where she was. Teresa tutted to herself and turned to close the door. A note had been stuck half in and half out of the letterbox, its corner caught by the brass knocker, the rest flapping in the wind. 'Well, what do we have here?' she said as she pulled it free, the corner ripping on the knocker.

Keeva folded her arms and looked back down towards the church and the village women coming out of their doors and rushing along the road to make the last bell. Each one would have raced to finish one final domestic chore before they tore off their aprons, replaced them with coats and shawls, and slammed the door behind them. 'Teresa, come on, would you,' she shouted as she turned around. 'I'm not going without you.'

But Teresa was no longer standing; she had slowly slid down onto a pot of winter pansies and her face had turned the colour of the sheet of paper she was holding in her hands. 'Keeva, get Father Jerry,' she said.

'I can't,' said Keeva as she unlatched the gate and ran up the path. 'Mass is about to start.'

Teresa gripped the sides of the pot and pushed herself up. 'Help me,' she said, 'this is serious. Mary Kate has been kidnapped and whoever it is, he wants money from American Joe before he will let us have her back.'

Mary Kate had woken on a hard floor, in darkness. As she tried to move her hands, she could immediately tell they were bound, and so were her ankles. She was in her nightclothes and seemed to have only one boot on. She lay on her back and blinked into the dark. Her instinct was to scream, but instead she froze, her throat thick and dry. There was an astringent smell that made her eyes water. It reminded her of St Angelus and Nicholas. She had dreamt of him for the first time and as she woke, her heart was full of him, as though he was with her, could see her. She half expected to hear his voice. What had she dreamt? She searched her mind, trying desperately to recall the details, and they came at her in a rush: her velvet ribbon, her emerald heart.

'Every time you feel this velvet ribbon against your skin, it is my touch, and I am there with you.'

Tears ran down her face. Lavinia Marcus, evil woman that she was, had stolen her velvet ribbon, had taken from her the most precious gift Nicholas had given her. As she lay there, bound and gagged, her heart filled with a hate and rage that threatened to choke her, a hate stronger than that which she felt for her kidnapper. She no longer cared if she died. What did it matter? She had nothing left, not even the one thing that most reminded her of him, her velvet ribbon.

She heard a noise and turned her head. Here was another smell too, the smell of something dead, of rotting flesh, of fear. She couldn't see her kidnapper, but she could hear his voice.

'You awake now, are you?' the man said.

She blinked, tried to move her tongue, to make her mouth work, but nothing happened.

'I can tell you are – I've done this before,' the man said. 'I'm your granddaddy.' There was a yelp of pain and then silence.

Eventually her voice obeyed her. She managed to push the tape away from her top lip, using her tongue and stretching her mouth, and she croaked in a thick rasp, 'Hello? Hello? Who is there, please? Who is it? What do you want me for?'

She began to weep as her emotions pushed through the barrier of fear. Her granddaddy was Seamus. That man was not Seamus.

She stopped breathing as she heard the sound of the waves beating against the rocks and the screech of the birds overhead. She knew those sounds; she was close to home, she had to be. 'Hello,' she croaked again. But there was no reply, only the stench of putrid flesh.

Chapter 19

Michael arrived at Bee's and found her and Bridget boiling herbs on the stove. 'Is Mary Kate with you?' he shouted from the doorway.

Bee dried her hands on a tea towel and walked towards him. 'No. Is she not with you?'

Michael looked confused. 'Not at all. The arrangement was for me to pick her up first and then collect Cat and Mrs O'Keefe before taking them all to Ellen Carey's for a visit.'

'I went for her earlier to see if she wanted to have her breakfast with us, but the cottage door was already open and she was gone. I thought she must be with you.'

Michael took off his cap and rubbed his head. 'Well, there is only one place she could be. She must have taken herself off up the hill to Mammy's. She probably decided to have breakfast with the ladies.' He shook his head and sighed. 'You know, don't you, that thanks to Dana Brogan, everyone in the entire village thinks she was married in Liverpool and has come home a widow.'

Bee hadn't known that, but it didn't surprise her. Stories took on a life of their own in Tarabeg, they were all aware of that.

'I know Dana meant well,' Michael continued, 'but everyone is now asking me why was it such a secret and I have no answers. Has she said anything about coming back to work in the shop, Bee? The sooner things get back to normal, the better.'

'No, Michael, she hasn't. But do you really think Mary Kate will want to work in the shop?'

'Of course she would. She hates the idea of Joe's hotel, so what else is she going to do? I'll be off to Mammy's then – you never know, I might get a second breakfast for my troubles.' Without waiting for a reply, he lifted his cap in the air, waved them goodbye and strode back down the incline towards his car.

Bridget came and stood next to Bee as they both watched him leave.

'She isn't at Nola's, is she?' Bee said.

'No, she isn't,' Bridget replied.

'Holy Mother of God, where is she?'

'I wish I knew, but I can feel her energy; she isn't far away. Annie is fretting and she has brought it to me. Wherever she is, she cannot have gone far.'

★

Father Jerry could tell that something was wrong the moment Teresa and Keeva walked into church. During communion, instead of taking the Host, Keeva slipped him a note. Once communion was over, much to the surprise of the congregation, he went straight to the dismissal in a matter of seconds. There was much confusion in the church as a result.

'Are ye feeling all right, Father?' asked Philomena, who made straight for the altar. Because her own son was a priest, she saw herself as being on the highest social rung in the village, second only to Father Jerry himself, much to the annoyance of many.

'Oh, get lost, Philomena,' said Keeva, in a way she'd never spoken to anyone before in her life. She pushed past her. 'Father, come on, we have to find Michael. Get your vestments off and your car out.'

'And I'm coming too,' said Teresa in a tone Father Jerry knew only too well and would not dare argue with.

Cat had received a note herself that morning, placed on the doorstep by one of the children. He'd been intercepted by Joe on his way out to the fields.

'What do we have here?' Joe asked as he held his hand out to the child. The boy obediently picked up the letter and passed it over. Joe immediately acknowledged the hunger in the boy's eyes, his cold, white face and threadbare coat, his clothes held together by patches of mismatched darning. 'Nola, have we something to give this young man for his troubles?' he shouted. He scanned the envelope and saw that it was addressed to Cat. 'Cat, it's the mail boy for you,' he yelled.

'Mail boy? What in God's name is that?' said Nola as she came to the doorway with a dishcloth in her hand. 'Oh, 'tis you, Malachy,' she said to the boy. 'Have you had your breakfast? Come on in, get some bread and rashers to eat on your way down to school.'

The boy grinned and, knowing Nola's kitchen almost as well as his own, ran to the table.

Mrs O'Keefe, who'd heard Nola's invitation, was already cutting the bread. 'There you go, young fella,' she said, handing him two soft white slices, still warm from the oven, and a thick rasher of bacon dripping with fat sandwiched in between. 'I expect you to get all your catechisms right today.'

Malachy grinned at Mrs O'Keefe, displaying a row of yellow teeth, and, taking the unexpected breakfast, ran out of the door, shouting, 'Thank you, missus.'

Joe, curious, hovered by the door, tying his laces and glancing up as Cat opened the letter. They had built a rapport over the past few days and he liked her very much, just not in the way he'd have wished. He watched her back as she retreated from the door, distracted by the envelope addressed to her in a bold script, head bent, legs bare, flat slingback shoes scuffing the floor. She removed the letter as she reached the table, and a smile spread across her face.

'Who is it from?' Mrs O'Keefe asked, surprised that anyone would be writing to Cat. Joan and Deidra back in Liverpool had the telephone number for the post office and Cat had already phoned the house twice to speak to them and check that the children were behaving themselves.

Cat folded the letter in half and laid it on the table in front of her. She looked up at Mrs O'Keefe and grinned. 'I've been asked on a date,' she said.

'What? With who?' Mrs O'Keefe dried the breadknife she'd just rinsed, laid it back on the breadboard, came round to Cat's side of the table and sat down.

On the step, Nola was talking to the men as they loaded up the cart.

'It's from the schoolteacher, Declan. He's asked can he walk me to the dance. Said he's bought two tickets and would I have one and be his date for the evening.'

'Who asked you that?' Nola shut the door behind her, blocking out both Joe and the wintery sunlight, and came to Cat's side.

'Declan.'

'Oh, would you look at that face.' Nola turned to Mrs O'Keefe. 'It's all written there, isn't it. It happens like that when it's meant to. That smile, as God may be my judge, is a forever smile. You can tell in an instant.'

Cat had no time to respond as the door flew open and in walked Michael. 'Is Mary Kate already here?' he asked.

The three women turned to look at him. 'Not at all,' said Nola. 'How could she be? You were supposed to be bringing her up to us. Did you not go and collect her from Angela's cottage?'

'Yes, of course I did, but she wasn't there.'

'Well what kind of eejit are you? She will have been having her breakfast with Bee.'

Michael snapped back at Nola, something he rarely did. 'I went straight to Bee's and she wasn't there either. Bee said that Mary Kate's door was open when she herself had called in for her, but she'd already left. I can't find her anywhere.'

'Right.' Nola unfastened her apron. 'There'll be no more bread baked here today. Hats on, ladies. Michael, let's get down to the village. Fetch Joe and tell him to bring his car too, and tell Seamus and Pete to come with him. I feel it in my bones, this is trouble.'

As they approached the village, Nola's prediction sprouted legs sooner than even she could have anticipated. Just as Michael was turning the car out onto the main road from the bottom of the boreen, Father

Jerry almost ran headlong into them. Michael slammed on the brakes and jumped out from behind the wheel. 'What's your hurry, Father?' he asked.

Father Jerry leant on the car with one hand and caught his breath. 'My car's in Murphy's stable or I would have been here quicker. Go and fetch American Joe, there's trouble. Teresa is beside herself. I've told her not to call the guard, we can't take the risk.'

'Father, what are you on about? Joe's already on the way down, with Seamus and Pete. Mary Kate has gone missing, Father – was she at Mass?'

'The guard?' said Nola as she opened the passenger door.

Michael took the letter Father Jerry held out to him. As he read it, his world shifted beneath his feet. His eyes met Father Jerry's and although he tried to speak, he couldn't on account of the bile that filled his mouth.

'No, she was not, but we have this. Read it, would you, Nola.'

Michael's hand was trembling as he held out the dirt-stained letter for Nola to take.

Cat's face was pressed up against the back window. 'I've no idea what's going on out there,' she said to Mrs O'Keefe, 'but whatever is in that letter has made Nola mad.'

Mrs O'Keefe was staring straight ahead, through the front windscreen. 'Yes, and Michael isn't too happy, either.'

Cat swivelled her head round and saw Michael vomiting on the side of the boreen. She almost fell out of the car as Nola jerked open the door.

'Move over, ladies, let me in beside you. Father, get in the front and come with us,' she shouted in a tone that it would have been futile to resist. 'Michael, pull yerself together, this is an emergency. Get in the car and drive.'

Michael stood, wiped the back of his mouth with his hand and, white-faced, returned to the driver's seat. Everyone was silent as the car turned into the village: Cat too scared to ask for any further information, and Mrs O'Keefe too concerned. The only words spoken were from Michael to Father Jerry. 'It's back, Father. The curse.'

The only acknowledgement Father Jerry gave was to close his eyes, and he remained like that until Michael brought the car to a screeching halt in front of the post office. Michael missed Mr Keene by only inches as the solicitor held open his car door for Matron to alight.

Her eyes had adjusted to the gloom, and although she could not see him clearly, just a grey form on the floor, she knew he was there by the smell, which appeared to be getting worse by the hour.

He could sense she was looking at him and he turned his head to face her. Through the last few hours there'd been times when he'd been too terrified to move, because of the ghosts. He'd seen Angela, the wife he'd murdered, standing there close to Mary Kate, with their daughter Sarah by her side. Mary Kate had lain whimpering, and a man had come to join them, running his transparent fingers over her hair and face as if to try and comfort her. McGuffey thought he must be delirious with the fever. They didn't look his way – it was as if he was the one who was invisible – and he barely blinked for the fear of them, until the ghosts slipped back into the wall of the cave and he and Mary Kate were alone once more. It was only then that he found the courage to speak as she cried out to him.

'Why do you want me?' she mumbled.

He forced his response, his eyes darting, searching the dark for more unwanted visitors. 'Quiet. We'll be gone and they'll be here for you soon, before tonight. Stop your crying. You aren't here for long.'

He could speak no more than a few words at a time. All of his focus had to be on fighting the pain and staying alive. He kept slipping in and out of consciousness. Only his mind could save him from what he knew was his fate; if he gave in to the fire coursing through his veins and the pain that had rendered him almost unable to think straight, he would no longer be in the cave in earthly form but trapped amongst the ghosts that were hovering and whispering his name, faceless in the shadows.

Jay scuttled in from under the curtain of vegetation, clicked on his torch and jumped back as his beam lit the terrified face of Mary Kate; it was as though he'd forgotten she was there. McGuffey jolted into consciousness again and his hand automatically reached for his gun.

Jay grinned at the sight of Mary Kate's obvious distress and then, ignoring her, he dropped to his haunches at the side of McGuffey. 'They have the letter. I hid behind one of the graves to watch after I put it on the door. Running about like fecking headless chickens, so they were.'

Mary Kate, her eyes open and petrified, groaned.

'Shut yer mouth,' he hissed, then turned back to McGuffey. 'They won't call the guard, not after what you wrote in that letter.' He winked.

McGuffey pulled himself up against the wall. 'Did you get anything for the pain?'

'No, I couldn't. But for the love of Jesus, the smell from your leg.' Jay placed his hand over his mouth and wretched.

'Is she all right?' McGuffey nodded towards Mary Kate.

'What do you care? There'll be a thousand pounds sat on Sarah Malone's grave at midnight tonight and then we'll be away. She can stay as she is until then. You aren't going soft on me, are you?'

McGuffey winced and wondered was he going mad

himself. He had never cared for another individual in his life. His childhood beatings at the hands of a violent and drunken father had made sure of that, and yet now, here, with death stalking him from the shadows, he felt confused. 'She has my blood running through her veins. It's different. Take the tape off her mouth and give her a drink.'

Jay took a step backwards. 'Do it yourself. She's money to us, nothing else. I don't give a shite if she's your granddaughter.'

McGuffey raised his gun. 'I may be in pain, but there is nothing wrong with my aim. Take the gag off her.'

Jay was about to protest but thought better of it. 'I don't need you now – I can take the money and run,' he spat.

'Do that,' said McGuffey, 'and when they do find her, I'll tell the guard it was you all along, that you kidnapped us both. I'll make sure you're locked up and the key is thrown away. You have no training in survival, you won't last five minutes.'

Jay hesitated, looked towards the entrance to the cave, bent swiftly, held Mary Kate by the hair and ripped off the tape.

She didn't make a sound, just turned her head and looked into McGuffey's eyes.

'Don't speak,' said McGuffey, laying his gun across his lap. 'I won't think twice about using this if you do. Sit up.'

She pushed her elbows into the floor and tried to heave herself up. 'I can't,' she croaked. 'My hands are tied.'

'Untie her hands,' said McGuffey.

'Are you fecking mad?' Jay almost shouted through clenched teeth.

'No, I'm not. Her feet are still tied, she won't be going anywhere, and I'll watch her.' His fingers clenched the barrel of his gun.

Jay dropped to his haunches and undid the rope behind Mary Kate's back.

She breathed deeply, fighting an overwhelming urge to scream. She knew she was in grave danger and had to weigh both her words and actions very carefully.

McGuffey held out the whiskey bottle to Jay. 'Give her this.' He turned his gaze directly on her. 'Can you speak?'

Mary Kate nodded, her eyes darting around the cave, searching to see how Jay got in and out. There was no obvious opening. She took the whiskey, but her hands were weak and she almost dropped the bottle.

'Help her,' barked McGuffey.

Jay looked daggers at him but did as he'd ordered and bent down and held the bottle to her lips.

She immediately began to cough and splutter and seized the opportunity to speak. 'Why am I here? Let me go, please,' she gasped.

McGuffey appeared not to hear her. His eyes were

closed as he swigged on the whiskey. Jay answered for him. 'We've left a note for your fancy American to pay us a ransom. He will leave the money tonight and then we will be off and living the life of lords. No one will find us.'

'How will they know where I am?'

'Because we'll leave a note in your own cottage telling them, that's how. I'm not a fecking eejit. Now shut up. If I'm to be up all night getting your granddaddy into a boat, I need my sleep.' He shuffled over to the wall of the cave, sat against it and failed to hear Mary Kate's response.

'My granddaddy?' She turned her head towards McGuffey. The only granddaddy she knew was Seamus. She'd only ever met a brick wall when she asked about her mother's family. Bee very occasionally spoke to her about her mother, but on the subject of Angela she never got a satisfactory reply. 'Oh, you don't want to be knowing about the past,' Bee often said. 'No good will come from it, and besides, I never wanted her to marry him anyway. Nasty man, he was.'

Mary Kate couldn't take her eyes from his face. Her granddaddy? He was unshaven, dirty and in pain, and his face was gaunt, with large bags under his eyes, but in the line of his jaw and the blueness of his eyes, which had reflected the torchlight, she could believe that he was. Despite everything, she no longer felt scared. He was her family. Surely he would protect her.

Chapter 20

They had stopped off at a small hotel in Castlebar, which was where Matron had tasted her first Guinness. 'I don't think it will be replacing the sherry in the sideboard any time soon,' she'd said to Dr Gaskell, wrinkling her nose in distaste.

'Elsie might object if it did,' he replied, taking a long draught from his own pot.

Matron had spent her evening writing out a list of questions for potential applicants to leave with the post offices along the way and had even designed her own posters. 'What do you think?' she said as she held one up for him to inspect.

Dr Gaskell removed his reading glasses from his jacket pocket and, leaning forward, squinted at the poster. 'I think you've spelt "probationary" wrong,' he said.

A look of horror crossed her face. 'Never,' she said as she turned the poster around and examined it herself. 'That's not spelt wrong, that is how you spell "probationary".'

He grinned at her and took another sip of his drink.

'Oh, you beast. Honestly! I'm going to tell your wife what a meanie you've been when we get back.'

Dr Gaskell studied her as she packed away her poster. It was doing her good to be away from St Angelus, and the prospect of finding a ready supply of new nurses willing to be trained and moulded to her own high standards had delighted her so much, there was a youthful glow to her cheeks.

'Are you happy for Mr Keene to organise the initial selection of probationers from over here?' he asked. 'I know you, you don't like to lose control of anything, but that is one thing you won't be able to do, unless you want to be hopping back and forth on the boat every five minutes, and I can't see you doing that. Once you've made your mind up, that'll have to be it. You'll have to put your trust in Mr Keene. He's a professional himself and he won't take kindly to you issuing him with instructions over the phone every five minutes.'

'What a thing to say.' Matron pushed her glass of Guinness to one side and folded her elbows on the table as she leant forward. 'Why do you think I've asked him to be responsible for the first sift of potentials only? The final interview will still have to take place at St Angelus. Can you imagine me trying to recruit without the board having a look-in? I don't have full control as it is – that assumption is a myth. I'm not a tyrant, Dr Gaskell.'

He was about to point out that by introducing this process, she was in fact controlling the quality of applicants who were put before the board, but they both knew that was what excited her so much about this. With the help of Mr Keene, she really would remain in control.

'Ah, good evening,' said Mr Keene, walking towards them with a pot of very dark liquid in his hands, which Matron now recognised as Guinness. 'I have good news.' He pulled out the chair next to Dr Gaskell. 'I have spoken to the postmistress in Tarabeg this evening, a Mrs Doyle. She is very excited at the prospect of our visit. She said they get a lot of visitors these days in Tarabeg. We will call in there on our way to Belmullet, and that will cover the area, more or less. I imagine you will be spoilt for choice, Matron. I have been to Tarabeg a few times, because of the property I told you about. It's a very quiet little village and the people are extremely friendly, honest and hardworking. Nothing of any note ever happens there. I'm very sure you'll have a good supply of young ladies wanting to hop over on the boat to Liverpool and take up a nursing career. Indeed, they will be so used to hard work, it will seem like a holiday to them.'

'Tarabeg? That was where Mary Kate, the young lady Nicholas Marcus was with, came from,' said Dr Gaskell.

'Excellent. Well then,' said Matron, 'it sounds perfect. Despite the circumstances, which we won't go into right now, Mary Kate was a very well put-together young lady, and she made such an impact on everyone in the ward. This is all going to be just marvellous. Now, can I tempt either of you to a glass of sherry?'

Mrs Doyle ran down the steps of the post office to greet the car. 'Mr Keene, is it?'

Mr Keene looked about him in confusion and an embarrassed Mrs Doyle answered his unspoken question.

'I have no idea what is occurring here today,' she said as Matron stepped out of the car. 'The place has gone mad.'

She scanned the gathered crowd and the women who were hurrying out of their cottages and tying their shawls as they trotted towards the post office. News travelled fast in Tarabeg and Mrs Doyle was usually the main source. It appeared as though the entire village had come out into the main street within mere minutes. She saw Philomena leave the front door of the butcher's and stop Ellen Carey, both turning to look at her, aghast.

'I thought you said it was a quiet village?' Matron said to Mr Keene, who was removing his driving gloves.

'It is – it was. Something is obviously very wrong.'

Joe's car pulled up with Pete and Seamus as passengers, and Michael leapt out of his car and ran over. 'We need a plan, we cannot call the guard,' he said as he handed the letter to Seamus.

Rosie popped up by his side. The villagers were huddling in a tight circle around Michael 'What's up?' she asked. 'Miss Gallagher came to the school and told me about the letter. This has to be some kind of sick joke, doesn't it?'

The letter was passed from one person to the next to read. The visitors watched on as the tension mounted palpably. They were largely ignored, much to Mrs Doyle's discomfort, who'd been rather hoping they would be treated like royalty upon their arrival.

Declan had heard the commotion and had followed Rosie out of the schoolroom and up the main street. He'd left Teresa in charge of fifty children, who he knew would by now be anticipating an early playtime. He ran over to stand at Joe's side and read the letter. As he did, he caught Cat's eye in the back of Michael's car and, despite the noise and bustle, held her gaze and smiled. She seemed to be fishing in her handbag on her lap for something. A few moments later, she held up his note from earlier that morning, grinned like she was about sixteen years old, blushed, nodded and mouthed the words, 'Yes. Thank you.'

Declan felt the blood rushing to his face as he grinned back. He was quickly brought down to earth by Joe.

'We need to organise search parties,' Joe said, and then, spotting Mr Keene, he shouted over, 'Mr Keene, what on earth are you doing here?'

Mr Keene was at his side in a few strides. 'I'm accompanying a hospital matron from Liverpool, helping her recruit new nurses from the villages. You seem to have a bit of a problem?'

'I do that,' said Joe. 'Someone has kidnapped Michael Malone's daughter and they've demanded that I leave a thousand pounds on the grave of her mother at midnight before we can have her back. The note says that if we call the guard, she'll be murdered in cold blood.'

Michael joined in. 'And it's signed by a man we know has murdered before – Kevin McGuffey, my father-in-law. He ran away after he murdered my mother-in-law, Angela, and he hasn't been seen since. They say he went to join the IRA.'

Seamus had earlier shouted for Paddy to get his gun. Keeva had answered his call and now came running out of the butcher's carrying the shotgun, followed by Tig.

'A gun,' squealed Matron, and the village women, who'd been talking amongst themselves, clustered round her.

''Tis a terrible thing,' said Philomena to Matron, not waiting for an introduction. 'My son is a priest and he says the Devil himself walks up and down this street when the fancy takes him.'

Matron held out her hand, her mouth open. Keeva joined them and pushed Philomena to one side. 'Don't be putting the lady off visiting us now, Philomena. Hello, I'm Keeva. Take no notice of Philomena, she was a friend of Angela's and she never recovered from the murder.' Her voiced dropped to a whisper as she looked about her to see had she been heard. 'Ghastly, it was. Not one of us slept for weeks in case he came for us in our beds. Anyway, hello, and a hundred thousand welcomes to you.' She grinned from ear to ear. 'We have become a tourist hotspot, or so Peggy says. Ah, here she is now. Peggy, we have more visitors.'

Peggy, at the sight of Pete Shevlin arriving in the back of Joe's car, had abandoned the shop and joined the rest of them. She'd already been told about the letter by Teresa, before she'd gone on up to the school.

''Tis a terrible thing, Keeva,' said Peggy, and to Matron, 'Hello, missus, how are you.' Matron's mouth opened and closed, but before she could reply, Peggy continued. 'Are ye staying up at the farm or passing through?'

Having recovered from being addressed as 'missus', Matron seized her moment. 'What exactly has happened?' she asked.

Peggy spoke to Matron as though she'd known her all of her life. 'Mary Kate has been stolen by her own grandfather, and he wants money before he will give her back, and it's a bit of a worry because the man's an evil murderer who sups with the Devil and fights with the IRA. He will be no stranger to murder so he won't.'

Matron's face turned pale as her blood pressure fell into her boots. 'Mr Keene, this is not the sort of place I imagined you were bringing me to. A grandfather has stolen his granddaughter for money? I think this may have been a terrible mistake.'

'Hang on a moment,' said Dr Gaskell, prising himself with some difficulty out of the back of the car. 'Do you mean Mary Kate Malone who has just returned from Liverpool?'

At the sight of Dr Gaskell, Cat and Mrs O'Keefe pushed open their car doors, and in doing so immediately answered his question. 'What on earth is going on?' said Mrs O'Keefe. 'That's Dr Gaskell and the matron from St Angelus.'

Dr Gaskell raised his hat to her but had no time to answer, as Joe took charge. 'Right, everyone, stop talking, please, now. QUIET! We all know what has happened, and we know why. This man that some of you know, Kevin McGuffey, has taken Mary Kate Malone and he wants money before he will give her back. I will get the money, and if by midnight tonight we haven't found her, I will do as he asks, but as God is my judge, I will be waiting for him. Right now, we need to organise ourselves into search parties – not to find Mary Kate, no one must approach this dangerous man, but to look for clues as to where he may have taken her. Mrs Doyle, I am taking over your post office as a headquarters until this is over. This is where we will operate from. If any of you see something untoward, you must return straight back here to let us know immediately. Seamus, I want you to remain in the post office and write down any and every bit of information brought to you.'

Joe looked over at Michael and Rosie. They appeared to be in their own world. Michael, with his arm around Rosie's shoulders, looked as though he was about to explode, whereas Rosie, normally so in control, was white-faced and trembling.

'I cannot say this loud enough: do not, I repeat, do not go anywhere near that man. Do you understand? Michael, you take Rosie back to the shop and stay with her. We will keep you informed of everything that happens.'

It was apparent from the expression on Michael's face that this would not be happening. 'I will not! I will search every corner of this village for my daughter.'

Joe didn't argue. With the arrival of Mr Keene, they had four cars between them, and that would be crucial in getting people about. He looked down on the sea of upturned faces: women wearing widow's weeds and men with brooding eyes peering back up at him from under the rims of their oversized caps. They were a motley bunch, but they were all he had to work with.

'Mr Keene, can we use your car please?'

Mr Keene touched his hat. 'You most certainly can. I am happy to drive. However, my advice is that, despite the instructions in the letter, you call the guard and you, er, lose the guns.'

'We will talk about that later,' said Joe.

As volunteers for the search parties put up their hands and split off into four groups, Mrs Doyle turned her attention to Matron and Dr Gaskell. 'Come along inside and let's get a cup of tea in you – you look very peaky,' she said to Matron.

'You go along inside with the postmistress,' said Dr Gaskell. 'I'll go with Mr Keene and see if I can help in any way. This appears to be a village in crisis.'

Peggy and Keeva ran in ahead of Mrs Doyle. 'Don't you be worrying, Mrs Doyle, we'll take care of everyone here,' said Peggy. 'Rosie has gone to fetch more milk and tea. She won't be staying in the shop with all this going on.'

Matron allowed herself to be led by the arm into the back of the post office, where Keeva pulled out a high-backed wooden chair. She was clutching her poster in its homemade cardboard wallet to her chest. 'I think I've made a terrible mistake,' were the only words she said for some time.

*

Bridget and Bee had slipped off their shoes and rolled up their skirts, tucked the hems into their knickers and, with lobster pots hanging from their arms, were combing the shore and the rock pools for seaweed.

'Holy Mother, 'tis freezing,' said Bee.

'Don't I know it,' said Bridget. 'I've used the last batch today and that leg ulcer of Nola's isn't going to heal itself, so I need fresh supplies. You can come with me tomorrow and I'll show you how it works in practice.'

Bee had been amazed at how quickly Nola's ulcer had improved, despite her ignoring the advice to rest her leg.

Half an hour later, Bee's basket was as heavy as she could carry and she began to make her way back to the shore. The sky was cloudless and deceptively bright, the cold wind having robbed the sun of its warmth. She pulled her shawl around her as she stood on the hard, wet sand and looked up at Angela's cottage on the cliff for any sign of Mary Kate. There was none. She had a bad feeling. Her blood had run cold in her veins all day and it wasn't just because of the weather. She had heard the whisperings and they disturbed her. No matter how hard she strained to hear and make sense of the ghostly voices, she couldn't make out what it was they were trying to tell her.

Turning back to the ocean, she watched as Bridget, standing knee high in the shimmering water, lifted out her last clump of seaweed and hauled it into her pot. Bridget waved to indicate that she was returning to shore and Bee waved back then walked to the rock where she'd left her shoes and stockings. She sat down to wait for her.

'My feet are so cold, they're numb,' Bridget said as she waded over.

'Have we enough seaweed now?' asked Bee.

'We have. We'll let it dry out and then I'll grind it to a powder. It's great for wet wounds. The dried seaweed absorbs the nasty pus and fluid and also has magic healing. The ulcer turns red at the edges and gets a bit smaller each day. Only the seaweed can do that.'

'I've seen it on Nola's leg,' said Bee. ''Tis a miracle.'

'Aye, and one you are about to learn how to make happen.' It was as Bridget stood up from fastening her boot that she stopped dead.

'What?' asked Bee. 'What's the matter?'

Bridget's eyes narrowed. 'Look, over there, at the foot of the cliff.'

Bee turned to follow her gaze just as Joe's car pulled up beside the path to the door of Angela's cottage. He jumped out of the car and began frantically waving his arms at them. Bridget felt the words coming at her before she heard them. She knew exactly what had happened before Joe could tell her, and she knew what she had to do next. She dropped the lobster pot onto the sand.

'Bee, over there, that red boot at the foot of the cliff, it's Mary Kate's, isn't it?'

Bee placed her splayed hand over her eyes. 'Aye, it looks like it. What's it doing there? 'Tis just the one. She wouldn't have took them off and only put one back on. Bridget...' Bee turned and put her hand on Bridget's arm. The whispers became clear to her for the first time. 'It's him – McGuffey. Mary Kate's in trouble.' Her nails dug into Bridget's arm.

'Shh,' said Bridget. 'Don't worry. She is in danger, but we are here now.'

They both looked up at Joe and Bridget waved him down to the shore. 'Joe isn't here waving like a madman to talk about his new hotel,' she said. 'He knows. Come on, let's go and meet him.'

'Shall we fetch the boot?' said Bee.

Bridget saw Joe almost slipping on the shingle as he raced down the cliff. 'No. Leave it to Joe. He'll know what to do.'

Chapter 21

If she drank any more tea, Matron thought to herself, she would float out of the door. She was flanked by Cat on one side and Mrs O'Keefe on the other.

'You could have knocked me down with a feather when I saw you get out of that car, Matron,' said Mrs O'Keefe.

'I didn't feel too stable myself,' said Matron. She looked around the post office in bemusement; it was filled to the door with women talking and she wondered how was it they found so much to say. 'Why are you here?' she asked them both. 'Is it something to do with the Malone girl?'

Cat lowered her voice and leant forward. 'We came to see was Mary Kate all right. They have very strict ways over here. Very prim and proper, they are.'

'As am I,' said Matron in a flash.

'Ah, yes,' Mrs O'Keefe interjected, 'but you, Matron, are also a woman of the world. You made allowances for Mary Kate because you knew she was in an impossible position. The same allowances wouldn't have been made here. They are the loveliest people, but they are most definitely not people of the world.'

She winked at Matron, who furrowed her brow. No woman had ever winked at Matron. She was a woman who made probationers tremble in their shoes and porters flee to the sides of corridors like cockroaches avoiding daylight when she approached. She pulled her posters tighter to her chest and sighed. 'Dr Gaskell has been concerned about her too. There's something about that girl – I could tell as soon as I laid eyes on her. We both think she would make an excellent nurse, once she's through her period of grieving. That's why we're here, in fact, on the lookout for girls like her, and like Nurse Brogan. They seem to be of a type, and we're having such trouble recruiting. Girls get married so young and then they leave and have families. I wonder sometimes how it is we'll be able to staff our wards.'

Cat was now right on the edge of her seat. 'I think she'd make a good nurse too. It's not just because she was so good with Dr Marcus when he was dying – she was lovely to all the patients on the ward, they all loved her.'

Matron's expression softened. 'Quite. I don't mind

telling you, though, I never thought to find her in this situation – having been kidnapped!'

Peggy approached them carrying a wooden tray. 'A drink, missus?' she said as she held the tray out to Matron.

Mrs O'Keefe saw Matron's back stiffen at the 'missus' and would have laughed herself if she'd not been so desperately worried about Mary Kate's disappearance.

'Er, what is it?' Matron managed.

''Tis a glass of whiskey, for the shock. We all need it. Keeva just fetched it over from Paddy's bar. We get that many visitors around here these days and go through that much of the stuff, don't we, Keeva?' she shouted over her shoulder to Keeva, who was setting down her own trayful of small glasses on the post office counter.

Mrs O'Keefe reached up and took one. 'Slainte,' she said. 'Oh, don't worry, Matron, it's amazing how quickly you get used to this. We have it in our tea at breakfast up at the farm. On our second day here, I thought I wouldn't make it through a third, but now I'm loving it.'

Matron watched in amazement as Mrs O'Keefe emptied a third of the glass in one mouthful. Holding her own glass to her nose, she smelt it, then took the smallest sip. She coughed, her eyes watered, and she sipped again. 'You live on the same avenue as the Marcuses, don't you? I remember you saying so in my office, on the night Dr Marcus died.' She took another sip and Cat saw the colour flood to the base of her throat.

'I do. I'm on the other side and a bit further down. I get the feeling Mary Kate misses it.'

Matron's head swivelled to face her. 'I can assure you she's been in the right place, here in Tarabeg. Or at least I would have thought so, had she not been kidnapped. Dr William is being hounded, the poor man. Lavinia Marcus has been back to the house and showing potential buyers around herself and she visits the practice nearly every day on some excuse or another. She sold her husband's desk out from under Dr William's feet, and I mean that almost literally. Had a man with a cart waiting outside. The agent hadn't been able to sell the house and so she came back to take over. One of my ward sisters bumped into her in town. I have to say, I don't believe the story about the agent, I think she came back to Liverpool to taunt Miss Malone. I think she was almost frustrated to find her gone.'

Mrs O'Keefe gasped. 'What a wicked woman. Can you believe that?'

'I'm afraid I can. Having dealt with her throughout that very sad time, I can tell you I would believe that and worse.'

The post office door opened and in walked Dr Gaskell with Tig, Paddy and Father Jerry.

'Did you find her, Father?' asked Mrs Doyle before the door had closed.

Father Jerry shook his head. 'We didn't, Mrs Doyle, and it's hard to believe that it is already afternoon.'

The women stopped talking and the sound of rosary beads clicking filled the silence.

'Is he a doctor?' someone whispered.

'He is. From Liverpool,' said Mrs Doyle, preening herself, proud to have such a prestigious visitor in her post office.

'Come here and have yourselves a sandwich,' said Keeva to Dr Gaskell. 'Peggy and I have made enough to feed an army.'

Mrs Doyle tutted. 'That girl, she wouldn't stand on ceremony to the Pope if he walked through the door.'

'She should have at least bent her knee,' Philomena whispered back. 'The cheek of her.'

Dr Gaskell's face lit up at the sight of the plate Keeva was proffering. He had never seen ham sliced that thick, and it smelt so good. In her other hand she held a glass of whiskey. He heard Matron's polite cough and ignored it entirely. 'Now then, Matron, just the one,' he said. 'It would be rude to refuse, and what's more, Mrs Gaskell doesn't need to know.' He smiled at Keeva as he took the glass.

'That'll warm you back up,' said Keeva. 'And besides, the missus has had two of her own, haven't you, missus?'

Dr Gaskell almost showered Keeva with the whiskey he'd sipped; he bit into the sandwich to prevent himself from laughing out loud as Matron's cheeks glowed red with indignation.

Bee, Bridget and Joe stood around the table in Angela's cottage staring at the red leather boot with its faux grey leopardskin lining. Pete Shevlin picked it up and looked at the underside. 'I doubt there'll be a route map on the sole,' said Joe. 'Who lives up here, Bee? The boot hasn't appeared out of nowhere. Which cottages are empty? We need to start searching them. Pete, have you a gun?'

Pete shook his head but held up his shillelagh. 'No, but I have my fighting stick. No one will get near me with this, and it can do fierce damage to a man's legs if need be.'

Joe picked up the stick, which had been made from a knotty length of blackthorn, and looked at it doubtfully. 'Do they teach you this at school?' he asked before handing it back. He turned his attention to Bee. 'Has this happened before, Bee? Only I thought this place was a one-horse town but today it feels more like downtown Chicago. Who lives out here?'

'Only us, Bob and me, and Mary Kate's been staying here since she came back. She's supposed to be living here permanently, but as God is my judge, I can't see that happening. What used to be the bar and the other fishermen's cottages are all empty now. There's my in-laws' cottage, the nearest to us, close to the cliff, but it's been empty since they died, more than five years now.'

They all jumped at the sound of a car engine outside. Joe ran to the door and held the gun ready but dropped it when he saw it was Captain Bob.

Captain Bob raced into the cottage, made straight for Bee and hugged her to him. 'I got someone to stand in for me,' he said in answer to the question perched on her lips. He'd left for work hours ago.

'I've only just heard myself, from Joe,' she said.

He could tell she had yet to absorb the full impact of the news and was struggling. He turned and saw that Bridget was sitting by the fire, clearly in a contemplative mood. He didn't need to ask what she was doing. Her lips were moving, but no sound came out. She was communing and it was not a process he felt inclined to disturb. In Tarabeg, the dead often had more answers than the living.

'The news is spreading up the coast,' he said, and, turning to Joe, he added, 'What can I do? Do we have any ideas?'

Joe held up the boot. 'Found at the bottom of the cliff.'

Captain Bob took it from Joe's hand and turned it over. 'It is hers,' he said. 'She was wearing these boots the night she came home. Not the kind of boots you'd be able to buy in Mayo.'

Bee walked down towards the end of the cottage, to where Mary Kate's bed stood against the wall. She turned back to the men. 'Bob, do you think there's a funny smell down here?'

He followed her and sniffed the air. 'There is,' he said. 'Like antiseptic, although not as strong.'

Bee bent over the bed and pressed her hands on the rumpled bed sheets, allowing her weight to sink into the mattress as it creaked and groaned beneath her. The blanket was in a tangle and the pillow had disappeared. She took a deep breath and in a choked voice said, 'Even Mary Kate wouldn't leave her bed unmade like this for the whole day.'

Still sniffing the air, Captain Bob dropped to his knees and looked under the bed. He pulled out the discarded pillow and sniffed that too. 'My guess is Mary Kate was taken from here.'

She had fallen asleep almost as if instructed, after Jay had given her her last drink of water, pulled her to her feet and taken her to the corner of the cave to relieve herself. Her abdomen had been distended and the pain had kept her awake for hours.

'Turn away while she goes,' she heard her granddaddy say from the other part of the cave.

'I'm not an animal,' Jay had replied. And then, in a lower voice, to her, 'You can't get away, so don't try. I'll move meself over a bit – you go just there.' He stepped back and was swallowed by the dark in an instant.

It hurt her to urinate and she felt faint from the effort. She tried to see but could only make out the uneven wall against which she pressed her hand to balance herself, and the dark sandy floor.

He took her arm to guide her back. 'None of us will be in here for much longer,' he said. 'Drink this.'

She held the cup to her lips and drank the water he held out to her.

'Now sleep, until it's time,' he said, and added, 'I will be, with a bit of help from this.' The whiskey bottle appeared before her face. 'Want some?' he mocked.

She shook her head and he laughed as he pushed her back onto the floor.

'We're going to be on the run for a few days and I need me sleep. I'm tying her hands back up,' he said.

Without him even asking, she extended her hands in front of her, pushing her wrists outwards to give herself some room. It worked. He was too impatient to notice. She could sense a new agitation in his voice and was glad when he moved away from her. She listened to his every movement; he was seven steps further into the cave before she heard him flop onto the floor.

'Here, drink this,' he said, she assumed to the grandfather she had only seen and heard in the darkness of the cave, but there was no reply.

Even though she fought to stay awake, a strange tiredness overcame her too and, lulled by the soporific beating of the waves against the shore, she fell into yet another deep sleep.

She awoke what must have been hours later, with her face in the direction of where she'd seen Jay enter and leave the cave and from where she caught the occasional whiff of fresh air. The rotting smell that surrounded her was overpowering. She strained her ears to hear every breath that was not her own, every cough and wince of pain from the man who'd told her he was her granddaddy. The panic rose in her chest and threatened to choke her as she shook off the half sleep and was once again fully aware of where she was and who she was with. She took deep breaths, and, closing her eyes, placed herself back in her home, with Nicholas, in the avenue.

'Nicholas...' She whispered his name, imagined her arm linked in his as they walked around the lake in the park, her holding Jet's lead as the mischievous dog trotted beside them, sensing their happiness, content. She pictured them sitting listening to the band on a warm Sunday afternoon as Jet dozed across her feet and Nicholas held one of her hands in his lap, using both of his. If she tried hard enough, she could imagine he was lying next to her and that if she just reached out her hand, she would touch him.

Her eyes opened wide. There was a noise, a crack – like a whip. No, it was a stone, a voice, a man's voice.

She pushed herself up onto her side; raised up like that, she could smell the whiskey fumes coming off Jay and filling the air. His chest rumbled in his stupor. She held her breath; there was no other noise, but she could hear voices out on the beach.

If she shouted out, she would alert her captors, but if she stayed quiet, how would she ever be found? She tried to shuffle along on her side, starting first with her bound feet, moving one heel and then the next a few inches to the side. She lifted her backside, and, finally, her shoulders followed. She had moved maybe four inches; she was yards from the entrance. Tears of frustration filled her eyes. Admonishing herself for being feeble, she did it again. Grit on the hard stone floor pierced her elbows like needles but she made not a sound.

Listening hard to see had she been heard, she was met by a black void of silence. She held her breath, blinked. His breathing had gone quiet. There was no constant gnashing of teeth or terrifying screams of pain. She focused her hearing; she was right. The loud whiskey-snores were coming from one man – Jay. She lifted her feet again and followed the same routine: another few inches. *Three moves, one foot; three feet, one yard*. She steeled herself for the next painful shuffle. *Not far to freedom*, she told herself: *ten yards, the entrance*.

The voices sounded closer now. Suppressing every instinct to scream out, she moved another few inches and stopped to listen again. There was nothing other than the rumble of Jay's breathing. She moved again. *Three moves*, she counted to herself. And then again. The voices were louder. *Four moves*. She could make one of them out. *Five*. There was a woman's voice. *Six*. It was Bee. And then another. *Seven. Bridget*. Yes, it was Bridget. *Eight*.

She was out of breath. How could she be? And then the voices moved away. They were retreating, becoming fainter not louder. She almost screamed out, 'No, don't go! Wait! Come back!' She lifted her ankles and moved once more, *nine*, and she almost gasped as she saw a long line of daylight on the cave floor. She was out of breath because she was moving up an incline. She could see the entrance; she was closer. She moved again, *ten*, and then she stopped dead, mid movement, as his voice pierced the darkness and made her blood run cold.

'I have my gun on you. Don't you make a sound.'

Chapter 22

'It's as if someone has died in here,' said Peggy to Keeva as they manned their station behind the table, slapping butter on overly thick slices of bread. Loaves were being baked by villagers to feed the search parties and were arriving into the post office still warm.

Peggy had voiced Keeva's inner fears and she immediately became distressed. She placed her hands over her eyes and pressed them hard. 'I can't bear to think about it,' she said. 'I've known her since the minute she was born. Sarah was like my sister. I just can't bear to think of it.'

'Stop.' Peggy took hold of one of Keeva's hands and pulled it down. 'I spoke to Pete as they took off up the hill. He said there's no way McGuffey will harm her because he's after the money. He said Joe will leave a note saying he can have the money but he has to hand over Mary Kate in return. He may be rich as Croesus, Joe, but he has brains too.'

Keeva took her handkerchief from the pocket of her skirt and began to dab at her eyes. 'I know, McGuffey is evil and it's money he's after, it always was.'

'Aye, true enough, and that's what'll keep her safe. Come on, look, we've made enough sandwiches to feed an army – Paddy will be running out of ham at this rate and will have to move on to cheese.' Peggy flopped a slice of bread onto the board in front of Keeva and changed the subject. 'What do you make of the doctor and the Matron. She's a funny one, isn't she?'

Keeva looked up and over to the chair where Matron had been sitting for the best part of four hours, back straight, smile stiff, always polite. 'Aye, she is. Mrs Doyle says she runs a big hospital, and those two ladies from Liverpool told me she knows Mary Kate.'

Peggy stopped mid slice with her knife in the air. A lump of butter splatted onto the wooden table. 'How in God's name does she know her? Did Mary Kate meet everyone in Liverpool when she was there? I mean, when I asked her had she seen the Conomys, she said she hadn't, and yet everyone coming here seems to have met her.'

Keeva clapped a slice of bread on top of a thick slice of ham. 'I don't know, Peggy, but I do know this: she went through a tough time in Liverpool, and when this is over, she won't be staying here with us. I think there is something to what she says, you know – the change, the hotel coming and all. The visitors, that solicitor, and even Mrs Doyle putting up advertisements to recruit nurses for Liverpool. Would you look at her.'

They both looked to the post office window, where Mrs Doyle was standing on the stepladder. Matron had joined her and was holding it for her. 'Be careful now,' she said as Mrs Doyle climbed the steps to fix the poster to the window.

'Don't let me go now, Matron, will you,' said Mrs Doyle. 'Mind you, I'm in the right place if I do fall down, with you and the doctor here.' She laughed out loud.

Peggy and Keeva looked at each other in astonishment. They had never heard Mrs Doyle laugh out loud before. 'See what I mean,' said Keeva. 'Mary Kate has been kidnapped, everyone is running around like headless chickens, Mrs Doyle is laughing like a kettle. It's all changing and there's nothing we can do about it. I reckon you have to be here to go along with it, you know.'

Peggy had no chance to respond as the post office door almost banged open and in strode Joe, carrying a boot. The stepladder rocked back and forth and Mrs Doyle held on for all she was worth. 'Holy Mother of God,' she yelled as Matron almost threw herself onto the ladder to steady it.

'That's Mary Kate's boot he's holding,' said Keeva, the colour draining from her face.

The crowd of waiting women, which had thinned out since earlier in the day, gathered around Joe and peered at the boot as though it were the Holy Grail.

'Find Michael, someone,' Joe said. 'We all need to head out to the shore. He took her from the cottage and it's unlikely he brought her back here, into the village. We're all looking in the wrong place. Bridget said she's close to the shore and I'm not going to argue with Bridget.'

The murmur of voices rose to a crescendo then halted as Father Jerry walked in. 'Everyone needs refuelling, so they're heading back here for food and drink, Mrs Doyle,' he said. 'There's nothing to be seen or heard of her anywhere.'

Behind him, the returning search parties began to arrive in the main street and make their way towards the post office.

'Right, let's get these sandwiches out there and on the counter,' said Keeva.

Matron approached them. 'Can I help, ladies? We are very used to dealing with crises at St Angelus – I'll help with the drinks, shall I.'

She was already rolling up her sleeves and Keeva knew it was a statement not a question. 'Well, if you don't mind, Matron. Most of this lot will wait to be served.' She nodded towards the older women in widow's weeds who were now examining the boot as though it was an exhibit from outer space.

'One of them told me she's borne thirteen children,' said Matron. 'I think they've done their bit. Here, let me carry those teas, Peggy.'

Peggy grinned. She liked Matron – she liked anyone from outside of Tarabeg. 'Thank you, Matron. It seems to me they won't be stopping searching until midnight and we're going to be busy. She could be anywhere out there.'

'Yes, well, I am very sure she is out there somewhere, and that young man, Joe, appears to be both in charge and fearless. You're very lucky he's here.'

Up at the farm, Nola and Seamus stood looking at the wall above the fireplace.

'We can't let Joe pay the ransom when we have all this money of Daedio's behind the fire,' said Seamus, placing his hand against the limewashed chimney breast.

''Tis up to Michael. It's his decision, he's her father, he has to decide,' said Nola.

Seamus removed his cap, a rare event, and then his jacket. He laid his jacket over the back of the rocking chair next to the fire and as he did so, it began to rock back and forth. They both stared at it, and both knew what it meant. Annie was with them. Daedio had slept in the kitchen for years before his death and had told them that Annie often came to talk to him at night, when they were all in bed.

Nola stretched out her arm and slipped her plump hand into Seamus's calloused palm. 'Annie agrees with me. Daedio always said that Annie would give us a sign when it was time to do what was needed with the money, didn't he?'

The rocking continued, steady.

'If Annie didn't want us to do this, she'd be rocking that chair like a madwoman was sat in it.'

They both stared at the chair as the rocking continued, back and forth.

'Come on, this is a sign – we knew it would come one day. It's Mary Kate's money, isn't it, Annie? And Finn's too. There is plenty to pay McGuffey, and it will be worth every penny if it means he leaves these shores and never shows his evil face back here again.'

Turning from the chair, Nola placed her fingers alongside the brick that gave them access to the safe in the wall, made by Annie many years ago. She began to wiggle it free. 'It needs a bit of strength behind it,' she said. 'Come here, Seamus, pull it free. 'Tis that long since it was opened.'

Seamus prised the brick away with very little effort and, placing his hand inside, removed the first roll of green dollars.

'How many dollars are there in that one?' asked Nola.

'The same as in the next one. Five hundred. Teresa Gallagher counted them out with Daedio when they checked them.'

Nola took the roll between her finger and thumb and examined it. 'Get the lot out,' she said.

Seamus's eyes popped wide open. 'The lot? I'm not even sure how much that all comes to. It hasn't been counted since long before Daedio died.'

'I don't care.' She threw the roll onto the kitchen table. 'It's time they saw the light of day.'

Half an hour later, they were both sitting on chairs around the kitchen table and staring at the pyramid of dollar notes in front of them. Nola's eyes met Seamus's over the top.

'What do you think it would buy, Seamus?'

Seamus scratched his head. 'I wouldn't be knowing. What do you need?'

'Me, I don't need nothing other than to get Mary Kate back and see McGuffey gone for good. And when that happens, which it will, we'll bring her up here and tell her to take what she needs and get herself away to wherever she wants to be.'

Seamus practically felt his chin hitting the wooden table. 'But she's come home! For good.'

Nola pressed her hands onto the table and levered herself up. 'No, she hasn't. Any fool can see that. She's here, but it's not where she wants to be. I've been thinking, Seamus, there's only one way to break Shona's curse, and that's for Mary Kate to get the hell out of here and make something of herself. She needs to take this money and put it to good use. We're too old to be selfish. We've had our lives, but hers is before her and it's about time this money was used. It does no good sat behind our fire. We must give it to Mary Kate now and give Finn's half to Michael to be put in a bank in Galway.'

'I'd drink to that,' said Seamus.

'You're about to,' said Nola as she placed two glasses on the table. 'Things are going to change around here and the thing that is going to change the most is that we are going to stop being terrified of Shona and stop letting her have a hold over us. Come on, drink, and then down to the village. I only came back up for butter. We have to get this money into the village and into Michael's and then find our Mary Kate.' She lifted the large bowl she had fetched from the dairy and held it to her hip like a baby as she looked out of the window at the horse, still harnessed to the cart, waiting patiently.

'We all have our day, Seamus,' she said, almost under her breath, 'and isn't it just a thing, you don't know it's here until it's gone.'

They both noticed at the same moment that the chair had stopped rocking.

'She's happy with what we've done, I can feel it,' said Nola. 'We're doing the right thing.'

'Come on, woman.' Seamus slapped his cap back on his head. 'They'll be needing that butter down in the post office before they run out of sandwiches. Ten men arrived from Ballycroy in the back of a van to help. I heard one of them shout, "I'm not lifting a finger unless the butties are spread with Nola Malone's butter."'

Nola grinned from ear to ear and blushed. 'Get away with you,' she said as she closed the cottage door behind them. 'I never thought the day I married you that I'd be condemned to years of your blarney.'

As she stepped up onto the cart, Seamus placed a hand on each of her buttocks and pushed her up. 'No, and I never thought that under that skirt you would have the nicest arse in Tarabeg. Life's full of surprises, missus.' He climbed into the cart next to her, but as they turned and looked at each other for a long moment the smiles disappeared.

'We will get her back, won't we, Seamus?' she said.

'Aye, we will. 'Tis the money he's after. He has no axe to grind with Mary Kate. Evil men like him, they worship the money.'

Mary Kate froze at the sound of his voice; her breath, laboured from the effort of moving across the cave floor, caught in her throat. She could smell the pus from the wound in his leg, but she couldn't see him. If her attention hadn't been so focused on her inch-by-inch shuffle towards the strip of light on the floor of the cave, she would have heard him approaching. Jay's breathing was deep and noisy. She had heard him glugging the whiskey from the bottle and had assumed her other captor was in the same state of unconsciousness.

Something cold and hard prodded her in the back and she gasped. Then he screamed so loud and so close to her, she let out a small shriek in response. 'Move,' he gasped. 'Move.'

His breathing was strained and she dared to turn her head to look at him. The part of the cave she had moved to was lighter and airier. Letting her breath go, she gulped in a lungful of the air, inhaling towards the light and away from the man who called himself her granddaddy. She might have been bound and virtually helpless, but she felt a new strength and determination running through her; she was no longer as afraid or disoriented as she'd been earlier. 'N... n... no, I w... won't move back into there,' she said with huge difficulty.

There was a loud, dull thud on the floor next to her and his body banged into the side of her. In a panic, she shuffled to the side and let out a stifled scream. As soon as she was clear of his hot breath, she pulled herself up into a sitting position, though she was trembling so much, she feared she'd fall back down.

Her grandfather was now on the floor of the cave, writhing in pain. He was holding onto one of his legs with both hands, teeth gritted, cursing. His gun had fallen to his side and it was as if he was unaware she was there. And then, in what must have been as much of a blessed release for him as it was for her, he slumped into unconsciousness.

Mary Kate stared at his filthy body and watched as his contorted face relaxed. She caught a glimpse of her mother in his face. She blinked; it was the face of her mother. She shook her head and tears filled her eyes. It had to be the dark, the cave. She was delirious.

'Mammy,' she cried. 'Mammy.' She looked again. She was there; Sarah was with her and it was not the body of her granddaddy she saw on the floor before her but the image of her mother.

'Brave girl,' said her mammy, and then came the voice of Nicholas.

'Count again, Mary Kate. One, two, three and you're there.'

Her head swung around. She couldn't see him, could only hear his voice. 'Nicholas...'

'Four, five... Go on, they're coming for you out on the shore.'

She gulped in more of the fresh air and as her shivering subsided, a calmness washed through her.

Sarah smiled. 'Go on. We're waiting, we won't leave you until you're safe.'

She allowed her eyes to believe, to feast on her mother's face.

'Jacob's ladder will always lead me to wherever you are,' her mother said. 'Nicholas and I will be your guardian angels. Get out of this cave and go back to Liverpool, there is a life waiting there for you. Go and do great things.'

'How? I don't understand. I can't.'

'Oh yes you can. You can because you're Mary Kate. Everything that is bad here in Tarabeg ends with your success. Go out into that world, Mary Kate, it's waiting for you. You're going to be someone special, as you were always meant to be. You will do good things. You will put an end to all of this by your actions. Always remember, Nicholas and I are here. We are all here.'

Mary Kate turned towards the daylight. She brought her knees up to her chest and pushed herself back. She was no longer afraid of being seen, no longer felt the fear; she pressed herself onto her back and wriggled along the ground. She took one last look at her captor. The hazy darkness had swallowed him, but as her eyes adjusted he returned and she could see that his breathing was rapid and shallow and he was still unconscious. Even if he did wake, he was in so much pain, she doubted he'd be able to follow her.

'Nicholas,' she whispered into the cave.

'One,' came the reply. 'Two.' She heard Nicholas counting along with her. 'Three,' he said, and the tears spilt down her cheeks as she laughed and cried and heaved herself along.

She stopped and took a breath – it tasted fresher. Pulling up her shoulders, she prepared to shuffle some more.

'One.' It was her mother and Nicholas together. 'Two,' they chanted, and she laughed out loud in sheer happiness. 'Three.' She was there, she had reached the curtain of vegetation.

She kicked out with her feet and it gave way in front of her. She edged slowly around until her back was pressing against the curtain and she fell straight through, out onto the shingly sand. Yelling out loud to give her the energy to push, she heaved herself onto her side and rolled and rolled, ignoring the stones that pierced her skin and the driftwood that jarred her bones and tore at her limbs until she was free of the rocks.

Stopping for a breath, she heard Nicholas calling her name. Lying on her back, looking up towards the sky, almost unable to open her eyes in the light, she heard more than one voice. It was no longer Nicholas.

The shingle vibrated as footsteps came closer and then there was an overwhelming sense of relief as she was scooped up into the arms of a man. Opening her eyes, she could see it was Joe, and not far behind him came her father. She inclined her head towards the cave. 'My granddaddy...' she mumbled. 'He said he was my granddaddy. And the other man, his name is Jay.'

'Come and get her,' shouted Joe to the other men running towards them. He set her carefully back down on the beach, took a knife from his back pocket to cut the ropes that bound her, and then pulled her up into a sitting position. 'Where did you come from?' he asked as he looked back towards the cliff face.

'It's green,' she said. 'It's the grass, it's grown over the opening.'

Joe stood, shielded his eyes with his hand and scanned the cliff. 'I can see it – you've pulled some away. Is he in there?'

Mary Kate tried to stand but wobbled. Joe reached down and steadied her.

'I have your other fancy boot,' he said and, despite the tension, he smiled.

Her father was already at her side and in the distance she saw the others drawing near.

Michael didn't speak. He tried, but his throat was too thick with unspent tears. The rush of relief was all he could deal with as he pulled her into his arms. 'My babby,' he whispered into her hair. 'My babby.'

Joe looked impatient. 'Are they armed?' he asked her.

She pulled herself free from her daddy's arms. 'I think only he is. He's unconscious though, there's something wrong with his leg. The other man, Jay, he drank a whole bottle of whiskey, he said he was going to sleep until tonight – he's dead drunk, so he is.'

Joe bent down, picked up the rope he'd cut from Mary Kate's ankles and turned to the men who had joined him. 'Pete, Tig, come with me. We have one more job to do. Michael, take Mary Kate back to the post office, Rosie and Nola are there, and then come straight back here in the van. I think we may have a couple of prisoners. And tell Mr Keene it's time to call the guard.'

Chapter 23

It had been the longest day of Michael Malone's life and he told Rosie so as he undressed for bed. 'I've just checked in on her, and Finn too. I've never felt the need to do that before, but I'm putting a lock on the back door tomorrow. Dana Brogan is on the mattress you put on the floor next to her.' He dropped his trousers to the ground and sat on the side of the bed, hands on his knees, trousers around his ankles.

Rosie's heart constricted as she looked at the man she knew had stared through the windows of hell for all the hours his daughter had been missing. 'She's safe,' she said as she sat down beside him and placed a hand on his knee. 'It was nice of Dana to come rushing over when she heard what had happened. She and Mary Kate seem to have a bit of a bond, don't you think?'

'I do. I must send a bottle of whiskey over to the daddy. He was a great help with his van, and bringing their farmhands too.'

'People were arriving from all over to the post office, the news spread fast.'

Michael rubbed his hands across his face. 'Thank the Lord those two are behind bars. No harm will come to anyone now.'

'That's true. And just think, McGuffey would be dead if Dr Gaskell and the matron hadn't been in the village. Wasn't that a strange thing.'

'How can such an evil bastard have luck like that?' The anger spilt from Michael in his voice. 'I wish they hadn't come. I wish he was dead.'

'Shh, neither of them will ever get out of prison. Father Jerry told me that kidnap is a very serious crime. They will be in Galway jail for life, is that not good enough?'

They both stopped talking as they heard a van pull up outside Paddy's and then a clamour of excited voices as the door opened and closed.

'Jesus, Tarabeg has suddenly become the centre of the feckin' earth,' said Michael.

''Tis true. And that's enough to take in as it is, without everything else that's happened.' Rosie bent down and pulled Michael's trousers over his feet.

He removed his cap and hung it on the bedpost, then fell back against the feather-stuffed pillow. 'I feel as though the world has turned upside down, Rosie. Nothing feels the same. It's as if the days when Angela was murdered have returned and, God knows, they were dark enough.'

Rosie pulled back the pink candlewick bedspread and slipped between the sheets. They were cool to the touch, chilled by the air from the Taramore river outside their open window. She switched off the lamp, propped herself up on one elbow and stared at his profile. His still black, wavy hair contrasted with the whiteness of the pillow in the moonlight and as he turned his face towards her his eyes reflected the starlight back to her.

'Maybe it's come full circle,' she said. 'Haven't you always felt, Michael, that there was unfinished business around here?' Without waiting for a reply, she continued. 'I always have. It was there before Sarah died, but it never went away. It was still there after, too.'

Michael's eyebrows almost met in the middle. 'And now?'

Rosie hesitated. Raising her eyes to his hairline, she began to run her fingers over his thick and slightly receding waves. She had untied her own hair and it fell across her shoulders and down onto his chest. 'I know this is going to sound weird,' she said, 'but it's gone. Whatever it was, it isn't here any more.'

Michael didn't reply. He turned his head to the window and, reaching out, pulled Rosie down into his arms. He felt her heartbeat close to his, stroked her hair down her back, pressed his limbs against hers. 'Rosie, I don't think I've ever said this to you before, but thank you.'

No sooner had the words left his mouth than she raised her hand and pressed her fingers to his lips. 'You don't have to say that,' she said.

His hand moved and began to rub up and down the tops of her arms. 'I do though. You came here, took over a new baby, a grieving man and a sad daughter, and you saved all of our lives, Rosie. I don't know what would have happened to us if it hadn't been for you. I would have lost the business and that's for sure. I know I've been the worst man you could have married, but I do love you, you know that, don't you?'

Rosie didn't speak, just gave the slightest nod and pressed her forehead deep into the pillow. Tears of happiness had filled her eyes and she allowed them to run and be absorbed by the crisp fresh linen beneath her face. It had taken so long, years of uncertainty, and now he had said it and she knew he'd meant it.

They lay in silence for what felt like an age until Rosie spoke. 'Michael, Mary Kate won't stay, you know that, don't you?' She held her breath as she waited for his reply, which seemed to take forever to arrive.

'I do,' was all he had to offer in response.

An owl hooted outside the window and the rush of the Taramore as it went on its way filled the room.

Michael's breathing became deeper and steadier. He was spent, as were they all. He kissed the side of her head through a curtain of hair. 'I love you,' he whispered again, and within seconds he was sleeping.

He had never before said the words she had waited years to hear and yet now they'd come twice in one night. She felt as though her own heart would burst with happiness as she smiled and wept all at the same time. *This is a special night*, she thought to herself as she pressed her skin closer to that of the man she had always loved. Wrapping her arms around him, she fell into her own deep, exhausted sleep.

Nola and Seamus had not had so many people in the farmhouse for as long as they could remember. Nola had been in a flap, fetching provisions and drink from the old house as Joe drove his car up and down the hill, more times than he would like to count, with Pete riding along for company. He turned a blind eye to the only thing so far that day that had gladdened his heart, Pete giving Peggy a kiss in the back of the car, whilst Tig and Keeva gabbled away in the front, oblivious. He had raised his eyes to the rearview mirror at just the wrong moment and turned his attention straight to Keeva next to him.

'Are you as tired as the rest of us?' he asked her. 'You made enough sandwiches to feed every man in Galway.'

'Go'way, would you,' she said. 'How can we complain about being tired after all you have done? They say you carried McGuffey and then dragged Jay out of the cave straight after him, is that right?'

Joe almost laughed out loud. 'It is, but it wasn't difficult. I thought McGuffey was dead, and Jay, well, he was just dead drunk. To be honest with you, Keeva, I felt cheated. They were no challenge whatsoever.'

Keeva moved her hand to her side and slipped her fingers into Tig's. They had left the children with Paddy and Josie, who had opened the bar on a night that was busier than usual as everyone dissected the events of the day. There would be people travelling from other villages in cars and vans to gather the news to take back home.

'I've never known a week like it,' she said. 'We have Mary Kate back, the visitors from Liverpool, you yourself buying the manor. I feel like Lady Muck meself, just being sat next to you, and as well as being lord of the manor, you're only a hero into the bargain now too, isn't he, Tig?'

'That's a fact, so it is,' Tig replied. 'And don't forget that solicitor friend of Joe's, Keeva, and the doctor and Matron turning up. And the guard – when was the last time he was in Tarabeg? He's grown a limp and a beard since I last saw him.'

Keeva shuddered. 'And McGuffey and Jay,' she added. 'I thought we'd seen the back of McGuffey years ago.'

Minutes later, they walked into the light and warmth of the farmhouse to find Cat frying potatoes at the range and being helped by a beaming Declan, who carried the bowls to the table. Mrs O'Keefe was draining vegetables at the sink and Seamus was removing the biggest leg of pork anyone had ever seen out of the oven. At the table sat Mr Keene, Matron, Bee, Captain Bob and Bridget.

'What was it that was wrong with his leg?' Bridget asked Dr Gaskell. 'I've never smelt anything like it before in me life. I have no potion for such a thing.' Between them they had tended to McGuffey before the guard loaded him into the back of his van.

'It was gas gangrene. The bacteria in the wound releases a gas into the tissues and is possibly the worst type of wound infection. The mixture you gave to Matron and me to clean him up, along with the opium for the pain, will only last long enough to get him to a hospital. The chances of his surviving for long are very slim. He won't make it to a court, let alone a prison, and I'm afraid all the money in the world can't save him.'

A hush descended over the room. Nola blessed herself and Bee stared at her. 'I have to,' Nola said. 'I don't forgive him for what he did, scaring the life out of our Mary Kate, and if he walked in here, I'd kill him meself, but we will have to pray for his soul if he does depart, we all know that.'

'Like hell I will,' said Keeva as she hung up her coat.

'Matron, are you ready to eat?' asked Mrs O'Keefe, holding out a plate of steaming pork with crispy crackling and fried potatoes. 'You must be starving.'

Matron smiled at Dr Gaskell and wondered, would anyone in St Angelus believe a word they said if they told them about their trip to Ireland to recruit new nurses.

Mary Kate woke to find herself in her old bedroom above the shop. She shuffled to the end of her bed, leant on the windowsill and stared down at the river. She knew it would be the last time she'd do that for a long while. She'd made a decision. The cave had been horrible and scary, the darkness, not knowing what was going on, but she'd not really taken her captors seriously, had never doubted that the money would be paid and that she'd get safely back home. Knowing almost nothing about her granddaddy, she'd believed that because he was her own flesh and blood he would never hurt her. The kidnapping hadn't frightened her into making her decision; she just knew that coming back to Tarabeg had been the wrong choice.

'Are you all right, Mary Kate?' She heard the rustling of bedclothes as Dana sat upright.

'I am.' She turned onto her side and leant her back against the wall. 'I can't sleep – there's too much going round in my head. I spent last night in a cave, and tonight you're here, sleeping on my bedroom floor. I can't believe you're here.'

Dana sprang to her feet, sat down on the bed next to Mary Kate and tucked the eiderdown around both of them. 'I can believe it,' she said. 'Do you not get that feeling sometimes that you knew you were meant to be somewhere? Have you not had that thing when someone has stepped into your life from nowhere and suddenly become massively important to you, even though you just can't explain how or why?'

'I have,' said Mary Kate. 'I met Mrs O'Keefe by chance on the boat from Dublin and I've seen her every day for the last two years. She's been the hugest part of my life. And Nicholas... he came to see me as a doctor, and that was it! I fell in love the moment I laid eyes on him.'

Dana squeezed Mary Kate's hand. 'I knew I was going to be your friend the moment I met you and found out you were from home. I just couldn't get over the coincidence. I mean, this place, it's so wee and no one ever goes anywhere. I just knew I was meant to be nursing your Nicholas, and I'm really glad I could be here today. We came as soon as we heard – the news ripped across the coast in minutes.'

Mary Kate smiled. 'I was amazed to see Matron and Dr Gaskell here. He was lovely when he checked me over after I got out of the cave. He told me they're here to advertise for nurses and that the solicitor's going to be handling the applications for them.'

'Yes, I take it as a compliment that they want more Dana Brogans at St Angelus.' Dana laughed and shook her head.

'Maybe I could help with that?' said Mary Kate. 'I wonder if they'd want to employ someone... I mean, I could travel back and forth on the boat, I could find girls who want to be nurses and go to Liverpool, couldn't I?' She turned to look at Dana. 'I'm desperate to go back. I made a big mistake coming here, so I did. It was all wrong, my head wasn't right, and when Nicholas said I was to come back, I'm sure now he meant for a visit.'

'Why bother helping Matron with finding the nurses, why don't you become one yourself? The hospital is growing, there are plenty of opportunities. St Angelus is the best place to work and I can't imagine a job more rewarding than mine. It's hard work though.'

'I saw that with my own eyes,' said Mary Kate. 'Do you think they would have me?' She felt a surge of life, of hope, in her veins, something she hadn't felt since the day Nicholas died.

Dana answered without a moment's hesitation. 'In a flash, I reckon. Especially as Matron is at your gran's farm tonight, being treated to some good old-fashioned Irish hospitality. Her and Dr Gaskell.'

Mary Kate groaned and put her hands over her face. 'Oh God, no, they'll be as drunk as lords by now and have the worst heads in the morning. Granny, nooo!'

'I wouldn't be worrying. I got the impression that after spending the afternoon with Mrs Doyle, Matron is smitten with the place. Why don't I make us both a cup of tea and then you can sleep on it. I'll go with you to ask Matron in the morning before she leaves, if you like?'

An hour later, Mary Kate was still lying on her bed, looking out of the window at the stars. She could hear Dana breathing deeply next to her once more, but her own mind was busy replaying the events of the past twenty-four hours.

'Nicholas...' she whispered up to the stars. She wanted him to speak to her, as he had in the cave. She heard nothing but the sound of the river. 'I'm going home, to Liverpool, and I will become a nurse, at the same hospital you trained in. For sure it will happen, I can feel it. I'll be close to you there, not here. You aren't here, my love.'

The window was partially open, the inky sky was clear and bright, and a breeze brushed her cheeks. 'I want to do what you did and help people who are sick, like Nurse Brogan helped you. That's what would make you proud of me, and me proud of myself too. Can you see me? Which star are you, Nicholas? Mammy? I love you both, I miss you both, I do.' As the tears filled her eyes, a million stars twinkled down at her.

Chapter 24

There was no sneaking away. This time, Mary Kate would leave Tarabeg in daylight and with the blessing of her father and the entire village.

'Do you have everything packed?' Rosie asked, and then quickly added, 'But you'll be back soon anyway, won't you?'

Mary Kate placed her case by the back door for Michael to load into the car when he returned. Rosie's question was easy to answer. 'I will. Matron said the next training school starts in a month. I'll be in the school for three months, and then I'll have my first holiday. I promise I'll be home then. It won't be like before, Rosie.'

Rosie wanted to say she understood that this time there was no Nicholas or grand love to hide, but it would have sounded cruel and made Mary Kate sad.

This morning, the light was back in her eyes and Rosie recognised it for what it was – hope. The smile on Mary Kate's face was a joy to see.

'Is Finn not up yet? I don't care if it's a Saturday, I'm off to drag him out of his bed. He can say goodbye to me properly.' Mary Kate grinned and ran up the stairs.

'Would you just look at her,' said Mrs O'Keefe. 'I reckon she's going to be just fine.'

Rosie was clearing the breakfast dishes into the sink. Wiping her hands, she turned back to face Mrs O' Keefe and Cat. 'She is that, and I couldn't be more delighted that she has the both of you in her life back in Liverpool.'

Mrs O'Keefe smiled at Cat. 'Well, I'm not sure how long this one is going to be around. I reckon you might be seeing more of her than me. She's not coming back to Liverpool until after the dance tonight. Declan is taking her to the station tomorrow – she's only coming along for the ride just now.'

'Oh, why is that?' Rosie looked confused. 'What delights can Tarabeg offer to keep you here for another day? I'm beginning to think that maybe we should all move to Liverpool.'

Cat blushed and looked at the floor. 'Honestly,' she said, 'trust you.' She folded her arms and, despite her shyness, jutted out her chin. 'Declan and I have taken a shine to one another. He asked me to the dance and I said I would go. I'm a big girl, I can find my way back on the boat tomorrow.'

A grin spread across Rosie's face. 'Well, would you get you! Peggy is as bad with Pete Shevlin – smitten, they are. The whole incident with Mary Kate threw those two together. He's been in and out of the shop for months before I guessed. Honestly, I am always the last to know anything around here. I tried to persuade Mary Kate to stay for the dance, but she didn't fancy it and I can't blame her, with all she's been through.'

The sound of a car pulling up outside the back of the shop brought Mary Kate running down the stairs. 'Joe, is it you?' she said. 'Where's Daddy? He was due back from his deliveries half an hour ago.'

'I've come to fetch you up to the farm to say your goodbyes,' he said. 'Michael is up there, they want to see you.'

'But I said my goodbyes at the family supper last night.'

'Nola did say she was looking to have a quiet word with Michael before we came down this morning,' said Cat.

'Aye, well, they have a leaving present they want to give you. It won't take long,' said Joe. 'Ladies, I'll be back with her in less than half an hour.'

Mary Kate was already outside and climbing into the passenger seat. Finn, who'd been holding her hand, jumped into the back. Once they started to climb the hill, Mary Kate turned to Joe. 'I'm sorry I was so horrible to you when I arrived,' she said. 'I don't know why it is, but I'm not as against the idea of a hotel as I was when you first mentioned it.'

'I'm glad to hear it,' said Joe. 'I've appointed a project manager from Liverpool and we will begin work soon. Tarabeg will have one of the best golf courses in Ireland before long.'

'Can I work at the hotel, Joe?' Finn leant forwards, resting his folded arms on the back of Mary Kate's seat.

Mary Kate sniffed, unimpressed. 'You might want to come to Liverpool, to me, Finn,' she said.

'Where are you going to live?' Finn was already imagining himself making the journey.

'With Mrs O'Keefe, until I can sort myself out. The hospital has a nurses' home and Matron said she would like me to live there, although they may have to find a new one for all the new nurses they'll have coming soon.'

'Maybe she'd like me to come and build a hotel,' said Joe with a wink over to Finn in the back.

'Never! I'm glad that I'm off to Liverpool and you'll be busy here.'

Joe roared out laughing. 'Mark my words, one day you will stay in my hotel.'

'Never. Not in a million years. I do wish you luck though, Joe. Try not to change the village too much – it's special, you know that.'

'Thank you, Mary Kate. Do you think Father Jerry would allow that to happen? The man thinks he's the architect, he's had something to say about every single proposal so far. He has a meeting on site himself with Mr Keene and the architect today. It's a pity my sleeping partner can't be there.'

They were pulling up outside the old house and Pete Shevlin, who was on his way from the farmhouse, waved to them.

'A sleeping partner?' said Mary Kate. 'What does that mean?'

Joe jumped out and opened the car door for her. 'Well, in my case, someone who is very difficult and stubborn at times. Come on, we don't have long.'

Finn was already out of the car and running to Michael in the doorway. Mary Kate stopped and watched as Michael enveloped him in a hug. Her heart filled with joy. He'd done the same thing to her so many times.

Joe placed his hand in the small of her back. 'Life goes on and it is good,' he said.

'It is,' she replied, and felt the warmth of his hand on her waist. She looked up to his face, the clean-shaven face she had despised until just a couple of days ago, and she met in his eyes a softness, an understanding and something more that she couldn't place.

'Do you think you'll be back in Tarabeg any day soon or will I have to come to Liverpool to find you?'

he asked. He amazed himself. He had thought her a stroppy stuck-up madam, but now, since he'd rescued her, he felt fiercely protective.

She frowned. Her emotions were all over the place: she felt sad one moment, uplifted the next, now that she had made her decision to become a nurse, and her feelings towards Joe were surprising her. 'Joe—' she said as he gently turned her towards the house.

'I know, I know, you don't have to explain. You're grieving – Rosie's told me all about it. And you're off to be a nurse and that's a great thing to be doing. I'm not one to try and change your mind, but please remember that I'm here. I have a feeling I'll be waiting.'

'I will. I'll be back soon, but not to stay. My life is different now.' They both walked towards the grinning Michael.

In the kitchen, Nola and Seamus were sitting expectantly at the table. Mary Kate did a double-take and gasped when she saw what was in front of them. Michael gave her a little push and Joe pulled out the chair next to Nola for her.

With a huge smile on his face, Seamus gestured at the pile of rolled-up dollars. 'This is for you, Mary Kate.'

She stared, trying to find her voice. 'How much is it?' she whispered.

'It's three thousand dollars,' said Michael.

'Three thousand dollars?' Mary Kate had never thought about money when she was with Nicholas.

She'd never needed to. Nicholas had provided her with everything she'd wanted. It wasn't until he died that she'd realised how little she had of her own. At the moment of his passing, she'd been left with just the clothes on her back and a few pounds in her purse. It was only recently it had become a worry and yet, despite the very poor money she would be paid as a nurse, it had never once crossed her mind to refuse the offer Matron had made to her.

'I'll be able to pay Mrs O'Keefe back,' was the first thing she said.

'You owe her money?' Michael looked less than pleased.

'No, not really, but she has kept me and done so much for me. I'd like to do something to repay that.'

'There was much more than this,' said Seamus. 'Finn, your daddy has your share, to match Mary Kate's. The rest of it we have invested in a business for both of you. A big business.'

Mary Kate glanced up from examining the green dollar bills. 'A business? What business?' She looked from one to the other, genuinely confused.

'You tell her, Joe,' said Michael, grinning.

Joe put down the mug of tea that Nola had just refilled. 'Mary Kate, as of this morning, you, Finn and I are partners. We are all one-third owners of the hotel.'

Nola thought Mary Kate was going to faint. 'Quick, get the whiskey, Seamus,' she said.

'How?' Mary Kate said, alarmed. 'I want to go back to Liverpool and be a nurse. Daddy, you can't do this. It's not for you to decide what it is I should do, or Finn, for that matter. Life is changing, times are changing – you just can't do that.'

Nola leant over her shoulder and slopped some whiskey into her tea.

'Aye, and you will, you will,' said Michael. 'Don't you see, being a partner in a business gives you the freedom to do whatever you want. You're a sleeping partner for now, and one day you may want to come back and see if there's a role you can play. But if you don't, it doesn't matter, you'll just keep taking the dividend from the profits as a sleeping partner and you will never want for money. When my day comes, I will die a happy man for knowing that.'

The penny dropped and Mary Kate grinned. 'Difficult and stubborn, am I?' she said, turning to Joe as Nola worked her way around the table tipping whiskey into tea mugs.

They all laughed so loud, Pete Shevlin came running back in to see what he had missed.

Elsie had missed Matron. She had polished Matron's sitting room and office to within an inch of their lives. What she hadn't liked quite so much was being in sole charge of Blackie, and they were both eagerly anticipating Matron's return later that day. Elsie wiped the condensation from the windows with vigour and looked down at the life of St Angelus as it played out before her. 'Ah, there's Nurse Brogan, Blackie, back from her holidays,' she said as she wrung out the cloth into the bowl perched on the windowsill.

Blackie growled.

'Oh, I do wish you would stop that,' she said. 'You make me nervous.' As she turned back to the window, she almost dropped the cloth. Dr Gaskell's car was coming in through the main entrance, with Matron in the front. 'Bloody hell,' she exclaimed. 'I'd better get the fire going. No walk for you, Blackie.'

The Scottie dog sat on his rear in disgust and continued to growl.

Despite the unexpected rush to get the room warm and ready, Elsie breathed a sigh of relief. With Matron back, life would now return to normal. 'Well thank the Lord for that, eh, Blackie,' she said as she bent down to put a match to the kindling. 'Oi, get away from my ankles, you little bugger.'

She pushed Blackie with her foot and unintentionally sent him skittling along the carpet, just as Matron opened the door. 'He was about to take a chunk out of my ankle,' Elsie exclaimed by way of a greeting. 'He understands English, that dog. I only said I couldn't take him for a walk because I saw you arriving and had to light the fire, and he went for me.'

Matron wasn't listening as she stooped to greet her beloved dog, who was attempting to run up her legs. 'I'll walk him myself,' she said. 'We got the overnight boat because the weather was due to turn today, so they said.'

'Would you like a bit of breakfast first? I got Cook to stock up your fridge ready for your return. Here, give me your coat.'

Matron had begun to undo the buttons on her coat as she spoke. 'Dr Gaskell was hoping you would suggest just that and he's on his way up here in a minute. We didn't dare eat on the boat. Honestly, it does terrible things to your constitution.'

'Is he behind you, Dr Gaskell?' Elsie looked out of the open door onto the landing.

'He will be. You know what he's like – Mrs Tanner had just opened the tea hatch and called out to him. He's becoming such a gossip as he gets older. I don't know what Mrs Gaskell would say if she could see him.'

As Elsie turned on the gas ring in Matron's small kitchen, she realised she was grinning. The hospital had been a strange place with both Matron and Dr Gaskell away, and everyone had felt it. She placed the frying pan onto the flame and waited for the lard to melt before she laid the bacon rashers down. The familiar sound of Matron on the phone came through the door.

'Oh yes, it was a very successful trip. I recruited one nurse there and then, and I don't care what the board says, she will be an asset to this hospital and Dr Gaskell agrees with me. Could you bring me up the bed statement in one hour and I would like a ward-by-ward report on each patient, please. Also, ask Theatre Sister to come with you, I want to know how the new theatre technician is working out. And this new swab regime I'm reading about in the first letter I opened, has that been put in place yet?'

Elsie turned the rashers and sighed with contentment. Matron was back.

A fortnight after her return to Liverpool from Tarabeg, Mary Kate hovered at the end of the driveway with the keys in her hand, her heart beating madly in her chest.

Mrs O'Keefe was standing next to her. 'Are you sure you don't want me to come with you?' she asked.

'Actually, I do,' said Mary Kate, dropping the keys into her pocket.

'I thought so. Only a madwoman, as your Granny Nola would say, would do this alone. Come on.' She hooked her arm through Mary Kate's and propelled her into a walk of purpose down the driveway of the house in which Mary Kate had spent the happiest days of her life.

'Lift your head up,' Mrs O'Keefe said under her breath. 'Don't stare at the pebbles. They all look the same.'

On the drive sat a Morris Minor and next to it a familiar suitcase. Before they reached the front steps, the front door flew open to reveal Lavinia Marcus. She stood there in her hat and coat, a cigarette in her hand, staring at them as though an infestation of cockroaches was about to invade the house.

'Get away from here,' she said, jabbing her cigarette towards them. 'I told you never to set foot on this land again or to come anywhere near my house. Are your ears made of cloth or what?' She placed her hand on the door and inhaled deeply on her cigarette.

Mary Kate and Mrs O'Keefe glanced round as they heard a car turning into the drive. The tension slipped from Mary Kate's shoulders. It was William.

As he leapt out of his car, Lavinia shouted down the drive, 'William, will you tell this trash to remove themselves. I don't want them here when the new owner turns up.'

William locked his car door, pushed the car keys into his jacket pocket and smiled at Mary Kate. 'Your new owner has arrived,' he said to Lavinia. And then, turning to Mary Kate, 'Did the agent give you the keys?'

Mary Kate was stiff with fear and could only nod in response.

'Good. We're on safe ground then.'

Lavinia marched up to Mrs O'Keefe and with her hands on her hips lurched forwards and staggered slightly.

'Have you been drinking, Lavinia?' asked William.

She began to laugh. 'If I have, what's it got to do with you?' She turned to Mrs O'Keefe. 'What have you bought this house for? William, you said it was a young professional lady who was buying it – I mean, you're hardly professional, are you?' There was a slight slur to her speech as she threw her cigarette to the ground.

'A young professional lady has bought the house,' said William. 'Meet Probationer Nurse Malone.'

Lavinia rocked back on her heels and squinted. 'You?' she said, her voice dripping with disbelief. 'You? How can you afford this house? I put it on the market at a high price. I sold it for five hundred pounds.'

Mary Kate fingered the keys in her pocket. 'Yes, and I paid the price.' Mrs O'Keefe squeezed her arm. Mary Kate had expected to feel anger, grief, distress, elation when she walked down the drive, but actually all she felt at the sight of Lavinia Marcus was pity. 'Mrs Marcus, would you like me to fetch your handbag for you so that you can leave? I bought the house with all its furnishings and fittings and I can see that your suitcase is ready by the car.'

'No, no, I wouldn't. I've changed my mind – you can't have it. I'll take back the sale. Now scarper, off my drive! William, tell her.'

William looked down at the ground and scuffed a pebble with his shoe. 'I'm afraid, Lavinia, that it's too late for that. Mary Kate paid her money and the deeds are now in her name. She is the rightful legal owner.'

'But... but... I left you to sell the house and take care of it, why did you sell it to that tart?'

William's face flushed red. 'Lavinia, I suggest you go now, before Mary Kate calls the police.'

'I didn't want to have to do this,' said Mary Kate, 'but you have five minutes.' She looked at her watch, just the way Lavinia had with her on the worst night of her life.

Later that morning, when Joan and Deidra arrived, they almost ran down the drive. Joan was carrying her suitcase of belongings and holding Jet's lead, and Deidra had a basket of provisions on each arm. They could barely contain their excitement.

'I never thought I would walk over this threshold again,' said Joan as she stepped into the kitchen.

'You won't be,' said Mary Kate. 'In future, you will have your own key and you will only enter or leave this house by the front door.'

'The front door? I can't do that!'

'If I can, you can.'

'What are you going to do about the nurses' home?' asked William. 'Are you going to live here now?'

Mary Kate grinned, but before she could say anything, Mrs O'Keefe interjected. 'Before you start on that, we definitely need a cuppa,' she said. 'Deidra, did you bring milk?'

'I did.' Deidra emptied the basket onto the table.

'Good, there was only gin in that fridge.'

Jet jumped up, placed his paws on the table and licked Mary Kate's face.

'Jet, get down,' she said as she playfully pushed him away.

'Someone is delighted to be back home,' said William. 'Come on then. I can tell you have something up your sleeve – what is it?'

'Well...' Mary Kate smiled and looked from one to the other. They were all watching her. 'I am going to stay at the nurses' home. I'm looking forward to it. I'll make new friends and there are six of us starting and living in. But I love this house too. I thought I could rent it out, but I don't want strangers in here. So I asked Cat and the children to come and live here. They will make good use of the place and they even have Declan coming over for Christmas – can you imagine? Planned already. He's been over this weekend to see them all.'

Joan clapped her hands. 'Will we have children in this house again? Will we?'

'We will.' Mary Kate laughed. 'A whole brood of them.'

'Well, now that you're settled in and there's no threat to your life from Lavinia Marcus, I'd better get back to the surgery, or else Bella will be sending out a search party.' William stood and took his hat from the hook on the back of the door.

'Talking about parties, William, I think we should have one. Not yet – at Christmas. We could make it a second house-warming.'

'Only if you're up to it,' said William. 'You've had a lot going on.'

'I am. I can face anything now that I'm back here.' She glanced round the kitchen and a memory from the first time she set foot in the room came back to her: the boys sitting at the table, Joan fretting over the stove, Nicholas walking in and his eyes never leaving hers as he kissed the top of his son's head.

'You look exhausted,' said Mrs O'Keefe. 'I've checked upstairs – she obviously hasn't been staying here the last few days and she's had someone in, I can smell the lavender of the furniture polish and I'm certain she wouldn't even know what that is. The bed is all freshly made up – why don't you go for a lie-down. Cat and the kids will be here soon.'

'I think I will.' Turning to William, Mary Kate kissed him on the cheek.

'Come over to our house for supper on Saturday,' he said. 'You're expected. I'll pick you up in the car at seven.'

'I'll be ready,' she replied. 'I'm ready for anything now.'

Sleep was elusive. She listened to the murmurings coming up from the kitchen through the floorboards and, throwing off the cover, walked over to the window.

Being in the house brought memories of Nicholas flooding back. In this room she could hear his voice, she could almost smell him, feel his touch on her skin. Her fingers flew to her throat, where the green velvet ribbon had once sat, and for the first time in a while, tears pricked her eyes.

She opened the dressing-table drawer to see if the box of tissues she'd always kept in there to remove her make-up was still there. It was, even though the rest of the drawer was bare. The box was almost empty, and when she picked it up, something rattled inside. Her heart did a somersault in her chest as she plunged her hand in. The moment she felt the plushness of the cloth and the coolness of the stone, she knew she'd found it – her green velvet ribbon.

She sat on the stool and raised her hands to fasten it around her neck. But the fingers reflected back at her in the glass weren't hers. She closed her eyes and swayed slightly as she felt his lips brush against hers. 'Nicholas,' she whispered. There was no reply. There would never be a reply. She was home, she was safe, she was wearing her green velvet ribbon. She was about to embark on a new life, as a nurse, and she knew that Nicholas, her guardian angel, would be right there with her, at her side until she was ready to step out alone.

Glossary of Irish terms

boreen – narrow country lane

brack – fruit loaf

colleen – girl or young woman

curragh – small wickerwork boat or coracle

dudeen – short-stemmed clay tobacco pipe

poteen – illegal home-brewed alcohol, made from potatoes

shillelagh – stout wooden walking stick, sometimes also used as a weapon